A Silver Medallion

A Crystal Moore Suspense

By James R. Callan

Pennant Publishing

A Silver Medallion
Copyright: © 2016 by James R. Callan

Cover designed by Nada Orlić - Erelis Design
(www.nadaorlic.com)

ISBN-13: 978-0692679227
ISBN-10: 0692679227
LCCN: applied for

Printed in the United States of America

Pennant Publishing

Some Readers' Comments on *A Silver Medallion,* Book #2 in the Crystal Moore Suspense Series

"**A Silver Medallion**_is a gripping, action-packed adventure from talented author James Callan. Crystal Moore is a tough and savvy heroine who knows no fear. ..."

—New York Times Bestselling Author Bobbi Smith

" ... reads like a gold-medal thriller from page one, ..."

—From BookLife Prize in Fiction, Critic's Report

A Silver Medallion ... is the thrilling sequel to A Ton of Gold. ... The page-turning suspense kept me up well into the pre-morning! "

—Alyssa Elmore for Readers' Favorite (Barnes & Nobel)

James R. Callan is a master of understanding human conflict and the raw emotions that everyone faces ..."

Caleb Pirtle, III, Editorial Director, Venture Galleries

This book by Mr. Callan kept me hooked from the very beginning. Drawing a plot that seemed to leap from the headlines, he writes with a page turning intensity that will leave the reader satisfied. Crystal Moore is a heroine you can fall in love with.

Amazon Review - Abookanight

Dedication

This book is dedicated to all the writers who have unselfishly helped me along the way, starting with the late Jory Sherman and continuing through so many others until today and I'm sure beyond. They are too numerous to list individually. It would make a book in itself. As the saying goes, you know who you are. This book is dedicated to you.

Acknowledgements

A book of this size does not come together without help from many people. I want to thank all of those. But there are seven that need to be mentioned by name. First, I want to thank Ann Everett, Mike Haise, and Ginnie Bivona for reading through a less than well edited version. Your comments were very helpful and much appreciated.

I want to thank Mary Burton King for some advise in the forensic area. Always good to have an expert check some of your facts. And a big thanks to Ana for making the cover great.

While I spend a lot of time in Mexico, I am not an expert in Spanish. My thanks to Carlos Garduño for checking my use of Spanish in this book, and keeping it appropriate for the person using it at the time.

Last, but far from least, a very special thanks to Earlene for proof reading the manuscript, not once, but multiple times. If you find this book relatively error-free, the credit goes to Earlene. Those errors still in it are most likely something I changed after she had made it error-free. I will try to pay her back with coconut shrimp and hot fudge sundays.

Author's Notes

By and large, my depiction of Puerto Vallarta is correct. However, I have taken a few liberties - I guess we call those literary license.

Most of the restaurants called by name exist and are, in fact, frequented by the author. However, The Sundowner is fictitious, and so directions from it to Plaza Mar, including the small, dark, narrow street, are also made up.

The terrible road to San Sebastian still exists, but has indeed been improved, somewhat, perhaps using Crystal's twenty pesos. However, there is now a much better road from Puerto Vallarta which passes very near to San Sebastian. The road described in this book was at least as bad as I described it not that many years ago.

Lastly, Puerto Vallarta and the people of Mexico are more beautiful that I can describe. If given the chance, visit. You won't run into José Rodriquez de Allende, but you will find many friendly and gracious people, more than willing to help you.

A Silver Medallion

Chapter 1

CRYSTAL Moore drove slowly along the sandy road that curved through the property she had roamed as a child. Her grandparents had christened it "The Park" when they purchased it over fifty years ago. To Crystal, they could have named it Serenity. The tall, stately Southern pines, the oak and hickory trees, the mirror-still lake, the peaceful quiet, all worked to cast a spell of tranquility over her.

Crystal's maroon LeSabre crested the hill. Two hundred feet ahead, her grandmother stood under a maple tree, its autumn foliage creating a golden halo above her grey hair. Eula Moore was staring at the small storage shed about twenty feet behind her cedar-shake house. She aimed a double-barreled shotgun at the door of the building.

Fifty feet from Eula, Crystal switched off the ignition, eased out of the car, and moved forward, careful not to crack a twig or crunch a dried leaf. Now she saw her grandmother's right index finger curled around the trigger. Whatever was going on, she did not want to distract her Nana.

Eula Moore pointed the shotgun at the shed, her wrinkled hands as steady as those of an eye surgeon. "Don't make no sudden moves. I got a nervous trigger finger. I might just blow your head off."

Nothing moved.

"Now, very slowly, come on out in the open, and keep them hands over your head where I can see 'em."

Experience told Crystal her grandmother had heard the car, but Eula's attention never left the shed. The elderly woman stooped down, gaze still fixed on the building, picked up a rock with her left hand and made a sweeping, underhanded throw. As the chunk of limestone arched skyward, Eula pulled the ancient shotgun up and once more trained it on the shed.

The rock struck the tin roof with a satisfying bang. No animal came bolting out the door. The noise echoed and died away. The birds stopped their chirping. All was quiet.

Crystal crept up beside her grandmother. "What's in there, Nana?" she whispered.

"Animal. Person. Beats me. But I didn't git to seventy-five being careless."

Eula Moore, five feet two inches tall, ninety-five pounds with short-cropped grey hair, held a strategic position. No one could leave the shed without coming into her gun's sight. And no one could see her without first revealing himself. Eula looked frail, but her voice was strong, her will stronger. "Better come out 'fore I start shootin'."

A slight breeze wiggled the leaves on a towering oak tree shading the area. A squirrel sat motionless. The scene was as peaceful as a painting of a country lane. Except for the shotgun.

A few moments passed. Then a single finger came into view. Gradually, it turned into a whole hand, waving in a small arc. "*Por favor, no dispare.*" The tiny brown hand fluttered again. The voice quavered slightly. "Please. No shoot. No shoot."

Eula didn't lower the gun or take her gaze off the shed. "*Por favor?* Spanish?" Eula said to Crystal. Then to the tiny hand, "*Manos arriba.*"

Now, two hands waved. But no body appeared.

"You need to work on your Spanish, Nana. He may not

know what you're saying."

Eula snorted. "*Pardon* me. I didn't go to S.M.U. Or Stanford. Maybe you can do better."

Crystal turned toward the shed. "*Salga con las manos arriba.* Come out with your hands up."

A foot materialized in the opening. "Hands up." Then a body began to emerge. "Hands up."

Was it a child? Little more than five feet tall and slender as broomcorn, she could have been a girl of fourteen. Her uncombed hair, nearly reaching her waist, appeared as black and shiny as obsidian. Pink and blue embroidery decorated the rough-woven, white dress hanging from her shoulders and stopping just short of her scratched knees. Well-worn leather sandals revealed feet accustomed to no shoes at all.

The small hands trembled slightly as the young Mexican edged forward, but she held her head high and her back ramrod straight.

Eula waggled the barrel of the shotgun at the girl. "Far enough. Hold it right there. *Alto.*" Eula focused on the girl, but spoke to Crystal. "Okay. So I don't remember my Spanish good enough to find out what I got here. See what you can do. But don't get in my line of fire."

A cloud drifted away, allowing the sun to play fully on the girl's face. This was *not* a child. Those large eyes could not develop such sadness, such pain, in such a short life.

"*¿Como se llama?*" Crystal asked.

The thin young woman maintained her focus on the gun. "Rosa. Rosa Bonita Lopez."

"*¿Habla Ingles?*"

"*Un poco.*"

"*Hablo Español un poco. Vamos probando con Ingles.* Let's try English," said Crystal. The young woman's expression did not change, nor did her attention waiver from the shotgun. "Okay. Your name is Rosa Bonita."

"*Si*. Yes."

"And what were you doing in the shed?"

The Mexican woman's forehead wrinkled and she tilted her head slightly to one side. *Is she puzzled by the English or by what kind of an answer to give?* Crystal tried Spanish again. "*¿Que hacias en el cobertizo?*"

After several seconds, Rosa looked at Crystal. "Food."

"You were looking for food?"

"*Si.*"

"Are you hungry?"

Eula made a small grunt. "Dumb question."

"*Si*. Yes."

"When did you eat last? *¿Cuándo comiste por última vez?*"

"*Ayer en la mañana.*"

"Yesterday morning!" Crystal turned to her grandmother. "She's probably starving. Let's take her in and give her something to eat. Then we can find out why she's here."

Eula didn't move or lower the shotgun but Crystal walked over, smiling, took the young woman's hand and led her into the house.

                                    #

Inside Eula's large country kitchen, Crystal gave Rosa a tall glass of orange juice while Eula put the finishing touches on a chicken and rice meal she'd been preparing for her granddaughter's arrival. Rosa drank the juice without stopping and her dark, wary eyes remained focused on the chicken as Eula moved it from pan to serving dish.

"Why haven't you eaten?" Crystal asked.

"*No dinero.*"

"Where do you live?"

"*No casa. No casa.*"

"No home?" Crystal glanced at Eula, then back at the Mexican girl. "*¿Por qué?*"

"I run away."

"From your husband? *¿Esposo?*"

"No." Her sad eyes closed for a moment, then softly, "No."

"Parents? *¿Padres?*"

"No. From *hombre malo.*"

"*¿Quien?* Who is the bad man?"

"*Señor* Blackwood." Rosa scrunched her mouth and eyes as if she had bitten into a piece of spoiled fruit.

"Who is he? What is your relationship to him? A relative? *¿Un familiar?*

The Mexican woman shook her head violently from side to side. "No. *No familiar.* I am ... his ..." She furrowed her brows and cocked her head to one side. "How to say *esclava?*"

Crystal looked down for a moment as she searched her limited Spanish vocabulary for a translation. Finally, she looked up at Rosa. "The only English word I can think of for *esclava* is ... slave."

Rosa's head bobbed up and down. "*Si. Si.* Slave. I am his slave."

Chapter 2

AFTER dinner, the three women sat on Eula's veranda overlooking the long, narrow lake three hundred feet down a gentle slope. Crystal and Rosa rocked slowly in the porch swing. Crystal's hair, as black as Rosa's, curled in toward the neck just short of her shoulders, while Rosa's stopped just short of her waist. Both women were slender, but Crystal stood six inches taller. While the young Mexican had jet black eyes, Crystal's might be called antique bronze. But nothing in Crystal could match the sadness and pain evident in Rosa's eyes.

Getting answers from Rosa during the meal had been impossible. She had devoured more food than Eula and Crystal together, barely allowing herself time to breathe. Grandmother and granddaughter merely looked at each other, shook their heads, and smiled.

Now, Crystal resumed the painstaking task of discovering what had brought this beautiful young Mexican woman to Eula's home.

"Rosa, why do you say you were a slave?"

"I forced to work for *Señor* Blackwood. No can leave."

"What'd you do for him?" Eula asked.

"I do all things. I cook. I clean house. I wash clothes. *Plancha.*"

"Iron," Crystal translated for Eula.

"I fix yard, grass. I wash car." She paused for a moment,

eyes wide. "I do all things."

"How much did Mr. Blackwood pay you?"

"He say he pay me minimal wage."

"I'd bet on that," muttered Eula.

"Was it *minimum* wage?" Crystal asked.

"*Si.* Minimum wage. But when I asked him for my money, he say he take money for food I eat, room I sleep in."

Crystal and Eula exchanged looks, but said nothing.

"I tell him I eat less. Other time, he say he take money for clothes." Her shoulders, her mouth, her very spirit, sagged. "Sometime I get five dollars. One time I get ten dollars."

Crystal frowned. "Five dollars? For a whole day's work?"

Rosa shook her head. "No day. *Un mes.*"

Shock wiped out the frown. "Are you telling me you never got more than ten dollars for a month's work?"

"*Si.* Sometime I get nothing. Most time, I get five dollars."

Crystal looked at Eula and shook her head in disbelief. "How long, *quanto tiempo*, did you work for Mr. Blackwood?" Crystal asked.

"Eleven months," Rosa said.

Crystal's mouth stayed open as she stared at the young Mexican woman.

"Why'd you stay so long?" Eula asked. "I'd of said, 'So long Blackheart. I'm out'a here.'"

Rosa furrowed her brows but said nothing.

"Were you free to leave?" asked Crystal.

Still Rosa said nothing.

Crystal tried again. "Would Mr. Blackwood allow you to leave?"

Rosa shook her head. "No. He say, I leave, or talk to people, Miguel have accident."

"Miguel?"

"Miguel *mi esposo* in Mexico."

A few seconds passed before the full meaning penetrated Crystal's understanding. Rosa could not leave without putting her husband in serious danger. Crystal clamped her mouth shut lest her anger erupt in a scream.

Eula swore under her breath. "Damn crook. Ought to be hung up by his—"

"Nana."

"She won't know what I'm saying. And anyways, he ought to be." Eula softened her tone and leaned toward her guest. "Why'd you leave yesterday?"

Rosa turned away and this time, tears overflowed her eyes and ran down her cheeks. The Mexican's consuming anguish enveloped Crystal and her eyes misted over even though she didn't know the cause. She wanted to take the young woman in her arms and rock her. Instead, she looked toward the tranquil lake, hoping it might uncoil her stomach, shield her from the anguish filling the veranda like a dense fog.

Darkness had descended, and to the east, a thin cloud sliced across the slender crescent moon . A dagger aimed at Rosa.

"Three days back, Lucita come work at house. She come from Mexico. We talk. She hear of Miguel, *mi esposo*. She tell me . . ." Her voice broke and moments passed before she could continue. ". . . he is dead." Once more tears ran down her cheeks.

"Dead?" Crystal felt like someone had hit her in the chest. "What happened?"

Rosa wiped her eyes and opened her mouth, but the crush of emotion prevented words from forming. A minute passed and then another before she could answer. "Lucita tell me he get hurt working at *hacienda*. Josè no let him go to doctor. Two weeks, he die. She tell me they bury him . . . *el mes pasado*."

"Last month." It exploded almost as a scream. Crystal could feel the vein in her neck throbbing.

She slid over and wrapped her arms around Rosa. The young woman, ramrod straight and somewhat reserved until now, melted against Crystal as sobs shook her small body.

Crystal rocked the swing slowly, gently patting Rosa. The woman's tears gradually subsided, but an occasional low moan confirmed her grieving continued.

Crystal held Rosa tightly, both to give the young Mexican woman comfort and to ward off a sudden chill she felt. Crystal was not married yet. But she had lost both parents when she was seven and her pain had seemed hopeless for such a long time. No one could comfort her. No one could comfort Rosa.

Softly, Crystal asked, "Did *Señor* Blackwood know Jose?"

Rosa nodded. "*Señor* José get me to Texas. Miguel must work for him until I send money to pay for my trip."

Bile rose into Crystal's throat. José and Blackwood did business together. Blackwood undoubtedly knew of Miguel's death long before Rosa found out. But of course he didn't tell her. That would break the lock on her chains. His slave might escape.

Suddenly, the chill was gone, replaced by rising heat. It enveloped Crystal's stomach first. It spread to her head. Her face felt feverish. She brushed a hand across her brow, expecting to find beads of sweat. Her breathing accelerated, now rapid and shallow, and her jaw twitched as she clenched her teeth. This Blackwood person had kept Rosa a prisoner, chained by threats and fear of what would happen to her husband if she left. And when Miguel died, this . . . monster . . . didn't even tell Rosa.

Crystal's nails dug into the palm of her hand.

Somehow, Blackwood must be stopped.

Chapter 3

AT some level of consciousness, Crystal knew it was a dream but she couldn't seem to step out of it. Naked and locked inside a giant oven, she called for help. The men watching just laughed.

In frustration, she jerked around and the covers came off. The cool morning air shocked her warm body. Her eyes popped open and she focused on the cedar squirrel her granddad had carved for her when she turned eight. She was at The Park. She could hear voices. To whom would Nana be talking at this hour of the morning?

The events of last night surged to the front of her mind, like a camera zooming in for a close-up. Rosa.

Crystal hopped up, dressed, and splashed water on her face. She detoured through the kitchen to get coffee. With steaming mug in hand, she joined her grandmother and Rosa on the dappled veranda. The early sun peeked through the trees, casting wavering shadows across the expanse of redwood planking. But Rosa's story from last night obliterated the joy of morning in The Park.

"Good morning, sleepy-head," Eula greeted her.

Crystal settled into a high-backed rocker. "What's happening?"

"Oh, Rosa and I were just visiting. I was asking her where she lived before coming to Texas."

"Miguel and I live in Santiago. With my parents."

"Does José live there?" asked Crystal.

Rosa frowned and jerked her head from side to side. "No. He have big hacienda no far from San Sebastian. It no far from Santiago."

"And Lucita?" asked Eula. "Was she from Santiago, or San Sebastian?"

"No. Lucita go to San Sebastian before she come to Texas. Other man tell her Miguel dead. Man say if she see me, tell me."

Crystal sipped her coffee and tried to get her mind around the circumstances Rosa was describing. "Why didn't Lucita escape with you ... leave Blackwood's when you did? Why didn't she come with you?" Crystal asked.

"She afraid."

"Does she have a husband in Mexico? Is he working for Jose?" Crystal worried Lucita's husband might be trapped like Rosa's.

"No."

"This is like pulling teeth," Eula muttered.

"Nana, you're not in a foreign country and just learned your husband is dead. Have a little patience."

Eula gave Crystal a salute. "Yes, ma'am."

Crystal turned back to Rosa. "Why is Lucita afraid?"

"Her *niñas*."

"Her children? Where are her children?"

"Mexico."

"She left her children in Mexico?" Crystal asked. "With the father?"

"No. He is dead," Rosa said.

Crystal's hand began to tremble, and she put the mug

down on the small table beside the rocker. Her shoulders sagged as she tried to imagine the desperation that would cause a mother to leave her children behind and go to uncertainty in a foreign country.

A dark foreboding saturated her spirit as various images paraded unbidden across Crystal's mind. In a low and hesitant voice, she asked, "Who is keeping the children for Lucita?" Unconsciously, she held her breath, afraid she knew the answer.

Crystal heard a sharp intake of breath. Eula also anticipated the answer.

"They are at house of *Señor* Jose. They stay until Lucita make money to bring them to United States."

"Hell's bells," Nana said, looking at Crystal. "We're letting the fox baby-sit the new chicks." She turned to Rosa. "Boys, girls?"

"Two girls."

"My God," whispered Eula. "How old?"

"One has five years. One has three years."

Crystal tried to speak, but nothing came out of her mouth. Lucita would never raise the money to bring the girls to Texas. If Rosa had been trapped with a husband in Mexico working for Jose, Lucita was shackled much more securely.

She swallowed and hoped her voice would not convey her fear to Rosa. "She has to work to pay for her trip, and then work to pay for bringing the children to Texas?"

Rosa nodded.

"And like you, she can't leave to take another job?"

"No."

"Did you tell her she might make only five or ten dollars a month? That she would never pay off the debt?"

"I tell her."

"But she wouldn't leave with you?"

"No. She say, *Señor* Blackwood tell her if she leave, or talk to anyone, children have accident or disappear."

Crystal's thoughts raced. How could a person do this to another human being? How could he force a mother to give up her children? To threaten her by holding her children hostage? And never plan to return them to their mother?

From what Rosa had told them, Crystal could imagine the children being slaves their entire lives. Even if Lucita saved every cent she was paid, she would never have enough to rescue her children. If she did manage to pay her debt, there was no guarantee, perhaps no hope, the children would ever be returned to her.

Crystal could hear her heart pounding, could feel the vice tightening on her stomach, could taste the anger taking control of her body. She jumped up and stormed off the veranda.

She stomped down to the dock. Quiet time, just floating in the boat or paddling around near the banks always eased her mind, diminished problems, relaxed tensions. She loosened the mooring, stepped into the boat, and used a paddle to push off. Maybe the lake could work its magic once more.

The narrow lake stretched nearly a half-mile long, yet never got within a thousand feet of The Park's boundaries. No passing cars or booming stereos disturbed the peace. Only the chirping of birds, or the splash of a big catfish, interrupted the silence.

The sun peeked through the tallest pines—an orange disk on a bright blue background. Scattered, puffy white clouds drifted lazily across the sky.

The deep, cobalt blue water enhanced the green of the trees. Some sumacs along the creek that fed the lake had already begun sporting their flashy, autumn colors. High in the pine trees on the east side of the lake, purple clumps of ripe Muscadine grapes promised a juicy treat.

Most problems just couldn't stand up to the beauty and serenity of floating around Nana's lake.

But Crystal's mind was trapped by the plight of the young mother. Twice, Crystal looked around, thinking she heard children crying. Or was it their mother? What an incredible decision to make, to leave her children behind. She could not have known what kind of man José was. He must have played the part of a savior, paying her way to a place where she could make enough money to take good care of her children. He would look after her girls until she got on her feet and could send for them. Crystal's whole body shook with revulsion. Even a rattlesnake warned you. José could not, must not, get away with this.

This man would *not* do to Lucita what he had done to Rosa. The evil could not be allowed to continue.

And yet, another part of her mind protested. *Don't get involved. Stay away from Blackwood. The man is evil. Stay away. This is not your problem. Besides, there is nothing you can do. Lucita will not leave Blackwood as long as her children are held hostage. Stay away. Put it out of your mind. Forget about it.* But the problem had taken up residence in Crystal's brain.

She had beached the boat when a commotion caught her attention. A smallmouth bass, probably chasing a minnow, had run aground. Now, it flopped around in a frantic attempt to find enough water to swim. Crystal bent over to pick it up and was rewarded with a slap of lake water in her face as the fish flipped its tail.

"Hey, guy, I'm trying to help." She eased one hand under the white belly and her other hand over its silver body, making a cage to keep it from jumping out. Then, stepping one foot out into the water, she slipped the frightened fish back into the lake.

Rosa was out of her element, too. Crystal could help her.

But Lucita was caught in a net.

Chapter 4

CRYSTAL climbed the grassy hill toward the house. On the veranda, Eula rocked slowly, cradling a tall glass of iced tea, a smile playing at the corners of her wide mouth. Rosa sat, twisting a piece of her dress around a finger.

Crystal reached the bottom step before she could hear what Eula was saying.

"No, I don't know what will happen to you, anymore 'n I know which way a fish'll turn. But you can bet your drawers I won't turn you over to immigration."

Rosa wrinkled her forehead and stared at Eula.

Crystal stepped up on the porch. "I don't think 'drawers' fits into Spanish the same way it does in your version of English, Nana." She dropped down into one of the rocking chairs.

"Well, pardon me. I didn't get a graduate degree from Stanford. We were doing okay without your help, thank you."

Rosa looked from Eula to Crystal, deep lines creasing her forehead. "You no call immigration?"

"No," said Crystal. "We won't call immigration."

Rosa grabbed Crystal's hand and held it tightly.

Eula arched her eyebrows. "Well. You got it all figured out? You usually work things out on the lake."

"I did get a few ideas, Nana." Crystal turned to Rosa. "I want to go see Mr. Blackwood. Will you take me there?"

The relieved look that had covered Rosa's face vanished

in an instant, replaced by a wrinkled forehead, squinting eyes and a gaping mouth. She dropped Crystal's hand as if it were a hot branding iron. The short, quick jerks of her head from side to side made her answer clear.

"Rosa, I would be going with you. I wouldn't let anything happen to you. Mr. Blackwood has no hold on you now. It will be all right."

"Bum idea," said Eula.

Crystal ignored her grandmother. "I want to talk to Lucita, Rosa. I want to see if there is something, anything, we can do to help her. Maybe we can get her out of there."

No tears seeped from the jet-black eyes, but a slight tremor ran down Rosa's arms to her tightly clenched hands. "I want help Lucita. But I no go to house of *Señor* Blackwood."

"He can't do anything to you. I'll be with you."

"Bum idea, if I ever heard one," Eula repeated.

"*Señor* Blackwood maybe do nothing, but *Señor* Argos do bad things."

Both Crystal's and Eula's eyes opened wide. "Who is Argos?" asked Crystal.

"He work for *Señor* Blackwood. Is bad man."

"How is he bad?"

"He hurt people. He hit people, knock them down. Kick them. Broke Pilar's hand. I afraid of him. I no go to *Señor* Blackwood." She continued shaking her head from side to side. "No go."

"You're shelling empty hulls there," Eula said.

Crystal nodded. "Okay. What is Lucita's family name?"

"Morales," Rosa said.

"Morales," Crystal repeated. "And can you tell me Mr. Blackwood's address? Where does he live?"

Rosa shrugged. "I know is in Dallas."

"Do you know his first name?"

"First name is Hunter. He is called Hunter Blackwood."

#

After lunch, Crystal powered up her laptop computer and minutes later had the information she needed. She located Eula and Rosa in the utility room moving clothes from the washer to the dryer.

"I found him. Only one Hunter Blackwood in the Dallas/Fort Worth area. Address is 1 Hunter Circle. Does that tell you something?"

"It tells you to tread carefully," said Eula. "Reckon he's got powerful friends."

"If he's doing what I believe he's doing, I'll stomp, not tread. Tomorrow, when I go back to Dallas, I'm going to pay Hunter Blackwood a visit."

"And say what? 'Are you a slave trader?'" Eula turned the dryer on and headed for the veranda with Rosa trailing behind her.

"I hadn't thought of that, but it sounds good to me," said Crystal, following them. "No. I'm just going to ask to speak to Lucita and then ask her if she is being held against her will."

Eula eyebrows arched up. "And then what?"

"Then I can tell Tom I know firsthand a young woman is being held against her will."

Eula plopped down in a rocker and motioned Rosa to take one. "Now, I'm not one to give advice."

Crystal rolled her eyes.

"But, you might want to rethink - or think, I'm not sure you've thought about it yet - such a foolish idea. This man sounds dangerous. I'd hate to have to come rescue you."

"What's he going to do? Pull me in the door and lock me up?"

"It happens."

Crystal had no comeback. People were kidnapped. People did disappear. But...what? It didn't happen in Dallas? It only happened to *other* people?

The three rocked in silence, absorbing the warm, fall sun. After awhile, Eula said to Crystal, "You could take Bull with you. Ask him to ride shotgun."

Dr. Mark O'Malley was the founder and principal owner of Intelligent Retrieval Systems, or IRS, the company where Crystal worked. He had been a professional bull rider when he was younger. Eula was the only person Crystal had ever heard call Mark by his nickname from the rodeo days: Bull O'Malley.

"I can't do that, Nana."

Eula pursed her thin lips and wrinkled her nose. "Don't know why not. Knowing Bull, I'd bet my first-born daughter he'd go."

"You didn't have a daughter. I'm not going to ask him to go with me, and that's final."

"Bad move." Eula sighed. "But I guess good judgment is learned from bad judgment." She rocked quietly for a few moments. "You could call him up and ask him out. Then say you have to make a quick stop."

"I'm not going to call him up and ask him out."

"Mistake. He's blue-ribbon quality. Somebody's gonna put a bridle on him if you don't."

Crystal sighed.

The only chance to end this conversation was to remain silent. Ever since Eula met Mark last fall, she had been after Crystal to go out with him. In truth, Crystal and Mark *were* going out, a fact she chose not to share with her grandmother just yet. Nana would start planning a wedding and talking grandkids.

But Crystal had involved Mark in her problems last year and almost got him killed. As comforting as it would be to have him along, she would not ask him to go to Hunter Blackwood's with her. Besides, Mark had his own problems right now. His mother was terminally ill and, at least while his sister was in Europe, he had the full responsibility of caring for her. Crystal would not add to his load.

Eula refused to drop the subject. "I've watched him around you. He really--"

The jangling of the telephone saved her.

"I'll get it." Crystal ran into the kitchen and answered the phone.

"Hello, Crystal. This is Dr. Krupe."

Dear God. Her hand shook and her knees felt weak. She slumped onto a stool.

She still vividly remembered the man from her past who nearly succeeded in crushing her. Against her will, her mind replayed visions of Dr. Krupe's sexual assault when she was just months from finishing a Ph.D. at Stanford. She successfully rebuffed him, but the very next day, he began an attack that drove her out of school. Crystal had believed him to be the world's greatest authority on information retrieval. When he said her research was worthless—that she had no ability for graduate school—she lost all self-confidence and left. She had worked long and hard toward a doctorate, only to have it snatched away because she refused to go to bed with her dissertation advisor, Dr. Lester Krupe. It had taken her until last year, with a lot of help from Brandi Brewer, her housemate, to regain her self-esteem.

She took a deep breath and spoke carefully, afraid her voice might betray her. "How did you find me?"

He laughed. "I *am* the leading authority on information

retrieval."

Of course. All her school records would have included Nana's phone number. She visualized his striking patrician profile, laughing in his condescending way.

"So why are you calling me?" Their last meeting, nearly a year ago, had ended with her accusing him of trying to steal her research, and pass it off as his own at a presentation at the University of Texas in Dallas. He had cost her a Ph.D. She had cost him a lucrative consultancy job. No, she corrected herself. *He* had cost himself that job.

He continued in his usual, self-confident manner. "In the face of your blistering attack on me when I was at IRS last fall, I didn't get to give my side of the story. You were so upset and out of control I felt it best *for you* that I not respond fully. But, we do need to clear the air."

"It's history. There's no need to rehash it."

Krupe continued, "It is customary that the advisor's name appears on the papers of his students. After all, the professor often provides the idea and always the guidance necessary to bring the idea into a publishable paper."

"My name was not on the paper. You did not provide the idea, and you provided extremely little guidance." Crystal tried to keep her voice level, even as her blood pressure rose.

"Oh, I'm sure both our names were on the opening slide." His manner remained as smooth as always.

"No. I was there, remember. Mark was there. Shall we ask him? Better yet, I'm sure I can find several faculty members at UT/Dallas who can verify it. Shall I go out and explain the situation to them and ask what they remember about it?"

Krupe hesitated. "Well, possibly the secretary made a mistake. You know how they are. Only thinking about quitting time and payday. I will check the slides. If she left your name off, I will reprimand her. Will that make you feel better about things?"

Crystal bit her lip. Had she opened her mouth, she was certain she would have yelled at the man.

"What I'm saying to you, Crystal, is I will try to set things right, make certain your name is clearly listed. But I ask you not spread any more misinformation around that I was not sharing credit. You know I would not knowingly—"

"Dr. Krupe, I'm not spreading anything around. I've put it behind me. But I will certainly use my paper when and where I choose. And you know how secretaries are. They might forget to put your name on it."

"Now Crystal, let's try to keep this on a professional level."

Her skin crawled as the memory of him groping her breasts and kissing her neck materialized.

"Will you agree," he continued, "if I personally guarantee your name is on the very first slide, you won't rehash the problem you perceived to have existed when I presented the paper last year?"

"I haven't been talking about it. I'm happy to forget about it completely. Just don't give my paper again."

For several seconds, Krupe remained silent. "I have been asked to speak at Carnegie Mellon University. You do know CMU is an important school for IR, don't you?"

"Of course."

"They heard about the presentation in Dallas and a Dr. Jamie Patrick at CMU has asked me to come and present it to the students and faculty."

Crystal had met Jamie at a conference. She judged him to be honest, reliable, and extremely bright. She chose not to share that information with Krupe.

"You can be absolutely certain your name will appear immediately below mine. I'll even make sure it is in the same size type as mine. Will that be agreeable to you? I promise your name will be on the paper when I present it at CMU."

Crystal was silent. Krupe had tried to take full credit for it in Dallas. Then, when she called him on it, he tried to claim it had really been his idea, his work. Now, the secretary caused the problem.

Having her work presented at CMU would be good for her professional standing. Except, Krupe would be doing the presentation.

"Crystal?"

"When?"

"Just about a month from now."

"I'll think about it."

He does not intimidate me. He does not intimidate me. But her hand was quivering as she hung up the telephone.

Chapter 5

SUNDAY morning, Crystal turned on her computer and tapped into her resources at Intelligent Retrieval Systems. An hour later, she had a picture of Hunter Blackwood, one that did not look dark or evil or threatening. Nor did it show any warmth.

He served on the Board of Directors for the Dallas Symphony plus several charities. Dallas society circles considered him a desirable and eligible bachelor. He appeared to be a one-man financial consulting service, who paid taxes—a lot of taxes—but had no office outside his home. A house with a property value of six million, he didn't need one..

The only thing remotely strange concerned the death of his wife four years ago. While the police classified it as murder, Crystal could find no resolution to the case. Otherwise, the man appeared as unremarkable as store-bought bread. Of course, to really ferret out information, she needed to be at her office.

She left The Park just after lunch, heading back to her apartment in Dallas. She had listened to Rosa's warnings and Nana's cautions. She had taken note of her grandmother's repeated suggestions that Mark accompany her, and silently dismissed them.

Though she tried to think of more pleasant things, her mind refused to dwell on any topic except Lucita and her children. When Rosa had first used the word *"esclava,"* Crystal hadn't really believed anybody was enslaved. Not in this day and age. Not in Dallas, for God's sake. The United States was the land of freedom. True, certain prejudices lingered, maybe even flourished in some places. But slavery did not exist. People used the word "*slave*" to stir emotions.

But the more she learned about what had happened to Rosa and Miguel, the more she began to believe. Rosa had not been held by chains, but by something stronger: the love for her husband.

Crystal slammed a hand against the steering wheel. Should she go straight to her friend Tom Hawkins—Brandi's boyfriend and a detective with the Dallas Police Department? Maybe he could talk to Blackwood. But at this point, what proof could she present? Crystal knew, could feel it in her bones, Rosa was telling the truth. Tom would say he needed concrete evidence. Lots of people thought they were not paid enough and exaggerated how little money they made. Certainly Lucita should pay room and board. He'd say the problem was for immigration, not the Dallas police.

By the time Crystal reached her apartment, she was thoroughly confused. What would she say to Blackwood? But she was positive about one thing: she *would* talk to Lucita.

In the apartment her housemate, Brandi Brewer, lay in the middle of the living room floor, her feet on a chair, a pillow covering her head.

"Let me guess," Crystal said. "Some new fitness routine Tom's talked you into."

"No." Brandi's voice seeped through the pillow. "I'm trying to get in touch with my subconscious, my inner self."

"And when you do?"

"I tell it what I want and it takes over from there."

"Sounds good to me."

"*I* thought so. 'Course, Tom, being the practical detective, said it was all a bunch of hogwash." The pillow came off Brandi's face, revealing copper-colored hair and bright, aqua eyes. "Have a good time at your grandmother's?"

Crystal dropped onto the couch. "I don't think 'good' quite catches the flavor of it. But interesting."

"Eula fixed you up with the preacher's son?"

"No. Believe it or not, that would have been better."

"Better?" Brandi sat up. "This I gotta hear."

Crystal filled Brandi in on Rosa's arrival and the story the Mexican girl had told them. Brandi sat, mouth open, not saying a word—an unusual state for her.

When Crystal finished, Brandi asked, "And you're going over there?"

"Yes, I am."

Brandi shook her head and sighed. "Okay. Give me five minutes." She picked up her petite, size four body and headed toward her bedroom.

"You don't—"

"'Course I do."

#

Brandi drove. Crystal gave directions off the GPS.

"Almost there. Take the second right and you should find Hunter Circle," Crystal said. "You really didn't have to come. Nothing's going to happen." *But I'm glad you did.*

"Good. And don't think I'm going in with you. I'm not that stupid."

"Then, why did you come?"

"I'm sitting in the car, doors locked, motor running, cell phone in my hot little hand. Anything doesn't look right to me, Mother Brewer calls in reinforcements."

"Motor running?"

"You bet. Doors locked. The way you told it, I believe these guys can make a person disappear. And I think two could disappear as fast as one. They come after me, I'm gone - for help, of course. The worst thing that can happen is for you to disappear and nobody knows how or who snatched you. I'm going to know. And they're gonna know I know."

Crystal laughed. "I've read those books. 'If I'm not back in an hour, the police will receive a letter telling all about you crooks.'"

Brandi's eyes turned serious and she raised her chin. "Just 'cause it's in a book doesn't mean it won't work. I'm just modernizing it a bit. Motor running, cell phone in hand."

Brandi turned the car into a cul-de-sac. "Wow."

Hunter Circle had but a single residence, an expensive, sprawling house that exuded all the warmth of a codfish. One-story wings extended on each side of a massive, two-story center section. The house presented no architectural interest other than its size. Bricks, trim, doors, and windows were a uniform off-white, more on the gray side than a warmer, yellow tint. Crystal could see no shutters, in fact, no ornamentation at all. *Looks like a prison.* Instinctively, she looked up to see if there were any guards on the roof.

A number of small, uniformly green shrubs hid the foundation, but offered no charm to the featureless building. They were clipped so perfectly they might have been plastic. The neatly trimmed grass looked lifeless, in keeping with its surroundings. Not a single flower graced the property. Not even a dandelion.

A black, wrought-iron fence surrounded the yard. Crystal shook her head. It added to the general impersonal, sterile feel of the place. As for security, it might keep out a boy chasing an errant football.

Today, the gate stood ajar. They would park on the street, and Crystal could simply walk up to the front door and ring the bell. A chill caused her to shiver.

"Now, there's digs that say 'I've got money.'" Brandi

giggled. "Not old money, mind you. Definitely new money. Old Blackie didn't want it to look like a plantation. Might give people ideas."

She stopped the car opposite the flagstone walk that curved up to the mammoth structure. "Gives me the creeps." She leaned over to look out Crystal's window. "You know I can't stand anything that's too neat. Reminds me of that movie, The Devil House. Remember that one? The house was possessed or something. People would go in and never be seen again. Couldn't even find bones or anything."

"You're not helping, Brandi." In spite of the bright, sunny day, Crystal felt as though she were about to enter a graveyard at midnight on a cold, moonless night. Even the hairs on the back of her neck stood on alert. "There's not even a bird anywhere around this place."

Brandi put a hand on Crystal's shoulder. "You don't have to do this, you know. In fact, I don't know *anyone* who wants you to."

With an effort, Crystal forced her gaze to shift from the house to her friend. "If I believe Rosa, then I have to do this. And I do believe her." She sighed. "It isn't going to get any easier if I wait." She opened the door, but her feet did not move.

"How long do you think you'll be in there? When should I panic and call in back-up?"

"Give me ten minutes. Probably won't be that long." She forced a little laugh. "I may not get past the front door." With that, she pulled herself out, closed the door, and headed for the house. The door lock clicked behind her.

Crystal rang the bell and waited. Up close, the house appeared no better. Millions of dollars and still it looked as appealing as day-old coffee.

She grasped her hands tightly behind her back and hoped her knees did not buckle. She clinched her teeth so tightly her jaw throbbed. She could hear a rapid thumping noise. Was somebody running in the house? *Dummy, that's your heart beating. Calm down. Relax. Breathe.*

The door opened and there stood a young Mexican woman. "*Sí?*"

It took a moment for Crystal to find her voice. "Are you Lucita?"

The woman's black eyes narrowed and a frown creased her young face. A simple dress hung from her shoulders. Her sandals looked much the same as Rosa's. A plain, silver clasp held black hair away from her round face. Her features were as delicate as spun glass. She jerked her head to glance behind her, then looked back at Crystal. She nodded once, so slightly Crystal almost missed it.

Crystal took a deep breath and reminded herself to speak slowly and distinctly. "If you would like to leave now, I can help you. We will go and get your children back. Rosa is with my grandmother. I will take you there. And we *will* get your children. But you need to come with me right now. *Ahora.*"

Lucita tilted her head to one side. She gave no response, no real indication she understood except her eyes grew even darker.

Crystal tried again. "Do you want to leave this house?"

Still the young woman made no sound, but her breathing accelerated and stress lines formed between her eyebrows. She took a small half-step away from Crystal.

From nearby in the house a male voice said, "Lucita. *¿Quien es?*"

Crystal stiffened. Before she regained her composure, a man appeared behind Lucita and placed his hand lightly on her shoulder. She moved aside and Crystal was facing a man probably in his late forties, well over six feet tall. His brown hair had only a little gray at the temples. Despite handsome features, he appeared unattractive. Perhaps it was the cold that radiated from his dull, grey eyes. The slight smile on his face added no warmth. In his left hand he held a large metal casting of some sort.

"May I help you?"

Once again, Crystal found it difficult to speak. She had wanted to talk to this man, to accuse him of cruelty to these Mexican women. Now, her voice failed her. When she managed to speak, the words rushed out of her mouth. "Are you Mr. Blackwood? Hunter Blackwood?"

"Yes, I am. And who are you?"

A simple question. One she didn't want to answer. But she was the one who had come here asking questions. "Ah, Ms. Moore. I was asking Lucita if she wanted to leave. I wanted to know if she was being held here against her will." Her voice betrayed her and cracked like a teenaged boy's.

Hunter Blackwood studied Crystal for several seconds. If her accusations offended him, no indication showed in his manner. But the look in his eyes hardened. He turned and took Lucita by the hand and guided her up beside him. "Lucita. ¿Esta usted aqui contra su voluntad?"

She shook her head violently from side to side. "No. No. Estoy muy a gusto aquí." Her eyes opened wide and deep creases formed across her brow. She continued shaking her head in short, jerky movements.

Blackwood turned back to Crystal and raised his well-trimmed eyebrows. "I don't know where you got the idea she wanted to leave. But you heard for yourself. She said she liked it here. Do you understand Spanish?"

"Enough."

"Then you know what she said. Was there anything else?"

Crystal didn't know what else to say. To verbally attack Blackwood would do no good. He seemed too cool to lose his temper and say something that might help her. She could tell him Rosa was at The Park and had revealed what he did to her. What would that accomplish? Simply tell Blackwood where Rosa was. Where to look for her.

His cold smile returned and he stood there waiting for her to answer. Her gaze wandered to the piece of bronze he held, shaped like a huge dollar sign, probably a foot long, and from the way he held it, heavy.

She blinked several times to break her stare and looked back up at Blackwood's icy eyes. "No. I just wanted to hear her say she was here of her own free will."

"Well, you did. Is there anything else?"

Crystal stood there, not knowing exactly what to do next. Anger overtook her brain and she wanted to lash out at this evil man. But fear was rising just as fast. Fear won out. "No."

"Then, good day." And he shut the door.

#

Crystal got in the passenger's side and Brandi had the car moving before the door closed.

"Well?" Brandi drove, but her attention stayed on Crystal.

"Just get us out of here. That guy and that place give me the creeps."

"I'll say. I was shaking out here in the car."

"Besides, I don't want to give him a chance to get your license plate number."

Brandi's eyes opened wide and she glanced at her friend. "Wow. He really did spook you." She whipped the car around the corner and sped down several blocks before making another turn, heading for the freeway.

Crystal let out a long breath. "I'm sure you saw the woman who opened the door. That was Lucita. I asked her if she wanted to leave right now. I told her we would get her children." Crystal shook her head. "She didn't say a word."

"Are you sure it was Lucita?"

"She nodded when I asked her. Then Blackwood came to the door."

"I saw a man." Thin traffic allowed Brandi to concentrate most of her attention on Crystal. "Nice looking, from what I could see. What did you say to him?"

"I said I wanted to know if Lucita was there of her own free will or if she was being held against her wishes."

"Wow." Brandi slammed her hand on the steering wheel, accidentally honking the horn. "Crystal Moore, woman of steel nerves."

"Yeah. I was shaking in my shoes."

After a moment of silence, Brandi said, "Well, come on, gal. Don't leave me hanging. What'd he say? Or do?"

Crystal furrowed her eyebrows. "Strange. I thought that question would get some sort of rise out of him. But he just turned to Lucita and asked her, in Spanish, if she was there against her will."

"And?"

"She said no. She liked it there."

"In Spanish?"

"Yes. But simply and slowly enough I understood her."

They drove another block. "How'd he ask it? I mean, did he say it in such a way she knew what she'd better answer?"

"No. He asked it as easily as you might say, 'Is dinner ready?'" Crystal rubbed the side of her nose. "But she was terrified. I could see it in her eyes. She was afraid to say anything else. I'm more convinced than ever. She is a slave. *Ella es una esclava.*"

"And how'd he treat you? Particularly after you asked

him that?"

"He was as pleasant as could be." Crystal shook her head. "No, not pleasant. Cold. Neutral. No emotion at all. He didn't seem to be upset with my question. Of course he wasn't upset with Lucita's answer. Then he asked if there was anything else. I said no and he said good day. He didn't get angry or even show any displeasure. He just smiled. A chilling smile."

Brandi squinted her eyes and half-turned to Crystal "That's it? He didn't ask you why you were there or who sent you?"

"No. Nothing. Well, he asked my name."

Brandi glanced at Crystal, lines of concern etched into her face. "Did you tell him?"

"I stammered and said I was Ms. Moore."

"I'd have told him I was Joan Doe or Sara Jane Smith. Or Hillary Rodham. I thought I'd taught you better."

Crystal remained silent. *That was a mistake. What was I thinking. Did I really think Lucita would just bolt out the door with someone she'd never seen before? Stupid. Nana was right. Dumb idea.*

Once more, Crystal shifted her head so she could see in the outside mirror. The street behind them was empty. The hand clamped on her purse relaxed ever so slightly.

Chapter 6

AT 1 Hunter Circle, Blackwood returned to his study and closed the door. Burgundy carpet and mahogany paneling gave the room its dark appearance. The desk and several low, lateral file cabinets were made of the same wood. He placed the bronze dollar sign on the desk, then sat in a high-backed, burgundy leather chair and placed his well-manicured hands on the desk. Three focused spotlights in the ceiling illuminated the desktop and the chair in front of the desk, but left him in the shadows.

"Her name is Moore. Brown eyes, black hair, late twenties. Get her picture from the security camera. Find her." He began sorting through some papers on the desktop. His well-modulated voice had revealed no anger.

The man seated before him nodded.

"I do not want to see or hear about her again."

Blackwood raised his head slightly, fixing the man with a steel-cold stare. "Ever."

Chapter 7

CRYSTAL sat in an overstuffed chair, upholstered in a nubby material of a color she called champagne and Brandi called granny white. A magazine lay open in her lap, but she was staring into space.

Brandi lounged on the couch, feet curled under her, flipping through a Dillard's catalogue and munching an apple. "Now, here's a little number that would grab Tom's attention. What do you think?" Brandi turned the catalogue toward her housemate. When Crystal didn't look, Brandi waved the page at her. "Hey, are you home, or having an out-of-body experience?"

Crystal blinked twice and looked at the cocktail dress vividly displayed in the catalogue. "Yeah. That would look good on you."

"Okay. Forget the sexy dress. Can't afford it anyway. What's sucking up all your brain waves?"

Crystal's dark mood saturated the room. "He scares me."

Brandi screwed her face into a question mark, then quickly changed to understanding. "Blackwood. Fortunately, you don't have to see him again."

"What about Lucita?"

"Did you ask her to leave with you? On the spot?"

"Yes, but— "

"But nothing. You gave her a chance. She said she liked it there. End of story."

"I can't ignore her, or her situation."

Brandi dropped the catalogue. "Look, you marched right into the tiger's den. You confronted the beast in his lair. That's hardly ignoring the situation. You went far beyond the call of duty and tried to get her to leave. She wouldn't. You can't force her. You don't need to feel guilty." Brandi crunched into the apple again.

Nothing Blackwood said sounded threatening. Bland or bored best described his look. Yet, his attitude, his eyes, his very being radiated such cold Crystal had felt chilled standing three feet away. Without saying a single menacing word, the man had terrified her. And made her angrier than she'd been in years.

"Who's going to help Lucita?"

"The same person who would of if Rosa had rummaged through somebody else's garbage can instead of Eula's." Brandi exhaled loudly. "She's not your responsibility, Crystal. And we are in agreement: you don't want to tangle with Blackheart." Brandi reached out and took her friend's hand. "What's happening with Rosa?"

"She's staying at Nana's. We'll work something out for her, get her some jobs. I've got to see about getting her a green card or visa or something."

"Okay. So, you're working to save Rosa, improve her life, maybe make her legal here. You gave Lucita a chance to escape. You confronted Blackwood. You've done a lot. You're not at fault 'cause you haven't done *everything*. You can't right all the wrongs in the world. Lucita won't leave." She hunched her shoulders. "Maybe she *shouldn't* leave."

For a long time, neither woman said anything. Finally, Crystal let out a long breath. "You're right. I can't force Lucita to leave. And we *are* helping Rosa."

But to herself, Crystal acknowledged her fear of Blackwood outweighed the other factors.

#

Crystal spent the next morning working on her current IRS project, a computer program capable of constantly analyzing all records in a hospital database to determine if any correlations existed between a disease and patient characteristics. Instead of long, drawn-out studies, her system would instantly check when new data was entered. She met with each member of her team, got reports, made suggestions, updated her progress chart, and adjusted her targets.

She spent the afternoon on Lucita and her children. Not that she planned it that way. But everything else got crowded out of her mind by pictures of imprisoned children. Nightmares plagued her all last night—images of mistreated girls, crying for their mother, not knowing if they would ever see her again, not knowing if she were alive or dead; visions of the mother, growing old under cruel conditions, weeping for her lost babies; pictures of Crystal at her parents' grave.

She threw her pencil down. "It's not my problem." *Let someone else deal with it, someone more prepared to handle this sort of thing.* She went back to her project notes. But neither her eyes nor her mind could focus on the project. Scenes of the children growing up as slaves for José blotted out everything else. What would they have to do? Work eighteen-hour days cleaning or working in the fields? Maybe they would be forced into prostitution when they were twelve. Her dark mood deepened.

When she left the office at 6:15, the grey drizzle only added to her depression. Brandi was working the late shift, so Crystal fixed a salad and plopped down in front of the TV, channel surfing, trying to find something, anything, to take her mind off Lucita's children. The comedies were insipid. A police show featuring kidnapped children, and she quickly flipped past that. She tried a game show, a pop psychologist, and a reality show. Finally, at nine she switched the set off, left her plate in the sink, and went to bed.

#

Crystal woke with a start. Light perspiration covered her skin and she felt chilled, but the trembling was not from cold. The dream had been so real her ankles hurt and she reached down to rub them. Legs chained, she had been forced to work, with no time to rest. Hunter Blackwood held a bronze piece, shaped like a dollar sign. Any time she slowed, he would touch her with it, blistering her skin. She couldn't remember what the work was, but she couldn't do it fast enough to suit him. After awhile, he no longer needed to touch her with the bronze. Just pointing it in her direction would cause immense pain. Even now, awake, she felt as though her arms were blistered.

She focused on the soft glow of the digital clock sitting on the dresser. Four-thirty. This made five nightmares that had terrified her since going to bed at nine last night. Children in chains; dead parents; Crystal as a child crying in an empty, dark room. She dreaded going back to sleep and facing yet another frightening vision. She switched on the light, went into the bathroom, and splashed cold water on her feverish face.

She considered going to her office to think this through, but opted for the kitchen instead. A few minutes and she would have this sorted out in her mind, be back in bed, and fast asleep.

An hour later, she determined her analytical skills, so carefully honed during years of graduate study, completely failed her now. Without thinking, she glanced in the direction of Brandi's room. She had helped Crystal sort things out in the past. Though Brandi had only a high school education, she amazed Crystal with her ability to cut through all the chaff and pick out the kernel of insight. Brandi's common sense was uncommonly good.

Crystal tapped lightly on the door. "Brandi. Are you awake?" She recognized that was a stupid question but it was the first thing that came to mind. When her housemate didn't respond, she tried again: "Brandi."

The lump under the covers stirred. Then a hand emerged, followed by a head. "Of course I'm awake. What else would I be at..." She squinted at the clock on the wall opposite her bed. "At 5:35? That's 5:35 a.m. on a day when I go to work in the afternoon."

"I can't sleep."

"Funny, I don't seem to be able to sleep either. Was somebody talking to you, too?"

"I'm sorry. I don't know what to do."

"About?"

"Lucita. And her children. I've had nightmares about them — all night."

"That's the topic for the 5:35 discussion group? Your nightmares?" She sat up. "Is this a quick consultation, or should I plan for extended care?"

"Unless you have some marvelous wisdom that usually only comes in a thirty-second commercial, I'll make a pot of coffee."

#

Ten minutes later, the aroma of fresh-brewed French-roast coffee filled the kitchen. Crystal sat on a stool at the marble-topped bar separating the kitchen from the dining room, a steaming mug nestled between her hands.

Brandi stood beside the microwave, waiting for a doughnut to warm. "Okay. Where do we start? Being such an analytical person, you probably want to make a list."

"Good idea. We can make a table showing all possible options, plus the good and bad points of each."

Brandi settled on a stool, doughnut in one hand, coffee mug in the other. "First entry: forget all about it." She took a bite of the doughnut and smiled. "Good points: we can go back to sleep. And we can stay away from the Devil House."

Crystal sighed. "I honestly wish I could." Her mind automatically listed the good and bad points. If she could forget about Lucita and the children, she could get back to a normal life, forget about modern-day slaves and dead husbands and children kept from their mother. And maybe get rid of the nightmares. *Not likely.*

One nightmare early this morning had brought back into sharp focus the instant when her own warm, safe, happy family had been snatched from her. First came sadness, quickly compounded by fright, loneliness, and then anger. Why did this happen to her? Why had her parents deserted her? She needed them. What had she done to cause them to go away, to abandon her? Why wouldn't anybody help her? Why couldn't someone see her pain, step forward, keep her from a life without parents?

Nana and Granddad had tried to comfort her, but Crystal had been beyond help. Her parents were dead. No one could bring them back.

Now, more than twenty years later, she still felt the pain.

But Lucita was not dead. Something *could* be done for her children. As much as Crystal might like to walk away, she knew as certainly as she knew how to boil water, she could not turn her back.

"No. That's out. I have to help her," said Crystal.

"Go to the police."

"A possibility. What are the pluses and minuses?"

Brandi held up a half eaten doughnut. "I'll give the pluses. It might get us back to bed and get rid of your nightmares. Shifts the problem to someone else, always a good thing. And, they have the resources—translate: muscle—to deal with Blackheart."

"On the minus side," Crystal countered, "we have no proof, no hard evidence, to induce the police to investigate. Tom will tell us there isn't enough information for them to do anything. Even if we got the police to go see her, Lucita would say she was happy there, she didn't want to leave. And of course, both Rosa and Lucita would be subject to deportation."

"Deportation might be better than staying with Blackheart. And it might get Lucita back to her children."

"Maybe. More likely, whoever has the children would just take Lucita as his slave. Or kill her for causing trouble." Crystal pressed her lips into a fine line and shook her head. "I don't have a clue what the police would do. They're not immigration, but they are the law."

"I'll ask Tom about it tomorrow." Brandi pushed the last of the doughnut into her mouth.

"I could go back and talk to Hunter Blackwood again, explain that I know what's going on and will expose him if he doesn't correct the injustices."

"Correct the injustices? You sound like a lawyer." Brandi snapped her fingers, sending powdered sugar across the bar. "That's it. Take a lawyer with you. Maybe a legal beagle could convince him to let Lucita go, help her get her children back."

Crystal took a sip of coffee. "If it worked, that would be great. But the probability of that happening is about the same as making a perfect soufflé during an earthquake. I have a better chance just spiriting her away."

"I like it. Quick, neat, and we can get some sleep."

"But the negatives are too great to enumerate. We'd probably have to drag her off. And what would happen to her children?"

"Good point. You save her and the guy in Mexico kills the kids." Brandi made a sound like a buzzer. "Wrong."

Sighing, Crystal said, "As appealing as it sounds, I'm afraid we have to rule that one out."

An idea had been floating around in the back of her mind for several minutes. Now, it waved a hand, demanding attention.

"I could go down to Mexico and get the children. That would solve both problems at once. The children would be safe and Blackwood would have no hold over Lucita. She'd be happy to leave under those circumstances." Crystal sipped her coffee, eyeing her housemate over the rim of the cup.

"What? Are you nuts? Go into a foreign country and kidnap children. And not just any country. Mexico. The cartels kill people every day." She shook her head. "You thought there were lots of negatives for snatching Lucita. This swamps that. Bad idea. Bad, bad idea. Where's the father?"

"Rosa said he's dead." She wondered briefly if the father had worked for, or had been killed by José. "It's a *great* idea. Not necessarily an easy one to carry out, but a great idea. I like it. Can you imagine the look on Lucita's face when I return with the children?"

"I'm imagining the immigration officer's look when you try to bring them back."

The night had been miserable. Now she had a plan. Crystal's eyes sparkled and energy flowed through her body. "I've got to talk to Lucita again. I've got to get more information on her kids. I don't even know their names right now, or what they look like or anything."

Brandi just shook her head. "Dumb idea, Crystal. Think this through again. This is the kind of stunt I'd pull. And you'd tell me it was—how would you put it—*ill-conceived*. That's what you'd say. I know I'm not as smart or educated as you, but I can tell a dumb idea when I smell one."

Crystal's mind played a picture of the two young girls, weeping for their lost mother. Only now, a third young girl wept with them, a seven-year-old, motherless Crystal. Even now, her eyes misted over. Crystal made a solemn vow: *these children will be reunited with their mother.* "I'd better talk to Mark tomorrow," she said. "I guess that's really today, isn't it? Thanks for the help."

"Think nothing of it. But I've got three favors to ask in return. One, give this a lot more consideration before you buy tickets. And double check on the father. Maybe he's not dead. Maybe he can handle this."

"Okay. And number three?"

"Don't wake me up again this morning."

Chapter 8

AS soon as she got into her office, Crystal retrieved the map she had purchased on her way to the office. A quick scan of the index proved San Sebastian a very popular name in Mexico. Dozens of towns had San Sebastian as part of the name, and they were scattered from Tijuana to Cancun.

A snippet of conversation popped into her mind. Rosa's hometown Santiago was only a few kilometers from San Sebastian. Crystal scanned the index again. It couldn't have been worse, unless it were San José. More than one hundred towns had Santiago in their names. Trying to find the right pair could take hours.

She mentally slapped herself on the forehead. *Duh. Your business is information retrieval. Let the computer solve this.* Within a minute she had scanned the map into a file on her hard drive. Then, with the speed and ease acquired through years of practice, she quickly typed a set of commands into the computer.

The idea was simple. The computer searched the scanned image of the map, located all towns with Santiago as part of their name, and put them and their coordinates into a file. It did the same thing for San Sebastian. Next, it determined the distance from every town in the first group to every town in the second group. The computer would use the coordinates to calculate distances for over ten thousand pairs of towns. She drummed her fingers on the desk as the machine raced through its task.

The intercom buzzed. "Crystal. Dr. Krupe is on line 2."

Crystal had put Krupe's call and request out of her mind. She was not about to let it interrupt her now. "Tell him I can't take his call."

Thirty seconds later, the intercom buzzed again. "He says it's important he talk to you now."

Not long ago, she would have dropped everything to respond to Dr. Krupe, the high priest of Information Retrieval and, next to her father and grandfather, the man she had most admired and respected. But that was before he had summoned her to his house on a cold, rainy night to discuss her dissertation.

"He doesn't know what important really means. I'm not taking his call, Pam, no matter what he says. Sorry to put you through this. Just tell him there's nothing you can do."

Crystal shook her head slowly. Just three years ago she believed he was one of the smartest men in the world. She admired him, hung on his every word, trusted him. What a difference a few minutes could make. What a naive, stupid young woman she had been.

The computer began printing. Crystal retrieved the sheet. Each line contained a town with Santiago as part of its name, one with San Sebastian in its name, the map coordinates of each and the distance between them. The list contained the fifty pairs of towns closest together. The shortest distance appeared at the top.

The last two days had been depressing. Seeing only a single pair of towns close enough together to match Rosa's description brought a smile to Crystal's face. "Yes!" she said, and stabbed the air with her fist. She knew which San Sebastian. Adrenaline surged through her veins.

She picked up the map and started for the door, then stopped. The task frightened her. Could Lucita be reunited with her children by some other means? No. Crystal had considered other possibilities. Lucita would never escape as long as her children were held hostage. And Crystal knew her own misery of the last two nights resulted directly from her hesitancy to do what she knew, down deep, she had to do.

"Enough stalling," she said. "You're going."

Crystal knocked softly at the office of Dr. Mark O'Malley, president of Intelligent Retrieval Systems. Mark was hunched over his large walnut desk. Ordinarily, she enjoyed a moment just looking at his rugged, six-foot frame, handsome face, and the broad shoulders developed during years of bull riding. Today, thoughts of slaves occupied her mind.

Mark ran a hand through his thick, chestnut-colored hair as he looked up from the work on his desk.

"Got a minute?" Crystal asked.

"For you, always."

She crossed the room and perched on the front edge of one of the dark blue leather chairs facing Mark's desk. "Mark, I need to take some time off."

He nodded slowly. "Okay. How much time do you need and when do you want to take it?"

"I'm not exactly certain. Two or three days."

"You want two or three days off, or you want to take the time starting in two or three days?" Mark asked.

"Oh, I mean, I'll want to start the time off in two or three days."

"And how long will you be gone?"

Crystal shrugged and tried a little smile. "Don't really know."

His sapphire eyes bore into her. She adjusted her position on the chair and cleared her throat. She did not want to tell him her plans, such as they were. He would find them questionable, and she understood why. She had her own doubts. One moment she knew it was the right thing to do; a minute later, it sounded foolish. To an outsider, it must seem foolhardy all the time.

She felt certain he would grant her the time off. Vacation time should cover it, if she didn't take too long in Mexico. Her project at IRS was running ahead of schedule and she would lay out a careful plan for her people to follow while she was gone. Still, she understood that on such short notice, and with such an indefinite time frame, he deserved more information.

The silence stretched too long. She had hoped he would break the quiet, say something she could respond to. Part of the reason she was hesitant came from the fear he would try to talk her out of going. Brandi had experienced the evil around Blackwood's place and still she thought the idea bad. Eula, always a champion of the downtrodden, labeled the visit to Blackwood's house a bum idea. What would Nana say about this new plan?

Crystal realized the difficulties, and also the real possibility of failure. Right now though, she did not want to think of those, and she did not want anyone trying to talk her out of going.

She sat up a little straighter and tried to look more confident than she felt. "I need to go to Mexico for a few days and take care of some business."

"Mexico?"

She nodded.

"I don't mean to pry, but what kind of business? I didn't know you had ever been to Mexico, or even knew anyone in Mexico." Mark tilted his head to one side, raised his eyebrows, and stared at her.

"It's a long story."

"I have time, if you want to tell me."

She had not planned to tell him anything, did not want to tell him anything, but now guilt stabbed her belly, and she squirmed in the chair. Mark had always been willing to help her, usually without being asked. He had put his life on the line for her, simply because she was an employee, a friend. And now, he was more than a friend.

Crystal was dating Mark. He deserved more.

She took a deep breath, swallowed, and tried to sound casual as she began describing her encounters with Rosa and Lucita.

Mark listened without interrupting, his expression never changing. When she finished, it was his turn to take a deep breath. "Sounds like a worthy project."

Crystal's slender hands, which had been clenched in her lap, relaxed a little. At last, someone sees the need to do this.

"But," he continued, "It sounds like a pretty tough one. You'll be a foreigner, in a country with a different language. Do you know Spanish?"

"A little."

"A *little* works for a vacation. What you're proposing . . . well, I speak Spanish pretty well and I expect I'd have a hard time." He had been holding a pencil between his forefingers and now he laid it carefully on the desk. "Then, there are other problems. From what little you've told me, it sounds like you're going to be dealing with a ruthless element, in a country you know nothing about, a police force not quite as disciplined as the one Tom belongs to. And all of this in a country whose laws you don't know. Are you sure this is the best approach?"

"I don't know, but I can't leave those children or their mother in slavery."

"Slavery sounds a little melodramatic, doesn't it?"

Her voice rose an octave. "What would you call it? She's forced to work for nothing. She can't quit, can't even tell anybody about her problems. She can't have her children here. Jose, in Mexico, probably caused Miguel's death. Lucita's kids will never get free, unless somebody does something."

Crystal's hands once more locked together.

Mark's voice remained soft. "This sort of thing is wide spread. Not just in Mexico, but in many countries. You can't save them all."

Her lips barely parted. "No, I can't, Mark." She forced her jaw to relax and tried to compose herself, hoping her voice would not fail her. "But, I can save three."

For several moments, he stared at her. She met his gaze unwaveringly.

"You know my sister's in Europe right now. That means I can't leave for maybe a month."

"I know. And I'm not asking you to go with me."

"If Mother were in better health…. Can you postpone this until Jean gets back?"

"Mark, I appreciate the thought. But this is my problem."

"Not really."

"Yes it is. I can't sleep thinking about those little girls. And after what happened to Rosa's husband, I just can't wait." She blinked rapidly, trying to hold back the tears.

For several seconds, Mark said nothing. Then, "What do you plan to do?"

Crystal folded her arms across her chest. "I'll start with the local police. They'll know where he is. Probably have a file on him already."

Mark stretched his lips into a thin line, and cocked his head slightly. "In all likelihood, this José owns the police, or at least pays them enough not to bother him."

"Then, I'll contact the federal police." Her chin rose a little.

"The Federales?" He wrinkled his forehead. "That could

be tricky. They might look at you as a gringo trying to steal Mexican children. You could stand a better chance of getting in trouble than José."

Crystal frowned. "Steal their children?"

"It happens." Mark pursed his full lips. "Maybe we could get the mother away from Blackwood. Then she could go get the children herself."

"She won't leave. If she did, she believes—and so do I— José would kill her girls. Or sell them." Crystal shook her head. Tears pushed to be let out. "I couldn't sleep the last two nights thinking about them. I won't sleep until I do something. It's not even so much I want to go." The tears escaped. "I *have* to go." Crystal fished a tissue out of a pocket and dabbed at her eyes, which, though filled with tears, burned with intensity. "I have to go *now*."

Mark stared off into space, worry lines growing around his eyes. Finally, he broke the quiet. "Of course, you can have the time off. Whatever you need. Get your group lined up so they know what to do while you're gone. And fill me in so I can help them if they get stuck."

"Thank you, Mark. I'll give you a written plan and I'll make certain JT knows exactly what I want done. She can lead the others." JT Gonzales had moved to Crystal's project only six months ago, but already Crystal thought of her as second in command.

"Where are the children being held?"

Crystal laid the map on the desk. "José has a hacienda near San Sebastian del Oeste." She placed her finger on the map under the town.

"I suppose Rosa is still around? You can check that with her?"

"Yes. In fact, I'll do it this evening."

Mark studied the map for a few seconds. "Looks like

you'll fly into Puerto Vallarta. You're in luck there." He raised his head, his eyes dull and sad. "I hope it's not the last piece of luck you have on this venture. You know I have a condo there, in Plaza Mar, a lovely building. You should stay in my condo. It's right on the beach, in a delightful part of town. I'll call and tell them you're coming."

"Thanks. I really appreciate it. That will make things easier."

He turned and looked out the window. A light rain was falling on the West End, a former warehouse area just blocks from the grassy knoll made famous by Lee Harvey Oswald. Some years ago the area had been revitalized and turned into a trendy place, popular with tourists and locals alike.

Crystal fidgeted, not knowing whether the meeting was over or not.

Mark got up, walked around his desk, and sat on the edge of it facing her. "I'll help you anyway I can. I'm no expert by a long shot, but I've spent a lot of time in Mexico and I know a number of people there. However, as an interested party, I ask you to think about this again. What you're setting out to do is not only difficult, but very risky. Sounds like you're going against a dangerous person. The fact that this person is in a foreign country, *his* country, makes it much more hazardous." He took a deep breath. "I can tell you feel strongly about this and I won't try to talk you out of it, though I wish I could. Or at least get you to wait until I could go with you."

Crystal shook her head, but said nothing.

"At least discuss it with someone else. Consider whether there might be some other option."

His eyes narrowed slightly, and Crystal sensed he was trying to gage her resolve. Concern had replaced the usual sparkle in his eyes. "To say I'm a little worried is to put it mildly. I don't want to sound like a father, or even an older brother. You're an intelligent and independent adult. But you're important to me, and not just as an employee." He raised his eyebrows and smiled. "I wish you'd reconsider it. Or at least wait four or five weeks until I can go with you."

"Now that Rosa has escaped, things might change. It was a fluke that she even found out that her husband had died. If I wait, it may be too late for these children." She looked down for a second, trying to get her emotions under control. "Maybe I'll only collect information on this trip. Find out where and how they are held, what it will take to rescue them. I *will* be careful."

Mark nodded several times, but said nothing for a few moments. "If you go, I want to ask you to do two things. In fact, as your employer, who's giving you time off, I want to *insist* on this."

He paused and pressed his lips together. "Puerto Vallarta is a very safe place. But you're going on a dangerous mission. It appears you will be challenging a powerful and ruthless person. So, do not spend the night any place other than my condo in Plaza Mar. I don't know much about the San Sebastian area."

"Okay."

"And before you do anything, anything at all regarding the girls, talk with Juan Grande."

"Juan Grande? Okay. How do I contact him?"

"You don't. He'll contact you."

Chapter 9

FROM the county road, Eula's driveway wound nearly a mile through a pristine forest, over a clear stream, and up a steep hill to the house. Today, even the sun sparkling on the peaceful lake could not catch Crystal's attention. A dark cloud had hung over her since she learned of the plight of Rosa, Miguel, Lucita, and her children.

Over Crystal's objections, Eula had insisted they have dinner before Crystal and Rosa sat down for a more serious discussion. With the meal finished, dishes washed and put away, the three women moved into the living room.

Two long, brown leather couches sat at right angles to one another, one facing a large, fieldstone fireplace, the other looking out through the glass wall toward the lake in the distance. A huge, square coffee table was positioned in front of them. Three comfortable leather swivel chairs completed the seating. Western oil paintings hung on either side of the fireplace. A Remington reproduction occupied its own pedestal, appropriately lighted to highlight the large, bronze horse and rider.

Crystal laid out the map on the coffee table. "Show me where San Sebastian is, Rosa."

The young woman's focus wandered around the map, top to bottom, right to left. Finally, she turned to Crystal and shrugged.

"This isn't twenty questions," Eula said. "Give her a clue."

"I didn't want to influence her choice, Nana." Crystal

turned to Rosa and asked, "What state did you live in?"

She cocked her dark head to one side and wrinkled her brow for a moment.

Crystal asked, "*¿Que estado vives?*"

For several seconds, Rosa said nothing. Then, her face brightened. "Jalisco."

Crystal placed her finger on the map just below the town of Santiago de los Piños.

Rosa bent slightly, her shiny black hair falling across the table, and studied the map. "*Si.* Yes. That is where I live before." Her finger moved from Santiago de los Piños to San Sebastian del Oeste. "San Sebastian is where we go meet José. His hacienda no is far. Is where Miguel work for José."

From the map, San Sebastian del Oeste appeared to be about eighty kilometers by road from Puerto Vallarta. Roughly fifty miles. "Can you tell me anything about San Sebastian?"

Rosa shook her head. "No. We go there at night, leave early next morning. I too scared to see anything."

"Do you know Jose's last name, his family name?"

Rosa shook her head slowly.

"Think you got all you're gonna get from Rosa. You're gonna need some help from Lucita," said Eula.

"That will be tough." Taking one of Rosa's small brown hands, Crystal asked, "Will you go with me to talk to Lucita? I need to ask her about her children, names, ages, what they look like. Get a picture of them if possible. Anything that will help me find them."

Rosa pulled her hand back and shook her head. "No. I no go near *Señor* Blackwood. He kill me if he see me." Still shaking her head, she moved away from Crystal a little.

"She's got a point," said Eula.

"I'll protect you, Rosa."

Eula snorted.

Crystal ignored Eula's intrusion. "I need you. Lucita doesn't speak English. My Spanish is not good enough to find out what I need to know from her."

"Lucita speak English more good than me. She afraid talk to you with *Señor* Blackwood there."

"Makes sense to me. Man's a horse apple if I ever smelled one," said Eula.

"But I've got to talk to her. I can't find her children if I don't know what they look like, what their names are, how old they are, something about them."

"You talk to Lucita in market. *Señor* Argos take her there every Wednesday, middle of morning."

"But will she talk if *Señor* Argos is there?" Crystal asked.

"*Señor* Argos stay in car. Never go in market. You talk to Lucita in market."

"There you are," said Eula with a short nod and a satisfied grin. "Just go sit on a crate of lettuce and when Lucita comes in, hand her a tomato and ask what her kids look like."

"That's exactly what I'm going to do." Crystal turned back to Rosa. "You're sure she speaks good English?"

"*Si. Muy* good English."

Chapter 10

SINCE Brandi was still working the late shift, she agreed to be the lookout while Crystal met with Lucita. Now, the two women waited inside near the front of the store where Rosa said Lucita shopped.

Crystal glanced at her watch for the twelfth time, but only fifteen minutes had crept by. A car parked on the first row and a moment later Lucita emerged and started toward the store. Crystal's stomach tightened when the driver's door opened and a tall, well-built man got out.

Must be Argos. A scowl covered his face. His eyes jerked from right to left, as if looking for someone to hurt. Muscular arms ended in hands balled into fists. Crystal understood Rosa's reluctance to get near him. She felt an urge to run.

He stomped to the front of the car and spoke to Lucita. She simply nodded and started for the store. He grabbed her arm, spun her around and jerked her back. He put his face close to hers and barked something at her. This time, she spoke a few words in answer. He said something else, then shoved her toward the store. Both Brandi and Crystal let out a small sigh of relief when the man got back in the car.

Brandi moved to the front of the store where she could watch Argos. If he started to come in, she would alert Crystal. From outside the store, one could not see the vegetable aisle. Crystal hovered there, as nervous as she had been at Blackwood's.

Lucita entered the store, got a shopping cart, and headed

for the vegetable aisle. *Perfect.*

Crystal wasted no time. "Lucita, I've talked with Rosa and I know you speak good English. I need to talk with you while Mr. Argos cannot see us."

The Mexican woman stiffened at the first word. She glanced toward the front of the store.

Crystal placed her hand on the woman's arm. "I want to help you. I am going to Mexico, to San Sebastian, and find your children. But I need to know as much as I can about them. Do you have a picture of them with you?"

During her encounter with Argos, Lucita had been strong, unbending, refusing to be cowed by the angry man. Now, with trembling hands, she looked all around, glanced back toward the front of the store. When she turned back toward Crystal, the young Mexican's eyes, more charcoal than black, narrowed and for several seconds she stared at Crystal, as if trying to decide whether this person could be trusted.

Lucita's voice came out high and thin, like a child's. "Why are you to do this?"

So I can sleep at night? So I can stop thinking of your children being held as slaves? "Rosa is with my grandmother. She has told us about Miguel and about your children. Because . . ." Crystal saw herself at her parent's funeral. Even now, that pictured tugged at her heart. "Because I lost my mother when I was seven. She was killed in a car accident. Nothing could be done. But your children still have a mother. There *is* something that can be done for them."

Lucita's sad, dark eyes showed a glimmer of hope, even as deep lines formed on her forehead. "My children. They must be safe. I must know they are safe."

Just hearing Lucita speak English caused Crystal's spirit to lift. She felt like cheering, but this was not the time. "I will do everything, *everything* I possibly can to see your children are safe and are returned to you. I promise you that." Crystal held the woman's gaze, hoping Lucita would know how committed Crystal felt.

Lucita's face, showing a mixture of emotions, appeared so brittle it might crack under the strain. Crystal's feelings welled up and her eyes filled with tears. She didn't trust her voice, but her time with Lucita was very short. She had to get the information now. "Do you have a picture of them?"

The Mexican woman hesitated a moment longer, then opened her purse and began searching through it. She took out several pictures and checked them for a moment. "I do not know what to do. I afraid for my girls." She closed her eyes and gripped the pictures as if someone was trying to snatch them away.

Crystal said nothing. What a tremendous leap of faith she was asking Lucita to take. If Crystal made a mistake, this young mother and her children would pay the price.

That thought made her knees feel weak, her stomach queasy. She knew so little. She had spent a year researching a project of far less consequence. But a year's delay was out of the question for Lucita's children. They might have been sold already. Each day was a risk.

Crystal could hear Eula saying, "Bum idea." Brandi, with such good instincts, had called it a dumb idea. Even Mark, with his reckless, bull-riding background, had felt it too risky. Was she asking too much of this young woman? What if Crystal made the situation worse? Suddenly her stomach roiled and she thought she might throw up. *What am I doing?*

Lucita took Crystal's hand and placed a picture in it. Her voice quavered. "Please. Do not take chance with my little babies." Her eyes were filled with fear and hope and tears.

"I will do everything in my power to return your children to you safely. Is there anything you can tell me about where they are, or about Jose? Do you know his last name?"

"I only know Jose, but he is powerful man in San

Sebastian. Has big hacienda in jungle. You can find him. He also very dangerous man, very bad man. You must be careful. He kill people." She grasped Crystal's hand and held it so tightly it hurt. "Please do not do anything cause him hurt my girls. I am so afraid."

Tears ran down Crystal's cheeks. She put the picture in her purse. "I promise you I will do everything I possibly can. The safety of your children will always be my main concern. What are their names? Ages?"

Lucita looked at one of the pictures still in her hand. She turned it toward Crystal and pointed. "This is Serafina. She has five years. This is Angelina. She has three years."

"The father is dead?"

"Yes." Again, she looked around, checking, fearful. "I must hurry. If I take too long, *Señor* Argos come."

"Continue to shop. I will walk behind you. If you think of anything that will help me in Mexico, turn around and tell me."

Without another word, Lucita resumed shopping. Twice, she turned and gave a word or two of information to Crystal, quickly and in hushed tones.

They had reached the dairy section when Lucita turned to Crystal once more. The Mexican woman reached inside her blouse, and pulled out a silver medallion on a chain. She slipped the chain over her head, laid the large medallion on her hand and looked at it for a moment. The silver disk must have measured four inches in diameter and over half an inch in thickness. She shifted her focus to Crystal's eyes. "They will know this come from me. They know is sacred to me and I only give to a friend." She pressed the medallion into Crystal's hand and held it there for several seconds. "*Vaya con Dios.*"

Lucita turned, picked up a gallon of milk and headed toward the checkout counter.

Chapter 11

SHE kept her eyes closed. Held her breath. Listened. Nothing. Careful to make no sound, she inhaled, testing the air for any lingering smell of gunpowder.

She opened her eyes slowly, first only thin slits. Without moving her head, she searched in the darkness, looking for anything out of place, a patch darker or lighter than it should be, any slight shifting of the shadows.

The dream had terrified her. But was it a dream? Still unsatisfied it was not real, nonetheless she moved her head to look at the clock. Two-thirty. Forty minutes since she last looked at it, forty minutes since she had checked under the bed, in the hall, in the bathroom. She had found nothing then. Maybe there was nothing, nobody this time either. She eased back the covers, hot in the cool air-conditioning, and tried to force her mind to another topic, any topic. Any topic other than the hostage children. Or the brutal Jose.

Earlier, it had been Crystal herself held captive by the sadistic man. Then, thrust naked into a room with several drug lords. She had managed to drive that image away before... .

Prior to that, pictures flooded her mind, pictures of her in the jungle. Snakes, scorpions, poisonous plants surrounded her. Watching, sneering at her had been Jose, with a small, almost comatose child clutched under each arm.

But the latest in the stream of nightmares was the most frightening. She had actually rescued the girls. Lucita waited nearby, arms outstretched, ready to receive her children. But as

Crystal hurried the two girls toward their mother, José appeared. He raised a pistol, and with a smirk curling his lips, killed the two young girls. The mother just reached them as they fell dead at her feet. The horror in the young mother's eyes was directed at Crystal, the one who had brought the children to the place where they died.

Crystal sat up, pulling the sheet around her to shield her fevered body from the cold air. Maybe she should not attempt to rescue the girls. For several hours, her mind had been sending her signals her attempt would end in disaster. The threats to herself disturbed her no small amount. She had never crawled through a jungle. She hated snakes and scorpions. But the thought of being a prisoner sent an electric shock through the middle of her body as real as if she had stuck her finger into a live socket.

When Dr. Krupe had tried to explore her body, she simply shoved him away and left. It had cost her a Ph.D. , but she could stop the unwanted advances. But what if she were a prisoner, unable to refuse anything? She shivered and now, not from the cold. The thought of being helpless frightened her more than snakes or scorpions. Having no control over her life was terrifying. The thought of being tied down, powerless to do or prevent anything shook her resolve.

As Brandi had pointed out, Crystal had tried to get Lucita away from Blackwood, had offered to take her at that very moment. And Crystal *was* helping Rosa. Surely that was enough. Crystal could renew efforts to free Lucita—without going to Mexico. Without going into the jungle. Without challenging a pitiless killer.

Was it not enough to confront Blackwood? He scared Crystal. She hoped never to meet up with him again. If she worked to free Lucita here, would she have to deal with Blackwood?

She had only heard about Jose, how cruel he was. She'd *met* Blackwood, looked into his cold, dead eyes.

Maybe it would be better to drop the whole thing. Mark, an ex-bull rider no less, warned her, asked her not to go to Mexico. Brandi, who seemed capable of facing down the devil, told her not to get involved. And Nana, who seemed to fear nothing, told her not to get sucked in. Perhaps she was foolish to think she could rescue two little girls being held by a powerful and ruthless man in a foreign country. Maybe the best approach was to work to eliminate the acceptance of such acts. She could do a lot to help, without getting in the crosshairs of two vicious men.

Suddenly she felt better, no longer shaking, no longer too hot or too cold. She could work behind the scenes. She did not have to be on the front lines, in a foreign country. She did not have to challenge two very evil and merciless men. She lay back down, closed her eyes and quickly fell asleep.

                                    #

She jerked up. The clock showed 5:15. The dream blazed in her brain, far too vivid. Now, it was the children who were tied up, helpless, no longer crying for their mother, but crying for themselves, for their lost childhood, for their lost freedom, their lost lives. Their large, sad, brown eyes begged for someone, anyone, to help them. But it wasn't anyone they were looking at; it was Crystal. She tried to close her eyes, to concentrate on other things—anything not to see them looking at her. No matter what she did, their beseeching eyes burned into her.

Though she tried and tried, the one thing she could not do was turn away from them. *I don't want to go,* she cried. *But I can't leave them. I can't walk away. I won't let a madman ruin their lives like he did Rosa's. He mustn't win this time.*

She swung her feet down to the floor and stood. There was no need to look under the bed; the malicious man was in Mexico, imprisoning innocent young girls. *I don't want to get involved, but I already am. I'm as much a captive of those beautiful children as they are of Jose.* She walked to the closet.

The only way I can get free is to get them free.

She pulled down a suitcase. And for the first time in twenty-four hours, no doubts swirled in her mind.

Chapter 12

CRYSTAL sat in a window seat on American Airlines flight 339, non-stop from Dallas/Fort Worth airport to Puerto Vallarta. She had been watching the landscape below her, but now, clouds provided only the appearance of a never-ending, featureless, snow-covered world.

Her mind replayed the trip to the airport with Brandi driving and imparting advice for the traveler.

"Don't wear any gaudy or expensive jewelry."

"Like I do here?" Crystal teased.

"Well, sometimes people buy stuff there and then flash it around. Mexicans think all Americans are rich, at least all who travel to Mexico. If you've got it, do not flaunt it."

"Yes, ma'am."

"And don't guzzle too many margaritas. They're stronger than you think and somebody will have to carry you home."

"You know I don't drink much."

"Yeah, but it's easier down there. You sit on the beach, gorgeous sunsets, tropical beauty, waiters who really try to give you whatever you want, and smooth drinks that go down so easy you know they won't affect you. So, you just have another. And another."

"I promise not to fall under the table."

"Personally, I don't eat stuff from the little street-vendor carts. I've got friends who do, but I don't. Except churos. They're great. Be sure to have some."

"What are churos?"

Brandi stopped at the tollgate and got a ticket to enter the airport. "They're little . . ." She wrinkled her small nose and waggled her head. "Things. I don't know. They take dough and deep fry it, kinda like a donut, only it's shaped like a Vienna sausage, then roll it in cinnamon and sugar. But better than any donut you ever had. You get them hot right out of the pot and you can eat a dozen of them."

"And where do you find them?"

"Street corners. The guy will have a . . .I don't know what, a round bottom pot with grease in it. And he squeezes the dough out of a little thing into the shape of a churo. Sometimes they have a hole in them and they put chocolate or caramelo in them. God, they're good. You'll know 'em when you see 'em. Have some for me. I love 'em."

"I'll force myself to eat some, just for you."

"And walk on the Malecòn at night. And be sure to go parasailing. Wow, I love to do that. Oh, and go to –"

"Brandi, this isn't a vacation."

"Well, you've never been there. You ought to at least see some of the sights. Oh, and ask about parades. They have lots of parades, all the time. And the girls wear such fantastic dresses, and dance down the street, and twirl these full, full skirts."

"I'll watch for parades."

"And the men wear tight pants, all decorated with silver. And huge hats, *sombreros*, that are works of art. Oh, and their horses. They have the prettiest horses in the world. And sexy men in those tight pants. Damn, I wish I was going with you." She pulled to the curb and stopped.

Crystal got out, retrieved her bag from the back seat, then stuck her head back in the window. "Thanks for driving me to the airport. I'll call you in a few days."

"Let me know and I'll pick you up."

"Will do." Crystal turned to go.

"Oh, wait," Brandi called.

Crystal turned back.

"'¿Donde esta el baño?' That's how you ask where's the bathroom. Very important thing to know."

Crystal retrieved a bag of peanuts from her purse just as the stewardess offered a variety of soft drinks. Crystal got a Dr Pepper and started on the salty snack.

Outside, the clouds had broken. The land below looked desolate. Hills dotted the area, but it could have been a desert. Crystal could see no vegetation or trees from this height.

The bleak countryside added to her depression. Many of the people around her were laughing, obviously eager to start a vacation. As driven as Crystal was to get there and start looking for the children, at the same time, she dreaded it. She imagined how excited Lucita would be when Crystal returned with the children. What if she had to come back and tell Lucita the girls were dead? Or nowhere to be found? She shuddered, then shook her head. She forced her attention on the landscape below. Those kinds of thoughts wouldn't do her, or the girls, any good.

Foliage appeared on the barren land. Ahead, a mountain jutted through wispy clouds. As the plane crossed over a ridge, the land turned green. Rivers found circuitous paths down the slopes, then meandered along the valleys. Here and there, the forest opened to small farms. Only occasionally could she find what she believed to be a road. She had not seen a highway in an hour. Yet people lived there, grew crops, raised families.

The pilot announced they would be landing in a few minutes. A stewardess came down the aisle, handing out declaration forms to be filled out for immigration. Crystal hastily wrote in the information, and once more turned her attention to the window. More and more land was given over to farming here. Roads began to crisscross the area and she could pick out trucks, cars, and even bicycles. In the distance, the deep blue water of Banderas Bay came into view. Ah. *Que bien!*

#

At 1 Hunter Circle in Dallas, Hunter Blackwood looked up at the gaunt man standing on the opposite side of the desk.

"I found Moore," the man said, looking satisfied.

"And?"

Eric Lithgow cracked the knuckles on his large right hand. A muscle twitched along his jaw but he did not look away. "Only caught up with her this morning. Her and another broad was moving. Followed 'em to the airport. The Moore bitch took a plane to Mexico." He clamped his mouth shut. When Blackwood said nothing, Eric added, "Airport wasn't a good place to –"

"Make contact. No."

"You want me to hop the next plane to Mexico? She was going to Porto Varta."

Blackwood looked past the man for several seconds. "No. That won't be necessary. What time did the plane take off?"

Eric looked at his watch. "'Bout an hour ago."

"And you're just now telling me?"

"Called and you wasn't here. Told Lucita to tell you I called." He swallowed. "And stopped to eat."

For several moments, Blackwood bore into his visitor with a laser-like gaze. Then, he picked up some papers and without looking at Eric, said, "I'll call you when I need you."

Eric left the office.

Hunter Blackwood picked up the telephone and dialed a fifteen-digit number.

Chapter 13

THE thirty-minute taxi ride from Puerto Vallarta's Gustavo Diaz Ordaz International Airport to Plaza Mar proved more interesting than staring down at the landscape from 34,000 feet. Though she had lived her entire life in Texas, with its common boundary with Mexico, Crystal had never visited the country, unless she counted a dinner once just across the border.

Nestled between the Sierra Madre mountains and the Pacific Ocean, Puerto Vallarta presented a very different image of Mexico from the one Crystal had gotten during her three-hour visit to Tijuana five years ago. Here, tall palm trees swayed in the ocean breeze. Flowers grew everywhere: in dusty paths and gravel roads, unattended flower boxes and cracked pots sitting on unpainted porches, and the occasional well-tended gardens. Many houses were painted in bright hues from across the entire spectrum, colors never used on homes in Dallas.

Part of the trip followed the curve of Banderas Bay. Rowboats and sailboats moved silently through the wakes of small motorboats and large sightseeing boats. A huge cruise ship was tied to a dock only ten yards from the highway. Young men, and a few women, bobbed on surfboards, waiting for the perfect wave. Jet skis zipped about like water bugs.

Above the deep blue water, highlighted against a lighter blue sky, parasails and a gaily colored hot air balloon drifted south over the coast. Two men battled for supremacy of the skies with their kites. The bright red and blue sail of a wind-surfer caught Crystal's eye, as he guided his board right up onto the sand.

Businesses crowded the other side of the road. Tourist traps used varied motifs to entice the passerby. Most of the establishments positioned a representative on the street actively trying to attract customers. The temperature was high, yet most shops and restaurants were open to the sea breeze. And everywhere, lively music filled the air.

The taxi stopped at the end of a street, only a few yards from the beach. "Plaza Mar. It is here," said the driver as he got out to retrieve Crystal's bag from the trunk.

In the Plaza Mar lobby, tropical plants luxuriated in huge Mexican pots. Large paintings depicted a cathedral, a fishing village and a street bounded by stucco houses with red tile roofs. Further in on the right, the lobby opened to a patio, bordered by a wide variety of lush, tropical plants. Several tables and chairs flanked a fountain gurgling in the middle of the courtyard.

At the reception area, a young woman in her early twenties, with hair shorter than Crystal's, was talking on the telephone. She had a button nose, eyes as black and shiny as cassis, and a mouth just a trifle too wide. As Crystal approached, the receptionist finished the call, looked up, and smiled. Crystal revised her thought; the mouth was perfect, the smile infectious.

"Hello. I'm Crystal Moore and –."

"Oh, yes. *Señor* O'Malley tell us you are coming. Welcome to Puerto Vallarta and Plaza Mar." The receptionist turned, picked a set of keys from behind her, and handed them to Crystal. "Is help necessary with your luggage?"

"No. I have only one bag, and it's on wheels. I can manage it."

"*Señor* O'Malley's unit is on sixth floor." She pointed to her left. "Take elevator. When you get off on sixth floor, turn left. His unit is at end of the hall. My name is Mercèdes. If I can answer any questions, or give help to you anyway, call me. Just dial o."

"Thank you. I'm sure I'll need your help." *And help from a lot of others.*

#

When Crystal reached Mark's condo, she unlocked a wrought-iron gate, but the interior door was open. Since she knew Mark hadn't been out of Dallas for several months, she expected the condo to be stale and stuffy. However, all the windows and doors had been opened and a gentle breeze brought freshness to the condo.

A mural depicting a vivid jungle scene covered the wall opposite the entrance. To the right was the living room with two long, built-in couches facing each other and a glass-top coffee table in between. A rattan chair with bright yellow upholstery separated the living room from the entry area. Over one couch hung a giant Aztec calendar made of inlaid woods from many different trees. On a table at the end of the other couch stood a large, bronze sculpture of a young woman in a long, flowing dress, her hair forever blowing in the sea breeze. An immense basket of *cupa de oro* flowers adorned the coffee table.

In the bedroom, she set her suitcase on a small stand. Bright Mexican art hung on the walls and the spread on the king-sized bed displayed large calla lilies that looked as if they were water color paintings. The adjoining bathroom was also bedecked with local art.

"This certainly isn't decorated like his house in Dallas," she said.

The doors to the terrace stood open and sounds of a mariachi band invited her out. Below, a large plaza filled the block in front of Plaza Mar. A bandstand was in the center, with walks coming in from all sides. A grassy area and a number of trees, some flowering, and all unfamiliar to Crystal, made it very inviting.

At one end of the plaza stood a larger-than-life bronze statue of some Mexican hero, eternally guarding the place. At the other end was a life size bronze sculpture of a burro, with a little boy offering the animal carrots and pulling him, while another boy was at the back trying to push the stubborn donkey. The life-like statue brought a smile to Crystal's face.

The mariachis were attired in bright red, with silver adornments on their pants and coats. Crystal leaned on the balcony railing, absorbed in the music.

When the song ended, Crystal began surveying the rest of her surroundings. In every direction, the views were breathtaking. To the west, lay the deep blue of Banderas Bay. Far out, the land curved its long arms around, protecting the bay and the beautiful town. Sailboats graced the horizon while smaller boats scurried in closer to shore. On the beach, children dug in the sand or played tag with the incoming tide.

To the south and east, verdant mountains rose to brush the sky, which Crystal decided was the exact color of Mark's sapphire eyes. As the mountains swept around to the West, they came closer and closer to the bay until finally, they simply sank into the water.

Crystal pulled a chair close to the terrace railing and absorbed the beauty, peace, and tranquility. The tension she had felt for nearly a week began to drift away in the cool breeze. A young man lifted off the sandy beach under a brightly colored parasail. He floated up soundlessly and gradually glided down the coastline. Ten minutes later, he came into sight again. For a time, he hovered over the beach, then slowly settled down, landing as easily as jumping off a chair.

The laughter of children drifted up from the park. Two young girls ran in the grass, falling down, getting up and running some more, all the time laughing with the pure joy of childhood. They could be the same ages as Angelina and Serafina. The smile evaporated from Crystal's face. Lucita's girls probably weren't laughing or playing now.

A jangling noise sounded behind Crystal. She spun around, only to recognize it came from the telephone. Who would be calling her?

"Hello?"

"*Hola.* I am Mercèdes, in reception. I am leaving for today. Is there anything I can do for you before I go?"

Crystal ran a finger along her eyebrow. "No. I can't think of anything right now."

"I will be back in morning. If you do not know where to eat tonight, there is very nice restaurant right on beach, I think you will enjoy. It is called 'Sundowner' and food is very good. Ask for table on sand."

"Sounds nice. Where is it?"

Mercèdes gave her directions. "If you go near seven, you will see a most beautiful sunset."

"Thank you. I'll try it."

"I am back at eight in the morning. If you need anything tonight, Alberto will be in reception. He will help you. *Hasta mañana.*"

#

A little before seven, Crystal was seated at a small table. In spite of what Mercèdes had said, she was still surprised some tables were placed right on the beach. The tide was coming in. *What happens if the water gets here before I finish eating?*

The sun perched on the edge of the world. A long, golden streak stretched from the huge orange ball at the horizon to the waves breaking on the sand. It shimmered and sparkled and danced as the sun slowly descended into the water. And then it disappeared, painting the western sky like so many roses.

Mercèdes was right. Crystal had never witnessed a more beautiful sunset. She wished Mark were here to share it with her. If she'd asked him, he might have come. She smiled wistfully. Why hadn't she? *His dying mother*, she answered.

She toyed with her drink, a lovely tropical concoction surely more lethal than it tasted. Yes, Mark would make this a perfect evening. She took a sip of the sweet drink.

A short, pudgy man approached her table. He held up a collection of brightly colored scarves, gently waving in the breeze. "Scarf, *Señorita*? Many colors to choose from. Almost free."

The vendor must have had three dozen scarves in different sizes, styles, and colors. He quickly displayed one after another. When Crystal showed the slightest interest in one, he draped it over the edge of the table. "You like this one?" He left it there and continued to show other selections. "How many you like?"

"How much are they?"

"For you, only one hundred pesos. Very good price."

Crystal picked up one of the scarves. She could feel the paint on the surface of the material. "Will the colors run if I get it wet?"

He furrowed his brows.

"If the paint gets water on it, will it——"

"Oh, no, no, *Señorita*." He reached behind his back and brought out a small bottle. He opened the top and poured some liquid on another scarf with a similarly painted design. "See." He rubbed the water into the paint with his fingers. "Paint good. Water no hurt. *Mi esposa* paint these. Very good paint."

Crystal looked at another of the scarves.

"Better price for two. I give you two for one hundred fifty pesos. Only seventy-five pesos for each. Cheaper than K-Mart."

She picked up another one. Though not hand painted, it felt as soft and silky as a cloud. Its gay colors mirrored the recent sunset. Crystal seldom wore scarves, but these caught her interest.

"For you, only one hundred and twenty for two."

She looked at the man. He was smiling, holding the scarves up, his entire attention on her.

"I might take one. How much for one?"

"Only one? They are so many beautiful ones to choose. Can you not find another you like?"

"Yes, they are all beautiful. But I think only one."

"For you, eighty pesos for one."

Crystal fished out a hundred-peso note and handed it to the man.

"For only twenty pesos more, you can have two, *Señorita*."

"No. Just this one."

He laid a twenty peso note on the table. "*Gracias, Señorita*. You will like it. Tomorrow, I sell you another one." He moved to a table of three women, all speaking English.

Crystal took another sip of her drink and returned her gaze to the water. The afterglow was fading but still beautiful. Forgetting problems would be easy here.

"Would *Señorita* like bracelets? Real Taxco silver. Made by hand."

Crystal turned. This vendor was not as neatly dressed as the scarf salesman. His clothes were rumpled. And he did not have the same bright smile.

He held up several silver bangles. "Only four American dollars. Better buy is three for ten American dollars." He slipped a bracelet out of the group and offered it to Crystal. A delicate pattern of flowers etched the shiny surface.

She waved her hand. "No, *gracias*."

"Here. Feel it. Best silver in Mexico. You like it."

"No, *gracias*," she repeated.

"Cheaper than K-Mart."

"Not tonight." She turned away and looked at the water, now turning from deep blue to black. The glow on the horizon had evaporated and no moon had taken up the task of lighting the sky. Night had descended over Puerto Vallarta.

She sensed the man had moved closer. Now, she could feel his breath on her ear. Her own breath quickened and her hand tightened around the glass. A brown hand waggled a silver bracelet in front of her. This time, he spoke softly, near her ear. "Come outside. We talk about missing *niños*."

Chapter 14

HER whole body stiffened and her heart rate shot up. She turned back toward the vendor.

He was gone.

Her stomach cramped and she didn't breathe until she spotted him walking out into the street. She jumped up to leave, then remembered she had not paid for her drink. She looked around. No waiter appeared to be in the entire restaurant. What could the drink cost? Her twenty pesos change from the scarf lay on the table. *Surely fifty pesos will cover the drink. The twenty can be a tip.* She grabbed a fifty out of her purse, dropped it on the table, and hurried out, scarf in one hand, purse in the other.

She scanned both directions. Her throat tensed when she did not see him. She scrutinized each person. *There he is, turning into that small street.*

She rushed up the dimly lit street after the bracelet salesman. Ahead, he swung to the right and turned into a passage between two buildings, not once looking in her direction.

The narrow entrance into the dark street revealed little. A chill surged down Crystal's back. She was in a foreign country, and alone. This would be a scary street in Dallas, but at least she spoke the language, knew the rules. What if it were not the man with the bracelets who had turned into this dark alleyway? Should she follow him?

Anxiety held her back; his words pulled her forward. She

had come to Mexico to find the children, to liberate them. Did she expect them to be sitting on the street corner in broad daylight, waiting for her? On the other hand, entering a dark street, little more than an alley, seemed foolish. But Mark had said Juan Grande would contact her.

Mustering up her courage, she stepped slowly into the unknown.

"Come quickly," a voice said.

Now she could see the man, waiting just a few yards beyond the light. He still had the bracelets in his hand. He began to walk, and she fell in step.

"Are you . . ." She hesitated. Her heart felt as if it were in her throat. "Are you Juan Grande?"

"No, no," he said with a small laugh. "You want meet him, go to Café des Artistes tomorrow night, eight o'clock. No tell anyone of meeting. No tell anyone of Juan Grande. No bring anyone with you. If you wish meet him, no forget come tomorrow. No tell anyone, even at café."

"Okay. And who are you?"

"Call me George."

"Okay, George. Now, why-—"

"Watch!"

She jerked her head around and managed to stop just inches from a concrete telephone pole positioned squarely in the middle of the sidewalk. She frowned at the inanimate object, wondering why on earth anyone would put this obstacle in the middle of a walkway. She stepped around it. "*Gracias.* Why . . ."

He wasn't there.

She looked around. Her eyes had adjusted to the low light in the street. The buildings, adobe with brick showing through in places, crowded the narrow sidewalk. Now, she noticed the poles wandering down the walk. Trash cans and pots of tropical flowers shared space on the concrete. Trees grew at the curb. Here and there, a child's toy decorated the walk. But no bracelet salesman. She turned around in a complete circle, studying each object in the small lane.

"George?" She spoke softly, but in the quiet of the dark street, her voice thundered in her ears, almost echoing between the buildings of the narrow passage. No one answered. Nothing moved.

With a conscious effort, she began to creep ahead. *Foolish. Get out of here.* Fear returned and her legs felt weak. Uncertain of her step, as if her ankles were trying to turn, she forced herself to walk briskly toward the light at the end of the block.

At the bright intersection, she paused to get her bearings. Plaza Mar should be one block straight ahead and half a block to the right. Here, the street was well lighted. Her breathing and heart rate returned to normal and she covered the block in little more than a minute. Turning the corner, she could see the Plaza Mar building.

She had taken only a few steps when a voice said, "*Señorita.*"

A young man, no taller than she, but wiry with well-defined muscles, stepped in front of her, a smile on his face. "Have you had dinner tonight?"

Crystal jerked to a stop, a frown on her face. Dinner? "Ah, no. I mean, I'm not interested in dinner." She started to step around him, but he moved in front of her again.

"Maybe a fiesta? I can show *Señorita* more . . . things."

The statement stopped her dead in her tracks. Every muscle in her body tensed. *Señorita Moore.* How did he know her name? No one in Puerto Vallarta knew her name. Except Juan Grande.

"What things?" she asked, her voice shaky.

"Whatever you want."

Her intuition told her this was not Juan Grande. Not one of his men. And yet, this person knew her name. José could not be aware she was in Mexico. *Could he?*

Plaza Mar stood at the end of the block, its warm amber lights beckoning. The Mexican stood still, smiling, saying something about breakfast and a condo.

"*No gracias.*" She stepped around him and almost ran the hundred yards to her building.

#

She still felt uneasy as she sat on the terrace half an hour later, drinking a Corona. What if that had been Juan Grande and she had lost her chance to meet with him? Still, George had said tomorrow. But then, was George to be trusted? Who was he? She picked up the phone and dialed.

"Mark, this is Crystal."

"How are you enjoying Puerto Vallarta?"

"It is absolutely beautiful. And your condo is fantastic."

"Glad you like it. What's going on? Any problems?"

Crystal grimaced. "Not really. Haven't been here long enough for much to happen."

"You sound a little unnerved. Is that just the poor quality of the phone line?"

Rats. She thought she had settled down. "Could you describe Juan Grande for me? So I'd sort of know what to expect when I meet him."

"Hasn't contacted you yet?"

"Not directly." Crystal related the meeting with George, but decided against mentioning the other man who stopped her on the street, though she didn't know why.

"I don't want to bias you in any way. You'll know him

when you see him. Besides, it's not what he looks like, but how he might help you that counts."

"But I might get the wrong person. Mistake someone else for Juan Grande."

"Won't happen. It will be clear. Besides, it's hard to go wrong at the Café des Artistes. If nobody shows, it's still a great place to have dinner. Nothing like it in Dallas. Wish *I* were going to have dinner there tomorrow."

Silently, Crystal wished he were too.

Chapter 15

FRIDAY moved at a snail's pace. She walked through Cardenas Park over to Basilio Badillo, the street Mercèdes called Restaurant Row, and turned left a block to Fredy's Tucan for breakfast.

Back at Plaza Mar, she stopped at its library and picked out a book she hoped would be light and happy. The next two hours she spent reading on the beach, a cool ocean breeze tempering the warmth of the sun, the sky deep azure. But in two hours, she only managed to read thirty pages.

Though not really hungry, she ate chicken fajitas at the Sea Monkey on the beach just a couple of blocks from Plaza Mar. After lunch, she stopped at the front desk and thanked Mercèdes for her suggestion last night. Then, trying to sound like the typical American tourist, Crystal casually asked about various restaurants, including the Café des Artistes. After Mercèdes gave it lavish praise, Crystal asked for directions.

"It is not far, but you may want a taxi. They all know Café des Artistes," Mercèdes said.

#

Sitting on the terrace of Mark's condo, she reviewed the incident with the man on the street last night. Probably the drama was in her mind. She certainly wouldn't have given it two seconds consideration if it had happened in Texas or she hadn't been down here on some sort of covert mission. That was it. She was providing this with the atmosphere of a CIA operation. She was going to return two kids to their mother, for God's sake, not assassinate some head of state.

Finally, at seven-thirty, she walked out the front door and strolled along Olas Altas. Lively music poured out of restaurants. She crossed over to absorb the pungent smell of Mexican cooking coming from Café Olla. Small children, some of whom could not be more than five years old, offered to sell her Chiclets or long-stemmed roses. She passed taxis parked and waiting for customers. Then, she turned around and selected one of the cabs that paid the least attention to her.

The taxi let her out at the foot of a few stairs leading to the Café des Artistes. A handsome Mexican man greeted her inside and asked if she had reservations.

"No. I'm meeting someone."

His focus bounced between her and his reservation book for several moments. "Are you *Señorita* Moore?"

"Yes, I am." *Does everyone in Mexico know my name?*

"Please make yourself comfortable. We will have your table ready in a few minutes."

She browsed around the long, narrow room with several openings on the left and doors to restroom facilities at the far end. Almost opposite the *maitre d'* station, an archway led into a bar, now half-filled with people. She wandered down toward the next opening, stopping every few feet to admire the abundant paintings artistically displayed on the walls. Scattered here and there were sculptures, ranging from small pieces to life-sized creations.

The second opening on the left revealed part of the dining area. Gardens were woven in among the tables and most of the area was open to the heavens. A small stream meandered through the flowering shrubs. The clear, pure notes of a flute came from somewhere out of her view.

"Your table is ready, *Señorita* Moore."

She followed the *maitre d'* to a small table for two,

situated under a magnificent tree. Tiny lights, twinkling in harmony with the stars beyond, embellished many of the limbs.

A waiter appeared immediately, placing a crystal goblet of sparkling water on the table and a small plate of *hors d'oeuvres* so artistically presented Crystal wondered briefly if they were real. She sampled one and found it exquisite.

She had finished a second and was reaching for a third when another waiter approached, bent low and spoke so softly she could barely hear what he was saying.

"*Señorita* Moore, taxi is at front door. It take you to more better place for dinner."

Crystal frowned. "Ah, I'm meeting someone here."

The waiter smiled. "Taxi take you see him."

She put the *hors d'oeuvre* down and stared at the little plate in front of her, not certain what to say. George said to meet Juan Grande here.

The waiter whispered, "*Señor* O'Malley like it always."

Crystal's head came up with a jerk at the mention of Mark's name.

"Taxi take you where you want go. No one meet you here."

Her mind raced. She expected difficulties and Mark warned of dangers. Her problem was, she could not tell friend from foe. Perhaps she had encountered no foes yet. The man last night probably was saying "more things" instead of Señorita Moore.

She looked at the Mexican standing beside her. His smile was so genuine she found herself getting up even as her mind told her to stay right there.

"How will I know which taxi?"

"You no get in wrong taxi."

On the sidewalk, Crystal looked through the car window

at the driver. *Not George.* Her hand trembled as she opened the door and got into the back seat, with no idea where she was going. Without a word, the man put the car in gear and moved away from the curb, turned left, and headed down the hill toward the bay.

"Where are we going?"

The driver glanced at the mirror, looking directly at her, but said nothing.

She tried to sound authoritative. "*Señor,* tell me where we are going. *¿Donde vamos?*"

This time, the driver did not even look in the mirror.

Chapter 16

THE driver turned at every intersection. The taxi bounced with such frequency and force she found it difficult to keep track of the direction they were heading, much less the route. She had the feeling they had made more than one circle. *This has to be okay. Right? They know I'm supposed to meet with Juan Grande.* But even as she tried to reassure herself, she was trembling. She reached in her purse for her phone. She could call Mark. Even as her fingers touched the cold plastic she was jarred by reality. She had no cell phone service in Mexico.

They were working their way up the mountainside. That much was clear. The lights on the boats bobbing in the dark water of Banderas Bay were getting farther and farther below.

Twelve minutes later, they turned off the paved roads and wound down a narrow lane, palm trees close on both sides, no lights visible except the taxi's dim headlights, which penetrated the dark only a few feet.

Abruptly, the road ended. On the right was an adobe wall with a wooden gate, which opened as the car stopped. A man filled the opening and beckoned her to come in.

Once more, she didn't know what to do. *If these are the bad guys, they already have me. Too late to balk.* She hadn't the slightest idea where she was but she was certain no help was near.

She opened the door and stepped out. The air was cooler here than in Vallarta, and the smell of the sea was replaced with a slight musty scent. A bird call she did not recognize pierced the quiet. She closed the car door and immediately it moved away, made a sharp U-turn, and headed back the way it had come.

She watched it leave with a sense of despair. She had felt uneasy about the taxi and its driver, but they were her only connections with the outside world. Now, they were gone. She could run; but where? She was alone with no idea where she was. Again, her body trembled and her stomach began to cramp.

The stocky man at the gate said, "*Beinvenido, Señorita* Moore. Please come."

The man did not look threatening, and just his calling her by name eased her tense muscles. She followed him down a long hall and into a small, windowless room. The furniture appeared to be handmade. The couch and two of the chairs had rawhide coverings, while two other chairs were covered in a hand-woven nubby cloth. Everything from the furniture to the wall hangings, even the walls, fell into the brown part of the color spectrum.

She had seen little else of the house, but her impression could be summed up in one word: mysterious. And yet, not threatening. Somehow, the house had a friendly feel to it.

The only occupant of the room put down a book and stood up. "*Hola.* I am called Juan Grande."

For the first time in the last hour, her hands relaxed. *At last.* This was the man she was looking for, the help she needed.

Juan Grande had no neck. His round, pudgy face sat right on top of his broad shoulders. If his droopy mustache grew any longer, it might touch the rough weave of his shirt. Although shorter than she was, he must have weighed over two hundred pounds. Shaped like a brick, he appeared to be just as solid. His coal-black shaggy hair brushed his collar in back and hid all but the lobes of his ears.

But the most striking features of the man were his eyes.

Shiny. Liquid. Black as obsidian. They focused with the intensity of a laser, penetrating the person. They connected with a force difficult to break. For the first time in her life, Crystal believed she might be hypnotized simply by looking into someone's eyes.

She tried to summon her confidence. *"Hola, Señor Grande."*

He motioned for her to sit on a couch, and he resumed his place in a large, bamboo chair. He waved a hand at the man who had brought Crystal and said, *"La senorita Moore no ha comido. Tráigale algo."* The man nodded and left the room. "Please, call me Juan. I do not know where 'Grande' came from." He laughed, a low, rumbling sound that made Crystal smile.

He laced his stubby fingers across an ample belly. His unlined face gave little clue to his age. Crystal guessed mid-forties. His unblinking eyes gave no hint of his thoughts.

Ever since she arrived in Puerto Vallarta, Crystal's hopes had been kept high by the prospect of meeting this man. Now, the optimism began to evaporate. The help Mark had alluded to seemed remote. While Juan appeared pleasant enough and his eyes were like none she had ever seen before, Crystal was not sure how much help he would be. His expression gave no hint of interest.

She refocused and could see he was appraising her in much the same way. She shifted on the couch under his steady stare.

"Why have you come?" he asked.

Crystal tilted her head to one side. Surely he knew why she had come to Mexico. Mark had talked to him, asked him to meet with her. "You talked with Mark?"

"Yes."

"Then—-"

"You tell me why you come to me."

Crystal nodded and began to tell of her meeting with

Rosa and the plight of Lucita and her children. He sat in total silence, not moving a finger, not blinking an eye. Was he even listening? She told of her decision to come to Mexico and try to rescue the children. "So, here I am."

A woman entered and placed a plate of tamales, beans, and rice in front of Crystal. She nodded and smiled at the woman, but turned her attention back to Juan Grande. She needed information more than food.

"Why are you in my house? There are no children here."

"Mark made me promise not to do anything until I talked with you." Juan only returned her stare. "I need your help."

"Who has children? Where are they now?"

"They are being held by a man named José near San Sebastian del Oeste."

He raised his overgrown eyebrows. "One fourth of men in San Sebastian are called Jose."

"This José is powerful. He employs many people. According to Lucita, he owns a large hacienda in the jungle just outside San Sebastian."

"This man, he sounds very dangerous. It would be very difficult to rescue the children."

"I will pay whatever it takes to get the children out."

Again, Crystal grew uncomfortable under his penetrating, intense stare. Finally, he said, "Would you spend the night with me to help these children?"

Crystal's whole body grew rigid. She had been begging this man for help. Now, her eyes flashed the outrage she felt. "*Señor Grande*, I am willing to pay money, work without stopping, take whatever risks are necessary to get these children back to their mother. Going to bed with someone has nothing to do with saving children. Obviously, I have come to the wrong person." She stood up. *What was Mark thinking, sending me to this man?* "Thank you for your time, but I will look for someone else."

Juan Grande's belly began to shake. Slowly, a rumble started to work its way up through his body. He leaned his head back and a booming laugh erupted from his mouth. His whole body shook.

Crystal's frown turned from anger to puzzlement. She clutched her purse, not knowing whether to leave or not.

The laugh subsided somewhat, but continued to reverberate through his body. "*Señor Toro* say you are serious. But I must know for myself how you think. To say no and look for other help, this tell me you are serious. No give up." He waved his hand at Crystal. "Sit. Please sit. And do not worry. Carlotta, my beautiful wife, kill me if I even think of sleep with another. And why would I want to, with Carlotta here?"

Crystal hesitated. Until he broke into laughter, Juan's face had been as one of the masks so popular in Mexico, registering no emotion. Now, it appeared softer, kinder, and less intimidating. "So, Mark tell you I help. *Gracias, Señor Toro.*"

"How do you know Mark?" She eased down to the edge of the couch, still undecided. And how did he know Mark was called Bull?

"We do much things together. It is long story. And we must discuss other things tonight. But I tell you one story. You know Conan?"

"Conan?"

"*Si.* Conan. They show on TV in your country."

"Oh, Conan, the Barbarian. Yes. A TV series."

"They make pictures here, only few kilometers from Vallarta. They need someone to ride bull, but no Mexican. Mark is here. I know he ride the bulls in Texas. I get him to ride for Conan. We no have ..." He stopped, searching for a word. "*Payasos* ... ah, clowns. Mark get off bull, and bull chase him. Mark jump over fence and in cactus." Juan's round stomach began to shake again. "We pick *espinos* out of *Señor Toro* for hours." Juan's booming laugh once more filled the room.

For the first time in hours, Crystal smiled. "Thorns?"

"*Si*, thorns." Juan's laugh slowly faded. "But, we need be serious. Tell me everything, even smallest thing you know about children, and Jose." He bent forward and rested his chin in his large, right hand.

Crystal added what little she had not already told Juan. For the most part he simply listened, only occasionally interrupting to ask a question. She showed him the picture of the two girls. As he handed it back to her, he muttered something under his breath in Spanish. Crystal did not recognize the words, but she knew it was a curse.

"That is not much," he said when she had finished. "Someone here know more about *you*. Know your name, know you are here, in Vallarta. Maybe they know what you try to do. Are these people of Jose? I do not know. Who is watching you?" He paused and looked at her.

She shrugged.

"I do not think they know you come to me. That is important."

"How do they know about me? I haven't told anyone."

"*No se*. I don't know. But they do."

A chill ran through her body. She had told nobody she was coming to Mexico, except Brandi and Mark, Eula and Rosa. None of them would tell anybody else. While she didn't really know Rosa, Crystal couldn't imagine the young Mexican telling anybody about Crystal's trip. Lucita certainly would not tell anyone; her children were most at risk. Could Blackwood have found out about her trip? How? And why would he care, unless he knew why she was here. He could not know that. Could he?

She looked up to see Juan Grande's unblinking eyes studying her. "What can you do?" she asked.

"First, I learn about Jose. I find where he keep *niñas*. Then, I find way to get them."

"And what can I do?"

"Now, nothing. I tell you when I find answers to these questions." He stood up. "Carlos."

The man who had driven her from the Café des Artistes appeared in the doorway. *"Lleva a la señorita Moore a Plaza Mar, por favor."*

Chapter 17

THE mercado sprawled over several blocks. A combination flea market, bazaar, and mini-mall, the Mercado consisted of hundreds of small, hot, crowded shops overflowing with items for sale. Most of the shops were contained in a huge two-story building that sat beside the Cuale River. Narrow aisles made it impossible to keep from continually brushing against people. Crystal hugged her purse as if it were a sick baby. Mercèdes had suggested the market when Crystal asked where she might pick up some gifts for friends back in the States.

Crystal could discern no pattern: jewelry was next to toys and toys next to pottery. A shop specializing in copperware might contain a display of Mexican vanilla. A booth with five thousand tee shirts also sold crystal bowls. And more than one shop had rugs and wall hangings featuring Dallas Cowboys designs. Sculptures, paintings, beautiful stained glass in a variety of forms, intricate beaded work, woodcarvings, and magnificent silver crowded the narrow aisles. One could buy elaborately decorated sombreros, bull whips, masks, small furniture, key chains, gold chains, and plastic yo-yos. Shops offered marble coasters, chess sets ranging from four dollars to four thousand dollars, paperweights of all designs, and figurines, both religious and vulgar.

At almost every step, someone would offer an item, promising the best price in town. The vendor might be a seventy-year-old woman or a nine-year-old boy. All spoke English well enough to make a reasonable sales pitch, but none seemed to understand "No."

After an hour, Crystal left with nothing and hurried back to Plaza Mar to check for messages. None.

At an Internet computer in the lobby, she checked her e-mail. Only one message caught her eye, a message from Dr. Krupe. "Crystal, please respond to me. CMU is expecting me. They would like to hear our paper. I need to make my arrangements for the trip to Pittsburgh. E-mail me or call me at your earliest convenience. Dr. Krupe."

Their paper. In Dallas, it was *his* paper. She was not mentioned. She hit the delete key and the message disappeared. She had to make arrangements, too. Arrangements to get two young girls rescued and returned to their mother. Lester Krupe and CMU and Pittsburgh would have to wait.

#

"Where shall I have lunch, Mercèdes?" Crystal asked.

"Hummm." The Mexican woman tapped her teeth several times with a pencil. "Señor O'Malley always go to El Dorado soon as he gets here. He says his Vallarta time not start until he has chicken-avocado soup and sangria at El Dorado."

"Then that's where I'll have lunch today. If anyone calls for me, I'll be back in an hour."

She followed the walk along the beach a few blocks. El Dorado sat under a steeply pitched, thatched roof and was open on three sides, the kitchen forming the back wall. Its western edge ended at the sandy beach. From there, tables, shaded by large palapas, spilled out onto the beach. Most of those were taken and Crystal chose a small table under the thatched roof, two rows back from the beach. Following Mark's tradition, she ordered chicken-avocado soup and sangria.

She had just tasted the drink when she noticed a vendor staring at her. He stood outside the railing that defined the restaurant, holding a case filled with silver jewelry. He was short, slim and clean-shaven with neatly trimmed hair. On this warm, humid day, his white cotton shirt and pants were immaculate.

He held up several chains. Crystal shook her head. Undeterred, he put the chains down and picked up a ring. Even from a distance, the ring flashed, immediately catching one's attention. When Crystal looked interested, he motioned to indicate he would bring it to her. Again, she shook her head. He tried another ring. This time, Crystal raised her hand and signaled him over to her.

With his case balanced on his hip, he selected the first ring and handed it to Crystal.

"Ninety-nine point four percent pure silver. Stone is topaz. I polish it by hand myself. You like?"

The ring sparkled. It would be perfect for Brandi.

"How much?"

"For you, only one thousand pesos."

At the Mercado, when she said no and walked away, the vendor always lowered the price. She handed it back. "That's more than I can pay. Thank you." She picked up her drink and looked away.

The vendor moved around so he was in her line of sight again. "You will be my first sale of the day. I make it eight hundred." When Crystal said nothing, he added, "And I give you this very nice leather jewelry bag for it." He produced a small leather pouch.

Crystal took the bag. Without meaning to, she smiled and her eyebrows arched up. The pouch was as soft as a week-old kitten. She looked at the ring, still held in front of her by the vendor. "How about six hundred pesos?"

The Mexican's face sagged and his eyelids drooped. "Oh, Señorita, I lose money. I cannot feed my family." But his hand holding the ring in front of Crystal never wavered. "Seven fifty, and I still give you the leather bag."

Crystal ignored the ring and began looking at other items

in his case. She should get something for JT and Sally at the office. Nana never wore jewelry. Crystal would have to think of something else for her.

She ran her finger over a pair of earrings. The silver looked as if it had been carved, so sharp were the edges of the designs. "How much for these?"

"Only three hundred pesos."

"And these?" She pointed to another pair of earrings.

"Very cheap at two hundred."

She put them down. "Do you work here often?" she asked.

"I work every day. I must feed my family."

Crystal tried to look disinterested, but had difficulty keeping her gaze off the ring. "Maybe I'll see you here another day. Maybe I'll buy it then, after I've had time to look around some more."

"Oh, Señorita, ring like this no be here tomorrow. I sell this today." He sounded sincere, not begging, not pressuring. He held the ring steady in front of Crystal.

She had already looked. His case did not contain another copy of it and she had not seen anything to compare with it during her morning outing.

"I make you deal. Take ring and pair of earrings for nine hundred fifty pesos and I give you leather bag for each."

Crystal reached in her purse and extracted two five-hundred peso notes and laid them on the table. "I'll give you one thousand pesos for all three. Plus three leather bags."

He put the ring in Crystal's hand and laid out the earrings she had looked at. "You very tough woman. I give you all three, but no leather bags. That take little profit I make."

"How much for the bags?"

"Three bags. For everybody else I take fifty pesos for one.

But for you, all three for one hundred pesos. They are handmade. Very soft. Very elegant. Very nice. Very good price."

Crystal fished out another hundred-peso note and handed it to the man. "Thank you. And my friends back in Texas to whom I will give these send their thanks to you also."

The man's eyes and mouth drooped and lines formed across his forehead. "You no get any for yourself? You are such nice lady. You should have one also."

Crystal laughed. "No, no. No more today. Perhaps another day."

"I am Diego. If you no see me, ask anyone. They find me. I make special ring for you. One as beautiful as you."

"Thank you, Diego. And my name is Crystal."

#

That evening, Mercèdes invited Crystal to walk along the Malecón, a wide pedestrian walkway that bordered the bay and was popular with both tourists and locals. "It is always fun to walk on Malecón, but Saturday night is most fun."

The south end of the Malecón separated Plaza Mar from the beach. Crystal and Mercèdes walked two blocks to a high arching pedestrian bridge over the Cuale River. On the other side of the bridge, large sail-like modern sculptures scattered along the walk emphasized the importance of the bay in Vallarta's history.

Five minutes beyond the bridge, Mercèdes pointed to an open-air theater. "They perform some of our traditional dances tonight. You like to watch?"

"Sure," said Crystal.

Mercèdes led the way over to the Los Arcos amphitheater. Facing the bay, half a dozen rows of concrete seats wrapped around the large stage, providing seating for several hundred, while standing room accommodated several hundred more.

Through the four arches at the back of the stage, the sun began its nightly dive into the sea. A beautiful replica of a pirate ship, its sails billowing in the breeze, glided majestically across the golden path laid down by the setting sun across the blue waters of Banderas Bay.

On stage, six women and six men danced to lively Mexican music. The women wore bright, full, long dresses and clicked an infectious rhythm with their castanets. The men, dressed in black with silver adornments, circled the women. Then the women caught the hem of their dresses and swirled the skirts, creating a kaleidoscope of color. The men hammered out a staccato beat with their boots. Dramatic. Magnetic. And somehow, very sensual.

When the dancers finished, Crystal and Mercèdes wandered around the immediate area. Artists of all types were selling their creations. One featured intricate pictures made from tiny, colored straw. To the side, a man used cans of spray paint to produce fanciful pictures. Within a fifty-foot circle, a person could buy oil paintings, watercolors, jewelry, ceramics, and photographic art.

For those who wanted to feed their bodies instead of their souls, food stands surrounded the artists. The pungent smell of corn roasting over charcoal came from a dozen vendors. Other stands and carts offered guava, papaya, and mangos, often carved into intriguing shapes. Vendors passed through the crowd selling drinks poured out of huge gourds.

The two women strolled down the promenade, here about thirty feet wide, bordered by the beach on one side and on the other, the bustling Paseo Diaz Ordaz, crowded with cars and taxis. Even though the walk sometimes stood six to eight feet above the beach and four feet above the busy street, no railings existed.

Bronze sculptures, some twenty feet tall, others only a foot, adorned the Malecòn. People climbed and sat on these works of art. *If these were in the States, police would surely have chased away the children, and the adults. I guess here, sculptures are to be enjoyed both by viewing and by using.*

Hundreds of people strolled on the wide walk—couples, groups of kids, and whole families. Some had babies in strollers; others had small children whose hands they held while the young *niños* learned to walk.

Soccer games and kite-flying shared the beach. Men cast lines into the water while teenagers bodysurfed. Couples held hands and watched the sunset. And a mother chased her little boy across the sand.

For an instant, the young woman looked like Lucita. Crystal closed her eyes. Why was she out here enjoying herself when Lucita's children were still imprisoned? *But what can I do? Until Juan Grande calls, the answer is—nothing.*

Perhaps she could start looking on her own. Where? San Sebastian? If she did not hear from Juan tomorrow, she would rent a car and drive there. Only fifty miles. She could ask questions, see what she could find out.

#

They ate at Tequilas, where a mariachi band entertained them with its unique music. They sat on the second-floor balcony, overlooking the Malecón and Banderas Bay.

As the sun sank toward the blue water, Mercèdes said, "Maybe you see the green flash tonight."

Crystal raised her eyebrows. "What's the green flash?"

"Just as sun disappears into water, sometimes you see a green flash of light, where water meets sky. Right where sun sinks into the water. Watch closely. It is only for a second. You do not always see it. Watch. It is almost time."

The last part of the sun disappeared beyond the horizon. Crystal saw nothing green. "I didn't see it. I didn't see anything."

"Sometimes you do. Sometimes you do not. But it is nice to see. Watch for it other nights."

"What causes it?"

Mercèdes shrugged. "Someone tell me refraction causes it. I do not know. But I have seen it many times. You must watch very closely, at just the right moment. You will see it. It brings good luck."

#

After dinner, they started back to Plaza Mar. Ten minutes later, they stood across the street from the Los Arcos theater where earlier they had watched the dancers.

"This is the Palacio Municipal. In United States, you call it City Hall. And this is the Plaza Principal or the Plaza de Armas." Mercèdes indicated the park beside them. "We have many activities here. Often there is music. And of course, many people use stage to give speeches." She laughed. "Not many people listen."

Crystal looked up at a large bronze statue on a tall pedestal. "And who is this?"

"That is Luis Vallarta. The town was named for him."

"Was he a priest, a missionary?"

"Oh, no. He was in government. A judge, I think." Mercèdes pointed across the plaza. "That is The Lady of Guadalupe Church. Most people call it The Cathedral. The crown on top is important to people of Vallarta. When it fall down in earthquake a few years ago, we were very sad until it again sat at top of cathedral."

Across the Plaza, a short block up the hill stood the huge, stone church, its massive doors open and people wandering in and out. High above, a large crown capped the bell tower. A bright light topped each point of the crown. From this angle and at night, they twinkled like stars. As she admired its beauty, her thoughts turned to the missing children and she said a silent prayer they were safe.

On the way back to Plaza Mar, Crystal stopped and pointed at a life-sized bronze sculpture. "They look like the dancers we saw earlier."

"They should," said Mercedes. "Jim Demetro, used two of those dancers as models."

"What a beautiful statue."

"He is a famous artist. He did the statue of the boys trying to get the burro to move, the one in front of Plaza Mar. He donated those to the city because he loves Puerto Vallarta."

"The burro sculpture is fun. And lots of people were photographing it when I was watching."

"It is very popular among the tourists and the locals as well."

#

Back in the condo, Crystal settled into a comfortable chair on the terrace, watching the people in the park. She picked up the novel she had started earlier, but the activity below and the waves cascading on the sand fascinated her, and the book remained unopened.

As usual, strolling musicians played lively Mexican tunes and children chased each other around sculptured bushes in the dim glow of ornamental lights. Tourists browsed at the kiosks that bordered the west side of the block.

For many of the children, no parents appeared to be watching. How nice to be able to let children play in the park at night without worry they might be harmed or kidnapped. Children here were freer than in the States. At least, some of them were.

Crystal jumped at the sound of the telephone. She walked into the living room and answered it.

"Come to Cathedral for ten o'clock mass in morning. Sit in third pew from back, on far left side."

"Is this—-"

"Yes. Please do not call my name."

"Okay. What if the pew is full?"

"There will be place for you. Ten o'clock. Tomorrow."

"I'll be there. Should I-—"

The line went dead.

Chapter 18

CRYSTAL hesitated at the Plaza Mar gate. She did not expect to see anything amiss, but prudence dictated she be aware of her surroundings. Everything looked normal. Not much happened in Cardenas Plaza at nine forty on a Sunday morning. None of the vendors had opened their booths this early. No children played in the small bandstand or under the trees. Only a few tourists strolled the walks beneath the palms.

She had allowed ample time, but still set out at a brisk pace. The Cathedral was not far, less than a mile. A gentle breeze floated off the bay, carrying a pungent smell of salt and fish.

She turned left on Ignacio Vallarta and almost immediately slowed her pace. Sharp contrasts were common in Mexico, but Crystal ranked the scene in front of her near the top. A man was using two burros to deliver supplies to a cyber café.

The street felt different from last night when all the shops were open and vendors tried to entice you into their stores. The cyber café had three customers, but other restaurants would not open until later. Even the Mercado had locked its doors to business this early on a Sunday morning.

She approached the Cathedral through the plaza by City Hall. While Cardenas Park had been almost deserted, Plaza Principal was filled with people. Vendors were selling food, children were playing, two men with guitars were singing on the steps to the City Hall, and standing in the bandstand, a man was giving a speech. Sure enough, no one was listening.

As she left the Plaza, she realized what last night she had thought was a street leading to the cathedral, was in fact a pedestrian walkway wider than most Vallarta streets. People moved at varying speeds up the slight incline. Beyond, wide steps led up to the large doors into the church. Crystal joined the crowd as the bells began to toll high above. Last night she had noted the massive crown sitting atop the bell tower. Today she saw three towers with many bells hung in them, all ringing, calling people to services.

At the top of the steps, she paused. Scores of people were entering the church, which looked to be full already. Occasionally, someone would stop and drop a coin into the hands of one of the poor people who sat on either side of the entrance. One woman, hands outstretched, silently pleading for donations, had a small baby strapped to her back. Crystal reached into her pocket and pulled out a hundred-peso bill, and placed it in the mother's hands.

"*Gracias. Vaya con Dios,*" the woman whispered.

The church was full, with many people standing around the walls and in the aisles. Crystal moved to the left and checked the third pew. People sat shoulder to shoulder in it. She walked over to the aisle, took a few steps forward and stopped, not certain what to do. Mexicans crowded the pews from the back row on up the aisle as far as she could see.

Juan Grande had said the pew on the far left. She checked around once more, making sure she had selected the proper aisle. This had to be the correct place. Self-doubt crept up. *Could he have said the right side? No, it was clear; left, third pew from the back.* She stood there, not knowing what to do. Now, panic was replacing the self-doubt. *What am I going to do?*

She glanced back at the third pew and blinked. The end seat was vacant. Just a moment before, it had been filled like all the others. Now, the space she needed was empty. She looked around, trying to see who had gotten up and left, but no one was standing or moving away.

She sat down in the empty seat.

Out of the corner of her eye, she peeked at the old woman sitting next to her. The woman's eyes were closed, apparently deep in prayer. No one had taken any notice of Crystal.

She surveyed the church. Made entirely of stone, it didn't seem as large as it had from the outside. Partway in from each side, a row of thick columns rose up perhaps three stories, then flared out and up to support the roof. Stained-glass windows depicted various Bible scenes. A row of small, crystal windows just below the curved ceiling ran the length of both sides. Behind the main altar, a gigantic tapestry had an image of the Lady of Guadalupe woven into it, with other small images along the edges. Gold leaf adorned much of the sanctuary and large gold candlesticks, perhaps five feet tall, were positioned on the altar. Hundreds of flowers decorated the area.

Two priests and four acolytes walked into the sanctuary at the front of the church. From somewhere above, the warm, rich tones of a pipe organ filled the immense stone structure.

The service had been in progress about five minutes when the old lady next to Crystal leaned over and whispered, "I no walk good. You help me, *por favor*?"

The woman stood up and held out her hand. Crystal swiveled her head around, hoping someone else might help the old woman. No one offered any aid.

What if Juan Grande comes for me while I'm gone? Crystal had no way to contact him. If she were not here, would he think she didn't show up, didn't care? Would he simply drop her from his plans?

Anxiously, Crystal checked again. Everyone was so intent on the service they were not even aware the old woman had spoken or stood up. She continued to stand there, smiling, holding her hand out. Crystal eased out of the pew, stepped into the aisle, and took the woman's hand.

The woman hobbled, but she guided Crystal to the side of the church and through a door that opened to a patio. They crossed the courtyard to a carved wooden door with a sign identifying it as the *Sacristia.*

Crystal assumed the woman was headed toward a restroom, but she didn't see one anywhere. Inside the *Sacristia,* the woman stopped and closed the door behind them. A chair was positioned beside the door and she moved it slightly so it blocked the door from opening, then eased into it without saying a word.

Crystal frowned. *Is this a trap? I could overpower the old woman and leave if I have to.* Candles, cabinets, and chairs furnished the room, obviously where the priests donned their vestments. The wall on the right had a door that probably opened into the church, most likely how the priests and acolytes entered the sanctuary. Crystal could make out the priest's voice, speaking to the congregation.

The opposite wall also contained a door. And as she tried to decide whether to stay or leave, the door opened and Juan Grande strode into the room. He pointed at two chairs standing in the middle. "Sit, sit." He took one of the chairs and Crystal sat in the other.

Before she could say anything, he leaned forward, and began, "I carry bad news."

"You haven't found the girls? But you've only looked a short while."

"No. I find children. They are held by José Rodriquez de Allende. He is very bad man. He do many bad things. Steal. Kill people. Bad man."

"Can't you get the police to arrest him?"

Juan smiled. "He also is very powerful man. Has many men. Some police take money from him. I think we no get police to arrest him."

Crystal's shoulders sagged. "How can we get the girls

away from him? We can't give up, just leave them there." Her hands twisted around her small purse.

"No, no. We no quit. First, I make plan. We bring children away in few days."

"Great. When do we go after them?"

Juan shook his head. "I and my men get them. You can not come."

Crystal sat up straighter. "I certainly am going to go with you and help. Remember, I asked for your *help*. I didn't ask you to do it all by yourself."

He pursed his lips behind the bushy mustache. "No. Much danger."

"Juan, I know it will be dangerous. But I have to go. I came down here to get the children. *Because* it is dangerous, I cannot ask you to do it and not be willing to take any risks myself. I will go with you."

"You no understand. José very bad. I can do many things to help you. I can protect you here in Vallarta. But, if José capture you, I can do nothing. If he get you, you disappear. Before I can get help, you will be gone. Where?" He raised his shoulders. "*No se*. No one ever see you again. You become slave. Toy for drug buyers. Not here. We no find you." He raised his eyebrows.

"The American embassy—"

"Can do nothing."

She cocked her head. "Surely the American Embassy—"

"American Embassy try, but can no help you. *I* can do nothing." He looked at her, again with his unblinking stare, as if seeing through her eyes and into her brain.

Am I being foolish? She expected danger. But Juan's intensity, his conviction, had a sobering effect. She swallowed. She had not consciously thought about the American Embassy as a solution before. But somewhere in the back of her mind, on some level she had not visited, she now admitted she had the notion, when all else failed, her government could protect her in a foreign country. This man in front of her had severed that small safety line.

She struggled to erase the mental image of her with drug lords, with no hope of escape. *If he intended to frighten me, he succeeded.*

An image from the past popped into her mind. A nine-millimeter pistol was aimed at her. A bullet fired just past her head, the next threatened the middle of her face. That had been over a year ago, and still a chill passed through her just thinking about it. Scared, she had not fainted or given up. She had been trying to protect her grandmother.

Once more, she felt her stomach twist and a little electric shock race through her body. Should she tempt fate again? This time, it concerned people she didn't know, had never seen. But two small children had no one to help them, no one who cared they were separated from their mother. And Lucita, a slave back in Dallas, a slave as surely as if she had iron shackles on her feet, could never leave, never be free, while José held her children.

The man in front of her didn't know the two girls or their mother, had never seen the anguish in Lucita's eyes, or heard Rosa crying for her dead husband. Yet, he was ready to go, to risk his life and those of his men.

Could she just let others take all the risks? Why not? Juan Grande was probably accustomed to dangerous situations. He didn't want her to go with him. Why argue? She admitted it. She was scared just thinking about it. The sensible thing was to wait here and let Juan Grande handle it. He knew how; she didn't.

In a corner of her mind, she could hear her Nana saying, "Don't plant the seed unless you plan to harvest the crop." She had planted the seed.

"Juan, I know what you're saying. I do understand the danger. But I must do this. I cannot come here and ask others to face the danger while I sun myself on the beach. I have the pictures of the girls, so I can identify them."

"Give pictures to me."

Crystal smiled, trying to be light-hearted. "Have you looked at yourself? You will scare the children. They might just refuse to go with you. You will frighten them." She touched the pendant Lucita had given her. "They will come with me." Her smile disappeared. She straightened her back and turned quietly serious. "I am most grateful for what you are doing. I understand the dangers and I am very ... nervous. But, I will share those risks. I will go with you." She leaned closer to the huge Mexican man. "I could not do this without you. But I cannot let you do it without me."

For a long time, Juan stared at her, liquid eyes so black no pupils showed. Crystal could feel Juan's focus becoming sharper, more intense, searching her resolve, her motives.

His gaze shifted and he looked over Crystal's shoulder for several seconds. Then he refocused on Crystal. "Most important is safety of children. If I take you, you must do what I ask."

Crystal nodded.

"With no hesitation. Hesitation can cost much. And if I must choose to save you or children, I save children." His dark eyes never blinked.

His words grabbed Crystal by the throat, lodged there, making her want to swallow, but unable to do so. "I am here in Mexico to rescue the children," she finally managed. "I agree with everything you have said."

His steady gaze probed inside her. She could feel it penetrating into her heart. Slowly, his intense focus relaxed. "I take you with me. I make plans. I call in three, four days." He stood.

"How much notice will I have? Do I need to sit by the

telephone until you call?"

"I give you plenty time," he said. "You ride horse?"

"Yes." She grinned. "I *am* from Texas." She said it with bravado, but her knees felt weak.

"Please think of dangers. You can change the mind and not go. Wait in Puerto Vallarta until children are safe. There will be no shame. You are brave woman." For a moment, he studied Crystal. Then he said, "You take my mother back to church, *por favor*." He turned and left.

Chapter 19

MONDAY crawled by. Crystal sat on the terrace, the telephone within arm's reach, trying to read a novel. But her mind refused to be involved in the story, reverting continually to the captive children and her lack of action. She threw the book across the deck. It ended up splayed open in the flower box. *When is he going to call? Is anything happening?*

She stared at the book sitting in the dirt. She had not thrown a book in years. "I don't care," she snapped. "I'm doing nothing. I came down here to help. And what am I doing? Reading."

On impulse, she picked up the phone and dialed.

"Hi, Nana. How're you doing?"

"Happy as a pig in slop. Rosa is a great companion. Good worker, too," said Eula. "I'd let you say *hola* to her, but she's out roaming around The Park."

"Just thought I'd check up on you."

"Things not perking too well in Mexico, I take it."

Crystal sighed. Of course, she could not fool Eula. "Mostly not moving at all. I'm spending my time waiting."

Eula laughed. "Waiting's always the toughest part. 'Course, it's often the most important part. Picking the right time's half the battle."

"It's just so frustrating."

"You can solve that immediately. In your head. And you

better. When the time comes, you need to be clear headed. Ready. Rested. Being frustrated sops up your energy, fuzzies your thinking." Eula paused a moment. "You know I wasn't in favor of your doing this. Still not. But I know you're determined. So, quit fretting. And here's a new word to add to your vocabulary: patience."

"I never was too patient."

"I love you anyway."

"I don't know what to do."

"A good time not to do anything. Unclutter your mind. Be flexible. The right time'll show itself."

Neither woman spoke for a minute. Then Eula said, "Do what you gotta do, then come on back to your Nana. Safe and sound."

#

Tuesday, Crystal was walking back to Plaza Mar after breakfast when a scruffy man stopped her.

"Only forty American dollars for Jeep. You buy gas. No extra charge for four hundred kilometers. You can drive all around bay."

"*No gracias*," Crystal said, hardly looking at the man.

She had taken two steps when it hit her. She could drive to San Sebastian. Only eighty kilometers, about fifty miles. An hour. Get a feel for the area. Maybe even see José Allende's hacienda. What if she actually saw the children? Just the possibility set her heart racing.

She turned back to the man. "Does that include insurance?"

" Yes, *Señorita*. For you, I include insurance for no extra dollars."

"I'll take it."

#

An hour later, she sat looking at her map in Las Palmas. Lost. A man in Ixtapa, the previous town, had assured her a sign in Las Palmas showed where to turn. She had found no such sign.

"*¿Donde esta el camino a San Sebastian?*" She held out her map in front of a young Mexican man, pointing to the town.

He frowned and tilted his head to the side. Then, slowly, the frown turned into a smile and he nodded several times. "*San Sebastián está a la izquierda de la señal.*" He pointed back the way she had come. "*Cinco cuadras.*

Crystal retraced five blocks and looked for a sign to San Sebastian. Half hidden by weeds, a small wooden sign, about a foot off the ground, pointed to the left and signaled the way. She turned into the small road. So much for the hour to get there. Of course, she had to cross Puerto Vallarta. That took some time. But, she had made the half-way point. Another twenty-five miles with no towns to slow her down: maybe forty minutes.

In her rear-view mirror, she saw a car turn onto the road behind her. Not close. She couldn't really make out much about it. She couldn't tell if it was grey or brown, a Jeep or some other open-topped vehicle. She had no idea who was driving it, man or woman, young or old, American or Mexican. But she knew one thing, could feel it in the pit of her stomach—that same car had been behind her in Ixtapa.

She slowed. He could go around her. The other vehicle slowed, staying a constant distance behind her. Of course, if he's going to San Sebastian from Ixtapa, or Vallarta for that matter, this was the only road. Naturally he'd be following her.

For a few moments that satisfied her and the small knot in her stomach faded away. Unbidden, a question popped into her mind. Since she got lost in Las Palmas, why was he still behind her? He had been close behind her when she entered the town. *Maybe he stopped for gas.* Consciously, she focused her thoughts on the countryside, the road, and the driving.

Within a mile, the road deteriorated. Pavement gave way to gravel, one lane replaced two. Forty miles per hour yielded to thirty-five, then twenty-five. Gradually, the road began to climb and soon Crystal felt as if she were driving on the roads they used in San Francisco movies. Only this one wasn't paved.

She could not help but grin when she realized she was actually in the jungle. An honest-to-goodness jungle. Parrots, yellow-bellied sap-suckers, and other brightly colored birds she had only seen in photographs perched on strange trees. Iguanas lounged on tree limbs or stood ready to cross the road. Wild goats stood on rock outcroppings, and more than once Crystal had to pause and wait until cattle or sheep moved off the road.

She made a sharp turn and slammed on the brakes, skidding to a stop at the edge of a stream. The sun-light danced on the rippling water and she had no idea how deep it ran. Not a good spot to have a car problem. She hadn't seen another soul since leaving Las Palmas. Except the car following her. Now, even that car had disappeared.

She got out, picked up a stick and approached the water. Looking down at it, without the glare, she could see it was less than a foot deep. She poked the stream bed with the stick. It felt solid enough.

She got back in the Jeep and eased it across the stream.

While the roadway didn't get any narrower, periodically the edge was washed away. A careless moment could result in a wheel dropping off the edge. Her hands gripped the steering wheel so tightly her knuckles were white and periodically one hand or the other would develop a cramp. She would have to remove that hand from the wheel and try to relax it.

The road rose and descended sharply as it clung to the edge of the mountainside, a sheer wall on one side and a five hundred foot drop to a river on the other. Each temporary descent would mean crossing another ford, and another steep climb.

She made a promise: she would be back over this road before dark.

Beautiful tropical flowers, often wild orchids, grew along the road and on the trees. Crystal was tempted to stop and investigate, but the road offered no place to pull off. *I could stop in the middle of the road. Who would care?*

A couple of times while making a hairpin curve, Crystal looked down and saw a small cloud of dust along the road she had traveled five minutes before. Once, she spotted a car through the trees, but could not tell if it was the same vehicle she had seen behind her in Ixtapa and later in Las Palmas.

Just over an hour had passed since she left Las Palmas. Checking the odometer, she let out a small cry. She had covered twenty kilometers. Just twelve miles in that time.

At last, she came to a stretch of level road and started to speed up as much as the rocks would allow. Before she reached fifty kilometer per hour, she was applying the brakes. A large chain crossed the road. She skidded to a stop, her mind confused, her nerves on edge. She could turn around, but not easily or quickly. And would she then meet the car behind her? Her breathing began to accelerate and panic was gaining control.

On her right, a small hut nestled under the trees. *Who's in that hut?* She jammed the gear into reverse, frantic to turn around and get away from this trap. In her haste, she killed the engine. As she started the car again, an elderly Mexican man limped out of the hut and toward her car. *He's limping. And he's smiling. Surely he's not a threat.* When he reached the car, he handed her a piece of paper. Crystal scanned it. Spanish, of course, and most of the words were unfamiliar. But near the bottom, she picked out an unlikely word: *autopista*. And twenty pesos. Her mouth fell open. This was probably the worst excuse for a road she had ever been on, and they were collecting a *toll*.

She fished out a twenty-peso note and handed it to the man. He smiled again, thanked her, and lowered the chain. She looked at the paper again. *"Para la rehabilitacion del camino.* For the rehabilitation of the road." She laughed. "It does need help."

The level road lasted only a few hundred meters more, and then the steep, winding, slender trail, littered with large rocks, resumed.

The scenery made up for the tortuous road. The dense forest included giant trees with smooth, deep red bark, others with bright yellow or orange flowers, trees laden with fruit of all sorts, and a wide variety of palms. Vines with multi-colored flowers climbed toward the sun. Bougainvillea and cupa de oro flourished. In the hour since paying the toll, only two places allowed her to pull off the road and admire the grandeur. Each time, she thought of the dangers around her, and quickly moved on.

The last forty kilometers, about twenty-five miles, took two hours, but at last she passed a sign welcoming her to San Sebastian del Oeste. On the left a white, stucco building was identified as the San Sebastian airport. Running parallel to the road was a narrow, short, but smooth grass runway, its sides marked by white-washed tires, upright, lower halves embedded in the dirt. Crystal saw no planes.

I made it. She allowed herself to relax a bit, focusing on the lovely town and trying to put the dangers out of her mind. She was in a town now. A town would have police. She felt safer already.

For about a quarter mile, the road into the town was wide, paved, and flanked by old, stately trees that filtered the strong afternoon sun. Then, it squeezed down to a single, narrow, cobblestone lane between adobe buildings. Small children played on a walk that filled the scant two feet between the road and the buildings.

A few blocks later, Crystal came to the town's central plaza. A tiny park with a gazebo surrounded by rose gardens occupied the middle of the square. The far side of the park was dominated by a stone building identified as the municipal office. On her right, stood a two-story hotel, constructed with irregular, hand-made bricks and rough hewn timbers, probably as old as the town itself. Behind her a long, low building housed a pharmacy on one end and the El Fortin Café on the other.

To the left a cantina and several other businesses occupied a one-story adobe structure. But what captured her attention was a graceful steeple towering over the building.

Instead of parking, she decided to investigate the church. She drove around the square, turning off on the far side and found the front of the church on the next block. She parked on the side street.

The church was constructed of the same limestone as the municipal building, but designed with more imagination, featuring buttresses, graceful curves, a bell tower, and of course, stained-glass windows. While the exterior was a dull, weathered grey, the interior used the full range of colors. The high-arched ceiling was adorned with delicate paintings. Statues, many clothed in rich fabrics, lined the sides and front of the church. And like the Cathedral in Puerto Vallarta, flowers graced San Sebastian's church. *How can such a small pueblo as San Sebastian maintain this beautiful church?*

Women knelt near the front, faded mantillas covering their bowed heads. Crystal knelt at the back pew and prayed the children were safe and would soon be free and reunited with their mother.

Outside again, Crystal wandered away from the square, down a narrow street, fascinated by this quaint village nestled high in the mountains, yet not far from the sea. She stopped to admire the large flowers with narrow, bright red petals, which towered over her head. She examined them closely and let out a low whistle as she recognized they were poinsettias, growing wild and over seven feet tall.

The dusty, four-hour trip had left her thirsty and now her stomach rumbled. *And I need to get a bottle of water for the trip back.* She walked around the block and headed to the town square, stopping once to pick some small beans off a tree she could not identify.

The El Fortin Café contained a total of three tables, all empty in the early afternoon, siesta time. Against the wall opposite the door, a cabinet made of course-cut wood displayed various items for sale: Mexican vanilla, a selection of liquors, and packages of food stuffs she could not identify. A large painting, framed with rough boards, decorated the wall on the left. Crystal sank into a chair at the closest table as a young woman came from the back and greeted her in English.

"I really need something to drink," Crystal said. "What do you suggest?"

"Many of people drink *racilla*," the plump Mexican woman suggested.

"Sounds interesting. What is it?"

"Is local drink, made from cactus. Very good. Like tequila."

Crystal laughed. "Oh, no, no. I have to drive back down that road. No alcohol."

"Okay. You like *agua de Jamaica*. Better than co-cah."

"I'll try it. And a bowl of soup. Can you tell me what kind of beans these are?"

The woman looked at the small beans Crystal had collected. "Coffee. Many coffee trees grow here. Make very good coffee. Many of people come to San Sebastian to buy coffee. We sell it here." She pointed to the packages in the wooden cabinet. "You wish try some?"

"Maybe before I leave."

The young woman left to fetch Crystal's order.

#

Half an hour later, Crystal had finished the squash-blossom soup and sweet *agua de Jamaica,* and was paying the bill. "Do you know a man here in San Sebastian named Jose?"

The waitress furrowed her brows. "Many men called José in San Sebastian."

"This man has a large hacienda, a short distance outside the town. And I am told many men work for him."

A dark cloud descended over the woman's face. She turned and hurried from the room without saying a word. *That was a mistake*, Crystal thought. But since she was expecting change from the two-hundred-peso note, she waited.

Two minutes passed before a beefy man came from inside. He smiled pleasantly at Crystal and laid her change on the table.

"Elena say you ask about a *Señor* Jose. Why you want know? Is he friend of you?"

"No."

"You do business with him?"

"No. I had heard he lived near San Sebastian, on a large hacienda. I was just curious, that's all."

For several seconds, the man stared at Crystal. She knew he understood; his English was good enough. After a moment, he looked out the window as deep grooves formed between his brows.

Without thinking, she slid her purse off the table and clutched it in her lap.

"Come with me to back. We talk there."

He stood perfectly still, made no move or gesture toward Crystal, yet she felt like a little girl being offered candy by a strange man.

Blood pumped through an artery at her temple, surging ever faster. Her left eye twitched. She moved her chair back and stood up, almost falling in the process. "I have to go," she stammered and started for the door.

He took a half step after her. "The change."

Crystal was out the door. "Your tip," she called without slowing down.

She ran across the street. Her car was several blocks away. *Leave. Now.*

A cool breeze swirled around her, but she only felt the chill from the café. She was looking down at the cobblestones, being careful not to stumble, and almost ran into a horse. Her head jerked up.

Blocking her path was a scruffy Mexican sitting on a large black horse. "*Senorita* must look where she walk."

"Excuse me, ah, *lo siento*," she said.

"Maybe I help. You like see big hacienda?"

The blood drained from Crystal's face. She tried to smile. "Thank you, but not today."

She moved to go around the horse, only to find another horse and rider blocking her way. The man moved his mount closer, forcing Crystal to retreat. A third man, round with a skimpy mustache, sat astride a burro there, leering at her from under a large sombrero.

"You ride with me," the first man declared.

Chapter 20

THE three animals now formed a triangle, with Crystal in the middle. The first man reached down, ready to pull her up on the horse behind him.

She swung her purse at the man's hand. He grabbed the strap, held it, laughing at her. She tugged on the purse to no avail. Now all three men were laughing.

Crystal swiveled her head around, looking for any help. Nothing but sweaty animals were visible. The man pulled the strap, slowly moving Crystal closer to him. For an instant, she considered letting go of the purse, crawling under the horse, and running. But the purse held not only money and credit cards, but her passport as well. And most important, the keys to her transportation out of this town. She yanked again. The strap broke and she stumbled, almost falling on the rocky street. This prompted a new round of laughter from the three Mexicans.

But Crystal had her purse.

A car skidded to a stop not a foot behind the horses. Its horn blared. The burro brayed and backed off. One of the horses bucked and ran fifty feet down the road.

"Come, I take you to car."

Crystal took in air, and her despair eased. Her hope died as she looked at a gray Jeep—the one that had followed her from Ixtapa.

The man was not smiling, but he was not fearsome. The Mexican on the large black horse was moving closer to her. "Come now," the man in the car said, "or they trap you again."

Crystal froze. The man with the thin mustache had settled the burro, was now trying to urge it back to pin her in. The second rider had his horse under control and inched the still-jumpy animal closer.

Can I make it back to the cafe? Then what? They drag me out.

She ran three steps to the Jeep and climbed in. Before the door closed, the car was moving. They turned and raced along the side of the plaza.

"My car," she began and pointed to the left.

The grey Jeep dashed straight ahead and Crystal's breathing stopped.

The driver accelerated down several blocks before turning left once more.

Crystal tried again, endeavoring to sound cheerful and trusting. "My car is back there." And she pointed back behind them.

The Jeep turned left again, only this time, not on a road. Her heart pounded, her breathing came in gasps. She could not keep Juan Grande's warning from blazing across her mind: *If he get you, you disappear. No one ever see you again. You become his slave.*

She looked at the speedometer. They were doing eighty kilometers over a horse path leading out of town. Even if she jumped out, she would be knocked unconscious, or worse. She could not escape. Her heart beat against her ribs. Her breathing was rapid but she felt like she couldn't get enough air.

They turned left, now heading back toward town. The Jeep bounced onto a street and slowed. Crystal was looking for a place to leap from the vehicle. *We're not far from the church. I can hide there.* She grasp the handle of the door, readying herself. Then up ahead she saw her car.

The grey Jeep slid to a stop opposite her car. The driver

turned to her. "Best leave *rápido*. They no take long to find you again."

She hopped out of the car and turned." Who are those guys? Who are you?" But the jeep was already speeding away.

#

Crystal spent most of Wednesday morning going over yesterday's events. *Who were those guys and why were they after me? José cannot know I am here. So what was that about? Did it have anything to do with the girls? And who was the guy in the jeep?* She shuddered, thinking about the man trying to pull her up on his horse. *I would have been just like Lucita's girls, a prisoner, trapped, unable to get away, and with no one to help me.* As much as she tried to think of other things, her mind wouldn't let go of the idea.

In the afternoon, Mercèdes called. "I have lesson this afternoon. Would you like to come with me?"

Without even asking what kind of lesson, Crystal accepted. She had done nothing but worry about Lucita's girls all day. *Maybe this will take my mind off yesterday. Juan Grande might call, but he said he would give me plenty of notice.*

At three o'clock, Crystal told Alberto, now at the reception desk, she would be back in two hours, if anyone called. Then she and Mercèdes left Plaza Mar.

"We catch bus at corner," Mercèdes said.

Four buses were lined up. They looked like the school buses Crystal had ridden to grade school, and they might have been that old. While most were blue, each had hand-lettered signs painted on the windshield, giving various points along its route.

Mercèdes selected the second one and they boarded, each woman handing the driver seven and a half pesos.

"What kind of lesson are you taking?"

"Flying."

"Flying! Wow, that sounds like fun. But difficult."

"Not airplane. I learn to fly paraplane."

Brows arched, Crystal asked, "What's a paraplane?"

"A powered parachute."

Crystal's mouth gaped. "A powered parachute? What on earth is that?"

"There is big parachute with little cart hanging below. Cart has motor and propeller like small plane. It is easy. I learn last week, in one day. Today, I practice. I already pay one thousand pesos for time."

Crystal grinned. "I never heard of such a thing. Sounds like fun."

"Maybe you try it?"

"No, no. I don't think so. I'll just enjoy watching you do it."

A young Mexican man boarded, and though plenty of seats were empty, he stood in the aisle near the front, facing the rear of the bus. A handsome man, perhaps twenty, he had a narrow mustache, neatly trimmed hair and wore a sparkling white shirt and black pants. As soon as the bus was moving again, he started singing. Most of the passengers, many of whom had been talking, stopped to listen. When he finished, he immediately started another. After the fourth song, he walked down the aisle, accepting donations. Quite of few of the passengers, including Crystal, tipped the singer for making the ride more enjoyable.

#

Half an hour later, Crystal and Mercèdes stood at the edge of a grassy area about the size of a football field. Spread out on the ground was a large, rectangular parachute, its bright orange and yellow hues providing a forty or fifty-foot splash of color against the dark, green grass.

While Mercèdes talked to a young Mexican man standing beside a faded blue pickup, Crystal walked over to inspect the parachute. A number of nylon cords ran from the chute to what could have been a go-cart with roll bars, except for the motor and propeller mounted on the back. Two seats, one in front of the other, accommodated two passengers. The motor was idling and the propeller rotated slowly.

When Crystal turned to ask a question about the rig, she found Mercèdes sitting on the grass, her head drooped down, her hands clasped together tightly in her lap. "Mercèdes, are you Okay?"

"I do not know. Suddenly, I feel very sick in the stomach."

"Perhaps we should go home. You can practice another day."

The young girl's face, always before radiating a warm smile, now was creased by pain. "No. I sit here for a while. I am okay in a little time." She put her purse down and rested her head in her hands. Then she looked up. "You take my place. You take lesson." She turned to the man and spoke to him in Spanish.

Mercèdes turned to Crystal. "This is Paco. He speaks English. He will teach you."

Crystal's eyebrows shot up. "Oh, no. I don't fly."

"I already pay one thousand pesos. Paco say he turn down other person to save time for me." Now, her voice pleaded. "Please. It is very safe." She turned to Paco. "Show her how easy it is."

Without a word, the man walked over, strapped himself into the front seat and put his feet on two bars. He reached down and pulled a rope, yanking blocks of wood away from the back wheels. Then he pulled a lever toward him. The propeller began to spin faster and the cart started moving along the grass. It had rolled only a few feet before the parachute caught some air and struggled off the ground. As the cart moved faster, the chute rose higher. The cart had traveled little more than a hundred feet when the parachute lifted it off the ground. Paco was flying.

By the time he reached the trees bordering the end of the field, Paco was eighty or ninety feet off the ground. He turned left, continuing to gain altitude, turned left again and zoomed past them, going in the opposite direction from his takeoff. A little past the road where Crystal and Mercèdes had gotten off the bus, he turned again. Now he was descending. The cart touched down and Paco brought it to a stop, directly in front of Crystal.

"See how easy? Please try it," Mercedes asked. "Paco is very good teacher. Very safe."

Paco flashed a brilliant smile at Crystal. "Come. I fly. You ride with me. Very safe. Nothing bad happen."

Before she realized she had agreed, Crystal sat in the cart, moving down the grassy field and then into the air. They made the same loop Paco had taken alone and in two minutes, they were back on the ground.

Paco helped Crystal out. "Fun? You like it?"

"Yes."

"Easy?"

"You made it look easy."

Paco's face split into a toothy grin. "Now, your turn. You sit in front. I sit in back. You fly."

Crystal was still deciding if she should do this as Paco helped her into the front seat and fastened her seat belt. He hopped in behind her and began yelling, to be heard over the noise of the motor, "Put feet on bars. Good. Now, see handle on left? Pull handle back to you, make engine run faster. Okay? Now, pull handle back."

Crystal pulled the lever back, sending more gas to the

engine, and the cart started moving forward.

"Pull back more."

She increased the power and soon the cart was off the ground. They were flying.

"More you pull handle back, higher you go. Not faster. Higher."

"This is high enough," Crystal yelled over her shoulder.

"Okay. To turn left, push left foot down. Try now."

Her feet rested on separate bars. Crystal pressed her left foot down. Attached to the bar, a line ran to the back tip of the parachute. When she pushed the bar down, the line pulled the tip of the wing—she now thought of the parachute as a wing—down and the wing began to turn to the left. The cart, swaying below the huge parachute, followed along.

They had turned almost in a circle when Paco said, "Pull foot up to stop turn."

Crystal shrugged. *Of course. Push down to turn, let up to stop the turn. Simple enough.* They straightened out for a minute, then Paco suggested she try a right turn. Crystal pushed down with her right foot and the parachute turned to the right.

Paco instructed Crystal and she maneuvered them around to the end of the field. "Now, push lever away. *No mucho.*"

Crystal complied and the cart began to descend. With Paco yelling instructions, Crystal brought the craft down to bump sharply on the ground, then roll to a stop.

Crystal started to unfasten her straps, but Paco put his hand on hers and shook his head. "No. We go around again. But first, I tell you again. Pull handle back, you go up. Propeller go faster, we no go faster. We go up. We always go same speed. Always forty-seven kilometers per hour. Engine go faster, we go up. Push handle away, go down. Engine go slower, we go down. No faster, no slower. In air, always same. On ground, make us go faster. Not in air." He patted her hand. "You take us up."

Crystal pulled the lever and the cart began to move. This time, Paco said nothing.

She had made several circles and was heading toward the beach when Paco leaned forward and yelled, "Pull handle back. Take us higher."

They were high enough for Crystal, but she pulled the lever back some more. She turned right, deciding not to go out over the water. They crossed over the beach again. Now, the people were only tiny figures, dots of color on the golden sand. The road became a dark ribbon with toy cars and trucks and a yellow school bus.

She turned the small craft back to the right and in the distance, she saw the airport, the sun reflecting off the shiny body of a jet. Beyond the airport, she located the marina with hundreds of boats bobbing gently, their tall masts waving to her. Far down the coast, Puerto Vallarta shimmered in the afternoon sun, green mountains and blue sky forming a backdrop.

The warm sun, and cool breeze blowing through her dark hair reminded Crystal of riding in a convertible. Only here, the view was much better.

She brought the paraplane back around to the left and sailed inland. Below, fields of crops formed green and gold rectangles, streams etched blue lines through the landscape, and thin trails that served as roads wound into the interior. A river snaked its way from the distant mountain to the azure waters of Banderas Bay.

Paco tapped her on the shoulder and said, "Take us back. You try to land soft."

This time, Crystal set the craft down with no instructions. She landed hard, the jolt knocking her teeth together.

They had not stopped rolling, when Paco said, "Take us

back up. Pull handle to you."

During the next fifteen minutes, Crystal made five more landings. By the last one, she managed to set the small cart down with only a slight bump.

They had barely stopped before Paco jumped out of the back seat. "You try one circle by yourself." He started away.

"No. Wait. Paco. I can't do that."

"*Si. Si.* Yes. You can do it. You no need go very high. Go. You have problem, I come get you." He turned and walked toward Mercèdes.

"How can you ..." The small cart was rolling across the grass. Looking down, she saw no brakes. She shrugged. "Oh, well." And she pulled the lever toward her.

Without Paco behind her, the cart lifted off much faster and in no time at all, she was higher than she had intended to go. She pushed the lever away slightly, leveling the craft. She turned, flew back to the other end of the field, then started her descent. With its lighter load, the parachute responded more rapidly to changes in propeller speed and she came down too fast. Before she knew it she was almost on the ground. She gave the lever a pull and instead of landing, the cart was gaining altitude again.

She eased off on the power and the cart descended again. Intent on watching the ground, when she did look up, she gasped. Still not on the ground, she was racing toward a barrier of tall trees. She yanked the handle back and pushed down with her left foot. Her eyes, wide as saucers, tracked the treetops as she slipped over them with only a few feet of clearance. She breathed again.

She circled back around and tried another approach. This time, she played with the throttle, a little nudge this way, a slight pressure that way. She managed to land with a mild bump and rolled to a stop only fifty feet past Paco and Mercèdes.

She started to get out, but the cart continued to move.

Paco came running up. "Switch. On right. Turn engine off."

She found the small toggle switch, flipped it, and the engine abruptly stopped.

Mercèdes walked up. "Did you like?"

"Yes, very much. I never heard of a paraplane. I mean, I think they have powered gliders somewhere around Dallas. But those always sounded too hard. You had something strapped on your back. And your feet were the landing gears." She laughed. "The way I landed today, I'd have two broken legs if they were my landing gear." She climbed out of the cart. "I think the powered parachute is a lot easier than a powered glider. At least for me. Of course, having Paco telling me what to do helped a lot."

"Maybe you come next week," Paco said.

"It was fun." Guilt flooded Crystal's mind. "I appreciate your lesson, Paco. But I won't be able to make it next week. That was probably my last flight in a paraplane. But, I did enjoy it."

Chapter 21

ALL day Thursday, Crystal huddled in the condo, the telephone never more than two feet away. Several times, she buzzed reception to ask if there had been any calls for her.

"I'm here. I will be here. If anybody calls, keep ringing until I answer. If for some reason I don't, send someone up. I'm expecting a very important call."

"*Si*. I understand."

Crystal picked at lunch on the terrace, alternately reading a novel and watching the activities on the beach far below her perch on the sixth floor. The portable telephone waited on the table beside her. When it rang shortly after 2, she snatched it up. "Hello."

"Taxi come at six o'clock. Wear dark clothes. Warm. No good clothes."

"Taxi?"

"*Si*."

"I, ah." She hesitated. "How will I know—"

"Is okay. Jorge drive."

The line went dead.

Was that really Juan Grande? I've talked with him twice, both times in person. That didn't really sound like him. She caught her breath. *Someone else knows I'm in Puerto Vallarta.* She racked her brain. And then it came to her. *That sounded like the man on the horse in San Sebastian!*

Ridiculous. Of course, it was Juan Grande. He said he would call. I was expecting his call. And it was exactly the kind of message I expected.

She dialed zero.

"Reception. Can I help you?"

"Mercèdes. This is Crystal. If someone is called George in English, what would you call him in Spanish?"

"Jorge."

"Thanks. That's all I needed."

#

She lay down and tried to sleep for a few hours. It could be a long night.

She tried to clear her mind, but it refused to shut down. She imagined the trip to San Sebastian at night over the treacherous mountain road. Would they be successful? Would José and his men shoot at them?

Rest. She tried some of the techniques she had read about but never found a need for in the past. Relax your toes. Now relax your legs. Now relax ... She even resorted to counting sheep. But her mind was as active as yeast in warm water. And while she could hold her eyes closed, she could not turn off her mind.

#

At six, Crystal stood in the reception area. She wore black jeans, a deep maroon knit shirt, and a dark blue denim jacket. The jacket was too warm right now, but she knew the elevation of San Sebastian was nearly 5,000 feet. At night, it could be cold. A black headband held her hair away from her face. She had selected a pair of black tennis shoes. Black socks completed the stealthy look.

Crystal was talking with Mercèdes, explaining the type of work she did for Mark when a taxi parked outside the front gate. The driver did not get out.

"Come over to the gate with me while I finish," she said to Mercèdes.

The Mexican woman came around the desk and walked over and stood by the gate. Crystal continued talking softly as she went out on the sidewalk, forcing Mercèdes to stay close in order to hear. Crystal bent down and peered into the taxi. It looked like George, but she couldn't be sure. "What is your name?" she asked through the window.

"Call me George, *Señorita* Moore," he replied.

She turned to Mercèdes. "I'll finish my story tomorrow."

#

Again, they traveled a circuitous route, eventually arriving at Juan Grande's house. During the drive, Crystal asked Jorge several questions about the rescue attempt, but he provided no answers, saying only Juan Grande knew the plans.

At their destination, Jorge guided her into a spacious room near the back of the house. Juan Grande and three other men stood around a table, studying a large drawing.

Juan stabbed various points on the map with a finger, almost whispering in Spanish to the men. The softness of his voice and the quickness of his speech made it impossible for Crystal to understand what he was saying. He moved his finger around the drawing, stopping here and there, issuing commands at each stop. The others nodded each time he looked at them.

At first, Crystal could tell nothing about the drawing, but finally picked out a house. At least, she thought it was a house. It appeared to have many rooms, and rambled around as if a child had designed it, adding rooms at whatever place her pencil happened to be. She identified several other buildings, all at a distance from the house, if the drawing was to scale. Certain lines were fences. But she could attach no meaning to other marks and symbols.

Finally, Juan Grande stopped talking, straightened up, and took a single step back from the table. The other men continued to study the map for a minute more, then left the room without a word. Only after they departed did Juan ask, "You have no change the mind?"

"No. I'm ready. A little scared, but I'll be all right. I will not faint. I will not scream." She regretted saying anything about being scared. "I'm ready."

He smiled. "Little scared is good. Only foolish man has no fear."

"Can we get in?"

"*Si*. No problem to get in."

Her grave look softened. At last, some good news.

"Problem," continued Juan, "is to get out."

The soft look morphed to intense. "Can we get out, then?"

"Some can. Important all can." He stared at her for several seconds. "You still can wait here. We bring *niñas* here."

Crystal shook her head. "No. I'll go with you."

Juan sighed. "Okay. You must do at once what I say. No hesitate." He held his hands, palms up, in front of his chest. He raised his left hand and said, "Alive." He lowered the left hand and raised the right. "Dead. One second between."

Apprehension took control and Crystal felt a little tingle in her stomach. She nodded.

Once more, he was silent; slow, even breathing, unblinking obsidian eyes probing, searching. Finally, he said, "You stay close to me. Others have jobs. You stay with me. I ask you do something, you do it fast. No questions. Okay?"

"Okay."

"Often, cause of death is hesitation." He looked at Crystal for a moment, then turned and left the room. She ran to catch up with him. She would stay close.

He stopped at a door and pointed to it. "*Baño.*"

Crystal shook her head. "No."

Juan nodded. "Yes. *Baño.* No *baño* later."

When she came out, Juan was not in sight. She returned to the room with the map, but no one was there. Her pulse accelerated. *They wouldn't leave without me, would they?* She retraced her steps and continued out the front door. Juan and the three men stood beside a jeep. Juan motioned to the front passenger seat as he was getting in the driver's seat. The other men piled in the back.

They left Juan's house at 8:20. The sun had long since hidden beyond the horizon and the new moon provided only a slight glow. Juan drove out the long road leading to his house without benefit of lights. He turned onto the public road and drove for thirty seconds before switching on lights. Crystal held tightly to the front edge of the seat with one hand and the door with the other. They were not even close to the dangerous part yet.

No one spoke until after the lights came on. Crystal couldn't understand what the men in back were saying but the talk sounded light and cheerful. Juan Grande did not participate in the conversation except for an occasional word or two over his shoulder.

The first thirty minutes took them through sparsely-settled land. After that, Crystal saw little evidence of civilization other than the road, which barely passed as manmade.

"Are there any people living in this area?" she asked above the wind noise.

"Yes."

"I don't see any lights, any houses."

"No electricity. Houses no built close to road." Juan glanced at her. "Many people live here."

"How long before we get to San Sebastian?" As soon as she said it, Crystal felt like a child asking, "Are we there yet?"

"We no go to San Sebastian. But we drive two hours, *mas o menos.*"

Crystal ran her tongue around her lips. Somehow, though she had planned to find out all about the rescue plan, she knew nothing of what they were going to do. She wanted to ask now. But the noise of the wind made it difficult to carry on a conversation and she doubted Juan would tell her anything.

A car passed, going in the opposite direction. They had not seen another car since they started. Never in her adult life had she been so unaware of where she was. Somewhere in western Mexico. Somewhere on a road between Puerto Vallarta and San Sebastian. Maybe. Tuesday, she had driven north first, before turning east. And according to the map, she had taken the only road to San Sebastian. This was not the same road. It was worse.

She closed her eyes. *Will the girls come easily, or will I have to convince them? Will they cry out? Will Juan and the others have to fight José and his men?*

Juan said José was a vicious man. Rosa indicated he was a ruthless criminal, not caring whether Miguel died, not willing to send for medical help. What if he or his men caught them? She had not seen any weapons, any guns. She didn't want guns around the children. But Jose's men would have guns. How would Juan deal with that? *How will I react?* She shivered. Rosa had said José was a powerful man with a large hacienda and many men working for him. Probably Jose's men patrolled at night. How did Juan plan to get past them? Juan said getting in would be easy. The problem was getting out. What if they didn't?

"Is best to think of other things," Juan said, as if reading her mind. "Think of your work. Or Christmas."

#

Crystal felt as if she had been bounced around in a food processor for hours. Her mouth was as dry as flour.

She sat bolt upright, as if hit by an electric current. Where would they put the children? The Jeep was full now. Two more, even if small, would not fit. One could sit on her lap. With the three jammed in the back, could the other child possibly sit on anybody's lap? Had Juan thought about that?

Juan veered off the road onto a dirt path. The bumping grew significantly worse. Trees crowded either side and grabbed at her right arm. What little light the moon provided did not penetrate here, and the dirt and trees absorbed the car's lights. She opened her mouth to speak just as they hit a large hole. Her teeth slammed down, biting her tongue. The warm, salty taste of blood filled her mouth. She decided to keep her mouth shut and tightened her grip on the door and the seat.

Juan switched off the lights and slowed. For several minutes, he drove in what seemed to Crystal like complete darkness. Then he stopped.

"We get out here," said Juan. "Stay near me. We walk ahead."

Crystal fumbled with the door, finally getting it open. She put her hand on the car and moved to the front of it. Her eyes were adjusting to the darkness. Now she could make out shapes, could see trees and where an opening existed. From somewhere not far away came a soft whinny.

Juan started forward and Crystal fell in behind. The sound of small twigs cracking mingled with the wind soughing in the trees. Were they near Jose's hacienda? A faint light bobbed ahead. Not a light; the glow of a cigarette.

"*Problemas?*"

"*No. Todo esta bien.*"

Juan turned and spoke to his men in Spanish. Without answering, the men mounted horses and moved away. Juan turned to Crystal.

"Is very dangerous from here. You stay here with Enrique. You are safe here. We come back here with children." He cocked his head and stared into her eyes.

"No. I'm going. Which horse is mine?" she asked with more confidence than she felt.

He handed her the reins of a small paint. "There is no road. Stay close. No get lost. If I tell you something, do quickly. Sometimes, only one second between alive and dead."

She trembled and stiffened, trying to hide it. "How far?"

"Not far. Perhaps one hour."

She put her foot in the stirrup and swung up into the large saddle, similar to the western styles she had used in Texas, but more comfortable.

Juan had told the truth about no road. Crystal frequently ducked to avoid branches. More than once, she had failed to see one and been slapped in the face. The first time, a slight moan escaped her. Juan turned in his saddle.

"I'm okay," she said.

"No noise."

#

They had ridden forever. Juan finally stopped, turned and motioned for Crystal to dismount. He held a finger to his lips. She swung down, pulled the reins over the horse's head, and walked up beside Juan. He tied the horses to a tree. He motioned for her to stay there, then he disappeared.

With the trees overhead and the undergrowth close on all sides, little light penetrated, but after scanning the area for a few minutes, she located the other three horses just five yards away. But no men waited near them. Her inner thighs throbbed. She rubbed each one, trying to soothe the mistreated muscles. It had been over a year since she last rode.

Juan returned, carrying a large bundle of grass and put it

on the ground in front of the horses. Then he moved beside Crystal and put his mouth near her ear. "We are near. Stay close to me. Make no noise. Do what I say, *rápido*."

Crystal nodded.

Juan started into the jungle and Crystal fell in behind him so close she worried she might step on his heels. Two of the men trudged ahead of Juan and the third stepped in line behind Crystal. For twenty minutes they crept through the thick scrub.

When Juan stopped, Crystal almost fell over him. They crouched down and peered ahead. Through the leaves, Crystal could make out shapes. A small building lay slightly to the right, and another farther to the left. A much larger structure, dark and daunting, sat straight ahead, dominating the scene. Excitement tingled her scalp.

Juan turned and once more placed a finger across his lips. He inched forward. Crystal cringed each time she put a foot down. Her footsteps sounded like crashing cymbals in the still night. Each crushed leaf reverberated in her ears. Surely, Jose's men could hear. At the same time, Juan, who weighed at least twice as much as she did, made no sound at all. She tried to put her foot down slower, letting it touch the grass and then carefully mashing it down.

They left the cover of the woods and started across an open area maybe three hundred feet wide. In the small house to her left, lights glowed and music drifted out. Directly in front loomed the biggest house. It seemed to grow larger as she watched. No light came from any of its windows, but a thin wisp of smoke escaped from a chimney and hung in the still air. The position of the structures matched the map she had studied at Juan's house.

She quivered with a short burst of adrenalin. Perhaps lights blazed inside the big house, but a cloud of malevolence absorbed and prevented any light, any hope, from escaping. A tremor ran through her.

How were they going to get in? How would they find the children? Would the girls cry out when awakened by strangers?

Juan changed directions, now heading toward the small house on the right. He had taken no more than three steps when he abruptly stopped. In slow motion, he squatted and pointed straight ahead. The other men crouched low enough to be sitting on the ground. No one moved nor made a sound. Her scalp prickled and her stomach felt queasy. She silently sank down until she believed she must be completely hidden behind Juan Grande. Hidden from what, she didn't know.

Crystal peered around Juan. What had stopped him? A thin cloud hid even the small illumination from the sliver of moon. No light escaped any of the buildings now. Crystal shivered.

Movement ahead. Something silently came toward them.

Chapter 22

JUAN Grande collapsed in on himself, becoming smaller and smaller, and inched toward her. Crystal's chest tightened and she clasped her hands together. Her breath came in short gasps and she was sure the world could hear her. She put her hand over her mouth and nose, trying to quiet the sound, trying to slow her breathing.

The men in front of Juan had virtually disappeared, forming only a slight bump on the ground. Her stomach roiled. She feared she might throw up. She almost lost her balance and discovered she was the one moving, leaning forward little by little. Juan was as still as a gravestone.

The cloud moved away from the moon. Its weak light reflected off a series of thin white blobs. Crystal's eyes went wide as she saw coming toward her a line of ducks. She relaxed. But Juan and the others still did not move. Juan did not appear even to be breathing.

The lead duck veered to the right and headed away from them. As soon as the line disappeared behind the small house, Juan turned to Crystal and pointed back toward the woods. *What?* When she did not move, he put his hand on her arm, pulled her up, and pushed her toward the woods. The other men passed her and were moving toward the shelter of the trees as fast as they could go without making any noise. Crystal moved out, with Juan right behind her.

When they reached the woods, she stopped. Juan pointed ahead. This time, she pivoted and stepped out. The other men were nowhere in sight.

As they neared the horses, Juan jogged ahead of Crystal. He whispered to the men. Hands clenched, he thrust his face inches from theirs. The men did not speak. They looked down, refusing to meet his eyes. He jerked his head toward the horses and without a word, they mounted and headed back toward the Jeep.

When they reached the Jeep, Juan spoke briefly to the man who took the horses. Crystal asked Juan a question. He ignored her, and ordered everyone into the vehicle. In less than a minute, they were driving back along the black, tree-shrouded path.

#

Sometime after 3, they arrived at Juan Grande's house. During the trip back, no one had spoken. Twice, Crystal asked Juan a question. His only response had been, "*Mas tarde*." Later.

In the house, Crystal again tried to question Juan. "*Mañana*," he answered. He called Carlotta, and when she came into the room, he spoke to her in Spanish. The only word Crystal could pick out was *cama*, bed. And then, before Crystal could say anything, he left.

"I am Carlotta, Juan's wife. We would like to offer you our hospitality for the night. Would you like to eat before retiring?"

"No. No food. But something to drink would be nice. Did Juan tell you what happened?"

"You were not there?" Carlotta asked, cocking her head slightly.

"Yes, I was. But I still don't know why we left so abruptly. Or why Juan was so unhappy."

Carlotta smiled. "Come. I will get you something while I explain."

Juan's wife was cut from the same mold as Juan, but with a face no artist could resist painting. While Juan's eyes were hypnotic, Carlotta's were flecked with gold and luminesced so her emotions swept over those around her. And she possessed a mouth most women only wished for.

She led Crystal down a short hall and into a kitchen. A bar separated it from a dining area.

Crystal perched on one of the tall stools at the bar. "We were in the yard, moving toward a small house when we suddenly stopped. All I could see were some ducks across the way. When they got out of sight, we ran back into the woods."

Carlotta poured a milky white liquid into a glass and set it in front of Crystal. "Not ducks. Geese. Very different. Geese are the best security. If they see anything moving around, they start squawking so loud they wake even those who died recently. If they had seen or heard you, they would have had all Jose's men coming after you."

"Well, Juan was not at all happy."

Carlotta laughed and her round eyes sparkled. "No. He is never happy when he runs into something unexpected. He plans very carefully. He is unhappy with his men for not knowing José had geese. Now, they are trying to figure out how to deal with the geese. You will go back tomorrow with a plan for the children, *and* the geese."

Crystal took a sip of the drink, expecting milk, but uncertain what animal produced it. Instead, it turned out to be quite sweet. "This is very good. What is it?"

"It is called guanabana. It comes from the guanabana fruit, which grows wild here. The skin of the guanabana is very unfriendly. But the inside makes a very pleasant drink."

"I want to compliment you on your English."

Again, Carlotta laughed a high, tinkling sound that reminded Crystal of tiny Christmas bells. "I should. I studied for four years at St. Mary's University in Texas." She paused a moment and then said with an appropriate Texas drawl, "Y'all know that school, don' cha."

"Shore do, pardner," Crystal answered with a grin. "What do we do now?"

"It is nearly three-thirty. I suggest we go to bed and get a good night's rest. You have another long night coming up. The men will figure it out."

#

At nine the next night, the Jeep pulled out once more. This time only one man, Pepe, accompanied Juan and Crystal. She started to ask about the other two, but Juan looked so grim, so deep in thought, she said nothing.

They followed the same route until they left the road. As uncertain of her whereabouts as she was, Crystal was positive this was not the same place they had left the road last night. But this trail could pass for the same path. Branches scratched the fenders, and tree limbs were brushed aside by the windshield. Only an optimist would even call this a trail.

When they finally stopped deep in the jungle, the same man held three horses, but the small clearing, the trees, and bushes were different from the previous night's rendezvous.

They rode slowly through the woods, no one speaking. Unlike last night, her thighs complained immediately.

The perfume of the forest, dank and heady, floated on the cool breeze. Insects buzzed and chirped. Night birds called to one another. And through the dark silhouette of the trees, the stars shone like distant sparklers on a moonless night

After more than an hour, Juan put up his hand and everybody stopped. They gathered grass for the horses, then started off through the woods, Juan in front, Crystal next, with Pepe at the back.

Forty-five minutes later, they arrived at the edge of the clearing surrounding Jose's collection of houses. Tonight, they were closer to the small house where Juan said the children were being held. Just inside the cover of the woods, Juan and Pepe sat down. Crystal followed suit. Juan rummaged around in a sack and pulled out three burritos. He handed one to Crystal and one to Pepe.

Far to the left, Crystal could just make out the house which last night poured forth music. Tonight, quiet. And only one window showing any light at all.

The front door opened and two men stepped out, looked around, and then stared in her direction. Crystal's skin tingled. They stepped off the porch and into the yard. Crystal's muscles tightened. Her breathing quickened. Her eyes opened wide. They continued to move in her direction.

Thick foliage concealed her, yet she could see them. Could they possibly see her? Did they know intruders were near the hacienda? A chill ran through her. She put her hand over her face, hoping to hide even the whites of her eyes. She opened a small slit between her fingers. A match flared as they lighted cigarettes. After a few minutes, they turned back and sat on the edge of the porch. Crystal's muscles relaxed slightly. Cigarettes. Five minutes later, they went back inside and shortly after that, the one remaining light disappeared.

As before, the big house was dark. If anything, it looked even bigger and more ominous than last night. Unlike one of the mysterious houses she read about as a child, with only the ghosts of murder victims inhabiting it, this one had real people in it. And rather than victims, it housed the murderer.

When Juan had described the danger of José capturing her, she had taken it seriously. But she had no reference point, no experience when her life could be threatened by such a man. Yes, Al had threatened her with a gun a year ago. But that had just happened. She had no choice. She made no decision to be there. She would have run away if she could have. But this time she had chosen to be here, in a similar position. She looked at the house. Its dark windows hid a man willing to kill, to enslave people, to threaten small children, a man who would happily kill her. And she wanted to run, run all the way to the airport.

She forced her gaze away from the sinister house and

settled it on the small building where the children were kept, little more than a hundred feet away. How terrible for those little girls to be there, in the presence of such evil, unable to run away or fly to their mother.

She looked back at Jose's house. She would not run. She could not leave those girls under his power.

#

Low clouds had rolled in and now blocked out the moon. The air felt heavy. A light mist began to fall. She pulled up the collar of her denim jacket and curled up to rest, her head down on her knees. She could see nothing. Her mind supplied much more vivid pictures.

They had walked a long way through thick underbrush tonight. How would they get the girls out through that in any reasonable amount of time? And without making any noise? That would be the toughest part. Probably Juan and Pepe would each carry one. Could they carry the girls that far and still move fast enough to stay ahead of their pursuers? Would the branches scratch the girls and perhaps cause them to cry out?

#

Juan's hand on her shoulder awakened her. She jerked up, momentarily uncertain where she was. How long had she slept?

He motioned for her to follow and laid his finger across his lips. They crawled out into the open. Juan looked all around and then began crawling toward the house, about a hundred and fifty feet ahead. The mist had given way to a thick fog. The ground was soft, almost muddy. Every few yards, Juan stopped and studied all directions before continuing.

They took fifteen minutes to cross the short distance. Now, crouched beside the door to the house, Juan reached into his knapsack, pulled out a can and a piece of cloth. He opened the can and poured liquid on the cloth. The pungent odor of ether assailed Crystal's nose.

Juan rose slowly, taking ten seconds to be standing upright. He turned the handle on the door. It opened. He entered and motioned for Crystal to follow. Pepe came in last, easing the door closed behind him.

Juan tiptoed into a bedroom. Very carefully, he laid the cloth across the face of the occupant.

Just as quietly, Juan retreated from the room and Crystal could see an adult form in the bed.

The next room contained two small, sleeping girls. Juan passed it and continued through the house, then returned to the girls' room.

The window in the girls' room faced Jose's house. Pepe found a serape and held it over the window. Juan pulled a small flashlight from his knapsack and flipped it on. Serafina slept on the side nearest to Crystal. On the other side was Angelina. Juan had said they would wake Serafina first, as she was the older.

Crystal rubbed the young girl's arm lightly and whispered, "Serafina. Wake up. *Despiértate. Despiértate,* Serafina."

A small fist poked out from under the covers and rubbed a tightly closed eye.

Crystal continued patting the girl. "Wake up."

The fist moved and Serafina's eyes opened to a small slit. Crystal and Juan had discussed what he would say and what she would do. Slowly and softly, Juan said in Spanish, "We have come to take you to your mother. She is waiting for you and wants you and Angelina to come with us. But we must go very quietly. Make no noise. It is a secret. Your mother sent her special medal so you would know your mother, Lucita, is sending for you."

Crystal held Lucita's medallion in the dim glow from the flashlight, close to the young girl. A hand reached over and touched the pendant, then took it in her hand. Then, Serafina looked toward Crystal.

Juan whispered in Spanish, "Are you ready to go to your mother? Will you do that?" he whispered in a gentle voice Crystal had not heard from him before. "Will you come with us very quietly?"

The tiny head nodded as she continued to hold the medallion.

"Will you tell your little sister, Angelina, to come with us also?"

Again, the head nodded. Serafina released the medal, turned over and shook her sister, none too gently. Angelina curled up tighter and ignored the shaking. Serafina shook her again and put her mouth near Angelina's ear. She spoke in Spanish, not as quietly as Crystal would have liked. The younger sister's eyes popped open and she looked over at Crystal. Angelina climbed on top of Serafina, reaching for the medallion. Juan continued to shine the light on it as Angelina turned it over in her tiny hands.

"*¡Ya vámonos, niños!*" Juan whispered.

Both girls got up and reached for some clothes on a chair. "Leave the clothes," Crystal whispered in Spanish. "It will be more fun to go in your pajamas. You can get new clothes with your mother."

Still somewhat groggy, the girls nodded. Crystal picked up Angelina and Juan lifted Serafina and put her on his shoulders. The light went out and they left the room.

At the outside door, Juan turned right. They had come from the other direction. They were walking away from the horses. *Is Juan confused? Sometimes people get directions wrong at night.* Crystal caught up and touched his arm and pointed behind them. Juan shook his head and continued straight ahead.

They had covered no more than fifty feet when he halted and put Serafina down on the ground. Crystal stopped, still holding Angelina.

Crystal thrust her head forward and opened her eyes wide, trying in the dim light to verify what she did not believe. Her mouth gaped.

Juan Grande was standing beside the small cart of a powered parachute.

Chapter 23

CRYSTAL put her face near Juan. "What are we doing?"

"You and children fly over hill." He lifted Serafina into the back seat.

Crystal shook her head slowly. She narrowed her eyes. "I ... I-- "

"Yes. You can." By now, he was putting Angelina next to her sister. "Do not frighten children."

"I ... I can't do this. You take them. I'll go back with Pepe."

Juan straightened up as he finished belting the two girls tightly into the seat. His belly shook but his laugh made no sound. He patted his ample stomach. "Never get off ground. You must go quickly. As soon as engine start, men will come. You must leave quickly."

Her voice shook. "Where do I go?"

"Straight over hill. No left. No right. Straight. On other side, you see lights. Land. Jorge waits for you. You can do this." He put his face in front of hers, barely an inch away. "Often cause of death is hesitation."

He guided Crystal in, helped her buckle the front harness, then flipped on the ignition switch.

"*Ahora*," Juan said.

Pepe pulled the prop. No sooner had it stopped moving than he pulled it again. In only a few seconds, the motor caught and roared to life.

"No can wait for warm up," Juan said. "Must go now. Increase engine speed."

Juan got on one side and Pepe on the other and they began pulling the cart, making it easier for the engine to lift the parachute and gain enough speed for lift off. Slowly, air began to fill the huge parachute laid out on the ground behind the little cart.

Lights came on in the main house. Even over the noise of the engine, Crystal could hear shouts. Another fifty feet and the lights of the small house were on. Juan and Pepe breathed heavily, still running as fast as they could pull the cart. The engine lent a hand. The chute, heavy from the mist, inched up in the air.

The cart had just risen off the ground when she heard more yelling. Men boiled out of the house like fire ants. An explosion erupted on the far side of the big house. Flames and debris climbed into the sky. Seconds later, another explosion ripped the night, this one off behind the smaller building. She turned her head and stared at the flames, momentarily confused. Then a small grin replaced her puzzlement. Juan Grande had planned a diversion.

Airborne, the engine sounding good, the ground receding. The hill threatened more like a mountain, rising up high in front of them, and not very far away. She pulled the throttle toward her, trying to gain altitude. "Dear God, please help me. Right now. Don't let me kill these innocent girls."

The mountain raced toward them. The misting rain had stopped. The fog was thinning. Thick, tall trees filled her vision. She held the throttle handle so tightly her hand ached. *Come on. Climb. Climb.* She checked the parachute to see if it had inflated fully. The night air was crisp. But it was not the cold that made her knees shake.

The top of the mountain loomed above her. The trees on

the ridge stretched a hundred feet above the ground. Even as the paraplane approached, the trees seemed to grow taller.

They wouldn't get over those trees.

She ripped her gaze from the towering trees directly in front of her, searched, but found no lower spot. A bitter taste filled her mouth.

Gunfire popped. Were they shooting at her? Or at Juan and Pepe?

She glanced at the tiny girls behind her. They didn't look frightened. Sleepy, maybe. They took no notice of the gunfire. They had had more than their share of unhappiness and their brief lives might end right here.

Crystal pressed her right foot down. Nothing happened. Her stomach contracted into a ball. Then, ever so slowly, the tiny craft began to turn. *Stupid. Why didn't I start sooner?*

The left wing cleared the trees by inches, and then began to pull away from them. Guns flashed. Panic tried to gain the upper hand. The little aircraft was headed back toward Jose's men, toward the guns.

But it had not crashed into the trees.

Mingled with the noise of the guns and the motor, she heard a different sound, like cloth tearing. She looked up toward the parachute. Near the center, the material had ripped and a piece of it now flapped wildly. One of the gunshots had hit the chute!

Chapter 24

AS soon as the small cart lifted off the ground, Juan Grande and Pepe headed toward the trees. Pepe, younger, more athletic, quickly pulled away.

Juan could hear Jose's men, rushing out of the houses, yelling, not knowing what had happened. The paraplane's motor had awakened them, but as they raced out, two explosions demanded their attention. Confusion reigned.

He glanced over his shoulder, could barely make out the parachute, its bright colors masked by the dark night. The mist had stopped and the clouds were disappearing. Just below the silhouette of the parachute, two white dots marked the pajamas of the two *niñas* being carried to freedom by a brave young woman.

The inside edge of his right shoe came down on a rock and his ankle folded over, sending Juan Grande crashing to the ground. He suppressed an oath that tried to erupt from his throat. Rolling over, he wiggled his foot and received an electric jolt up his right leg. Slowly he got on his hands and knees and used his left foot to push himself upright. When his right foot touched the ground for balance, pain stabbed him again. But, the ankle was not broken.

Suddenly, he was looking at his own shadow. A bright light swept the area, and Juan stood, fully illuminated. He tried to put weight on his sprained ankle. Running would be impossible. He might limp on it, but could he make it nearly a mile to the horses? Not before Jose's men captured him.

He pulled a pistol from his waistband, turned, and fired two shots toward the mountain. "The plane! Someone has stolen the plane," he hollered in Spanish to the men running toward him. "Someone has stolen the paraplane."

He turned toward the mountain. To his horror, the paraplane was coming back toward them. What was she doing? She had been almost over the mountain. Now she was flying back. She would be shot. Or captured. What could he do? He swallowed. Nothing.

At that moment, another gunshot sounded close behind him. Juan turned his head and could see several of Jose's men rushing toward him. He raised his pistol.

"Come," one of the men shouted to Juan in Spanish. "We must shoot it down."

Juan limped along as they passed him. If she landed, maybe he could give her time to escape. In his heart, he knew that was impossible. Even if she did not land, she would be shot.

The bright lights emblazoned a large area of the ground, but the little plane remained almost invisible against the black sky. For a moment, he thought it was turning away. He looked for the white dots that identified the two girls in their pajamas. He fired another shot, careful it would go nowhere near the plane.

Chapter 25

A LUMP formed in Crystal's throat. The cart moved slower. Was the hole slowing their flight, or making it unstable? They had not gained enough altitude to clear the mountain, but they were high enough to be killed if they suddenly crashed. She looked down at the trees below. Her stomach sank. The hole in the wing was dragging them down.

She forced herself to look away from the ground. She pulled on the throttle, already as far back as it would go. She took several deep breaths. She couldn't really tell any difference in the feel or sound of the paraplane. Maybe it wasn't sinking. Maybe it was flying alright. She studied the landscape below. *Yes, yes!* Gaining altitude again. But what if the material really ripped out and that section of the wing collapsed? What if bullets hit more sections of the wing? Again, she fought to keep panic from taking control. She leaned forward, willing the craft to move faster.

The noise of the guns grew louder. Crystal jumped. My God, what if they hit one of the girls? She pushed harder on her right foot, berating herself for turning back. But if she hadn't, they'd have crashed. The bullets might or might not knock the paraplane down. The trees most certainly would. *Please God, don't let any bullets find these children.*

As she began to come back around toward the trees, the paraplane had gained enough altitude to clear the canopy. Now, if she could only get back on the right heading so she might find George. She glanced back and down. Jose's house glowed in the dark landscape directly behind her. Jeep and truck lights illuminated much of the area. Flashlight beams reached into the sky, trying to find the small paraplane carrying two of Jose's captives toward freedom.

This time, they were above the trees. A major victory.

She could see nothing. Nothing but another mountain in front of her. Adrenaline shocked her arms and legs until they tingled. Juan had said "over the mountain." He hadn't said two. Was she going in the right direction? She looked around but could see no other possibilities. She scanned the ground below. No clearing, no lights, no place to land.

They raced toward the next mountain, even higher than the one she had just barely cleared.

Chapter 26

BACK at the hacienda, Jose's men ran back toward Juan, excited and yelling to one another, and then to Juan. "We must get horses, find Jose's plane. He will be very angry." Juan fell in behind them, unable to keep up, hobbling as best he could, his ankle punishing him with each step.

But, he had not been identified as an intruder.

Chapter 27

A GUST of wind lifted the small cart and both the girls let out a small gasp of excitement. Crystal let out a cry of relief. They were well above the trees now. For a moment, Crystal's hand on the throttle relaxed a little and she breathed more easily. Please, let me find George on the other side, she prayed.

Behind Crystal, the two girls were whispering to each other, and once or twice, Crystal heard a tiny giggle. The medallion had convinced them they were going to their mother. This was just an exciting ride. Only Crystal felt the danger.

They passed the crest of the second mountain ridge. Crystal searched the area below, looking for lights, some indication of where she could land. Only black treetops were visible. Lights or no lights, she needed a level place with no trees.

They were drifting to the right. She jammed her left foot down. That sent them turning to the left. *Calm down, Crystal.* It would go straight if she just let it. *Unless there's a crosswind.* And how would she know if there was one or not? She eased both feet up, so they were barely touching the bars. Were they going straight now? She had no idea, no reference point. And if they weren't, she might never find George. She tried to pick out a point on the horizon to aim for, but she could find nothing distinct.

What was her backup plan? She shivered as she realized no backup existed. If she didn't find George, what did she do with the girls? Her hands began to shake. Her feet were getting heavier. She eased them down on the bars equally, so as not to turn either right or left. She took in great gulps of the cold mountain air. *If I don't find George, he will find me. He will find me,* she repeated. *He will find me.* And with each repetition, it became more of a prayer.

Out of the corner of her eye, she saw a pinpoint of light. It could be anything. It didn't look like a landing light, but Juan Grande had not said what kind of a light to look for. Turning slightly back to the right she headed straight for the dot of white standing out against so much black, like a diamond on black velvet. Or a flame attracting a moth.

The light grew brighter. Another appeared just a few yards to the right of the first one. She had been maintaining her altitude, not knowing if a third mountain might tower in her path. Now she eased the throttle back, and dropped closer to the trees. Ahead, the tree line stopped. In the faint beams of the lights, the ground appeared flat.

Crystal now worried about landing the craft gently for two small girls. She remembered how hard she had jolted down before. She didn't know how to tell the girls to close their mouths. And how did one say in Spanish. "Brace yourself"? Paco had known he was about to hit the ground. He knew how to absorb the shock. Now, she had two young girls who knew nothing about this, two tiny girls who put their trust in her, two children whose lives rested in her shaking hands.

She gripped the throttle and eased the plane down little by little. When she passed the tree line, she was only ten feet above the top branches. The lights were brighter now, though still only thin beams. Holding her breath, she tried to make her glide slope as gentle as possible, easing off on the power by the slightest movements. And then they were bouncing along the ground, sliding and bumping and slowing.

Jorge ran up to the little craft, still rolling, and flipped off the ignition switch, which Crystal had forgotten, then tossed a box under the cart. "*Perfecto*," he said as he started unbuckling Serafina and Angelina. "Must hurry. José and men come soon."

Crystal released her harness and climbed out.

"Take children to horses. I come *muy pronto*."

At the horses, she turned to look for George. He had picked up the two large flashlights and was running toward her. Behind him, fire began to consume the parachute.

"You're burning it?" she asked.

"Yes. With clothes and bones. They discover no is children. But it slow them some *minutos*. Get on horse." He pointed to a piebald. Quickly, she mounted and Jorge hoisted Angelina up on the horse behind Crystal. "And they no fly it and look for us."

He and Serafina led the way on the other horse. The ride here was not as difficult as the one Crystal and Juan had taken earlier that night, but the darkness and the narrow trail still made it a challenge. Branches slapped at their legs, but with less fury than before.

They entered a shallow river and followed it downstream. After ten or fifteen minutes, they left the river and continued through the thick forest. No sign of a trail existed, but Jorge never hesitated.

They had been riding for more than an hour and the muscles in Crystal's legs ached with each step the horse took. Angelina had not made a sound. "Are you okay? *¿Esta bien?*"

The tiny head bobbed. "*Si.*"

Chapter 28

JUAN Grande sat on a stump, out of the light, hoping no one noticed him. His ankle now bulged over his shoe and even a few steps caused him to break out in a sweat.

When José learned his paraplane had been stolen, he screamed and yelled, fired a pistol into the air, promised to kill the person who stole his plane, kill the thief's family and friends. He dispatched four men on horseback to search for the plane.

Now, more than three hours later, the riders returned and José emerged from the big house to hear the report. He stood nearly six feet, with a barrel chest and narrow waist. He had a well-trimmed mustache. His thick hair had a slight curl and one might have described him as handsome if it were not for the cruel look permanently etched on his face.

One man came forward timidly and in a soft voice told José they had found the cart, but the parachute had been burned. Jose's hand shot out and he slashed the man across the face with the barrel of a pistol. The man fell to the ground and cried out in pain.

"And where is the person who stole it, who burned it?" José asked.

"No one was there. It was too dark to track him. We will look as soon as it is light," the man whimpered. He lay on his back, his face turned up, but his eyes remained closed.

José looked as if he might explode. "You should have found him tonight." José put his boot on the man's neck, stood on it and crushed his windpipe. The man's hands grasped his throat, tried to move the boot. His body writhed and he made a wheezing sound for a minute. Then his body went limp.

After a few moments, José asked, "Who was in charge of security tonight?" No one answered. His voice roared throughout the hacienda. "I asked who was in charge of security tonight." The mongrel that hung around the big house tucked its tail and slinked off.

Finally, the man standing next to Juan Grande said in a low voice, "I was, Señor Jose."

Jose's gaze slowly swung around to the man. "Tito, you were one of my favorites. You have served me well for many years. Why have you done this to me now?"

The man opened his mouth to answer just as José shot him in the head.

José pointed the gun at Juan Grande. "Who are you?"

Chapter 29

DEEP in the mountain jungle, Jorge held up his hand and reined in his horse. Then he moved forward very slowly for several minutes. Again he stopped. "*Como estás?*" he said softly.

Out of the darkness came, "*Bien.*"

Jorge dismounted and lifted Serafina down. "We take car now," he said to Crystal.

"Good," Crystal replied as she eased her sore legs to the ground, then helped Angelina down. "I'm ready to sit on something a little softer."

A shadow led the horses off into the trees.

They put the two girls in the back of an ancient VW. Crystal settled in the passenger's seat while Jorge drove. The dirt road rose and fell sharply, twisted right and left and back again constantly. The holes were many and deep. Frequently, when they made a sharp turn, the lights caught only the edge of the road. Crystal could imagine a five hundred foot drop to a river below. Nonetheless, she was glad to be off the horse. Finally, after what seemed to Crystal like half an eternity, they turned onto a paved road.

"Do you think they are close? Jose's men, I mean."

"*No se.*" Jorge shrugged. "He has many men in many places."

Even if Jose's men had followed them through the woods, they would not have a car at the end to continue following. But maybe they could get a car as easily as Jorge had. Maybe they had called ahead to have people stop them. She turned to look out the back window. Not far behind, a car sped toward them. She checked on the two girls. They had curled around one another, bouncing and shifting and sleeping.

The car closed on them rapidly, its lights blinding her to any details. Truck, Jeep, car, whatever, it swung out and began to pass them.

What if they recognized her? She bent down in the seat, getting her head under the dashboard.

The car raced by.

Chapter 30

JUAN'S hand rested on his pistol, but he knew he would have no chance. Even if he managed to shoot José before being shot, which was not likely, there were probably fifty of Jose's men standing around. All of them had guns.

"I am called Juan, *Señor*."

José sighted down the long barrel of the pistol, looking at Juan. The nose of the barrel wavered. "Take Tito's body out into the field, Juan, away from my house. Do not bury it. Leave it for the animals." With that, José turned and stalked into his house.

Another man came over and helped Juan move the body away from the houses, out into the open field where earlier a colorful parachute lay.

Afterward, Juan asked one of the women for ice and a towel. He found a secluded patch of grass and lay down, his injured ankle elevated, the towel holding ice against it.

Chapter 31

THE eastern sky was beginning to lighten when George brought the car to a stop in front of Juan Grande's house. The gate opened immediately and Carlotta ran out.

"Were you successful?" Carlotta asked.

"Yes," Crystal said. "Here, in the back seat."

The two women reached in, got the girls, cradled them in their arms, and ran to the house.

Crystal carried Angelina and followed Carlotta, carrying Serafina, down the hall and into a small bedroom. Within minutes, the girls were tucked into bed. They had barely opened their eyes and were already asleep again by the time covers were pulled around their tiny shoulders.

Carlotta took Crystal's hand as they left the room.

"Come. I give you something to drink. Then we must all rest. I know you have had a difficult night. You can tell us about it after some sleep."

"Is Juan back yet?"

"No. I do not expect him this soon."

Chapter 32

JUAN Grande had dozed off, lying on the ground in a secluded spot, the cold towel still wrapped around his ankle. He was awakened by cries of anguish. A young woman was running from the small building where the children had been kept, toward the main house.

A man stepped out of the door, stopped the woman, tried to calm her. They talked for a minute. Shaking his head, he returned to the house. The woman remained outside, crying, quivering. She leaned her head against the side of the house, her whole body sagging as if she might collapse at any moment.

In less than a minute, José de Allende stormed out the door, a small, honey-colored dog at his heels. "Look at me." The woman turned toward José and raised her head slightly, but kept her eyes focused on the ground. "Look at me," he bellowed.

By now, several of Jose's men had moved closer. Juan Grande eased up behind them, testing his ankle, finding it much improved over last night.

The woman raised her red-rimmed eyes to look at Jose.

"What did you tell Hernando?"

In a faltering voice and unable to maintain eye-contact with Jose, the woman said, "The children ..." A sob escaped. "The children are gone."

"Gone? Gone where?" José yelled.

"I do not know, Señor. When I get up, they are gone. Their clothes, shoes, everything is there. But no *niñas*."

"You searched?"

"Everywhere. They have disappeared." Once more, the woman started crying softly.

Jose's eyes narrowed, his jaw twitched, and his hands tightened into hard fists as he glared at the woman. For a moment, he said nothing.

One of the men standing nearby whispered to the *vaquero* next to him, "The paraplane."

Jose's head jerked in their direction. Slowly, his eyes opened wider, his thin lips parted. His face turned red as he sucked in air. His voice escalated into a roar. "They stole my plane *and* the girls?" He turned his attention back on the woman in front of him. "You let them steal the children? Do you know how much they were worth to me? Do you know how hard it is to get children that age?" The woman was cowering. He pulled a pistol from his belt cocked it and aimed it at the woman's head.

Juan spoke without thinking of the consequences. "Do not shoot her."

Suddenly, total silence.

All eyes shifted to look at Juan Grande. All, except Jose's.

Again, Juan knew he had no chance to fight. Why had he spoken? He knew why. The woman faced immediate death because Juan had spirited the children away.

His mind searched for words. "She is worth much more to you alive than dead, *Señor*. Maybe you get back some of the money she has cost you."

For a moment, Jose's focus remained on the woman. Then without lowering the gun, he turned, following the gaze of several men, to pick out the impudent fool who dared give José Rodriquez de Allende advice.

Juan believed he could look into a person's eyes and see his soul. But one did not need to search for Jose's character.

Besides, Juan did not want José to feel any challenge. Juan lowered his eyes, let his shoulders slump. He could feel the intense glare now focused on him. The gun swung away from the woman and slowly arced toward him. The men on either side edged away. The gun barrel lined up on Juan.

Gradually its nose sank until it pointed at the ground. "You are right. In three weeks, my friend from Columbia comes. Perhaps I can trade this ... traitor ... for much cocaine." He gave a mirthless laugh, then turned deadly serious as he spoke to the man nearest him. "Lock her up. See she does not escape. And do not mark her. She must look good when my friend arrives."

José holstered his pistol, then stooped and picked up the dog, cradled it on his arm and smoothed its fur with his other hand. He turned and carried the dog into the house.

The men drifted off, singly and in groups, in various directions, but none spoke to Juan. His ankle felt stronger. Time to wander off and disappear. He had three weeks to save the young woman.

Chapter 33

CRYSTAL opened one eye and looked at her watch, then opened both eyes to check again. She sat up and blinked, trying to clear the sleep away. Once more she looked at her watch. Nearly noon.

She splashed water on her face, dressed, and rushed into the kitchen.

"*Buenos dias,*" Carlotta said, wiping her hands on her apron.

"Good morning. How are the girls?"

"They are fine." Carlotta put a plate with scrambled eggs and bacon on the table. She set a mug of coffee beside it. "Have some breakfast. You must be hungry."

Crystal ignored the food. "Are they up? Can I see them?"

Carlotta sat down. "They are not here. We felt it best to move them. I know José will not find this house, but to be extra safe, we moved them."

Crystal gasped. "Not here? Where are they?"

The Mexican woman shook her head slowly. "I cannot tell you. It is best if you do not know. They are safe. And will remain safe until their mother can come for them."

"Why ... why can't you tell me? I certainly won't tell the wrong people." Crystal remained standing, her hands gripping the back of a chair. "Is Juan here now?"

"No. Juan has not returned." Carlotta looked directly into

Crystal's eyes. "You would not *want* to tell anybody. If you do not know, you cannot. It is best for the girls."

Crystal looked at her watch again. "Where is Juan? Have you heard from him?"

"I have not heard from him and I do not know where he is. He will return when he can." She picked up her mug and sipped some of the dark, steaming coffee.

Crystal had left him in the middle of Jose's hacienda, with men pouring out of houses, shooting guns. That was—she looked at her watch—ten hours ago.

"Has...." Crystal didn't know what to say. She did not want to worry Carlotta, but surely she knew the dangers. "Has anything happened to him?"

Carlotta smiled, but Crystal saw it was only to mask doubt. "I do not know. But I believe he will be okay."

Crystal sank into the chair. She had gotten him into this. He had sent her to safety while he had stayed back with the enemy.

"Jorge is waiting to take you back to Vallarta. It is best if you get back to Plaza Mar. You should not be gone too long. And you should make plans to return to Texas as soon as you can."

"But the girls?"

"They are safe."

Crystal stood up. "Carlotta, I came down to Mexico to see these children were rescued from Jose."

"Yes. And you have done that. They are no longer under Jose's control. They are safe." She looked at Crystal, eyes unblinking, intense, certain. "You have accomplished what you came here to do. It is time for you to return."

"I'm not leaving until I find out about the two girls. I intend to take them back to their mother."

"That is impossible. And by staying here, you endanger not only the girls, but all of us."

"But—"

"I will have Juan call you when he returns. He can answer your questions."

The front door closed and Crystal turned, hoping to see Juan walking down the hall. Instead, Jorge appeared. Carlotta got up and ushered Crystal out. She started to protest again, but Carlotta kept repeating that Juan would call.

#

Jorge drove her into Puerto Vallarta, stopping at a residence two blocks off the Malecòn. He got out and opened the door. They were not near Plaza Mar.

"My friend will drive you from here. Better I no be with you."

The taxi driver smiled and nodded. Two grocery sacks sat on the back seat.

"He take good care of you. I promise. You carry packages in Plaza Mar. Look like you go shopping." Jorge opened the door of the taxi and waited.

Crystal stood in the street. Jorge just smiled and said nothing. The girls had been spirited away from Juan Grande's while she slept and now she was being shuffled into a different taxi, with a different driver, one whom she had never seen before. She did not get in.

The new driver leaned his head out of the window. "*Señor* Bull always happy to ride with me." He smiled.

Does everybody down here know Mark? And how does everybody know he was called Bull O'Malley years ago? She shook her head slowly and got in the taxi.

#

Mercèdes met Crystal at the Plaza Mar gate. "Let me help

you. It look like you have bought many things."

"Ah, well, ah, yes. I do have a few things here. But they're not heavy. I can manage. Thanks, anyway." Crystal headed for the elevator, then stopped and turned around. "Have there been any calls for me, Mercèdes?"

"No calls."

Crystal took the elevator up to the sixth floor and carried the packages into the condo. *Might as well see what I bought.*

In the first sack she found soft drinks, cookies, bananas, papayas, mangos, bread, and some delicious-looking pastries. Protruding out the top of the second sack was a bright wrap-around skirt. Crystal took a moment to tie it around her waist, then stepped over to look at it in a full-length mirror. The gay, Mexican design lifted her spirits. Whoever picked this out had good taste. *At least, it matches my taste.* She returned to the package and pulled out a large bag of potato chips, a bottle of shampoo, and some laundry soap.

Beneath the small box of detergent lay another bundle wrapped in tissue paper. She lifted it out and carefully unwrapped it. Inside, she found several Polaroid photographs. The first showed Serafina and Angelina eating at the small table in Carlotta's kitchen. Both wore huge smiles. The girls had on pretty dresses, not the drab pajamas they wore when Crystal flew them away from Jose's. The second picture showed the girls standing, showing off their new clothes. The younger girl was looking up at her older sister with such an expression that Crystal knew why she was named Angelina.

Crystal let out a small gasp at the third picture. It showed her sleeping on the small bed, with the two girls standing beside her. Serafina had a hand on Crystal's shoulder, and Angelina was resting her head on Crystal's hand. She pressed the picture to her cheek. She had to work to keep from crying.

A small, handwritten note beneath the last picture said, "Please do not show these to anyone except their mother. And you must not lose them. It could be highly dangerous to you, the girls, and to us. We are grateful more than you know for what you have done." And at the bottom, simply the letter "C".

#

She walked through the park and a block past a school to a German restaurant one of the Plaza Mar residents had recommended. The small place sat back from the street amid palm, banana, and papaya trees.

Crystal enjoyed a wiener schnitzel while Mariachis serenaded the diners. For a while, she forgot the troubles of the last two days and enjoyed the atmosphere, food, and music.

Just after 9 she started back to Plaza Mar. She turned on Pino Suarez and was passing the school when a taxi slowed.

"Taxi, *Señorita*."

"*No, gracias,*" she replied and continued walking.

The driver hopped out and grabbed her by the arm. "You come." He began pulling her to the taxi.

Crystal struggled, trying to pull her arm free and keep from moving closer to the open door. The man spoke rapidly in Spanish. She understood nothing. Except the danger. By now, he had her next to the door and was trying to push her inside. Crystal stiffened and grabbed the roof, desperately trying to keep her body out of the vehicle. Light glinted off the blade of a knife in his hand.

They were beside the school, all of its students and teachers gone for many hours. Directly across the street was a large restaurant, closed for repairs. On the corner behind her, music and laughter drifted out of The Margarita Grill, its patrons enjoying a pleasant night, troubles and problems blown away by the sea breeze. They would not hear her but even so, Crystal tried to scream. Her voice came out as a thin, soft cry no one more than twenty feet away would notice.

She grabbed the hand holding the knife, trying to force it

away from her. He snickered. Instead of knocking her hand out of the way, he toyed with her, then slowly exerted his superior strength to force her arm down, bringing the knife closer and closer to her face. She felt her heart being squeezed. Her breathing was rapid, her mouth dry.

Juan Grande had said she would be lost forever if they captured her. No one would ever see her again. Her legs folded beneath her as the driver shoved her into the taxi.

Chapter 34

SOMETHING smashed against the windshield of the taxi. Flames erupted all over the front half of the vehicle. Crystal, practically inside the car, was shielded by the door. Her attacker had no such protection. Burning liquid splashed on him. He let out an angry stream of desperate Spanish. The knife clattered to the pavement as he began slapping at his hair and clothes with both hands.

She ran.

Dozens of people strolled in the park only a hundred yards away. As she neared the corner, she turned her head to glance behind her. The man was scooping up handfuls of dirt and throwing it on the car, trying to put out the fire. Crystal did not stop running until she reached the entrance to Plaza Mar.

Even after she got to the condo, she was still shaking. She opened a Corona and walked out onto the terrace. She could not quite see the place where the taxi had been. The school building, though only one story, hid a small portion of the street. She could see no flames or even the glow of a fire, but a small patch of smoke drifted up above the trees.

She sat down, still breathing hard. For a long time, she watched the waves crash on the beach. The lights along the walk highlighted the frothy water as it spent its energy on the sand. The rhythm was soothing.

She finished the beer and a slight grin worked its way across her face. At least she didn't hesitate. The moment she had the chance, she ran like hell. Juan would have been proud of her. And then the smile faded. Where *was* Juan? Was he safe? Was he alive? Or had he disappeared once José found him?

#

The next morning did not find her mood improved. She walked to Fredy's Tucan for breakfast, staying hidden within crowds of people, and keeping a careful eye on any taxi that came within a block of her. But even Fredy's *Pan Francis*, piled high with fruits and nuts and fresh whipped cream, did not raise her spirits.

She spent the rest of the morning on the beach after extracting a promise from Mercèdes she would come get her should a phone call come from ... anybody. She had almost said "Juan Grande," but remembered his admonition not to mention his name.

She took the book she had started earlier, but after reading the same paragraph the fourth time, she abandoned it. She had no way to call him, no way to get a message to him, no way to contact him at all. She had been to his house twice, spent two nights there, and had no idea where it was located. Mark would know. She suddenly realized she had not thought of Mark in days, and now she missed him, wished he were here to hold her.

Carlotta had suggested Crystal make plans to return to Texas. No way. Not without talking to Juan and finding out more about what had happened to the young girls.

A chill ran down her back. What if Juan didn't make it back? What if Jose's men captured him? She might never hear anything. What would José do to Juan? She tried to put that thought out of her mind. Yet it kept nagging at her. José would treat Juan Grande no less harshly than he would have treated her. And Juan told her she would never be seen again.

Her mood grew dark. She and the girls were safe. But what of Juan? And Pepe? They had risked their lives because she had asked them to help. They had sent her to safety while they held off Jose's men. Arms wrapped around herself, she trembled. Was there anything she could do? Could she and Jorge mount a search for Juan and Pepe? That was not realistic. She shook her head and closed her eyes to hold back tears. Realistic or not, if Juan did not come back, she *would* search for him.

And last night, how lucky someone had thrown a Molotov cocktail at the taxi. Her eyes opened wide and her mouth gaped. Luck had nothing to do with it.

Often, she thought she had a guardian angel watching over her. Here in Mexico, she had the distinct feeling the guardian angel was a friend of Juan Grande.

Now, much more alert to her surroundings, she noticed everything, everybody. She would recognize the taxi driver who threatened her with a knife. She had asked Mercèdes how to say "Help!" in Spanish and had repeated it until she was certain she would not forget it. She would not hesitate to scream. A loud scream, not the thin little girl's voice that came out last night. And following Juan's advice, she wouldn't wait even one second before screaming, running, fighting, or doing whatever she could do.

She also believed she could pick out George, should he be on the street near her. If she could find him, he could tell her if Juan was safe. No. Not good enough. *If I find George,* she resolved, *I'll make him take me to Juan's house.* She looked at every Mexican man closely, hoping to see George.

For lunch, she ate at the Yucateco Restaurant adjacent to Plaza Mar. The small restaurant featured recipes and spices of the Yucatan region. She selected a sampler plate with several different items. The food was unlike anything she had eaten in Vallarta, but it was absolutely delicious. *I'll come back here.*

Until she heard something from Juan, she would not stray far from Plaza Mar and the telephone. Again, Mercèdes promised to come get her should a call come in.

She changed into a bathing suit and swam in the rooftop pool. She tried relaxing on a lounge chair and reading, but found concentration impossible. Finally, she returned to the condo, showered, and dressed, ready to go ... wherever.

The sun had settled low in the sky and she was reading a book on the terrace when a soft knock came at her door. Juan Grande stood there smiling. For a second, she was too stunned to speak.

"May I enter?" he asked.

"Yes. Yes. Of course," she stammered and swung the gate open.

He closed the gate and the wooden door behind him. He looked around, then pointing at the open window in the kitchen, said, "May I close window?" He walked over and closed the stained-glass window.

"Would you like something to drink? Coffee, beer, soda?"

"*No, gracias.*"

They sat on opposite sides of the coffee table in the living room, Juan leaning back, relaxed, Crystal perched on the edge of her chair, every nerve tingling.

"When did you get back?"

"This morning."

"This morning? What happened? Did Jose's men capture you?" She looked for any sign of injury.

Juan's stomach began to vibrate and the deep rumble of his laughter escaped. "No, no. They not capture me. I join them."

Her concern turned to confusion. "You joined them?"

"*Si.* Yes. When they come out, I join them. I yell and point. I fire pistol at you." He stopped laughing and for a moment, his tone turned serious. "I am careful not to shoot close to you. But I worry when you turn and start coming back."

"I had to circle around to get more altitude, get higher, to get over the mountain."

"I worry. Then you turn and go away." He smiled briefly, then the twinkle left his eyes. "José is very mad. He send men on horses to find you. When they come back, they tell him parachute is burned. He is much mad. He kill man who tell him they no catch you."

"Killed him? Just because ..." She could not finish the sentence.

"Yes. I saw him do it."

"Didn't he know you were not one of his men?"

Once more, Juan's deep laugh filled the room. "I no be here if he know. There are many men. Much confusion. He ask me my name. I tell him I am called Juan. He not know I am enemy." His laugh stopped and the sparkle disappeared from his eyes. "He kill man who was guard at night. He shoot him." For several seconds, Juan was silent.

"It is morning when he find children are gone. He is mad again. Almost kill woman who watch children. He scream and yell at men. Find niñas! Bring to him! Bring to him person who take niñas. I am with men. I hear him like I hear you. He roar at sky, 'I am José Rodriquez de Allende. No one take my possessions.' His men afraid. Move away from him. Try to hide. He say to them, 'Bring me person who does this, or dig your own graves.'"

He paused and a dark cloud descended over his round face. "He know you are here. He tell Cèsar Aquilar to bring you to him."

"How does he know about me?"

Juan shrugged. "He know. He know before you go to San Sebastian. Then, men see you in San Sebastian. He want you."

"Last night, someone tried to drag me off the street and into a taxi cab."

"I must think he was Cèsar Aquilar. He is bad man. Do not let him take you. We no find you if he does."

A tiny icicle materialized in her brain. She shook her head. *Best not to think of that.* "How did you get the paraplane onto the hacienda before we got there?"

"It always there. We know it is there before we go. It belong to Jose." Juan laughed again.

"Why did you think I could fly it? I mean, until a week ago, I'd never *seen* one."

Juan just smiled.

Suddenly, her face brightened with understanding. "Oh. But—"

"I know."

Crystal nodded, "Okay. And Pepe? Did he get away?"

"Pepe *esta bueno*. You must leave Puerto Vallarta now. Is no safe for you."

"Why does José care so much? He must be very rich. Can the children, or the paraplane for that matter, be so important to him?"

"Not about money. About power. *José* decide what happen. *José* decide when happen. You take some power. *You* decide what happen to children." He paused and tilted his head to one side. "Also, you ..." Juan leaned his head to the opposite side, trying to find the English word. "... humiliate him. In eyes of his men, he is smaller. Nothing make him more angry. You must be very careful."

"But he doesn't know I took the children," Crystal protested.

"No. He no is certain is you. But he need goat to blame."

Crystal settled back in the chair. "I can't leave yet. I need to get the children and take them with me back to Texas."

Juan frowned and shook his head. "No. You try take

Mexican children out of Mexico and Federales take you to jail."

"I want to take them to their mother."

"You no have proof. Some people steal Mexican children, take to United States. You will no get children out of Mexico. If you try, you go to jail. Mexican jail no is good place."

Crystal stared at Juan. They had rescued the girls from Jose, but she couldn't take them back to their mother. She had failed. "Where are they? At your house?"

"No."

"In a convent?"

"No. Convent first place José look. He probably already look in many convents. Nuns no could hide children from Jose. They try, but José is powerful. Children are safe. He no find them."

"But, --"

"When Lucita come to Mexico, she get children. But no in Vallarta. Too dangerous."

"She won't leave Blackwood's. She is afraid her children will be hurt if she leaves."

"Carlotta give you pictures of children?"

"Yes."

"Lucita will know they no with José now." He reached in his pocket and extracted some pictures. "These are for Lucita, also."

Crystal took the pictures. One photo showed Serafina and Angelina, smiling and apparently happy. No adults. On the back of another picture, several Spanish words had been printed, obviously by a child. *A salvo de José*: safe from Jose.

Reaching across the table, Juan took one of Crystal's hands. In his massive hand, hers was like a child's. "She will know children are safe if you take these to her. You must be safe from José also. If you no take these to Lucita, she no will know children are safe. She no escape without these. Important you take pictures to Lucita. Can you call airline now?"

Crystal sighed. He was right. She had freed the children. Her job now was to free the mother. She picked up the telephone and made reservations for tomorrow's flight from Puerto Vallarta to Dallas.

"How will Lucita find the children when she comes back to Mexico?"

"When she ready, you tell Señor Bull. We tell her what to do." He stood and took her hands in his once more. "You are very brave woman. Carlotta and I proud we know you. Jorge take you to airport tomorrow. Be very careful tonight. José want you. He no certain you do it. But, he tell his men you do it. If he get you, he save face with his men."

"I don't know why he would suspect me."

"*No se.* But I know he does. And you do more than take *niñas.* You make him look weak. José not forget that. You watch your walk."

Chapter 35

MERCÈDES had invited Crystal to go to dinner with her and several friends. About half an hour before sunset, they all strolled along the beach to Coco Tropical, a lovely beachfront restaurant two blocks south of Plaza Mar.

Crystal decided, on her last night in town, to have one of the drinks Puerto Vallarta was famous for. It came in a whole pineapple. The top of the pineapple had been cut off, part of the inside hollowed out and the drink poured in. Then, the crown was replaced, with a small hole cut for a straw. A tiny umbrella and several Mexican trinkets adorned the concoction. One sip told Crystal it was very strong, yet smooth as whipped cream. She took another sip. A good selection. She might be forced to have another. An image of Mark O'Malley popped up in her mind, bringing a warm smile to her face. It would be nice if he were here to share the sunset with her.

"*Hola, Señorita*. I am Diego. I look for you. I make special ring just for you." Diego rested his heavy jewelry case on his knee, reached in his pocket and removed a ring. "For you, *Señorita*."

Mercèdes told the vendor they were not buying tonight, but Crystal took the ring. The odd-shaped topaz had a brilliant fire which leaped from the stone. The unusual silver setting complimented the stone perfectly. She kept her focus on the ring even as she spoke to the vendor. "This is exquisite," she said and handed it to Mercèdes. "How much, Diego?"

"For anyone else, one thousand five hundred pesos."

Mercèdes laughed. "*Demasiado*. Too expensive."

"You good customer. For you, only twelve hundred pesos. And I give you leather bag for free."

"Seven hundred," Crystal said.

The vendor's face wrinkled, his eyes drooped, and became moist. "*Señorita*, I must feed my family. I have many *niños*. But I like you. One thousand."

"*Demasiado*," said Mercèdes. She handed the ring back to the vendor. He took it, but his attention never left Crystal.

Crystal reached into his case and picked up a pair of earrings. Each was a hummingbird, with such amazing detail etched into the silver, one could almost feel the wings fluttering. "How much for these?"

"Four hundred pesos, for you."

"How about one thousand pesos for the ring and the earrings both?"

"I no do that for anyone else. But for you." He handed her the topaz ring.

Crystal opened her purse and fished out some bills. "Thank you, Diego. And because you have been such a good salesman and this is my last night in Puerto Vallarta, here is an extra two hundred pesos, for your many *niños*."

"*Gracias, Señorita. Gracias.*" He reached in a pouch tied to his waist and produced two soft, leather jewelry bags and handed them to Crystal. "You good customer and good person. Please come back to Vallarta." He started to walk away, then turned back. "And remember Diego."

#

Mercèdes had selected a table on the raised level of the restaurant, so they looked over the people strolling along the walk. With the exception of a few swaying palm trees, nothing obstructed their view of the bay. The sun moved rapidly toward the horizon, creating a wide golden path from the water's edge to the edge of the earth. The orange ball began to disappear into the water with amazing speed. Then it was gone.

And at that split-second, Crystal saw a brilliant, Kelly-green flash of light at the point where the sun had vanished.

She blinked. Gone. It had lasted only a fraction of a second, but her heart beat faster. Crystal had believed the green flash was just a bit of paradise hype. But she had seen it. She had felt it.

Or did she imagine it?

But her rapid pulse and the happiness she felt were definitely real.

#

Sunday morning, she packed, then strolled along the beach to La Palapa for breakfast. The food was good, the ambiance marvelous. Fresh fruit, artistically arranged, topped a bright green papaya leaf. Chilled coconut milk was served in the original shell. A slight hint of cinnamon invaded the delicate crepes. Crystal's chair faced the blue waters of Banderas Bay. To her right, the only real wall of the restaurant featured a magnificent mural of a jungle scene so carefully rendered she could almost hear the tropical birds calling to one another.

She might easily have sat there enjoying the atmosphere for another hour, but George would soon be coming to take her to the airport. She paid her bill, then ambled up the short block from the beach and turned left on Olas Altas. Plaza Mar stood four blocks away at the end of the street. She tried to breathe in as much of the town as possible before she left Puerto Vallarta. Had it really been only ten days? She smiled as she thought of flying the powered parachute, of riding a horse down a river on a moonless night with Angelina clinging to her. And her meetings with Juan Grande. The girls had been rescued and were safe now. All in all, a wonderful trip.

She was three blocks from the condo when she saw a car

parked at the curb, its rear door open. Her pace faltered. A careful scan revealed no driver in the car nor on the sidewalk nearby. In fact, she saw no one in the entire block. She quickened her pace.

She focused on the small Japanese car as she hurried past. Still no one there.

Something smashed into her right side. The force knocked her toward the open door. Before she could regain her balance, she was halfway in the back seat.

Frantically, she grabbed at the doorframe, desperate to halt her momentum, trying to claw her way out of the car. Something hammered her hand. She lost her grip. She jerked her head toward the outside. A fist slammed into her jaw. Crystal fell back against the seat.

She heard the door slam, then another, and felt the black vehicle bumping down the cobblestone street. In seconds, Crystal's head cleared. Her jaw hurt, her hand throbbed, and she had trouble focusing, but her brain registered clearly what was happening.

Cèsar Aquilar.

She had not gotten a good look at the man but she was sure this was the same man from two nights ago. And her gut told her without hesitation or doubt, Cèsar Aquilar was driving.

She reached for the door handle, ready to jump out of the moving vehicle. The door and window handles had been removed. No handles on the other door either. She looked around for anything she might use to escape. A dirty sock, a crumpled cigarette pack, and some food crumbs were all she found. In front of her, Plexiglas separated the front and back seats. She pounded on it, succeeding only in hurting her fists.

Juan Grande's warning roared through her head. "If he get you, you disappear. Before I can get help, you are gone. No one ever see you again. You become his slave. Toy for his drug buyers."

Terror surged through Crystal's veins. Her breathing came in gasps. Fear twisted her stomach until she thought she might throw up. She screamed and banged on the window. But the street was deserted.

Cèsar glared at Crystal, then turned up the radio so loud even if someone were on the street, they would not hear her over the music. Nonetheless, she yelled, "*Auxilio!*" several times, and "*Ayudarme!* Help me!"

She leaned back and started kicking the side window with both feet. The glass did not break. She twisted and kicked the front seat, knocking the driver into the steering wheel. The driver slammed on the brakes. Crystal was thrown to the floor. Before she could regain her balance, the man jumped out and opened the back door. A large, burly hand grabbed her hair and jerked her head back. His other hand slapped her across the face. A low growl emitted from his mouth. Crystal could not translate the Spanish but the meaning, clear in any language, terrified her.

He slapped her again and in the instant before her eyes closed in anticipation of the blow, she saw it, stuck in a leather sheath, attached to his belt. A hunting knife.

He let go of her hair and backed up. Her chance was gone.

She spun around. As he shoved the door closed, she kicked it with both feet, knocking it open. She shrieked at him as she struggled to get out.

The huge Mexican reached in and grabbed her again, this time by the throat. His thumb wrapped around her windpipe, cutting off all air. Crystal's hands clawed at the thumb on her neck, trying to get some breath to her lungs. He easily resisted her frantic effort, a twisted smile on his face. A painful, rasping sound seeped from her throat as her body urgently worked to bring in air.

As he pulled her closer, Crystal's right hand slipped away

from her throat, reached in, and yanked the hunting knife free. Even as it cleared the sheath, the huge man stepped back, his focus shifting to the knife, then back to Crystal's eyes.

Crystal grasped the knife more firmly, trying desperately not to show the fear gripping her heart. She slid toward the door, slashing back and forth with the knife.

His mouth became a sneer, his black eyes eager. His position shifted slightly, but he did not back up.

Crystal continued to brandish the knife in front of her in what she hoped was a menacing manner. She eased a foot out onto the cobblestones, careful to keep her balance.

The man's foot lashed out, catching her on the shinbone with the hard leather sole of his boot. A jolt of electricity shot through Crystal from leg to stomach. A slight cry escaped her lips. The driver grabbed her wrist, squeezing and twisting it. In two seconds, the knife clattered to the pavement. The next moment, his fist caught Crystal's left cheekbone, knocking hope out of her heart.

Chapter 36

THE force of the blow knocked Crystal back into the car, her eyes barely able to focus. The massive brute kicked her leg to get it inside, then stepped back to slam the door.

He lurched forward. His head banged into the car. His legs buckled and he grabbed at the roof in an effort to keep from falling. He jerked forward again. Then he was knocked to the side, falling on the street near the rear of the car.

Diego reached in, took Crystal's hand. "Come. *Ràpido.*"

Crystal blinked her eyes and shook her head slightly, trying to regain her sense of balance. With an effort, she scrambled out, then stopped to look at Cèsar Aquilar. She would not forget this man. He lay face down on the cobblestones, breathing, but not moving. She kicked the knife under the car.

"Thank you, Diego. Thank you, thank you, thank you. I thought he was going to kill me."

Diego had already started moving away. "Come. He no out long. We must go."

Legs unsteady, Crystal still managed to hurry. "Would you walk with me to Plaza Mar?"

"*Ciertamente, Señorita* Crystal."

They had reached Plaza Mar's gate and stepped inside before Crystal stopped trembling. "He's a big man. How did you ever knock him down?"

"I hit him with *joyelero,*" Diego said, holding up his

jewelry case. "Is solid, heavy."

Crystal reached in her purse, fumbled around, and produced two five hundred peso notes. "This is for you, Diego. I think you saved my life."

The small Mexican man looked at the money as if it were a tarantula and shook his head. "Diego no take your money. You are *mi amiga*. I sell jewelry. No take money to help friend."

"But, — "

Diego moved back a step. "No."

Crystal looked at the man, proud, dignified, and reserved. For a moment she said nothing. She wanted to wrap her arms around him in gratitude. That would be inappropriate and would only embarrass him.

Finally, she smiled. "You *are* my friend and I thank you for your help. Now, I would like to buy some jewelry before I leave. Will you sell me some?"

Diego beamed. "*Si*. Yes. Diego always sell jewelry." He opened the case, balancing it on his knee, and studied it for a minute. "Here is very nice necklace."

Crystal took the necklace and laid it across her hands. Three different colors of gold strands were woven into a gleaming loop which must have been twenty-eight inches around. It had a heavy feel to it, but was as delicate as meringue. "This is absolutely beautiful. How much does it cost?"

"One thousand pesos."

"I'll take it," and she handed Diego the five hundred peso notes.

Diego produced a small, soft leather jewelry bag, placed the necklace in it, and handed it to Crystal. "You come back to Puerto Vallarta. And remember Diego."

"I won't forget you."

#

Thirty minutes later, Jorge arrived, driving into the basement garage, so Crystal did not have to appear on the street at all. A locked, iron gate kept out people and all cars not specifically granted access to the underground parking area.

At the airport, Jorge carried Crystal's suitcases in and left her at the ticket counter. "Many police here. You safe here," Jorge told her and then departed.

Crystal checked in and immediately went inside the secure area to await departure. Twice, she checked her purse, making certain she had the pictures of Serafina and Angelina. She imagined her meeting with Lucita, warming at the prospect of freeing the pretty young Mexican mother. Finally, Crystal pulled out the novel she had been unable to finish.

She had been reading awhile when a disturbance occurred at the security check. The alarm sounded, followed by a heated discussion. A large column blocked Crystal's view of the area and she leaned out to see what was happening. Several people stood in the way, and she could manage only glimpses of the dispute. A large Mexican man was arguing with the guard. After a moment, the man handed something to the guard, along with a stack of bills.

Crystal had not seen the man's face, but something about his bearing sent a tremor through her.

"What was the money about?" an elderly man sitting behind Crystal asked his wife.

"He said he forgot he brought it with him. He gave the guard some money, for the guard to hold it until he got back. Did you see the size of the blade?"

Crystal was sure she had seen it, and held it, this morning. And the man was likely the same man who, but for Diego, would have kidnapped her.

Fear swept over her. She turned away and shrank back in her seat, hoping the man would not see her. She knew he no longer had the knife. But his powerful hands could snap her neck as easily as she could break uncooked spaghetti. And while police stood nearby, she might be dead by the time they subdued her attacker.

#

On the flight home, Crystal had not seen Cèsar. However, the more she replayed the scene at the security check, the more convinced she was the man with the knife was indeed Cèsar. That did not mean he had boarded this plane. Many flights left Puerto Vallarta in mid-afternoon. He could have been going to Houston, Minneapolis, Los Angeles, or half a dozen other places in the United States. Dozens of flights left for cities in Mexico. One of those was the most likely destination for him, she tried to convince herself.

She sat near the front of tourist class, staring out the window, but this time she took no notice of the landscape below. Diego had risked his life for her, someone he barely knew. She would not forget him.

#

When the plane landed at DFW, she was one of the first to get off. She breezed through customs, with only a brief question on whether she was bringing back any food. She said no, without really thinking about it. The agent just looked at her without saying anything. But he did not return her passport.

"Oh, except these cookies," she said sheepishly, pointing to a package of cookies sticking half out of her carry-on bag.

"I wondered if you were going to disclose those," he said with a grin and handed her passport back. "Welcome home."

#

"Okay," said Brandi as soon as they were in the car and headed home. "What happened to your face?"

A large, ugly, red bruise decorated Crystal's left cheek and her throat still hurt from Cèsar's attack. "I had a run-in with one of the bad guys." She tried to laugh a little. "You should see what he looks like."

"Sounds like you had a real adventure, and I do want to hear more about it. But first, what about the kids?"

"We rescued the children. We got them away from José and they are hidden safely, waiting for their mother." She settled back in the seat, her body relaxing for the first time in days.

Brandi stopped at the tollbooth, handed the woman money and the ticket, then pulled back into the traffic. "Okay. Details, gal. Details. How did you get them away from José Whoever?"

Crystal proceeded to give a rundown on Juan Grande, Jorge, and the powered parachute. Brandi interrupted continually with questions about each incident. "So, how did Big John get out?"

Crystal repeated much of what Juan Grande had told her about his night at Jose's hacienda. Through this, Brandi listened in wide-eyed silence, her mouth agape. They pulled into their driveway by the time Crystal finished the story of Cèsar.

Chapter 37

THE next morning, Crystal arrived at Intelligent Retrieval Systems early to begin catching up. Her work schedule would be disrupted this week as well. Missing the last week and a half of work, she needed to make certain the project was on track, that her people were not straying off on tangents.

Shortly after eight, Sally came into the office. "Welcome back." She flopped down in a chair. "Well, let's hear the good stuff. How was your vacation? And what happened to your face?"

Vacation. Crystal smiled. She told about the restaurants, parasailing, shopping, and passed off her bruises as a slight accident. Then she reached in her purse for a small leather bag and handed it to Sally.

"You shouldn't have. But I'm glad you did." She opened the bag and took out the earrings. "Wow. These are beautiful." She took off the earrings she was wearing and replaced them with the large, silver dolphins Crystal had brought her. "These must have cost a small fortune."

"You're worth it."

JT Gonzales tapped on the doorframe.

"Come in, JT. I brought you something from Puerto Vallarta." She retrieved another leather pouch and offered it to JT.

"Oh, I didn't...." JT looked embarrassed. "Thank you."

"Well, open it up and show us what you got," Sally said.

Mark O'Malley came in. "Welcome back."

"Oops. The boss is here." Sally eased up out of the chair. "I'd better get to work. Call me and we'll go to lunch together." She cut her eyes in the direction of Mark, then back to Crystal. "If you don't get a better offer."

"I'll come back later," JT said. "I think you will be pleased with what we got done while you were gone."

Mark sat in the chair Sally had vacated. "How was the trip? Did you accomplish your goals?"

Mark listened to her one-minute report, but somehow, Crystal had the feeling he already knew most of what happened. He hadn't even asked about her discolored face. She really wanted to give him a big hug, but they wouldn't do that at the office.

"I know you want to get settled, after your trip. But in the next day or two, I'd like to hear all of the details," Mark said. "Maybe over dinner?"

"I'll tell you everything, once I get caught up. Still need a half day off to wrap up things?"

"Certainly. Tie up the loose ends. Then, I want your nose to the grindstone." Mark was grinning as he said this. "Your people did a lot of work, but they need your guidance."

"Yes, sir." She gave a little salute.

An hour later, Crystal was deep in thought when the intercom buzzed. "Crystal. Dr. Krupe is on line 1. Will you take it?"

Crystal started to say no. But, it needed to be done. "I'll take it."

"Hello, Lester." She found it strange calling him by his first name, instead of Dr. Krupe. But her former advisor no longer cowed her. "How are you?"

"Ah. Well, ah, better, now that I have finally gotten

through to you. When we discussed this a couple of weeks ago, you promised to think about it. I need your answer, Crystal. I've assured you, your name will be displayed as prominently as mine. I've already had the slide prepared. It looks good. I will give you ample credit." He paused and when Crystal said nothing, he continued, "This will be good for both of us, Crystal. CMU is a top center for information retrieval. You'll get excellent exposure. And I think you will agree, having your name coupled with mine on a paper won't hurt your professional standing either. Plus, it will add another presentation to your resume. All positive things; no negatives."

She didn't really want to think about it right now. She'd been out of the office for ten days, and she wasn't finished. Lucita still remained under Blackwood's control.

"Lester, as you know, I've been away for awhile. And I have some very important matters to deal with right now. Let me think about this and I'll get back to you as soon as I clear up this other project."

"And when will that be?"

"With luck, Wednesday."

"I need to make travel plans. And of course, CMU must finalize their plans. Wednesday at the latest," he said with his usual self-confidence.

"I'll do my best."

Crystal dropped the phone back in its cradle and closed her eyes. *What to do?* After a few minutes, she got up and walked to Mark's office.

She tapped on the door frame. "Got a minute?"

He motioned her in. "What's up?"

She filled him in on Krupe's request, trying to present only facts and none of her emotions. He listened without interrupting, then sat quietly, rocking gently in his chair.

"And you believe he will really give you full credit?"

She nodded.

"Well, it never hurts to have your name attached to a presented paper, particularly an invited one. Is this for the workshop Dr. Patrick is hosting?"

Crystal cocked her head and straightened up a bit. "I don't know. Krupe didn't mention a workshop."

"Either way, I don't see how it can hurt you. Professionally. Only you can determine how it affects you emotionally." He raised his eyebrows and looked steadily at Crystal for several seconds. "But after he passed it off as his own here in Dallas, you certainly would be within your rights not to let him present it again. Strictly up to you. How do you feel about it?"

"I don't know. With all that's been going on, I haven't had time to think about it. One part of me says tell him no, unequivocally no. He's forfeited any right he might have had, and I think that was little to begin with. Another part of me says, forget it. Don't be petty. And it won't hurt me professionally." She shrugged. "I don't know."

"When does he need an answer?"

"Wednesday."

Mark gave her a confidence-building smile. "Give it some thought, then call and tell him your answer. I'm sure it will be the right one."

#

Crystal left IRS after six and immediately drove to The Park. Dinner was just being put on the table when she got there.

Eula had a million questions but Crystal did manage to get in a few bites of spaghetti in between answers. Rosa listened intently, but did not ask anything.

"Sounds as exciting as when the hogs ate my little brother," Eula said.

Rosa's brows furrowed, her mouth fell open, and she let out a small gasp.

"Only kidding, Rosa. Joking. Not real." She turned her attention back to her granddaughter. "So, what's the plan to liberate Lucita?"

"I thought I'd go see her at the grocery store on Wednesday. Try to get her to leave from there."

"Reckon you'll duck out the back door?"

"Yes, Nana. I'm not going to parade her in front of Blackwood's man."

"That's using your noggin. I don't think he'd take kindly to that."

Crystal turned to Rosa. "Do you think Lucita will be willing to leave from the store? I mean, would she need to go back to Blackwood's house for anything?"

Rosa looked at the ceiling for a moment, then back at Crystal. "If she know children safe, I think yes. No need go back. Better no go back. But, must know children safe."

Crystal got up and retrieved her purse from the living room couch, extracting an envelope. She withdrew the contents and handed them to Rosa. "Will this convince her to leave immediately?"

Rosa studied each picture carefully. "Yes. I think she come now."

Later, the three women sat on the veranda. A light breeze blew from the south and a few puffy clouds dotted the deep blue Texas sky. The trees prevented them from seeing the sun sink below the horizon. Crystal would see no green flash tonight.

"Rosa. Would you come with me Wednesday to see Lucita? You could help me convince her to come with me. Convince her the children are safe. Will you come?"

"No." The Mexican woman shook her head violently. A shadow crossed her face. "No. I no want get near *Señor* Blackwood." She continued to shake her head. "No. I wait here. You show Lucita pictures, she come with you."

"You've come this far on your own," said Eula. "Guess you might as well finish plowing the field."

Crystal thought about Juan Grande and Jorge and Pepe. She had not done it alone. She *could* not have done it alone. She might never know for certain, but she truly believed Jorge saved her life. She knew positively she wouldn't be here tonight if it weren't for Diego.

#

Tuesday morning, Crystal went to Mark's office.

"I'm hoping to get Lucita tomorrow morning. If I do, I need to get her on a plane and out of here as soon as possible. Juan Grande said I should tell you when she was ready. And he would tell us what to do."

"Think you can get her away from Blackwood that quickly?"

"I hope so. If she'll come. I'm going to approach her at the grocery store and try to get her to come with me right then."

Mark drew his lips into a straight, thin line and nodded. "I'll try to contact him this morning. I'll let you know what he says."

Mid-afternoon, Mark entered Crystal's office and sat down in front of her desk. "Good news and bad news. Or complications. Juan is wondering if she has any papers that will let her get out of this country and into Mexico. Does she have a passport or a visa or anything?"

"I've no idea."

"Important. As you know, when she picks up her tickets, they're going to want to see identification. Usually, that's a passport." He raised his unruly eyebrows.

"She won't have a passport. What kind of ID do you think would work?"

Mark leaned back and stretched out in the chair. "Driver's license, at the minimum. Something government-issued with her picture on it."

"They checked my passport, both in Dallas and in Mexico. I don't know what they do if you don't have a passport. But I can almost guarantee she doesn't have one. But, she's a Mexican citizen. Do you think she'll need one when she gets to Mexico."

"Didn't they look at your passport when you got back to DFW?"

Crystal nodded, then put her head in her hands and closed her eyes. After a minute, she looked at Mark. "I'll work on getting her on the plane. But I don't know what I can do on the Mexico end. Can Juan Grande do something there?"

Mark pursed his full lips. "He usually can. He seems to have many resources. I'll tell him you'll get her on the plane if he can get her into the country."

"What's the worst they could do to her? Send her back? I mean, she is a Mexican citizen, after all."

Mark shook his head and let out a short breath. "Who knows what they might do? Put her in jail for a while? Probably not. But I have no idea. What I *do* know is, if there's much of a fuss, José will hear about it and she'll be in big trouble. How about waiting to get her away from Blackwood until we get this sorted out?"

Crystal shook her head. "We can't wait. Even now, José might have told Blackwood the children have been rescued. They might tighten the security on Lucita. Or sell her to someone in another state. Or kill her. And Juan Grande assured me José would search everywhere for the kids. So, we need to get the mother to the kids and get them all to someplace safe, as soon as possible. Preferably yesterday."

Mark nodded. "I'll put the problem in Juan's lap." He got up to leave. "However, you haven't gotten her away from Blackwood or on a plane yet."

Chapter 38

WEDNESDAY arrived with dark clouds casting a gloom over Dallas. A steady drizzle fell and a light breeze made certain everything got soaked and people got chilled. From the moment she looked outside, Crystal's spirits were dampened. No cause and effect existed here, but nonetheless, she worried the dismal weather might be an omen.

Brandi drove while Crystal told her of Dr. Krupe's request.

"What do you think?" Crystal asked.

"He's the guy who tried to get in your pants, and when he couldn't, drummed you out of graduate school? Then tried to steal your paper? I think, no way, José."

"It could be good for me."

"Yeah, like an enema."

"No. He'd put my name on it, prominently. I'd get credit. And an addition to my resume."

"Well, you asked what I thought. If the guy was drowning, I'd throw him a life ring. But I wouldn't pull him in. No way, O.J."

#

Crystal and Brandi got to the supermarket well before they expected Lucita to arrive. They had laid out a strategy last night, and now checked everything to see if there were obstacles they had missed.

"Looks doable," Brandi said.

"I think so. But I wish the rain would stop and the sun would come out." Crystal looked at her watch. "We still have a little time, but let's get in position, just in case Argos decides to bring Lucita early." Crystal remembered how Rosa reacted to the mention of Argos, Blackwood's enforcer. "Of course, she might be late. So don't panic if it takes a little time." Even as she said it, a vague uneasiness settled in her stomach.

Brandi patted Crystal on the shoulder. "I've heard about the way you handle these dangerous situations. I'm not worried."

"I am. Go on. Move the car. And say a prayer this works. I don't have a back-up plan."

Crystal hovered around the fresh vegetables, planning to intercept Lucita there. At one point, a store clerk approached her and asked if he could help. She offered a weak "No thanks," and moved to another aisle.

She checked her watch again. Maybe it had stopped. Keeping an eye on the door, she wandered up near the front where she could see the large digital clock on the bank across the parking lot. Her watch was correct.

Lucita, scarf pulled around her neck and up over her head, ran through the rain toward the store. Crystal moved back, not wanting to have any contact with her where Argos might see them.

Lucita entered the store and stopped to shake the water off her jacket and scarf. She brushed her hand across her black hair. Crystal's heart beat faster. She had to hold herself back to keep from running to the Mexican woman. As Lucita took a cart and started toward the vegetable area, Crystal stepped out. They made eye contact. Only the slightest widening of the eyes indicated Lucita recognized her.

Argos burst through the door. Fear leapt onto Lucita's face. Crystal turned away, her knees almost buckling; her breathing stopped and she bit her lip to stifle a moan. She picked up a tomato, trying to look like any other shopper. She almost dropped it. She placed it in her cart and examined the cucumbers.

Agros marched to the express lane and bought two packs of cigarettes.

Lucita moved into the vegetable area, as if she had not noticed Argos. She studied the selection of lettuce, glancing at Crystal only for an instant. She was just putting a head of lettuce in her shopping cart when Argos started in her direction.

"Lucita," the man snarled. "Git over here."

Crystal's stomach tied itself in a knot. She forced herself to breathe and reminded herself, unlike in Puerto Vallarta, she did know how to yell "Help" here. What if he took Lucita away right now? Had he seen Crystal? Had he recognized her from her visit to Blackwood's house or her contact with Lucita two weeks ago?

What if she ran to Lucita and pulled her away? Argos could not make a big scene in the grocery store, could he? Of course he could. Worse, he could follow Lucita and Crystal wherever they went. He would know where they lived, where they took Lucita. Crystal's remark to Brandi flashed across her brain: *I don't have a back-up plan.*

Lucita left the cart and took several steps toward Argos. Crystal refused to look in his direction. She inhaled deeply, trying to ease the cramps in her stomach, arms, legs, and heart. She picked up a stalk of celery, hoping that might stop her hands from shaking.

"You gonna be long today?"

Lucita hesitated for a second. "*Si. He comprado mucho hoy.*"

"You better hurry. I don't wanna sit out in the goddamned rain all day." He turned and stomped out.

Lucita watched him until he was out the door, then turned and pushed her cart past Crystal. "Come."

Crystal walked toward the front of the store and watched until Argos got in the car. Then she followed Lucita to a spot totally hidden from outside. Lucita was gripping the handle of the cart so hard her knuckles were white. Her lower lip trembled slightly. Her eyes, at once hopeful and afraid, began to tear as they searched Crystal's face for the answer to a question Lucita could not ask.

Crystal put her hand on Lucita's shoulder. "The girls are safe."

Lucita gasped and her hands flew to her face and tears began flowing. "Serafina? Angelina?"

"Yes, both are safe from Jose. You must come with me now."

Lucita drew back away from Crystal's touch as if she had been burned. The tears stopped and deep lines formed between her black eyebrows. A woman moved slowly by them, looking first at Lucita, then at Crystal, who smiled a thin, weak smile at the lady.

"How do I know they are safe? How do I know you . . .?"

Crystal opened her purse and pulled out the photographs and handed them to Lucita.

The tears started again in earnest. Lucita pressed the pictures to her cheek. She studied the picture of the two girls standing beside Crystal, then looked up and smiled. On the next picture, the child's writing on the back had made creases. Lucita turned the photo over and read the words. Again, she pressed the picture to her cheek and whispered, *"Gracias."* Crystal was not certain whether it was directed to her or to God. She didn't care.

"Lucita, you must come with me now." Crystal put her hand on the woman's arm.

Lucita looked over her shoulder, toward the street and Argos.

"Come with me. Do not go back to Mr. Blackwood's."

"I . . . I don't know."

"What don't you know? If you go back there, José might call and say the children are gone. Then Blackwood will never let you out of his sight."

"But, *Señor* Argos will see me. He will come after me. He is very bad man."

"He won't see you. Or find you." Once again, Crystal put her hand on Lucita's arm.

"What if José finds my children?"

"He won't. Juan Grande has hidden them very well."

Instantly, Crystal regretted using his name. It seemed to mean nothing to Lucita. Still, should Blackwood get his hands on Lucita, he might force the name from her. But, Crystal could not pull the words back.

"How did he get them?"

Crystal did not want to explain things right now, here in the store, here where Argos might barge in and find them and force Lucita to return to Blackwood's.

Reaching into her pocket, Crystal pulled out the medallion Lucita had given her just two weeks before and handed it to her. The Mexican woman took it and pressed it to her breast. Slowly, Crystal began to guide her toward the rear of the store. "I'll tell you all about it after we get you away from here. We must leave before Argos comes in looking for you."

Only moments ago, when Lucita learned the children were safe, her black eyes sparkled and her smooth, brown face glowed. Now, dark shadows clouded her eyes and deep lines creased the flawless complexion. Her lips trembled slightly. "He will see me."

Crystal slipped her arm down around Lucita's waist. "We are not going out the front, so he will not be able to see you. Your two beautiful girls went with me with no hesitation and I took them to safety. I will do the same for you."

Obstacles lay ahead. Many things could go wrong. Crystal thought of the taxi driver trying to get her in the cab, when no one should have known she was in Mexico. Dangers hovered at every corner, but she could not place those on this woman's shoulders, already burdened with so much.

Lucita had been offering resistance to Crystal's steady pull. Little by little, Crystal began to feel the Mexican woman relaxing and soon they were moving at a normal pace.

At the end of the aisle, they turned right past the meat display. Shoppers picking through the selections, paid no attention to the two women moving along silently. Past the meat section, two swinging doors provided access to the storage and workrooms in the back. Crystal pushed through these.

A young man looked up from his work. "Can I help you?" he asked.

"No. We're just going out that door there."

He stared at them, brows knitted, clip board dangling, then started in their direction.

"It's all right," Crystal said without stopping. "The manager knows." The man, barely in his twenties, took a step forward, stopped, leaned as if to move again, but didn't.

What if he knew Blackwood and sounded the alarm that Lucita was skipping? "She's about to be sick," Crystal said. "The manager said the back door was closer."

The young man stood there, caught between the risks of alienating customers and not protecting the store. He said nothing else, just watched the women cross the storeroom.

She and Brandi had checked this part of the store earlier, so Crystal knew exactly how to negotiate the area and get to the outside door. She pushed it open. Rain still fell, and the wind flung cold water in her face, causing her to stop and draw back for an instant. She pulled Lucita out into the rain and closed the door behind them.

Her adrenaline shot up. Neither Brandi nor the car was in sight. Her heart pumped, a vein pulsating in her throat.

Chapter 39

A CAR'S headlights flashed on near the end of the building and started moving toward them. Lucita gasped and began to back toward the door.

The car skidded to a stop in front of them. "Sorry." Brandi reached back and opened the rear door.

Crystal grabbed Lucita's hand and practically dragged her to the car. "Get in and lie down on the seat," she ordered. As soon as Lucita was in, Crystal slammed the door. She raced around and hopped in the front seat. Brandi put the car in drive and eased down the alley.

"What happened? I almost panicked when I couldn't see you."

"Oh, some jerk came out and told me I couldn't park here. I argued with him, but he finally said he'd call the FBI or Homeland Security or somebody and get me arrested. So, I left. Parked down at the end so I could see you come out."

"Let's get away from here. Lucita is really afraid of Argos. He gives me the creeps, too. He came in the store and I almost passed out." She turned to the rear of the car. "Lucita, lie down out of sight until we get away from here. It won't be long."

The wind whipped the rain against the windows. A tremendous crash of thunder shook the car. Lucita did not move, nor did she utter a sound.

#

Forty-five minutes later, all three women sat around the

kitchen table sipping hot spiced tea and munching on brownies. Brandi and Crystal had changed into dry clothes. Lucita had slipped on a blue and green stripped terrycloth bathrobe Crystal provided. Rain still beat against the windows.

Lucita's charcoal eyes were shining and her face was animated as she talked about her two little girls and how smart they were. Both were learning English already. A few Spanish words popped up in Lucita's speech here and there, but generally, her English was good. Periodically, she would scan the room, check behind her, while doubt wrinkled her smooth face. More than once, when a car door slammed outside, she jerked around to look out the front window, her hand gripping the mug too tightly.

She turned to Crystal. "How will I get to Mexico? To see my *niñas*? When?"

"We're working on that. Probably by air and probably tomorrow, but I haven't worked out all the details yet."

"On airplane? I never go on airplane before."

"It's the way to go," said Brandi. "You'll love it. They'll give you drinks, magazines to read. And you'll be back in Puerto Vallarta in two hours."

"Two hours! We take three days to come in truck, and only stop for fuel."

"Do you have a passport, or some other kind of identification?" Crystal asked.

The Mexican woman shook her head. "Nothing. I never have passport. *Señor* Blackwood take all papers I have."

"Okay. I'll work on ID."

"And she needs something to wear," Brandi said. "Don't think she'll fit into my clothes and yours are way too big. She's about the same size as JT. Maybe she could borrow some of JT's."

Crystal's eyes opened wide. "You're a genius, Brandi. You

may have solved my biggest problem." She opened her purse, pulled out a credit card, and handed it to her housemate. "Can you take her to Penney's this afternoon and buy her several outfits?"

"Guess so."

"And get her a small suitcase. Might look suspicious if she's headed to another country without a bag of any kind." Crystal got up. "I've got to run to work."

"You know Blackheart and Argos are going to be looking for her."

"We're ten miles away. He can't be looking everywhere. But, go to Big Town Mall. Better yet, the Irving Mall. That'll be twenty-five miles from Hunter Lane. And thousands of people shopping. And he won't expect her to be shopping."

"Remember, I've got to leave for work by six."

"You've got time. I'll be back by then."

"And how am I a genius?" asked Brandi. "I don't get to be that very often."

"Tell you later—if it works out." She faced Lucita. "I'm so happy we got you away from Blackwood. Tomorrow or the next day, we'll get you to your girls."

Lucita grabbed Crystal's hands and kissed them. "*Gracias. Gracias.*" And her eyes glistened.

"In my country," Brandi said to Crystal, "If you rescue someone, you're responsible for them from then on."

"Your country?" Crystal cocked her head and squeezed her lips into a thin line. "*This* is your country, same as mine. And I never heard anything like that."

"You didn't see as many movies as I did."

Lucita looked from one of her rescuers to the other, forehead wrinkled, looking bewildered. "You not responsible for me. You save my children. You save me. I am always to owe you."

Crystal patted Lucita on the shoulder. "Thank you. But you owe me nothing. Just seeing those two lovely girls of yours safely away from José was payment enough." She turned a satisfied eye toward Brandi. "You. You just help Lucita get some clothes. And Lucita, don't let Brandi talk you into getting anything you don't like."

Crystal ran to her car and headed toward her office. After all the fretting, it turned out to be pretty easy. Somewhere in the back of her mind, a small voice said, 'Too easy.'

Chapter 40

CRYSTAL arrived at Intelligent Retrieval Systems just before noon and immediately left with JT for lunch. When they returned, Crystal went to see Mark.

"Okay. I have the ID. What did you find out from Juan Grande?"

"She's to fly into Leon."

"Leon? That's nowhere near Puerto Vallarta."

Mark smiled. "Exactly. There's an excellent chance José will be watching the PV airport. Maybe even Guadalajara. But he can't watch them all. There are good flights from DFW to Leon. Anyway, it's Leon. Maybe that's just where Juan has the best contacts. She's to fly as an American named Marie Navarro. They'll be expecting her."

"How about a change of name?"

"Oh? What ID have you come up with?"

"Juanita Teresa Gonzales." She smiled with satisfaction.

"JT?"

"Don't know why I didn't notice it sooner, but Lucita looks like JT. They could be sisters. I've already talked with JT. We'll trim Lucita's hair just a little."

"What? JT will buy the ticket and then give it to Lucita? She'll still need an ID to get through security."

"No. JT is giving her passport to Lucita. Then, once she's in Mexico, Lucita will send it back."

"JT agreed to that? She knows that's against the law?"

"She knows. I reminded her. She said she wanted to help, and was willing to take the chance. She said the real criminal was Blackwood. If anything happens, she can say her passport was stolen."

"I don't like it."

"I don't either, but we haven't come up with anything else that works." Crystal shifted and leaned her elbows on the edge of Mark's desk. "So what happens when she gets there?"

"When she gets to immigration, she should look for the agent who has a stuffed iguana sitting on a shelf behind him. That agent will check the papers they give her on the plane. She must be certain to fill those out on the plane so no time will be wasted at the immigration booth. He will pass her on through. Beyond the booth, she should look for a man with a toucan embroidered on his shirt and a nametag that says 'Jorge'. He'll be watching for her, so they shouldn't miss one another. Oh, and she should wear a shirt that says 'St. Mary's University' on it. He'll take her from there."

"Is that the Jorge I know?"

Mark shrugged. "I have no idea."

"I hope so. Then I know she'll be safe." She frowned. "Where do I get a shirt with St. Mary's on it?"

"That's my contribution." He opened a desk drawer and took out a knit shirt with a school logo large enough to be read from ten feet away. "Hope it fits."

"It will do. Anything else?"

"Will she have any luggage?"

Crystal nodded.

"Good. Have her carry it on so they do not have to wait at the baggage carousel. Juan would like her to spend as little time in the airport as possible."

"Okay. I'll see if I can make the reservations for tomorrow. You let them know they're looking for Juanita Gonzales."

"Yes ma'am. And tomorrow afternoon, you and I need to talk about your project. Saving people in distress is only one of your jobs."

#

Thursday morning, Crystal and Lucita left for the airport early. The attendant behind the counter checked her ID. If Lucita felt nervous, Crystal could not detect it.

They went to a coffee shop. Neither said anything about Blackwood or Argos, but both checked every man who entered, or even looked in through the glass windows. *If they're here, they'll be looking at the flights to Puerto Vallarta.* She hoped.

At the security checkpoint, Crystal gave Lucita a final hug, then stepped behind the barrier and watched her walk through the security metal detector.

The alarm rang out.

The Mexican woman turned to look back, her mouth half open, brow furrowed, eyes filled with terror. The agent stepped toward her and for a moment, Crystal thought Lucita might run.

"Ma'am, you leave on any jewelry, anything in your pockets?"

Lucita looked from Crystal to the man and back, her eyes now moist.

"Maybe a watch?" he said.

Lucita said nothing, still looking at Crystal, her eyes pleading for help. Crystal sucked in air as it came to her—jewelry. "Lucita, the medallion. The medal. Did you forget to put it in the tray?" Crystal made motions around her neck to indicate the chain.

Lucita's eyes opened wide and she nodded. She reached

in the neck of her blouse and took out the medal and showed it to the agent.

"That'd sure set it off. If you'll just put it in this tray and then step back through the detector, Ma'am," he said.

Lucita took the medallion off, but kept it and walked back through the metal detector and over to the barrier where Crystal stood.

"You take this. For all you do for me and my babies."

Crystal's nose and eyes tingled and she felt warm all over. "No. No. That's so nice, but it is your special medal, your patron saint who watches over you."

Lucita pressed it into Crystal's hand. "It is for you. It has special powers from Our Lady of Guadalupe. It keep you safe. It make you safe when you rescue my babies. It help you fly the plane."

"Oh, Lucita, I can't take this. It is very precious to you and your girls. And you may need it."

"No. *You* were special protection for me and for my children. I must know you have it. You give life back to me. This is all I can give you. Please wear it." Her face was flushed and her moist eyes sparkled. She reached over, kissed Crystal on the cheek, then turned and walked back through the metal detector.

Even after Lucita was through security, Crystal waited. What did she expect? That Blackwood or Argos would come dashing in, force their way through security and drag Lucita out of the airport? Still, she watched until the 737 taxied away from the gate. The American flight to Leon was scheduled to leave at 11:06. Crystal glanced at her watch: 11:08. Everything was going according to plan.

Sometime after noon, Crystal got to IRS. She scanned her e-mail, her U.S. mail, and three notes stuck to her desk. At 1:00 she had a meeting with the members of her project, who brought her up-to-date on the progress and problems.

After the meeting ended, she mulled over the problems her team had presented. Three weeks ago she had been fully immersed in the project, but now she felt as if she were starting from scratch. Troubleshooting the difficulties took most of the afternoon.

Then, she and Mark went over the project in detail, Crystal describing its status and proposing a solution for each problem. Most of the time, Mark just nodded. On two, he suggested other possible approaches.

Finally, they finished.

"Good work. You seem to have gotten back up to speed quickly."

"Thanks. Now, on another topic, have you heard anything from Mexico?"

Mark shook his head. "No. I don't expect any information today. Maybe tomorrow."

"So, we don't know if she got in or not."

"Not really. We'd be more likely to hear if something went wrong." He placed his hand over hers. "Patience."

"Not one of my strong suits." She stood. "Mark, thanks for all your help. It wasn't your problem, but you were a tremendous help. And I would never have gotten the children free without Juan Grande. He is terrific."

"He is. The best friend a person can have."

"How did you meet him?"

"It's a long story. I'll tell you another time. Over dinner tomorrow night?"

"I'd like that."

Back in her office, Crystal dialed home.

"Hi. What time do you have to go to work tonight?" she asked Brandi.

"Off tonight. No work. What you got in mind?"

"Nothing. I want to kick off my shoes, put my feet up, and do absolutely nothing. I'm about ready to leave. Order us a pizza from Giuseppe's and I'll be there by the time it is."

Chapter 41

BRANDI poured a Lone Star into a glass and picked up the TV listings. She had scanned half the night's programs when the doorbell rang. She glanced at her watch and headed for the door. *Pretty fast tonight.* A check through the tiny security lens revealed a man with a Giuseppe's cap on. *New man. Same pizza box.* She slipped off the guard chain and opened the door.

"Pizza. Fifteen dollar."

Brandi tilted her head to one side. "Fifteen?"

He opened the storm door.

"It only cost $13.50 last week."

"Fifteen dollar." He stepped inside.

Brandi did not like his pushy manner or his stepping into the house without being invited. "You wait here and I'll get the money." She turned to get her purse.

In an instant, she was flying through the air. She crashed onto the floor and pain stabbed her between the shoulder blades. She struggled, half crawling, trying to get up, get away. The man kicked her, knocking her against the wall. She tried to push herself up. Her shoulder rebelled.

He tossed the box on the floor, grabbed her legs and twisted her over to face him. "Where is Moore?"

She opened her mouth sending pain along her jaw. "More what?"

He placed his boot on her foot and stood on it. Her ankle

felt like someone had put a hot branding iron on it and she screamed.

"Where is Moore woman?"

Brandi did not answer. Sharp jabs ran up her ankle. *He broke my foot.* Her stomach heaved and she thought she might throw up.

The burly Mexican pulled out a knife and without another word, reached down and slashed it across her forearm, cutting a deep gash. "You tell. Where is she?"

She shrieked and wrapped her other hand around the wound, trying to stop the blood that poured out. The pain was intense. But her mind raced. What to say? She cowered and whispered, "She's at 1400 Lamar Street. 1400 Lamar Street."

"1 - 4 - 0 - 0 Lamar Street?"

"Yes." That was the address of the police station, where Tom worked. *Let the bastard go there. That's where he belongs.* She would alert them he was coming.

He nodded. But instead of leaving, he bent over and swung the knife toward her. She tried to dodge.

The knife sliced deep into her chest.

Brandi screamed. She gasped out a low moan, then fell silent. Her eyes closed and her head slumped to the floor. The Mexican man towered over her, watching. She wasn't breathing. He kicked her in the side. She made no sound.

For a few moments, he did not move. He kicked her again. Still no sound, except his footsteps across the room and the door slamming.

Silence.

Nothing moved, except blood. It ran from her arm onto the rug. It gushed out of the hole in her chest, spreading a red stain over her shirt.

Her right eye opened, no more than a slit. She had heard

the front door close. She could not see the man anywhere. She had been holding her breath and now her lungs burned. She breathed in fresh air and was rewarded by a searing pain in her chest. In spite of her resolve, she let out a moan. Now the left eye opened. Her vision was blurred, nothing in focus. But the bastard was not in the room.

She eased over, tried to get up. Bolts of fire raced through her body. Her foot would not support any weight. Putting pressure on her arm lashed her with throbbing pain. Each breath caused her to wince from the burning in her chest.

I'm bleeding to death.

She could feel her life seeping out, spilling onto the floor. She tried holding her left hand over the wound in her chest and her right hand over the deep cut on her left arm. The bleeding continued.

If I don't get up, I'm going to die. She tried again to sit up, but the pain held her as if she were strapped down. *Ignore the pain. My mind can override the pain. I will get up. I must get up.*

But she could not raise her body off the floor.

To her right a few feet, she saw the cord to the telephone. Groaning through clenched teeth, she managed to reach the wire and pull the phone off the table. It clanged to the floor. Her hand was trembling so much it took her several seconds to dial 9-1-1.

"9 – 1 - 1. What is your emergency?"

Brandi could feel herself fading fast, on the slippery edge of passing out. "Stabbed," she managed. The room began to rotate around her and the lights grew dim. "Dying." The phone slipped from her hand as blackness descended over her.

"Please stay with me. Don't hang up. Ma'am? Are you there? Ma'am?"

Chapter 42

EVEN the traffic couldn't dampen Crystal's spirits. The children were rescued from José the Horrible, as Brandi had christened him. Now, Lucita was on her way. In fact, she was there by now. In Mexico. In all likelihood she was with her two girls at this very moment. A little traffic could not compete with that. Juan Grande would have the kids close by. In her mind's eye, Crystal pictured Lucita, with one small girl straddling each of her legs. Her eyes, black and shiny as jet, would be sparkling with joy.

And the girls. For young children, time passed so slowly. Their separation must have seemed like years. Now they were reunited with their mother. Just the thought of that scene caused Crystal's eyes to mist over.

As usual, she had been stopped on the way out of the office. Now, she was late and Brandi would complain the pizza was getting cold. But then, they'd talk about Lucita while they reheated the pizza in the microwave, and Brandi would be excited Lucita got on the plane with no problems.

She inserted the key in the lock and opened the door. "Sorry I'm late. Got—"

Crystal's eyes went wide. She gasped. Across from her, blood covered a large area of the carpet near the wall. A pizza box lay in front of the couch. The telephone was on the floor.

"Brandi! Brandi!" She raced to one room after another, switching on lights, looking in closets. Near panic, she stood looking around. Brandi's car was parked in its usual spot. The pizza was there. Crystal's legs felt weak and she placed her hand on the wall to steady herself. What to do? What had happened here?

Crystal focused on the blood and her stomach roiled. She swallowed, trying to keep from throwing up. Beside the red stain the telephone lay upside down, the handset tossed to the side. She grabbed it up, ready to dial. She put the phone down and ran into the kitchen. Posted beside the wall phone was a list of numbers. She ran her finger down until she found Tom's work number and quickly punched it in. *Please be there*, she silently prayed. *Please*. A woman answered on the second ring.

"Detective Hawkins, please. It's an emergency." She waited, expecting a voice to come on the phone and say he was not in the office, gone on vacation, couldn't be reached. Leave a message after the tone, or call back tomorrow.

"This is Detective Hawkins."

"Tom, this is Crystal."

"What's wrong?"

"Something's happened to Brandi. She's gone. There's blood all over the floor. Her car's out front." She began crying.

"How much blood?"

"Lots."

"Let me see if 9-1-1 has received a call from there."

Crystal sank onto the couch. *Where could she be*? She jumped up and ran out the front door. Brandi's car was locked, but she could see in. Nothing. She ran to the house on the right, the only neighbor Brandi might visit, or ask for help. When the lady answered the impatient knocking, Crystal tried to sound casual as she asked if Brandi had been over today. No, the lady said. She hadn't seen Brandi in three or four days. Crystal left without giving any explanation.

As she cut across the lawn, she jerked to a stop. There by the oleander bush was a Giuseppe's Pizza cap. Strange. She'd tried to talk the delivery guy out of one several times and he made it very clear they were charged for any cap they gave away—or lost. She walked over and picked it up. Just beyond it, she saw a tennis shoe under the bush. With some trepidation, she lifted the lower branch. The body of a man lay there. He was not breathing. Dried blood caked his chest. Hesitantly, she pressed a finger to his wrist. No pulse. Crystal dropped the branch and ran for the porch.

The phone was ringing as she entered the living room.

"9-1-1 got a call fifteen minutes ago. They took a female stabbing victim to Baylor emergency. I'm heading there now."

"Tom."

"Yes."

"There's a body under the bushes in the front yard."

"A body? Alive or dead?"

"Dead, I think. I don't know. I couldn't see all of him, but he wasn't breathing. I couldn't find a pulse. And the blood on his chest looked — I don't know. No blood was coming out."

"I'll send someone out."

"Do I have to stay here?"

"Do you know anything about the body? Who it is? How it got there? Anything? Anything at all?"

"No."

"Meet me at Baylor emergency."

#

Crystal got to the emergency room first. No one would tell her anything, except they did bring in a young, female victim. She was alive. No, she could not see her. No, they could not tell her anything else.

When Tom got there, his detective status allowed him to get both him and Crystal in to identify the victim. Crystal clamped a hand over her mouth and bit her lip, but her body jerked with silent sobs. Brandi was unconscious and covered in blood.

Monitors beeped and jagged lines raced across a green scope. Tubes were attached to both arms, one trying to replace the blood that had been stolen from Brandi, the other dripping clear liquid from two plastic bags hanging on a silver metal stand. A doctor was adjusting a larger tube, inserted into her mouth, coming from a machine that made an awful, wheezing noise. A respirator. Brandi could not even breathe on her own.

Finally, Tom got the doctor aside. "She has a severe gash across her left forearm. More damaging, she has a deep stab wound to the right chest, most likely from a knife. She's in a hypoxic condition, probably a result of a hemothorax."

"Hold it, Doctor," Tom said. "In English, please."

"Sorry. Blood has invaded the right lung cavity, collapsing the lung. As a result, she is not getting enough oxygen into her blood."

"But she's going to be all right?" asked Tom.

The doctor shook his head slowly. "Right now, we think we have the bleeding under control. We're trying to aspirate the blood from the lung cavity." The young doctor's grey eyes revealed little. "She's lost a great quantity of blood and she has not been conscious since the paramedics found her. The only good thing is the knife, we're assuming it's a knife wound, missed the pulmonary artery. If it had been severed, she would have been dead before she reached the hospital."

"But she is going to be all right?" Tom repeated.

The doctor took a deep breath. "For now, we're just trying to keep her alive. And I must tell you, we are not assured of success. Your friend has been severely traumatized. Essentially, she has only one lung right now. She's lost most of her blood. The prognosis is not good." He shook his head. "I'm truly sorry. We're doing everything we can." He looked from

Tom to Crystal, then turned and walked back to the cubicle that held Brandi.

Now the tears flowed freely down Crystal's cheeks. Tom put his arms around her and for several minutes, she sobbed softly. Finally, she raised her head. "She will live, won't she?"

Tom guided her to a chair in the waiting area. "I'm going to check in. Be back in a little bit." His detective's demeanor kept his voice unemotional, but the wrinkles at his eyes were more pronounced and he blinked too often.

Crystal curled in on herself, winding into a tighter and tighter ball, eyes closed, body shaking. She remembered a doctor once before saying, "We're doing all we can." She was seven years old and her parents lay in an emergency room. They both died. She clutched herself tighter, trying to squeeze out the pain.

#

She was still shaking, trembling, when Tom returned. "Would you like some coffee?"

She looked up to say no, but he was holding a cup for her and she took it. "The pizza delivery boy was dead. The investigative unit is headed out to your house, to see what they can find."

Crystal managed to nod slightly.

Tom lowered his weary, six-foot two-inch frame into the chair next to her. His hazel eyes were bloodshot. "I couldn't find out anything new on Brandi. They're still working on her." He stared at his shoes for a long time. "She's strong. Tough. She'll make it."

His voice sounded hopeful, not confident. She put the coffee down and slowly began to wind into her tight ball again.

In the darkness of her inner sphere, she was totally unaware of the world around her. All she could see was black. Etched black upon black was the image of her parents' bodies being lowered into their graves. Then, Brandi was saying, "Dr. Krupe is a big fat poop," and laughing. And the scene dissolved into Brandi lying on the gurney with tubes in her, and long faces on the nurses. Brandi was telling her to be a wild woman. Then her eyes were fixed on the flat line on the monitor as her granddad lay on the hospital bed. Crystal was screaming, "No. No." But sound could not escape the black hole she had made.

#

She awoke with a start. "What's happening? Where's Brandi?"

Tom had his hand on her shoulder. "They've just taken her up to intensive care. They have her stabilized."

"Stabilized? Is she awake? Can I see her?"

"No. She hasn't regained consciousness. But they at least have her stabilized. Her heartbeat is regular, but very weak. Blood pressure is still low."

"Have they operated on her?"

Tom shook his head. "She isn't strong enough. They think they've got the internal bleeding stopped. For now, at least." His eyes had dark blotches under them and his whole face sagged. Tonight, he looked much older than his thirty-five years. "The collapsed lung can heal by itself—if she gains some strength. So, right now, they don't think they'll operate. That's about all I know." He paused for only a moment. "It's after 3:30. Why don't you go home and get some sleep? I can have someone take you."

"Go home? Oh, no. No. I can't leave her. She's here because of me."

"What do you mean, 'because of you'?"

"He came to kill me. I wasn't there, so he tried to kill Brandi instead." Tears began again. She thought of Juan Grande's words: "You do more than take *niñas*. You make him look weak. José never forget that."

"First, she's not going to die. Okay?" He sat beside Crystal. "She'll pull through. You know how tough she is."

Crystal tried to smile but it didn't come.

"Second, how do you know the guy was after you?"

"I just know. It was the same man who tried to kidnap me in Mexico. I'm sure he got on the plane to Dallas. He's here, looking for me. And he found Brandi." A shiver ran through Crystal's body.

"You don't know that."

"Was it robbery? Did he steal anything? Did they find any reason for the attack?"

"Well," he started, looking across the room, then down at his hands, and finally back at Crystal. "They won't know if anything was taken until you check the place over. But, no, her purse wasn't touched. Nothing obvious missing."

"Somebody wanting to rob the place wouldn't kill a pizza delivery boy just to get in."

For several minutes, neither spoke. Then, Tom said, "If you're right, you might not want to go back to the apartment. Is there some place else you can stay tonight?"

Crystal wiped her face with the back of her hand. "Tom, I'm staying right here. I'm not going anywhere."

Tom nodded. "Okay. Come on; let me walk you up to the waiting room outside intensive care. You might as well be there, so they can find you when she regains consciousness."

They took the elevator and Tom told her what the Criminal Investigation Unit, or CIU, had found thus far. At least four different sets of fingerprints adorned the pizza box. "They'll check those against the delivery person and others who worked at the pizza shop last night. As I said, her purse wasn't bothered. They didn't notice any obvious things missing."

"What about the delivery boy?"

"Dead. Stabbed. So we have two stabbed victims at the same location. The autopsy might give us a clue if the same knife - at this point we're assuming it was a knife - was used. They searched the grounds but didn't find the weapon. There was a bloody fingerprint on the door, probably where the attacker closed the door when he left."

"She hasn't regained consciousness? Does that mean she's in a coma?"

"Technically, yes."

They walked through a small waiting room and up to a nurse's station. Tom introduced Crystal to the nurse.

When they were back in the waiting room, Tom said, "Since you insist on staying, I'm going to run down and see how they're doing on the evidence. I'm betting we've got a good set of prints. And when Brandi wakes up and can identify him, we're going to lock him away forever."

"I can identify him right now."

Tom studied her for a long minute. "Try to get some sleep on the couch there. I'll be back in a couple of hours." He started to leave, but stopped. "Do *not* blame yourself. Even if the bastard was looking for you, he's the one who stabbed Brandi. Not you. Nobody made him stab her. And I guarantee we will catch him."

Crystal stretched out on the couch and tried to sleep, but her mind kept flashing scenes of all the funerals she had ever attended, all the dead people she had seen. And in between, scenes of Brandi lying on the gurney with tubes running in and blood running out. She did not know whether she was asleep or not. She only knew she was not resting.

Tom returned at 8:20. Crystal was sitting up, sipping coffee out of a paper cup.

"How is she?" he asked.

"No change. They let me go in for a minute while a nurse

checked Brandi's IV's." Tears welled in her eyes. "It was hard to tell she's alive."

"Her body is using all its energy to recover. Nothing wasted on external things. Brandi's smart. She's going to survive."

Crystal thought he smiled a little too brightly. His voice was too upbeat. He hoped Brandi survived. But did he believe it? The nurses remained very guarded. The most positive thing they told Crystal was that Brandi was stabilized. Not getting better. Not making progress. Not even a half-hearted, "She'll pull through," or, "These things take time." Brandi was not going downhill; she was already at the bottom.

"The bloody finger print on the door matches one of the prints on the pizza box," Tom said. "They're running some tests now to prove the blood on the door is Brandi's. And someone is tracking down the people from the pizza place, to sort out the other prints on the box." He drank some coffee. "Who knows when the autopsy on the delivery boy will be done? But, the CIU guys are convinced the wounds on the boy were made by a knife and will match those on Brandi."

"Tom, I don't care right now. I just want Brandi to wake up and be all right. Then, I'll worry about catching the ..." She wasn't certain what she wanted to call the man who had left her best friend at death's doorstep.

"Why don't you go get some rest? I'll stay here. I'll call you the minute Brandi regains consciousness."

Crystal's lifeless eyes stared without seeing. "Go where? I can't go back and sleep at the apartment."

"Right." He nodded. "Besides, it's still a crime scene. They wouldn't want you rummaging around in there anyway." He took another sip of coffee. "How about your grandmother's? If any place can relax you, The Park can."

She closed her eyes for a minute and rubbed her forehead with the heel of her hand. She opened her eyes. "I'll think about it—if you're going to be here. Right now, I think I'll run by IRS. I need to fill Mark in on what's happened. I've been gone so much lately, and now ..." Her voice trailed off. She remained just a word or a thought away from tears.

"He'll understand."

"I know he will. But I need to at least report in, tell him what's going on. Besides, he'll want to know about Brandi. I should have called him hours ago. I'll be back in a little bit."

She got up to leave.

"Crystal. If you're right about this guy really being after you, he's still out there. Watch yourself. Don't take any chances."

She nodded. "Promise me you'll call the minute there's any change?"

Tom put a hand over his heart. "Promise."

"You've got my cell number?"

"I've got your home number, your cell number, the IRS number, and The Park. I'll call the instant I know anything."

#

As soon as Crystal got to Intelligent Retrieval Services, she went to the Ladies Room, washed her face, and applied some lipstick. Her hair was a mess and her clothes looked like they had been slept in, which of course they had.

She told Mark about the attack on Brandi, steeling herself, knowing how difficult it would be to describe what had happened. Even so, she broke down and for several minutes she could not continue.

Mark sat in stunned silence. He did not press her. He went around the desk, put his arm around Crystal and pulled her in close.

Finally, she was able to go on, and related what little the doctor and nurses had told her. Brandi was still in a coma and the hospital was making no predictions.

"How is Tom taking it?"

"Better than I am. At least on the outside. He sounds confident she'll pull through. He says the words. I think he's pretty shaken up. He's always so strong, and of course, he's used to seeing acts of violence and victims."

"But this is Brandi."

"Yes. He still sounds like a cop. But he doesn't look like a cop, you know, unemotional, uninvolved. I think inside he's crying."

"You spent the night at the hospital? Have you eaten anything? Other than coffee?"

She shook her head.

"Okay. Let's go get you something to eat. You can tell me anything else you want to, but I know how hard this is for you. If it's too painful, you don't have to talk about it. Outside the office I can hold you closer."

#

Crystal's group had barely left the office when Sally came in and slumped in a chair. "I heard something about Brandi being attacked. What happened?"

Once more, Crystal had to relive the details. She stopped a few times to compose herself, but this time she got through it without breaking down. Was she becoming calloused? Did she feel less? Or was she just coming to terms with what had happened?

Crystal made one last stop by Mark's office, telling him she was going to the hospital. She might be late coming in tomorrow. Mark told her to take whatever time she needed. And, of course, he would check with Tom on Brandi's progress.

Crystal stopped by the ladies' room and at 4:35, she left IRS, heading for her car.

Mark burst out the door, JT right behind him. "Crystal," he yelled. "Come back for a second."

Crystal turned just as a shot rang out. She fell to the ground.

Chapter 43

MARK and JT each grabbed one of Crystal's arms and carried her inside the building.

"Are you all right?" Mark asked. "Are you hit?"

"I, ah, I think I'm Okay." Her voice was shaky. "It scared me and I fell. But I don't think I was hit."

Mark looked through the glass door, down the block. "JT, make sure she's not hurt. Call 9-1-1. I'll meet you in my office in a few minutes."

"Where are you going?" Crystal asked.

But he was gone.

#

Less than five minutes later, a police car skidded to a stop and two officers rushed into the building. They took statements from Crystal and JT separately then went outside to check the area .

"Let's get a drink and wait in Mark's office," Crystal suggested.

Twenty minutes later, Mark walked into his office, Dr Pepper in hand. "How are you feeling, Crystal?"

"I'm okay. I wasn't hit, but I actually felt the shock wave," Crystal said. "That was frightening." She tried a smile, but it didn't work. *The worst part was somebody tried to shoot me.* "Did you find anything?"

"Not much. The shooter was on the roof of the Hatley

building. He left a shell casing and a few scratches in the gravel. Nothing else. Not a candy wrapper, or a drink cup, or a business card. But from the marks in the gravel, I'd say he'd been there awhile. Waiting for you."

Crystal shivered. "Thanks for that image. The police have already been here, taken our statements and said they were going to check around outside."

"Yeah. I talked with them. They found the slug hanging from a brick. Too smashed to do them much good. I found a shell casing on the roof of the Hatley building and gave them that. That's about it. They said they were going to check the Hatley building, but they won't find anything there"

Mark picked up the telephone and dialed. "Hi. How's Brandi?" He listened and then repeated to Crystal that Brandi had not come out of the coma. "Tom, someone just took a shot at Crystal." He paused. "No, just missed. Luckily, she turned just as the shooter fired." Again, he waited. "Yeah. We called 9-1-1. Police have already been here and taken statements. I talked with them. Davidson and Bentley." He listened a moment. "At IRS." Mark smiled encouragement to Crystal. "Good. We'll be here."

Crystal asked, "Glad you came out the door and called me. What were you going to say?"

"Oh, in all the confusion, I completely forgot. I just got a call from Mexico. Lucita and her children are together. I can't tell you where they are. That is . . ." He looked down, and a slight pink colored his cheeks. "I *can* tell you they are not in Puerto Vallarta or San Sebastian or Santiago. And probably never will be. The important thing is, they're together. The girls and mother are all in good shape and happy."

Crystal's eyes glistened as she grinned, afraid if she spoke, she would lose all control of her emotions.

"Carlotta found a nice little house for them and Juan has lined up a good job for Lucita. Oh, and Carlotta has sent a

FedEx letter to you. "

Crystal looked at JT. "That's probably your passport." Crystal put her arms around Mark and JT and squeezed. "Thank you both. Those poor children would never have seen their mother if you hadn't helped."

"You deserve the credit. Juan said—I believe I'm quoting him exactly— 'She is tough, like burro'." Mark nodded once toward Crystal. "You're the one who made it happen."

"No. Juan Grande. I will love him forever for what he did."

"Well, don't tell Carlotta. She might just kill him," Mark said with a laugh. "I've never seen it, but Juan tells me she has a temper like a firecracker."

JT smiled.

Crystal tried. But instead, she shivered. *Someone tried to kill mer. And Brandi.*

#

It was a little after five when Tom arrived. "I think this guy meant to kill you, just as he did Brandi."

"Thanks. I needed to hear that," Crystal said.

"I talked with Bentley, one of the officers that responded to the 9-1-1 call. He said it was a two twenty-three. That was not a warning shot. You need to go away until we get this guy in jail."

Crystal took a deep breath. "When will that be? Do you have anything to go on? Will the slug or the thing Mark found help?"

Tom hung his head down, as if studying the floor, then shook his head and looked up, directly into Crystal's eyes. "Not much. The slug, even the shell casing, is probably useless, as far as catching the guy. We *have* isolated the fingerprints on the pizza box that probably belong to the perp. Haven't gotten an

ID on those yet, which surprises me. But I'm sure we will. When Brandi wakes up, we'll have her identification of him." He rubbed his nose. "We'll get him, Crystal. I promise. In the meantime, you've got to stay safe."

"Maybe I'll go to The Park tonight."

"Good. Plan on staying there a few days. Mark?"

"Right. Stay there until the police wrap this up."

Crystal started to protest, but Mark cut her off. "Crystal, you're no good to IRS dead. Besides, if he shot you, JT wouldn't be any good either. Nor Sally. The best thing you can do for IRS is stay alive. And right now, that means getting out of town. That's an order from your boss." He put his arm on her shoulder. "Now, I know you. You'll have your portable with you. So, if you want to take some work along, I wouldn't stop you."

"Thank you, Mark. But Brandi—"

"*I'm* keeping an eye on Brandi," Tom said. "I'll guarantee she's safe from further harm. And I'll let you know the moment there's any change. Besides, I'm convinced now: *you* are the real target. So, go to The Park."

"Can I get some clothes from the apartment?"

"I'll follow you there, check the place out, make sure it's safe. The crime-scene people won't be too happy about it, but you deserve some creature comforts."

"Give my best to Eula," Mark said as Crystal and Tom left.

#

Forty minutes later, Crystal had packed a small suitcase. "You're going back to the hospital now?" she asked. Tom nodded. "Call me on my cell phone as soon as you get a report."

Tom agreed and they left, locking the house.

During the drive to the Park, Crystal's mind flitted between Brandi and her own brush with death. The unplanned timing of Mark's calling her probably saved her life. She got only a scrape on her knees, not a hole in her chest. Brandi, a bystander, was locked in a battle with the grim reaper. The doctors still offered no words of encouragement. How unfair could life be?

Crystal slammed her hand against the steering wheel. All of this precipitated because one person wanted to make a slave of another. "I hate that man," she screamed.

She had never seen José de Allende, hoped she never would. Did he look like the devil? Or just a successful businessman, jaunty in an embroidered shirt, tight black pants, and a colorful sombrero, sitting on a beautiful, buckskin stallion? Could you tell a depraved person by looking at him?

#

Crystal walked in the kitchen and dropped her overnight bag on the floor. She wrapped her arms around her Nana and gave her a big hug. Over her grandmother's shoulder, Crystal saw Rosa come in from the dining room. "Hi, Rosa."

Eula hugged her granddaughter then gave her a playful swat on the bottom. "You left here to rescue Lucita, and I haven't heard a word since. If Mark hadn't called, I wouldn't even know about Brandi. How's she doing?"

"Still no change. The doctors are very guarded in their comments. They say stock phrases that don't mean a thing. I'm so scared, Nana. What if she doesn't make it?"

"Take a more positive attitude. How about, I hope she's awake and ready to go home when I get back to Dallas? She's a tough cookie. Have they caught the snake that stabbed her?"

"No. Not yet." Crystal teetered on the verge of tears.

Eula gave her a hug. "She'll make it. Now, you've been gone five days. What's happened about Lucita?"

"Four days."

"Heavens to Betsy, gal, Rosa and I are in on this too. Even

two days is too long. What's going on?"

"Lucita has her girls now. I'll fill you in on all the detail while we eat."

"Don't know why, but I made your favorites: fried catfish, fried okra, and fried corn on the cob. And fried apricot pies for dessert."

"Oh, Nana, I really need that tonight."

"You bring your fancy camera?" Eula asked.

"It's in my bag."

"Why don't ya get it? Mine's on the fritz and I haven't gotten a single decent picture of Rosa." Crystal dug her camera out of the bag while Eula and Rosa put dinner on the table.

The three women sat down and ladled food onto their plates. Eula held up her hand. "Tonight's special; so if you don't mind." She bowed her head and said, "Thanks, Lord, for getting that mother and her kids back together. And for watching over Crystal. And please help Brandi recover quickly. Amen." She looked up. "Okay. Now, let's show Rosa how to eat catfish."

Crystal picked up a squeeze bottle. "Nana cheats a little, Rosa. We ought to have fresh lemons."

"This is a lot easier," said Eula.

"Just squeeze some lemon juice on the catfish. Improves the flavor." Crystal passed the bottle to Rosa.

The Mexican woman turned the bottle over and gave it a hard squeeze. The juice shot out, drenching not only the fish, but the corn, okra and part of the table as well. "Oh. I am sorry."

"Not to worry," said Eula. "It'll be good on all that stuff."

Dinner conversation consisted of Eula asking for details on Lucita's escape and Crystal answering in between bites. Rosa paid close attention, but said nothing until Crystal announced that Lucita and the girls were together in Mexico, in their own house, this very night.

"*Donde??*"

"I don't know where. For safety they aren't telling anybody."

"You girls go ahead and finish up. I'm going to roll out the dough for the fried pies." Eula walked into the kitchen. "But you got to speak up so's I can hear what you're talking about. And get a couple a pictures of Rosa, Crystal."

Rosa helped herself to another piece of fish and Crystal picked up the camera. "Show us your beautiful smile, Rosa," Crystal said with a laugh.

She raised the camera. A board creaked. She looked toward the entryway by the back door.

Crystal stopped breathing.

Not ten feet away, glaring at her, stood Cèsar Aquilar.

Chapter 44

HIS eyes were like smudge pots, dark and smoldering, radiating anger from beneath overgrown eyebrows. His mouth was clamped shut, the muscles in his jaw tense, and his face resembled a huge beet. His wide body filled the doorway, his arms like elephant trunks, his barrel chest rising and falling slowly as he breathed. His right hand gripped a deadly knife.

Was it the same knife he had used to stab Brandi?

Rosa gasped softly. He turned his focus from Crystal to Rosa and a slight smirk snaked across his face.

Cèsar's gaze swept the room. He started toward Crystal. She wanted to run, but could not get out of the chair in time. As he reached the corner of the table, his hand came up, positioning the knife level with Crystal's heart.

Her hands shook as she thrust the camera toward him and pressed the button. The flash erupted only a foot from his eyes, the brilliant light blinding him. His hand shot up but the light had already done its damage. He slashed out with the knife, striking the camera and knocking it from Crystal's hands. It clattered to the floor as he swung the dagger again, missing Crystal by less than an inch. He blinked rapidly, while hacking back and forth with the deadly stiletto.

Crystal ducked and turned. Barely avoiding the blade, she struggled to scoot the chair back from the table. The chair stayed in place, its legs now caught in the rug. He stopped swinging the knife and looked at her. His vision has returned.

Crystal scanned the table for anything to defend herself.

A fork? A spoon? She grabbed the bottle of lemon juice, jerked it up, and squeezed with both hands as hard as she could. Lemon juice sprayed into Cèsar's eyes, and on his face. He inhaled sharply, sucking the acidic liquid into his nose and mouth.

Gagging, unable to see, he dropped the knife. Both hands rubbed his eyes. He staggered back a step, still choking.

Eula rushed out of the kitchen carrying a maple rolling pin. She raised her arm and hit him on the head with the heavy hardwood utensil. He dropped to the floor and lay there as still as death.

"I always wanted to do that," she said. "But was afraid I'd kill somebody. Guess this happened too quick to worry about anything 'cept this rattlesnake and his knife. So I conked him." She got down on her knees and felt along the side of his neck. "Blood's still flowing. Get some rope and let's hogtie this slop chaser."

Crystal ran to the shed and came back with a coil of rope. Rosa had picked up the knife. The menacing look in her eyes worried Crystal.

"Here, Rosa. Let me take that. The police will want it."

Rosa's eyes narrowed. The muscles in her jaw tightened. Her body leaned slightly toward the unconscious man. She shifted the knife in her hand.

Eula glanced up at the young woman as she took a step closer. "Rosa, let me have the knife so's I can cut this rope."

Rosa looked at Eula kneeling on the floor, her hand reaching for the weapon. Without a word, Rosa handed the knife to Eula.

"Looks like he could go bear hunting with a stick," said Eula as she started tying his hands behind his back. When she felt she had a good knot, she tied his feet together. Then, she pulled his feet up behind his back and ran a rope between them and his wrists. "Crystal, call Billy Goat and tell him we got a varmint here and the animal control people won't take him. I'm going to sit here with my rolling pin, and if he moves, I'll whack him again."

#

Cèsar opened his eyes and looked around. He tested the ropes. The more he struggled, the tighter the ropes bound his hands and feet. Eula sat a few feet away, dangling the rolling pin from one hand. "Don't wiggle too much or I'll slap you upside the head." She pointed the heavy wooden kitchen tool at him. He growled deep in his throat, but said nothing.

Rosa watched from a distance, hatred flashing in her dark eyes.

Thirty minutes later, Bill Glothe, the county sheriff, arrived with his deputy, whom he introduced simply as Slim. The sheriff was short and stocky, with a face that looked like it had been left out in the rain. Ears that matched his girth peeked out from grey hair a little too long for a police officer. Except for the patch on his shoulder, his attire could have passed for a ranch hand. "What've you got here, Eula?"

"Varmint sneaked in the back door and tried to kill Crystal. And I reckon he would have done the same to Rosa. Me too, if I'd let him."

Glothe looked at the rolling pin, still in Eula's hand. "And you, ah, subdued him?"

"Damn straight. 'Course Crystal softened him up for me."

Glothe bent down and looked into Cèsar's face, then straightened up. "Boy, his eyes look right mean."

"Well, Crystal shot him in the eyes with some lemon juice." She laughed.

"That'd slow you down all right. Know why he picked on you women?"

Crystal answered, "I think his name is Cèsar Aquilar and he came up from Mexico to kill me. I think, I'm almost positive, he stabbed Brandi—that's my housemate—last . . . yesterday. She's still in a coma at Baylor Hospital in Dallas."

The sheriff cocked his head and pulled his bushy, grey eyebrows down, half covering his eyes. "Crystal, I've known you since you was knee-high to a pup. I just can't imagine anybody wanting to kill you, much less traveling all the way up from Mexico to do it."

"It's a long story. And I'll fill you in some Sunday when Nana fixes dinner for you. But, if you can take his finger prints and send them to Tom Hawkins, I think the Dallas police will want to take him off your hands."

"Tom Hawkins? That the detective I met last year?"

"Same one."

"This the knife he threatened you with?" Bill picked up the knife and looked at it.

"Yes. And you can see where he hit the camera I was holding." Crystal showed the camera to the sheriff.

"Well, we'll take the trash out for you, Eula. First thing in the morning, I'll get those prints faxed in to Dallas. I'd be obliged if they come get him. Save me a lot of time and trouble. Food, too."

#

After Bill Glothe and Slim left with Cèsar, Crystal called the hospital. The switchboard transferred her a few times until they finally found Tom.

"How is she?"

"Not much change. Actually, the doctor almost said something encouraging tonight. Her vitals are a little stronger. They've taken her off the ventilator and removed the tube from her mouth. The endotracheal tube. How about that? You didn't think I knew that, did you? 'Course, I didn't an hour ago."

"What's that mean? Must be good, right?"

"Means she's breathing on her own now and that's good. But she hasn't come out of the coma—yet. They let me go in and see her for a few minutes. I thought her eyelids moved a little bit, but the nurse didn't see it."

"I think we caught the man who stabbed her."

"*What*? You did *what*? We who? Where are you? I thought you went to The Park."

Crystal explained the events of the evening. "I'm positive it's the guy. Bill Glothe, you remember he's the sheriff here, he's going to send you fingerprints in the morning."

"Damn. How did he find you at The Park?"

"No idea. I mean, he must have followed me out here. Maybe saw me when I got clothes at the apartment. All I know is, he came charging in with a nasty-looking knife in his hand."

"You're something else, Crystal. When are you coming back?"

"Tomorrow. With Cèsar captured, I'm feeling better already."

"Good. You can stand watch here, if I have to go get this Cèsar person."

Crystal hung up and turned to Eula. "How about those fried apricot pies you promised?"

"Anybody still interested, I can whip 'em up."

Crystal took Rosa's hand and started for the kitchen.

"We're both interested. You can work up an appetite capturing big, bad killers." Crystal laughed a little, but she didn't feel all that cheery.

#

The three sat around the kitchen table, eating the hot pies. Rosa said little, her jet black eyes showing no spark, no joy. Finally, Eula asked Rosa what she thought about Cèsar.

"I like him better dead."

Eula raised her eyebrows and stopped chewing. "Well, that's clear enough. Why?"

"He one of Jose's men who let my Miguel die. I hope he never get out of prison."

"I can agree to that completely," Crystal said with a nod. "And if Brandi dies, I hope he gets the death penalty." Her eyes misted over.

"You told Tom you'd be back tomorrow. You're leaving so quickly?" Eula asked.

"Got to, Nana. Brandi's still in a coma. I feel so bad. She got stabbed because of me. He was after me and Brandi just happened to be in the way." The high of capturing Cèsar had evaporated.

"Now, don't you go blaming yourself, Crystal. That animal stabbed her. You didn't make him. He didn't have to. He just did. Like a rattlesnake. Don't you take his blame."

Crystal nodded. But she did feel responsible for Brandi's problems. And if she died, . . .

Chapter 45

CRYSTAL spent Saturday and Saturday night in the hospital waiting room. On Sunday, Tom told her the CIU guys had removed their tape and she was free to use her apartment again. So while Tom stayed at the hospital, Crystal returned to her apartment briefly to shower, change clothes, and catch a quick cat-nap.

Now, the nurses let Crystal go into Brandi's room for short periods. Crystal would sit next to the bed, hold Brandi's hand, and talk to her. She told her about capturing Cèsar and how Bill Glothe had sent his fingerprints to Dallas. The prints matched what the police had found on the pizza box, plus the one bloody print on the door.

She explained how Tom had wanted to go himself to bring Cèsar back to Dallas, but Tom's captain wouldn't let him. Crystal laughed lightly, saying the captain was afraid Tom might kill Cèsar before getting back to the Dallas jail. She patted Brandi's hand and said the police had a good case, airtight if Brandi would wake up and identify Cèsar. The danger was gone. She could wake up now. They could go back to the apartment and feel safe.

Whenever a nurse came in and caught her talking to Brandi, Crystal felt a little foolish. But one of the nurses told her it really helped to talk to patients, even if it appeared they couldn't hear you. "The mind is aware of things, even if the patient appears not to hear. A lot of us now believe that a baby picks up a lot from what's said while it's still in the womb. You go ahead and talk to her. As her mentation gets lighter, she might even be able to respond to commands."

After that, Crystal talked to Brandi about everything: what was happening in the news, what Eula and Rosa were doing, and how much Tom missed her.

Tom held Brandi's hand too, but he never said anything to her—at least when Crystal was in the room.

#

Monday morning, Tom asked Crystal to accompany him to police headquarters, where she was introduced to an assistant district attorney, Lisa Swanner, and a member from the Mexican Consulate.

"This is a one-way window. He cannot see you," said Swanner. "Detective Hawkins tells us you know this man. Take a close look and then tell us what you can about him."

Even with Cèsar locked up, a chill ran down Crystal's back and her arms tingled. "His name is Cèsar. He's the man who attacked me with a knife."

"Can you tell us his last name?"

Crystal screwed up her face trying to bring the name into focus. "I can't think of it right now. But I'm sure it will come to me. Juan ... ." She stopped. Juan Grande would not want his name mentioned unless absolutely necessary.

They looked at her expectantly.

"His name will come to me. Just give me a little time."

"How do you know him?" asked the older, white-haired man from the Consulate.

"I was in Mexico a couple of weeks ago, and he tried to abduct me off the street, maybe twice. Then—"

"Why would he do that?" The Mexican asked.

She didn't want to say she was trying to abduct Mexican children. She decided to only hint at the truth. "I was trying to reunite some children with their mother. I believe the man who held the children illegally, a José de Allende in San Sebastian, wanted Cèsar to keep me from helping the children. Allende is not the father. Not a relative at all."

She fidgeted with her purse and had trouble looking the man in the face. "But, more important, we know from the fingerprints that he stabbed my roommate."

"Were you there?" the Mexican asked.

"No, but the fingerprints—"

"Please, just tell us what you *personally* experienced."

Crystal took a deep breath, trying to settle her nerves. The Consulate official wasn't conducting the investigation, wouldn't try the case. Why didn't he butt out? "He followed me to The Park, and—"

"The Park?"

Crystal wanted to yell at him to quit interrupting her, but refrained. "He followed me to my grandmother's house in East Texas, near the town of Wooden Nickel. He came into the house without knocking or anything, and tried to kill me with a knife."

"And what happened?" asked Swanner.

She thought how best to put it. "We subdued him, and held him until the police arrived and took him to jail."

The man from the Consulate raised his silver eyebrows and cocked his head slightly. "He looks like a formidable man. Who is 'We' and how did you ... ah ... subdue him?"

Crystal again thought out her answer before responding. "I squirted some lemon juice in his eyes just as he was about to stab me. Then my grandmother hit him on the head with a rolling pin."

"A rolling pin?" The assistant DA broke out laughing. "I thought that only happened on TV."

The man from the Consulate did not laugh. "You are

certain this is the man?"

"Absolutely." She tilted her head to one side, then smiled. "Aquilar. Cèsar Aquilar. That's his name. And José Rodriquez de Allende's hacienda is located in San Sebastian del Oeste."

"Are you willing to testify at trial?" asked the assistant DA.

"Yes. I certainly will testify that he came into my grandmother's house and tried to stab me. He swung a knife at me several times. The police have the knife. If it hadn't been for the lemon juice, I'd probably be dead now."

"Lemon juice?" The ADA frowned, two vertical lines forming between her blond eyebrows.

"Was all I could find. We'd put it on the catfish we were having for dinner."

Tom, the ADA, and the man from the Mexican Consulate excused themselves and walked some distance away to confer. Crystal could not hear what they were saying. But at one point, Tom's voice rose and Crystal was certain he said, "Not if Brandi dies."

Chapter 46

HUNTER Blackwood studied the man in front of him. "I have heard the Moore woman is still walking around."

Eric Lithgow shifted his weight from one foot to the other and looked at the front edge of Blackwood's desk. His gaze moved to Blackwood, then quickly back to the desktop. "Took me awhile to find her. Then she went to Mexico. She's back now."

"And you had a shot at her and missed."

Eric's head jerked up. "How ... Who told you that?"

Blackwood puffed on his cigar, but said nothing.

"Bad luck. Just as I squeezed off a round, the bitch moved."

A thin smirk appeared on Blackwood's face. "Perhaps you should ask her to hold up a bull's-eye and be very still. You could only get off one shot?"

"Well, ah, this guy came out."

"He had a gun? He started shooting at you? He was a policeman?"

"Ah, no." Eric shifted again. Moisture began to form on his upper lip. "I'll cap the bitch."

"When?"

"Soon. I'll try to find her tomorrow."

Blackwood stared at the man for a full minute. *Let the stupid bastard sweat.* "Do I need to get someone else, someone who can handle a woman? Even if she moves?"

"No sir, Mr. Blackwood. I can do her." A drop of sweat rolled down his chin and he brushed it off with the back of his hand.

"Good. Good-bye."

"Ah, Mr. Blackwood. Could I get a couple a lines?" Blackwood looked up from the paper. Eric tried a small laugh. "Might help me get a better shot at her. You know, steady my hands." He grinned nervously.

"When I think you need something to steady your hands, you'll be out. Finished. For good." He returned his attention to the paper in his hand.

Eric turned and slouched out of the room, closing the door very quietly.

Chapter 47

TOM sat hunched over in the small car, driving Crystal back to the hospital. He had refused to say anything until they were out of the parking lot.

"Okay. What was that all about?" Crystal asked. "What were the ADA and the man from the Mexican Consulate talking about?"

"The Consulate guy was there because we have locked up one of his citizens. And we may execute him, which they wouldn't like. You really got the guy excited, though, when you mentioned José de Allende."

"They know him?"

Tom grinned and nodded. "That they do. They've been after him, well, the *Federáles* have, for a long time. But he's too well connected — and protected. Nothing goes back to him directly. Always a lot of people in between. You say Cèsar is a direct link. They want us to work with them, cut him a deal if he can give them enough to get old Mexican Joe."

"What about the pizza deliveryman?"

"Yeah. So far, we only have circumstantial evidence. Fingerprints on the pizza box. Nothing actually on the body. But I'm sure we'll turn up something to strap Cèsar to that murder."

Crystal looked straight ahead and bit her lower lip. "I heard you say something about Brandi."

"Yeah." His voice took on a hard edge. "I said plain and

simple, if she dies, Cèsar gets the needle. No dealing."

"What did the ADA say? I mean, you can't—"

"No, *I* can't. But I can twist Swanner's arm, and she knows it."

"You go out with her?"

An embarrassed grin made its way across Tom's face. "Yeah. Before Brandi. We're still friends. She knows Brandi."

"But Brandi's not going to die."

"No."

Tom clenched his teeth. Stress lines formed around his hazel eyes. His worry invaded her, casting a chill on her heart. For four days now, whenever she closed her eyes, she saw red spots, patches of blood on the living room floor.

The doctors were still very guarded. Ninety-six hours, and still Brandi was in a coma. They were making no predictions, no guesses, no suggestions, no hope as to when she might regain consciousness. They said she *might*, she *could*, but never *she would*.

Crystal felt her mind losing its grip on the belief that Brandi would recover.

#

Brandi still remained in a coma. A tube remained in her nose, down her throat, into her stomach. IV's dripped antibiotics and nutrients and hydration into Brandi's arms. Her left foot was in a soft cast. The nurses said Crystal and Tom could sit and talk to her as long as they wanted. Tom stayed nearly an hour before returning to work. Crystal left only long enough to down a cup of soup in the hospital cafeteria.

Now, she was back, talking to Brandi, just as if she could hear, telling her about how she and Nana and Rosa had captured Cèsar. Crystal even laughed when she explained how she shot the lemon juice in his eyes, and how Nana came in wielding the rolling pin like Marjorie Maine in some movie. Crystal told about the rifle shot he took at her when she was coming out of IRS and how Mark had chased the shooter.

"He was lucky the guy didn't stay and shoot him. But you know Mark. Still a little of the bull rider in him. But that's all over with now. All we've got to worry about is getting you back in good shape."

She gently rubbed Brandi's hand and looked out the window, looking for a sunny day, trying to keep hope alive.

"Not . . . over."

Crystal jumped and her heart skipped a beat. Brandi's eyes were closed, her breathing shallow but steady. Someone had spoken, and yet no one was in the room but her and Brandi. She got up and walked to the door. She searched the hall in both directions. The only person she could see was the on-duty nurse, sitting in the nurses' station down the hall. He was pecking at the keyboard of the computer, intent on the task at hand. It couldn't have been him. Besides, it sounded like Brandi. Well, not exactly.

She walked back into the room and looked at Brandi. "Did you say something? Please tell me you said something." Once again, she felt foolish. Crystal sat down and put her hand in Brandi's. "If you can hear me, just squeeze my hand."

She waited, trying to will her roommate to squeeze her hand. Even the slightest pressure would be fantastic, a positive sign that Brandi could hear her, really would get better. But no squeeze came.

She had been wishing so hard that Brandi would wake up, look at her, speak to her. Could she have imagined that Brandi had spoken? She remembered yesterday, thinking that Brandi's eyelids had fluttered. She had strained, trying by force of will to help Brandi open her eyes. Nothing happened. Then she wasn't sure whether the eyelids had moved or not.

Maybe she was hearing her own mind projecting words

on the comatose body. But if that were the case, it should have been something she would understand, something that made sense.

Had she heard anything? She didn't know. Somber reality replaced the euphoria of just minutes ago. But Crystal clung to the idea that Brandi had spoken to her. Hope was all she had right now.

Brandi's mouth opened. "Not . . . over."

Crystal could not remember such joy. This time she had seen Brandi's mouth form the faint, slow words. The tube down her throat made the words and the voice strange, almost unintelligible. They did not sound like Brandi, but her mouth had moved. She had spoken. The words may not have meant anything, but she had spoken. Crystal did not care if it meant anything or not.

She turned and moved closer to the bed, still holding Brandi's hand. She had to restrain herself from hugging the slight figure before her.

"Oh, Brandi. I was so scared. I kept telling myself you'd be okay, get better, and things would be like they were before. But, then . . ." Crystal began to cry in spite of her joy. "I love you. And so does Tom. He's been here a lot. He's gone back to work right now, but he's been here and is worried sick about you. 'Course you know how he is, the macho man who can't be afraid. But he was, Brandi. He was scared to death you weren't going to pull through. We both were."

Tears streamed down Crystal's face, curving around a big smile, as she squeezed her roommate's hand. And then, she felt a slight bit of pressure on her hand. She squeezed back and laid her head against Brandi's arm. "Take your time," Crystal whispered. "Take all the time you need. Don't force yourself. I'm here. I'll be here, as long as it takes."

When a nurse came in to check Brandi's vital signs. Crystal told her about Brandi speaking. The nurse simply raised her penciled eyebrows and continued to write on the chart. As she left the room she said, "Don't get your hopes up. Friends and family believe the patient wakes up or speaks or looks at them, when she didn't. These things sometimes take weeks. Sometimes, the patient never wakes up."

Crystal started to object, but the nurse was gone and the door was closed. Her euphoria disappeared, swept away by the cold, harsh words. Her eyes glazed over and tears wanted to run. *Sometimes, the patient never wakes up.* Why had the nurse said that?

"Because she was not here", a tiny voice whispered in Crystal's mind.

Crystal blinked, refocusing. The nurse was not here, but Crystal was. She *had* heard Brandi speak.

Crystal curled her mouth up, trying to smile. She did not imagine it. Brandi had spoken.

#

A little after 6:00, Crystal went to the hospital's cafeteria, ordered a sandwich, and a Dr Pepper and took them back to Brandi's room. While she ate, she talked to the unconscious figure in front of her.

"I was starving. I didn't eat much last night, skipped breakfast this morning and had only a cup of soup at lunch. Maybe that's why the hospital sandwich tasted so good. It isn't what --"

"I'm ... hungry ... too." Brandi's eyes opened half way.

Crystal dropped the drink. It hit the floor and splashed up her legs, but she didn't even notice. She pressed Brandi's hand between both of her own and kissed it. She trembled as tears ran freely. "Oh Brandi, thank God you're awake. I've been so worried." Sobs took over and she could no longer speak. She put her head next to her roommate's and let her fears run out on the pillow.

Finally, the shaking subsided and Crystal sat up. She brushed her hand lightly across Brandi's hair. "What can I do for you? Do you want anything?"

"Drink . . . something . . . to . . . eat." Crystal could tell each word required an effort. "Feel like ... haven't ... eaten ... in two days."

"You haven't. In fact, you haven't had any real food in four days. Do you remember what happened?" Crystal pressed the buzzer for the nurse.

Brandi stared into space for a moment. "Not really." She exhaled, as if exhausted by speaking those two words. "Pizza man ... came in." Deep lines formed across her forehead and she drew her lips into a thin line. "Hit me."

She closed her eyes and for several minutes said nothing. She squeezed her eyes tighter. Crystal continued to rub her fingers gently over Brandi's hand. Finally, she opened her eyes. "I remember." Another pause. "Stabbed." She looked at the tubes in her left hand, raised her right hand to touch the tubes coming out of her nose. "Hospital?"

"Yes."

When the nurse came, Crystal repeated Brandi's request for food. The nurse checked Brandi's pulse, blood pressure, and wrote on the chart attached to the foot of the bed. When the nurse finished, she left, returning shortly with a glass of ice chips which she handed to Crystal.

"Let her take these and melt them in her mouth. She can have as many as she wants."

"She wanted something to eat," said Crystal.

"Let's see how this goes. Then, we'll get her some juice. We don't want to shock her system."

Half an hour later, the nurse returned, removed the tube from Brandi's nose and left some apple juice. When Brandi asked about some solid food, the nurse smiled and said, "We're probably not quite ready for solid food yet. I've talked with your doctor. Normally, he wants to see you first, but I'll see what I can do."

Tom arrived a little later and could hardly contain himself. His eyes danced. He sat down, stood up, patted Brandi's arm, kissed her cheek.

"I'll be here all night. Until about 7:00 in the morning. Maybe longer. I just might not leave until I can take this woman home."

"'Then, I think I'll run along, give you two some time together." Crystal looked very sternly at Tom. "But no hanky-panky here in the hospital. Okay?"

"Promise. Besides, if that big, red-headed nurse caught us, she'd throw me out the window. I don't think she likes me even a little bit."

#

Crystal arrived back at the hospital a little after 9:30 the next morning. She had stopped by IRS, talked with her group briefly, given Mark an update on Brandi, then headed for the hospital.

Brandi was awake and feeling much better. She had slept well during the night and been given a solid breakfast and a sponge bath. Her copper colored hair had been brushed. And while she still showed the effects of her near-death trauma, her eyes were beginning to regain some of their sparkle.

"They can complain about hospital food all they want, but breakfast tasted wonderful to me."

"Well, you certainly sound better."

"I got some broth and a little icky green gelatin last night. My throat was still sore from that garden hose they had stuck down it. But I'm feeling a lot better this morning. You just missed the changing of the guard. They put a new bandage on my chest. Guess I'm out as playgirl of the year. Clearly, that doctor was no seamstress. Even I can sew better than that. Did the guy use pinking shears on me?"

"Nobody told Cèsar neatness counts. Did Tom tell you we caught him, the guy who stabbed you?"

"Yeah. Said he came after you and Eula hit him over the head with a rolling pin." She laughed slightly and then grimaced. "Please don't make me laugh. It hurts like hell to jiggle, even a little."

"Okay. No laughing. Seems like I haven't laughed in a long time."

"Soon as I'm not so sore, we'll giggle and act like school girls." Brandi adjusted her position in the bed and groaned as she did. "One of the nurses told me I said something to you before I came out of the coma."

"Yeah. Twice."

"What'd I say?"

Crystal laid a finger across her lips and rested her chin in her hand. "It's funny. I was going to say it was gibberish."

"And now you've figured out it was profound. I always wanted to say something profound. What was it?"

"I'd been talking to you ever since they let me in your room. One of the nurses said she thought it helped, talking to someone in a coma, that your subconscious would hear and it would encourage you to pull yourself out of the coma. So I told you all the things that had happened, and that we had finally caught Cèsar. So, now things were all wrapped up." Crystal fell silent.

"And?"

Crystal shook her head. "I thought you said, 'Not over.' Of course, another nurse said that probably came from my mind. I wanted you to come to so much that my mind projected words on to you. Does that make any sense?"

"You're asking me, the 'know-nothing girl'?"

"Would you stop saying that? You're very smart."

"Yeah. So what did I mean by 'Not over'?"

"I have no idea. And maybe you didn't say anything. But I thought I heard you say it twice."

"Twice profound. Wow! If only we knew what I said and what it meant. Okay. Tell me all the details. Everything that has happened while I was sleeping it off."

Crystal ran down the events. "Tom did tell you that you called 9-1-1 after Cèsar left you?" Brandi nodded. Crystal told about Cèsar's attempt to shoot her when she came out of IRS, and how he followed her out to The Park. She warned Brandi not to laugh, then related about shooting the lemon juice into Cèsar's eyes and Nana hitting him with a rolling pin. "I'm sure Tom told you Cèsar's fingerprints matched those on the pizza box and the bloody print on the door facing."

Brandi nodded.

While recounting the meeting with the ADA and the man from the Mexican Consulate, Crystal mentioned the possibility of a deal being cut so they could get José Allende. "Tom said there would be no deal if you died. Cèsar would face the death penalty."

Brandi closed her eyes and remained silent. After a bit, Crystal asked, "Are you Okay? Should I call the nurse?"

"No. I'm just thinking. Well, not really thinking, just letting pictures float by. But they don't make sense. I'm confused." She wiggled her head. "No news flash there."

"About what? Why the DA's office would consider a deal?"

Brandi's eyes remained closed but her face was creased, her brows knitted. "I'm beginning to see this Cèsar guy again, seeing him break my foot, cut my arm, and then stab me."

"Don't think about that. It's over, finished. Thinking about it will only make you feel worse."

Brandi opened her eyes and looked at Crystal. "In my mind, I can picture him busting through Eula's back door and coming after you with his big knife. I'll bet he didn't even notice Rosa. Had his eyes on you. I can see it clearly." Her breathing became labored and she said nothing. Once more her eyes closed and Crystal thought Brandi might have gone to sleep.

After several minutes, her eyes still closed, Brandi said, "I'm trying. Really trying. But I can not bring up a picture of him shooting at you with a rifle. From a distance."

Crystal frowned. "What do you mean?"

For fully a minute, Brandi said nothing, a frown creasing her face. Then, "I may be wrong. I'm no psychologist or psychiatrist or whatever." Several more minutes passed before she continued, "I've looked into that man's eyes. Up close."

Again, she paused, as if talking extracted too much energy. "I think he's an up-close-and-personal bastard. He broke my foot. He cut my arm. He got some information. Then he stabbed me. And he followed you to The Park... to stab you."

"Yes."

Brandi opened her eyes. "He tried to *stab* you." Again, deep lines formed around her eyes. Her lips pressed together tightly. "Up close."

Crystal's frown deepened. Her eyes darkened and became thin slits. "And you think he wouldn't use a gun, a rifle."

"I have no trouble picturing him coming into Eula's, knife in hand, ready to stab you. I can't even *force* myself to see him lying on top of a building waiting to shoot you."

She had been staring at the opposite wall. Now, she turned her head toward Crystal. "He wants to look in your eyes. He wants to terrify you. Not just kill you. Terrify you *first*, then kill you. He wants to feel your fear. He can't do that from two hundred yards. That's not the Cèsar I had my close encounter with." She cocked her head to the side. "Know what I mean?"

Once more, Brandi struggled to shift her body into a comfortable position. Crystal tried to help, with little success.

"I'm Okay. Just a little numb on that side. And they've got my foot in this soft boot, but it still hurts if I move it." She finally settled down. "Tell me again what happened in Mexico."

"I'm almost positive it was Cèsar who tried to pull me into the taxi the first time. I was half in when a Molotov cocktail hit his car."

Crystal grew silent. The corners of her mouth turned down. "My God, I see where you're heading. At one point, when he was trying to kidnap me, he could have crushed my resistance; but for a minute, he didn't. He toyed with me, watching . . . my fear. Enjoying it. Like you said, he took pleasure in seeing my terror."

A shiver ran through Crystal's slender body. "The man who shot at me wasn't Cèsar." Her eyes opened wide and her face began to pale. "Two people are trying to kill me."

Chapter 48

NEITHER woman spoke. Even with Cèsar in jail, Crystal had no doubt José could send another assassin. She shivered slightly.

"Crystal, I'm sorry. I know I've made you worry more. But the dark truth of the matter is, it isn't over. It's only one down and still one to go." She reached out a hand and patted her housemate on the arm. "You still have to look behind you, watch everybody, expect someone to be out there with a gun."

"Not over. That's what you said before you woke up from the coma. But how could you know? How could you say that when you were unconscious?"

"Don't ask me. I was out, remember?"

"I told you everything that was happening. Somehow, your subconscious figured it out."

"I think better when I'm in a coma. Should have tried that in school."

Crystal was silent for several minutes, her dark eyes half-closed and seeing nothing. "Who is the ... second guy?" She almost said "shooter."

"Maybe another guy from Jose?"

Crystal shook her head slowly. "Possibly. But that doesn't feel right. Why send two? He'd expect Cèsar to handle it."

"Backup? Just in case?"

With knitted brows, Crystal studied her fingernails. She

shook her head and looked at Brandi. "I don't think so. I mean, there's no rush, no deadline. It's a pride thing. We made him look bad. If Cèsar doesn't get the job done this week, there's always next week. Send someone else after Cèsar fails."

"Then who? And why?"

The two housemates were silent, trying to find the answers. Crystal slapped her forehead with her hand. "Duh. What are we thinking about? Who else has lost in this deal? From whom have we rescued people, besides Jose?"

"Blackheart! Of course. Why did it take us so long to figure that out?"

"Hunter Blackwood has lost two slaves, Rosa and Lucita. That could make him pretty mad."

"Mad enough to kill?" Brandi arched her perfect eyebrows and tilted her head. "With Mexican Joe, a *girl*, that's you, came into his house and took his slaves. If word got out about that, he'd lose more than just face. He'd lose power. But with Blackheart, he just lost his slaves. He can get more."

"Maybe. It cost him money. I can imagine that would be enough. On the other hand, we know nothing of the world Blackwood travels in. Maybe *he* could lose power and position. What if *he* has a boss and that man—"

"Or woman," Brandi said.

"Or woman. But I always think of bad guys as ... guys. Anyway, he could have a boss who might say Blackwood isn't tough enough, or careful enough, or reliable, or something. He could lose his power. The only way to salvage the situation is to kill ..."

For some minutes, neither woman said anything.

#

Shortly after noon, Tom and Mark sauntered into the hospital room.

"Hey, Brandi," Mark said. "It's good to see you with your eyes open and all that hardware removed." He bent down and kissed her on the cheek.

"Imagine how good it feels from this side." She looked at Tom. "No kiss from you?"

"I'm here on official business. No kissing while on duty."

"Glad to hear that, since I'm not usually around when you're on duty."

"What's the official nature of this visit?" Crystal asked, trying to sound like an official.

Tom reached into his portfolio and pulled out a handful of photographs. "If you feel up to identifying your assailant, it would make the ADA happy."

Brandi put her hand out and wiggled her fingers toward the pictures. "I feel up to that. Let's see what you have."

She took the photographs and began to sort through them. She pulled out the fifth one and handed it to Tom. "That's the bastard. No doubt about it."

"You haven't looked at the rest."

"No need to. This is your 'assailant'."

Tom took the photo. "Okay. But will you just look through the rest. Pat went to a lot of trouble to assemble all these."

Brandi scanned the remainder of the stack. "Haven't changed my mind. You've got some good-looking studs here. If you have the phone numbers to go with them, I'll keep a few for my file. But the one in your hand is the s.o.b. who stabbed me. And I'll swear to that in court."

Tom bowed slightly, and smiled. "Thank you, ma'am, for your cooperation. However, I must return all photos to the evidence room. And we don't give out telephone numbers." Tom took the remaining pictures and tucked them back into the folder. "Now that the official business is over, how you feeling?" He bent over and kissed her lightly on the lips.

"Feeling better, but Crystal is feeling a bit sick."

Both Tom and Mark turned to stare at Crystal. Mark asked, "Why are you feeling sick?"

Crystal explained the scenario they had developed regarding the man who had shot at her, with Brandi interrupting several times to clarify some point. When Crystal finished, she and Brandi waited for a reaction.

Mark pursed his lips and rubbed his strong chin. "Hunter Blackwood? Hard to believe. He's big in Dallas society."

"Mark, we know he kept the women slaves. I've rescued one, talked to another, and know there's a third."

"Coercing them to work for him and paying them next to nothing is one thing. Murdering someone, or contracting to have someone murdered, is quite a different thing." Mark shook his head. "He could argue that he paid a lot of expenses for the women, bringing them to Dallas, furnishing room and board. He was trying to retrieve his money. Murder? Can't explain that away."

Tom jumped in. "I checked on him after Brandi told me about the Mexican workers. First, Hunter Jason Blackwood is a big contributor to the Policeman's Benevolent Society. He's one of *the* most eligible bachelors in Dallas. He serves on boards of several charities. Big backer of the symphony." Tom shrugged. "Not the usual person to hire a hit man."

"I don't care if he *plays* in the symphony," said Crystal. "He's a crook. Right now, we're just arguing over how bad a crook."

"And I'll bet if you check, you'll find he's a bachelor because he murdered his former wives," added Brandi. "Instead of Blackwood, he's really Bluebeard."

"He did have a wife," said Tom. "And she died under

mysterious circumstances."

"Which the police never resolved," said Crystal.

Tom looked surprised. "Hunter was never a suspect."

"Sloppy police work," muttered Brandi.

"Tom, he held those women against their will," Crystal said. "He threatened to harm their families if they left. He paid them nothing. Rosa said she sometimes got five dollars a month, for sixty and eighty hours of work *each week*. He *enslaved* Rosa for a *year*." Crystal sighed in frustration. "If nothing else, he employed illegal workers."

"Okay. Okay. I'll do some checking, see what I can come up with. If we find anything, anything at all, I'll try to build a case against the man."

"How about trying to protect Crystal?" Brandi moaned as she straightened up and leaned toward Tom. "Somebody's still out there trying to kill her. You don't have the shooter."

"I'm not convinced we don't have the shooter in jail right now," said Tom.

"Well, get convinced. How about some police protection?"

Tom let out a long sigh and turned both palms up. "Brandi, I don't have enough evidence that a threat exists to *get* police protection."

"That sounds peachy fine. Let's hear it for the Dallas Police, here to protect and serve." Brandi turned to Crystal. "Hey, don't worry. When the guy shoots you, I'll be sure to remind Tom and Mark that we told them so. Maybe I'll get up and say it at your funeral."

Tom looked to Mark for some help, but got none.

"Tell you what," Brandi continued. "If you two big, macho guys can watch after Crystal until I get out, then, if the shooter hasn't already killed her, I'll take over and make sure no one sneaks up on her. But until I can get out of here, you're going to have to step up to the plate."

"She could stay at my place," said Mark.

"I was suggesting *protecting* her from predators."

Only a slight touch of pink inched up from Mark's collar. "I'll offer only as much protection as she will allow."

Crystal broke in. "Enough, you two. I'll stay at my place, thank you. And I can watch after myself."

"Hold it." Tom held up his hands. "Let's get back on a professional track. Let's think this through. Possibilities: one perp or two perps. If it's only one, you're in the clear. For safety's sake, let's consider the worst-case scenario. Let's assume there are two guys after you. If they're not connected in any way, probably, *possibly*, your grandmother's place is okay. But if they are connected, since Cèsar found it, you gotta figure the other guy knows about it also. That makes Mark's offer sound sensible."

Crystal started to speak, but Tom held up a finger. "I'm about to come around to your position, that there may be two killers. But I think they're working together. Even if Cèsar is working for Mexican Joe, and the shooter is working for Blackwood—still questionable, in my opinion—they could be sharing information. They have a common target: you. Why not share?"

"Thanks, Tom. I really needed to hear you call me the target."

Tom made a small gesture with his hands and scrunched his face. "Sorry. But you're the one who thinks there's another guy out there aiming at you. If you really believe that, then you better take precautions—hide out. Mark has a big house. I'm not suggesting anything as lurid as—"

"We've got the message, Tom," Brandi said. "Besides, it doesn't sound lurid to me. But, what about the rest of the time?"

"She can ride to work and back with Mark."

"So, Mark's a twenty-four-hour babysitter?" asked Crystal.

"Try bodyguard," Tom suggested. "Sounds better. But basically, as the only professional criminologist here, that's my recommendation."

Chapter 49

WEDNESDAY afternoon, Eric watched Crystal get into a truck. The gunman had seen her and the same man leave together yesterday and then arrive together this morning. Now, they were leaving together. *Nice work if you can get it*. He sniggered, imagining what he would do if that beautiful piece went home with him.

As soon as the big Ram truck entered traffic, Eric started his car and followed. He had no trouble following the truck, even at a distance. When it entered a private drive, he did not follow, but parked a quarter mile away.

As twilight settled over the area, he began to pick his way through the underbrush, staying clear of the drive, lest someone come driving in or out. Vines grabbed at his pants and shirt, causing him to curse under his breath. Twice he stumbled and considered turning back, finding a better place to kill the bitch. But he remembered the frigid look on Blackwood's face and the veiled threat. Eric swore again and kept going. *Oughta be a law against driveways this long.*

About five hundred feet from the street, he saw the lights. A little bit further and he could see the yard, illuminated by several floodlights mounted high on the house. The drive circled in front and branched off to a basement garage. But, he noted with satisfaction, the driveway went to this house alone and there was no other way out. On the circle in front of the house stood the red truck.

For a long time, Eric crouched in the deepening darkness, studying the house, working on a plan to dispose of the Moore woman. Music seeped out of the house. Classical garbage. Maybe he should just walk up to the door, ring the bell, and when they answered, shoot 'em both. *There could be more than two. Could get messy. This is the same guy who charged after me when I_shot the bitch the first time.* He pulled on his nose, scratched his head. *Be professional. The job was to off the woman. Don't screw it up with personal feelings. Think of a better plan. Get it over with and get back on Blackwood's good side.*

Twenty minutes later, Eric started working his way back to the street.

#

The sun was just peeking over the horizon Thursday morning as Eric parked and crept through the woods once again. This time, he carried his scoped, Remington 700 rifle. He selected the perfect spot, well away from the clearing, but with a good line of sight to the front door. He ran his hand over the sleek, polished, walnut stock. Of all his weapons, this was his favorite. He positioned the tiny barrel-support legs, checked once more the line of vision, and settled in. It could be a long wait.

Every few minutes, he looked through the scope, checking that nothing would prevent him from getting a clean shot. At two hundred yards, he could make this shot without a scope. But with this position, he could lie and wait and use a scope and be certain. He would not miss this time.

He'd been there over an hour when the door to the house opened. If she hadn't laughed, they might have been behind the truck before he saw them.

But she laughed. Her last.

Erik steadied himself and sighted through the scope. He wavered between a head shot and one to the body. The headshot was more dramatic and he moved the crosshairs up to the head. Just then, a leaf fluttered briefly somewhere between him and the woman. He could still see her. But what he needed this time was absolute certainty. He lowered his sight. *Right between her boobs*, a leer on his face. He squeezed the trigger.

Chapter 50

THE over-night stay at Mark's had been good. Not one time had Crystal worried someone was about to shoot or stab her. They agreed not to talk about work or slaves, which left ample time to enjoy the warmth of each other.

They had talked for nearly three hours. They had discussed wildlife and politics, flowers and economics, art and the educational system. Crystal was genuinely pleased that even when Mark had a different view on a topic, he listened carefully to what she had to say, and acknowledged the merits of her opinions.

Just after 8:00 the next morning, they left to go to work. A little smile played on Crystal's face as she thought about last night. When he had taken her into his arms and lightly brushed his lips across her cheek, she had almost melted. Even as he started to step back from her, she had difficulty taking her arms off his muscular shoulders.

Now, as they walked toward his truck in the bright glare of the morning sun, he still caused her heart to tingle.

She had taken three steps when she was slammed to the ground.

Chapter 51

THE morning was so quiet that even with the silencer, the discharge sounded loud to Erik. He snickered as he saw her hurled back and thrown to the ground. As she fell backward, he heard the sound. Not exactly a cry. More like a moan from the two twenty-three hollow-point expanding as it entered her body, knocking the air out her mouth, ripping organs and flesh and arteries. Killing. Hollow points killed. He kept the scope on the scene, watching to make certain this time. But he knew he'd hit her right in the center of her chest.

The man turned, dropped to his knees and studied her, put his hand at the spot where the bullet went in. *Why do people do that? Always want to get blood on their hands.* Eric could see that the man was talking. *He's calling, but she ain't gonna answer.* Eric smirked at his cleverness.

The man turned and looked into the woods. Eric was certain he couldn't be seen, but he felt a slight rush of adrenaline. This fool had charged after him the last time. As quietly as possible, Eric folded the legs under the rifle, eased to his feet and began to pick his way back to the street. Twice, he turned to make sure that crazy guy wasn't coming after him. *If the damn fool does, I'll stop and shoot his ass, too.*

Chapter 52

HER chest burned. Pain radiated from the center outward. She tried to call Mark, but nothing came out her mouth. She could feel her heart pumping hard, but she couldn't breathe.

She gasped, trying to get air into her lungs. Her chest felt on fire. Heat pressed down on her entire body. Her stomach roiled. Still she could not breathe. Her eyes opened as wide as saucers. Her hands flailed at her throat. Panic seized control.

Mark dropped to his knees. He slipped his hands under her waist and raised her lower back off the ground six inches. He lowered her, then repeated the lift. On the fourth try, she shook violently and sucked in a great quantity of air. For a minute, she just lay there, sucking in oxygen, trying to calm her nerves. Each breath brought pain.

"What happened?" she asked, continuing to breathe deeply. Her voice sounded a little raspy. "I lost my breath, couldn't seem to get it back." She started to sit up, winced, and lay back down. "What knocked me down?"

"I think you were shot, but I'm not sure."

"Shot?" She reached down and touched her chest. "I hurt like I have been." She tried to raise herself up again and let out a small cry. "Can you help me?"

"Maybe you ought to just lie there for a few minutes, until we know what happened to you."

She lifted her head to survey herself, and her eyes narrowed and her lips tightened. "That smarts." She groaned and eased her head back to the ground. "I don't see any blood. I feel more like I've been kicked in the chest than shot. Help me sit up."

Mark put his hands behind her back and supported most of her weight as she struggled to sit up. In spite of her clamped mouth, small moans seeped out.

"It hurts to breathe." She examined the front of her dress, then undid the three buttons at the top and pulled her dress open.

Lucita's medallion lay nestled against her breastbone, a rifle slug lodged in it. When she moved the heavy silver disk, a large, angry red bruise marred her chest.

Crystal objected, not strongly, when Mark insisted on taking her by the hospital to have a doctor check her.

#

"You're lucky," the doctor said as he motioned for her to put her dress back on. "The sternum is very strong. Has to be. It protects the heart right behind it, and holds your rib cage together. Even with its strength, it looks like yours was almost fractured. The x-ray shows the costal cartilage has been severely stressed. The good news is, it doesn't appear to be torn."

Crystal struggled into her dress. Even slight movements of her arms sent jolts out from her chest. She clamped her mouth shut, determined not to moan or cry out.

"I'd say you were one very blessed woman. Undoubtedly, that medallion saved your life. You're going to be sore there for several days, maybe a week. Any over-the-counter painkiller should be sufficient. I wouldn't do any heavy lifting." He smiled. "Definitely no bench-flys. No bear hugs, no boxing. Give the cartilage a chance to recover for several weeks. Otherwise, I think you're fine. Call me if you notice anything other than a little pain and discoloration as that bruise heals."

He rubbed his left eye with the end of a pencil. "We are required to report any gunshot wound to the police. This really isn't a wound—"

"It was attempted murder."

Crystal and the doctor both turned.

"Hi, Tom. You made good time," said Crystal. "Doctor, this is Detective Hawkins. Mark called him on the way here."

Tom produced his ID and said he would take care of the paperwork. Mark walked over and put his arm around Crystal, ever so gently.

"Well, I won't object to that," said the doctor. "If you'll just sign this paper and put your badge number on it, I'll turn this young lady over to you and Mark."

#

Crystal was adamant about going to work. Now she, Mark, and Tom talked in her office at IRS.

Tom held the medallion in his hand. "You are one lucky lady. Next time I go to Shreveport to play a little blackjack, I want you to come with me." He shook his head. "First, I can't believe this stopped the bullet. No, first, I can't believe the bullet hit this disk and not some other part of you. Look at this. It's a two twenty-three, and those can go through body armor. Then, it's a hollow point, meant to tear you up inside." He cocked his head slightly. "Of course, that may be what saved you."

Crystal frowned. "How's that?"

"The hollow point is meant to spread when it enters your body. Do more damage as it burrows in. This hit the medallion and spread, so it didn't go through the metal. Look at the thickness of this piece. I've never seen a pendant this thick before. Lucky."

"Keep telling me how lucky I am. Someone trying to stab me, now somebody else is shooting at me. I sure do feel lucky." She started to get up, but stopped and groaned. "What I really feel is sore. I know it didn't go through and kill me, but it sure did bruise me."

"Can I see?" Tom asked with a big grin.

"No, you can't."

Chapter 53

"OKAY, Mr. Blackwood. She's dead. A two twenty-three hollow point right in the heart. Clean." Eric Lithgow smiled, obviously pleased with himself.

Hunter Blackwood reached over and picked up the telephone, dialed and waited. "Ms. Moore, please." A moment later, he put the phone down.

Eric grinned and shifted his weight from one foot to the other.

"She's alive enough to answer the telephone in a rather pleasant voice," Blackwood said. "I would have thought if she were dead, she wouldn't have been as cheerful. What do you think?"

Eric backed up a step. His shoulders slumped and complete bewilderment replaced the grin. "I hit her. I seen her go down. I used a hollow point. She's gotta be dead." His mouth hung open. "You sure that was her?"

"She answered 'Crystal Moore.' But then, maybe she doesn't know she's dead. Some people are slow to catch on." He fixed Eric with an icy stare. "Maybe Sammy can—"

"No, Mr. Blackwood. I can do this." Eric's ruddy face had turned ashen and he placed a hand on the back of a chair to steady himself. "I don't know what's going on, but I *will* off her. This time I'll blow her head off and watch the blood run out of the bitch. I promise you. I will see her in a grave. You don't need nobody else."

Hunter regarded the man in front of him with contempt,

and his voice conveyed his impatience. "Eric, do not come back to this house, do not call me, until Crystal Moore is ... no more." His lips curled up at his wit, but his look remained cold.

Chapter 54

CRYSTAL stared at the telephone in her hand. "Weird. No one there." She put the telephone back in its cradle. "Okay, what's happening on the case against Cèsar?"

"We're still working on it," answered Tom. "Right now, we've got him on assault with intent to kill. That's for Brandi. Then, assault against you. Both of those are rock solid."

"No intent to kill Crystal?" Mark asked.

"Should be able to make that. But since Crystal and her grandmother took him out before he did anything, it's harder to prove."

"What about the pizza deliveryman?" asked Crystal.

"We've got a lot of evidence. Brandi says he had on a Giuseppe's hat and the pizza guy didn't. He had the pizza box—his prints are on it. Giuseppe's has identified the box as the same one the delivery guy took. Still had the ticket in it. Then, Cèsar was there at the right time. But all circumstantial."

"Circumstantial?" Crystal looked puzzled. "Opportunity, means, motive. What more do you need?"

"It's a body of evidence, but something concrete would make it open and shut. Like Cèsar's footprint next to the body."

"How about the same knife killing the deliveryman as stabbed Brandi? And that he tried to use on me?"

"The forensic lab is working on that. But unless we're really lucky, it won't be conclusive. Another piece of the puzzle. A little added weight the jury will have to consider. I'm sure the

DA can get a conviction."

"Forensics is *working* on it?" Crystal snapped. "It's been a week."

"Not really. We only got the knife a few days ago." Tom tilted his head to one side and shook it. "Of course, the Mexican authorities are still trying to work a deal. They think he can give them Allende. Personally, I'd like to see him rot in our jails for what he did to Brandi. And if we can get any hard evidence chaining him to the pizza deliveryman's murder, I'd hope he'd get the death penalty."

"Putting José out of business would do more good," Crystal said. "I know what you mean about Brandi. But she's going to make it. Think how many won't if José gets them."

Tom drew his lips into a thin straight line. "If I trusted the Mexicans to really lock him away for good. What if we give up Cèsar and José is out in six months? Would that be a fair trade?"

"You about ready to go out and search the woods?" Mark asked.

"The crime scene? Yeah. Just came by to tell Crystal to get out of town. I'm serious. Leave now. And, until we catch this guy, stay gone. Mark, you're her boss. Give her an order."

Mark grinned. "Okay. Crystal, take your portable and get out of here. And don't come back until I tell you to." He looked at Tom. "Was that good enough?"

"Depends on whether she goes or not."

"I'll go. Frankly, I'm sore. And a little scared. I have no doubt the medallion saved my life. I don't want to push my luck."

Chapter 55

CRYSTAL, Eula, and Rosa had finished lunch and were sitting on the veranda watching the birds and squirrels. Crystal had told them about the shooting, showed them her bruise, and the damaged medallion.

"Lucita say it have magical power," said Rosa.

"Well, I reckon," said Eula, eyes open wide, nodding. "Not only did it lure that bullet to hit it, but it was strong enough to stop it. Sounds pretty magical to me."

"I don't know about magic, but it clearly saved my life," said Crystal.

"And you think old Hunter is behind it?" Eula asked.

Crystal nodded. "I do."

"*Señor* Blackwood bad man."

"You can say that again," added Eula.

"*Señor* Blackwood *mucho* evil." Her dark head bobbed up and down, her hands balled into little fists.

Crystal cocked her head to one side and narrowed her eyes. "Rosa, is there something else that Blackwood does that you haven't told us about? Something bad or evil?"

Rosa nodded.

Eula stopped rocking and peered at her houseguest. "Well, tell us, gal."

Rosa looked away.

Crystal leaned over and put her hand on Rosa's arm. "Rosa, if you know something, please tell us. Why not tell us?"

"I afraid."

"Afraid? Afraid of what? You know we won't let him bother you."

Rosa swallowed several times and her body twitched ever so slightly. She clutched her hands together and looked down at the porch. "They make us do it." Her voice was almost a whimper. "They kill us if we not do it."

Crystal whispered. "Do what, Rosa?"

"They make us all ... carry drugs. We all must carry drugs in." This time it *was* a whimper.

Crystal's eyes were like saucers. "Blackwood did this?"

Rosa nodded. "Man in Mexico force us to bring them; say we must give them to man in Texas. If caught, our problem." She raised her head and her sad eyes were moist. "When we get to Dallas, first thing *Señor* Blackwood ask is where is drugs."

"So old Blackwood's harvesting more than one crop," said Eula. "He gets his slaves *and* he gets his drugs."

"Rosa, how much did you and the others bring in with you?"

She shrugged and shook her head. "*No entiendo.*"

"*¿Cuànto?*" Crystal held her hands together, forming a cup. "How much did you carry in? A few grams?"

"*Màs.* I carry maybe a kilo."

Eula whistled.

Crystal put her hands on her knees and leaned closer to Rosa. "Did each person bring in drugs? Each person who came in the truck with you?"

"Yes."

"Did the others carry as much as you did? A kilo?"

"Yes. Some more. I think men carry more."

"And how many of you were there?"

"Me and Teresa, Berto, Ignacio." She crossed herself. "And Antonio."

"Could have been seven or eight kilos, maybe sixteen pounds," said Eula.

Crystal took one of Rosa's hands in hers. "Do you know what marijuana is?"

The young woman nodded.

"Did you carry marijuana?"

She shook her head. "No. Drug is white powder. White powder in *bolsas*."

"Bags of white powder," Crystal said.

"I'm guessing Cocaine," said Eula.

Crystal got up and walked to the edge of the veranda. Slaves, drugs. What other evils did Hunter Blackwood deal in?

Eula rocked and Rosa sat very still, staring out into the shaded yard. After a minute, Crystal went back and sat beside the young Mexican woman.

"Rosa, did Lucita carry in drugs?"

"Yes."

"How many people came in with her?

"I think seven. Maybe eight."

"And they all brought in about the same as you did, a kilo?"

"Lucita say more. Lucita say two kilos."

"And all the drugs went to Blackwood."

"Lucita say all go to *Señor* Blackwood."

Once more, Eula whistled.

"Rosa, were there other groups of people brought up from Mexico, besides the ones you and Lucita came with?" asked Crystal.

"*Si.* Maybe one group each month."

The three women sat in silence. Crystal's mind focused on Blackwood and the drugs. He not only enslaved innocent people, he dealt drugs as well. Just another way to shackle people.

#

"Tom, this is Crystal."

"Of course it is. You think I don't know your voice by now? What's up?"

"On top of everything else, Blackwood's a drug dealer, too."

Crystal told him everything Rosa had said about the drugs, including the amount and frequency of the deliveries. "Can you search his house? Rosa didn't know where he kept the drugs. But she knows they came into his house."

"That's tough. My reason, my only reason, to ask for a warrant to search a respectable socialite's house is the story of an illegal. Don't think a judge will go for it."

"Come on, Tom. The guy's scum. If you can't get him on the slave trade, go after him on drugs."

"I need something more."

"How about Cèsar? I'll bet he knows the drugs are sent from Mexico to Blackwood. Rosa knows they get here. She's seen them come into Blackwood's house."

"Great. Now I have two illegals testifying, and one is a murder suspect. *If* Cèsar corroborates Rosa's story." He sighed. "Okay, first, let me see what Cèsar says. Then, I'll see what I can do. I'll let you know."

#

The telephone rang just after ten P.M. Crystal answered it on the first ring.

"Hope I'm not calling too late." Tom said.

"No, we're all up. What's happened?"

"Well, you had good information. Found nearly seventeen pounds of pure heroin. Arrested Blackwood, though I'm sure he'll be out on bail within the hour."

Crystal's smile evaporated.

Tom's voice was upbeat. "And we got Argos. He even took a swing at Glenn just before we dug the stuff out of a barrel of chlorine."

"Argos?" Her voice came out as a whine. "Blackwood's the real villain here."

Tom laughed. "Yeah. But I've already managed to turn Argos. So, now I have not only two illegals, but a bona fide Texan to testify against Blackwood, one who can name Blackwood's customers, give us times and places. The young Mexican girl there, probably a teenager, was too scared to tell us anything."

"How'd you turn him so fast?"

"Just expert work on my part." He chuckled. "Actually, every bag of heroin was covered with his fingerprints. I just explained that Blackwood would dine at the country club while Argos did thirty-five years in prison. I guess he didn't think that was fair."

A smile lit Crystal's face, then faded. "You said Blackwood'd be out in an hour."

"Yeah. But once we get a lot of this verified, interview some people, do all the grunt work, we'll pick him up and keep him."

Chapter 56

FRIDAY morning, Crystal walked into the hospital room to find Brandi sitting up in a chair.

"I hear rumors you might be going home tomorrow."

Brandi looked up from her book. "Yep. Getting ready to blow this joint. And what are you doing in town? I thought you were in hiding."

"Tom hasn't told you? They've arrested Blackwood. Found seventeen pounds of heroin at his house. Arrested Argos, too."

"Yeah, he told me. But they'll be out on bail today. At least, that's what Tom thinks."

"So, how you feeling?" Crystal sat on the edge of the bed and changed the subject.

"Great." She stuck out her tongue and made a face. "Well, maybe that's overstating it. But I feel well enough to go home and the doctor said I could go tomorrow if all today's tests look good. And if I promise to stay off my broken foot. So, I'm packing."

"Tell the nurses to burn what you arrived in. You don't want to see it." Crystal reached in the bag she had brought. "I stopped by Dillard's and picked up some things for you to wear home."

"Oh, you dear. I was so excited to be going home I hadn't even thought about what I had to wear. You're right. I don't want to see that old stuff, ever again." Brandi looked in the bag.

"You could have just gotten some stuff out of my closet."

"I thought maybe something new was appropriate for your return to the land of the living."

Brandi pulled out a lace bra and held it up. "Wow, this is gorgeous." She wrinkled her nose and frowned. "I'll love it in a week or two. Or a month. But not tomorrow. I'm still so sore, lace is out of the question. But it is beautiful."

"Okay by me if you don't wear a bra at all," said Tom from the door.

"What are you doing here? This is girl talk," said Brandi. "And don't get any ideas. The doctor said no wrestling matches for awhile."

"Should I leave you two?" Crystal asked, with a grin.

"Definitely not," said Brandi. "I may need protection."

"We are here to protect and serve," said Tom as he walked over and gave Brandi a kiss. "I guess you're feeling a little safer with Blackwood in jail," he said to Crystal.

"Blackwood wasn't trying to shoot her," said Brandi, shaking her head and gesturing with her hand.

"No, but we've grilled him on the contract. It would be really, really stupid to continue after he knows we suspect him. And while most crooks are dumb, I don't think Blackwood is."

Crystal moved to the window and stared at the parking lot below. Without turning, she asked, "What'd he say, about the contract, I mean?"

"He denied knowing what I was talking about." Tom hunched his shoulders, and opened his eyes wide, a study of innocence. "In fact, he didn't remember ever hearing your name. Who were you, anyway? Of course, he made the same claim about the drugs. Said he never had anything to do with pool chemicals. Servants handled that. Maybe it was their drugs. Couldn't *believe* we found any on his property."

"Maybe you arrested the wrong person," Brandi said.

Tom nodded. "That's what he said. And as a contributor to the Policeman's Benevolent Society, he couldn't believe we'd really think such of him. Certainly couldn't imagine we'd arrest such an upstanding citizen. He was hurt." Tom grinned. "I was so touched, I almost apologized."

"Blackwood didn't shoot Crystal," Brandi repeated.

"No, but he hired someone to do it." Tom frowned and studied Brandi, waiting for something else.

Brandi exhaled loudly and cocked her head to one side. "Am I the only one who wonders if anybody told the shooter? Did old Blackheart use his one call to notify the shooter the contract was off, leave Crystal out of his gun sights?"

Crystal had turned back to face Brandi, and now the smile drained away from Crystal's face. "You mean, if no one calls the contract off, it's still on?" She turned to Tom. "Does that happen?"

Tom scratched his misshapen nose and looked away. "It can happen that way. It's possible, as far as the ..." He looked at the ceiling, and wagged his head, searching for a description that didn't sound as threatening as hit man. "The hired man knows, Blackwood still wants you dead."

"I heard," said Brandi, "sometimes these hit men have so much pride that they want to finish a job even if there's no need to."

Crystal frowned as she looked from Brandi to Tom.

"Thanks, Brandi," said Tom. "But that kind of hoodlum pride is mostly in books and movies. Still, she has raised a very legitimate point, Crystal. I'll make it clear to Blackwood he'd better call it off, if he hasn't. That we know he's behind it and he'll be tried for conspiracy to commit murder if anything happens to you."

Crystal smirked. "Oh, that makes me feel a lot better."

"Go back and stay at Mark's."

"Are you kidding? The guy already knows that place."

"Yeah, but Mark said he should have taken you in and out through the basement garage."

"He'd have shot me through the window of the car. No. And I can't go back to our apartment. I'll go back to The Park, thank you."

"Cèsar found The Park," said Brandi.

"Yes, but Cèsar's in jail. And I really don't think Cèsar was working with anybody. This is an independent guy. And I hope the . . . shooter . . . was that Argos guy you've got in jail."

Tom pressed his lips together for a moment. "Maybe. Argos is nasty enough, maybe vicious. We've questioned him about the shooting. So far, we haven't gotten anything to tie him to it. But, we're working on it."

#

Crystal dashed by the apartment and grabbed a few things. Just as she started back into the living room, the doorbell rang. Her heart skipped a beat. Staring at the door, she could see what she already knew: she had forgotten to put the safety chain on. Beads of perspiration popped up on her forehead.

The bell rang again, more insistent this time. She took a single step, then stopped. She didn't have to answer it. She wasn't expecting anyone. No one knew she was there. She hadn't told Brandi or Tom she was coming to the apartment.

Her feet moved her closer to the door. She could look out the security viewer without being seen. Except, whoever was there would probably hear her knees knocking together.

The bell rang twice in quick succession. She had reached the door. She felt clammy all over. One part of her wanted to hide in the closet, not even peek. Another part of her said if she were very quiet, she could look out and no one would be the wiser. Except her. She would know. If she didn't like the looks, she would not open the door. She could dial 9-1-1, and tell them … what? Someone she didn't know was at her door.

"Package for Crystal Moore."

Crystal froze. The bell rang again. She eased up to look through the small round spyglass. A UPS deliveryman stood there, package in hand. At least, he was dressed like a UPS driver. Brandi said Cèsar had on a Giuseppe's hat. Should she respond or not? Right now, the person probably didn't know whether anyone was in the house or not. She slipped the chain in place, trying to make no noise. "Just leave it by the door, thank you."

"Can't. Requires a signature."

She placed her shoe where the door would hit it at the same time the chain stopped it. Maybe she could hold the door even if the person tried to break in. She chided herself. A UPS deliveryman would be okay. But a picture of Cèsar wearing a Giuseppe's hat kept flashing in her mind like a neon sign. He knew she was in the house. What was she going to do?

Her hand shook as she reached for the doorknob. She eased it open a crack. "Hand me whatever I need to sign." She could hear the tremor in her voice.

The man gave her a strange look, but slipped his electronic board through the slender opening. Crystal scribbled her name in the appropriate spot and passed it back, wedging her foot tighter against the door.

"What about the package?" he asked.

"Just put it down there. I'll get it later." She felt silly. Giving a little laugh, she said, "I'm not fully dressed yet. I'll get it in a minute. Thanks."

The man set down the package, turned, and hurried down the walk, shaking his head as he went. Only after he had driven off did Crystal take the chain off and retrieve the package. She tore the paper off, turned it over, and immediately dropped it.

It fell to the floor, as Crystal stumbled back a step and gasped. Lying there, face up, was a book, its title taunting her: *Death in the Afternoon.*

Slowly, her breathing returned to normal and she bent down and retrieved the volume. With all that had been happening, she had forgotten she ordered the Hemingway classic several weeks ago. She planned to give the leather-bound book to Mark as a birthday present next month. Today was not a good day for it to arrive.

She locked the door once more, slipping the chain into place. She sat down on the couch, shaking all over.

After a bit, she got up, chiding herself over the entire incident. She had been terrified of opening the door for the UPS man. *Pull yourself together. You've been through a lot more than this lately. Get a grip*

#

The sun ducked in and out of clouds as Crystal drove up the long tree-shaded drive into The Park. As she crossed over the wooden bridge her grandfather had built, she remembered the computer-controlled security system Mark had installed for Eula last year, when thugs were trying to run her off her land. *Maybe I should reactivate it. Wouldn't hurt to have it in place again, at least for awhile.*

Nana was in the kitchen, rolling out some dough, getting ready to make dumplings. "How's Brandi?"

"Going home tomorrow, and is she ever excited about it."

"You going back to take her home?"

"Tom wants to do that. In fact, he's trying to talk Brandi into staying at his place until all this mess is wrapped up. Poor guy. He's really been worried sick about her. Big, tough Tom. Fretting over her like a mother hen."

"Macho don't mean unfeeling. Your granddad was one of

the most macho guys I ever set eyes on. But with me, you'd a thought he was carrying a soufflé. And let me get sick, he'd bend over backward to take care of me."

"Where's Rosa?"

Eula finished rolling the dough and picked up the knife to cut the dumplings. "Down at the lake, I think. Least ways, she was a while ago. She loves The Park, but she's really missing Miguel. Sometimes at night, I hear her crying."

"You think she'll stay here? Miguel's dead. Is there anything or anybody to go back to Mexico for?

"She's never mentioned anybody to me."

"Or will the INS deport her?"

"I ain't telling INS nothing. She can stay here with me long as she likes. She's pleasant, helpful, grateful. She's kind and thoughtful. And handy as a pocket. You've up and left me. I like having her around."

Crystal ignored Eula's small jab. "Has Bill said anything?"

Eula snorted. "Old Billy Goat ain't going to turn her in. He hasn't asked and you can bet your britches he knows she's illegal."

The back door opened and Crystal turned to greet Rosa.

A gaunt man stood in the doorway to the kitchen. He was tall, with nondescript brown hair cut short. His nose had been broken sometime in the past and listed to the right slightly. But the most prominent feature was a chrome-plated revolver in his right hand, pointed directly at Crystal.

Her mouth opened, but no sound came out. Eula froze.

"You're a tough broad to kill. But I'm gonna make sure this time."

Crystal's throat constricted. The gun grew, taking over her entire field of vision. Caught in its dark power, she could not break away. Like the eye of a tornado, it drew her into its vortex.

"And who might you be?" asked Eula.

"You can call me the executioner." He sniggered. "Or a problem solver. This bitch is a problem. I'm going to eliminate the problem." He laughed.

"So, what's with the toy gun?" asked Eula.

The man looked at the gun in his hand, then back at the woman behind Crystal. "Toy? You dumb bitch, this is a Smith & Wesson .646 with hollow point slugs in it that'll stop a charging bull."

Eula grunted and shook her head. "I doubt you've ever seen a bull, charging or otherwise. You're a city boy, I can tell. But what I'm asking is, you've been using a rifle. 'Fraid to get close to the target, I reckon. So, why a little handgun now? Why an up-close gun?"

The man stared at the old woman, his pock-marked face twisted by a mix of anger and confusion. "Who the hell are you anyway? I'd like to know 'fore I shoot you." The barrel of the gun moved right to point at Eula.

"I'm this young woman's grandmother and she's pretty important to me and I'd like you to leave her alone. I know Blackwood wanted you to kill her, and he was your boss. But he's in jail. Can't order you around, tell you what to do any more. Ain't no reason to harm Crystal now. You can think for yourself; ignore old Blackwood; do what's right."

"Mr. Blackwood don't order me around." He stretched up a little taller. "I do what I wanna do. I'm doing Moore cause it'll make me feel good when Mr. Blackwood hands me all that money." He sneered. "She's worth more dead than alive to me."

"Blackwood ain't going to give you any money. He's in jail."

The gunman gave a nervous laugh. "Yeah, and I'm in Tahiti."

"Sure wish you were. But you ain't. You're here and old Hunter's in the can, worrying 'bout his own skin."

"You're lying, bitch. Mr. Blackwood ain't in jail. And if he is, his lawyer'll have him out in no time."

The grandfather clock in the living room chimed and for an instant, the man's head turned to look at the clock. Crystal thought about charging him, but he refocused on her. Juan Grande's words echoed in her head: *often the cause of death is hesitation*. She glanced at the clock. Three-thirty.

The nose of the pistol shifted left slightly to point directly at Crystal. Her pulse rate shot up. "Why *have* you changed from the rifle to a hand-gun?" she asked. Her mouth was as dry as the floured dough rolled out on the counter, and she sounded almost drunk as her words slurred from a tongue made sluggish by fear.

Again, the puzzled look descended over the gunman's face. "Plain and simple, I want to make sure you're dead this time. Mr. Blackwood was unhappy last time when I told him I offed you and you turned up still alive."

"You're afraid of Blackwood. And he's in jail," Eula said.

"Shut up, old bitch, or I'll shoot you first." His pig eyes never left Crystal. "Why ain't you dead? I knowed I hit you outside your boyfriend's house."

"Boyfriend!" Eula screeched. "Who's that, Crystal?"

Crystal's gaze was riveted on the gunman. "I was at Mark's."

"Hot dawg. Some good may come out of this yet."

"You two just shut up. I'm tired of all your yapping. Now tell me, before I shoot both of you, why ain't you dead?"

In spite of Nana's distracting banter, a tremor ran through Crystal. They were delaying the shooter, but no help was on the way.

"I asked you a question," he shouted.

Her heart pounded in her chest. Her mind searched back, trying to remember the question. "I, ah, I was wearing a medallion. It stopped the bullet from killing me."

The gunman's face screwed up into a question mark. "Some medal saved your life?"

"The woman who gave it to me said it had mystical powers."

"They say it's magic," added Eula. "It has the power to protect the person who wears it. And, here's the best part; it does bad things to whoever tries to hurt the woman wearing it. Think about that 'fore you do something foolish."

Crystal's mind raced, trying to come up with some way to keep the thug from shooting. She could rush the man, try to grab the gun, knock it aside. A futile plan. Blackwood wouldn't hire a novice. The guy would shoot her before she got close.

She cut her eyes to the right and left, trying to see anything she might use as a weapon. A fly swatter and a wastebasket. On the wall above the wastebasket hung a beautiful cardinal her grandfather had carved out of cedar for her. Any other time it would have brought a flood of warm memories cascading over her. Not now.

Some small part of her sensory perception picked up a tiny noise, possibly a creak from the back screen door, caused by the wind, perhaps.

"Don't believe in magic stuff. I believe in guns and bullets. And Franklins. Lots of Franklins." He laughed but his beady eyes remained cold.

"Money ain't going to help you this time. They already got Blackwood. If Crystal turns up dead, they're going to come straight after you." Crystal heard Eula step a little closer.

"And why's that, stupid bitch?"

"Cause they'll suspect Blackwood. They already know he

put out the contract on Crystal. And since he's in jail, they'll come down hard and fast on him. Now, I want you to concentrate on this. Pay attention." Eula could have been instructing a child instead of a man holding a gun on her and threatening to kill her. "What's he gonna do? He's gonna strike whatever deal he can. Right now, they got him on drugs. Rather than face murder charges, he'll turn on you like a dervish."

She paused only a moment. "Oh, sorry. Didn't mean to talk over your head. He'll turn on you fast as a frog snatching a fly. You'll be in jail. Now here's the good part." Eula gave the gunman a big smile. "You're sitting in a cell, facing murder. And since you been stalking Crystal, you're gonna get the death penalty, sure as taxes. Blackwood'll get out of jail cause he gave you up to the police. So, you get the death penalty and Blackwood gets off scot-free. He might come see you." She paused a beat. "When they stick the needle in your arm and say Sayonara."

The nose of the gun had been lined up on Crystal. It moved right, toward Eula. Fire erupted from the barrel, shattering the night, and Crystal's heart. She screamed.

Chapter 57

EULA'S head was turned away, but she was still standing. No blood was visible. But at this distance, the gunman could not miss.

Eula turned back, untouched by the bullet. Tears came to Crystal's eyes and she could hardly breathe. She started toward Eula.

"Stop! Take a step and I'll shoot you in the back."

Crystal stopped in mid-stride.

Eula never hesitated to push. "You jackass. You shot a hole in my vent-a-hood."

"And the next shot will be in your head, you don't shut up."

Crystal stopped shaking. On the outside. Inside, she continued to tremble. Her muscles felt like the elastic had gone dead, her stomach as if she had just gotten off a giant roller coaster. She could see the confusion on his face, his forehead wrinkled, his eyes squinting. But most prominent in her vision was the Smith and Wesson. They had no help, and talking him out of killing them did not seem very likely.

"You got two choices, as I see it," said Eula. "You can put that gun down, or you can regret not doing it for the rest of your life, short as that might be." She took one more small step closer to the gunman. Now Crystal could feel her Nana's breath.

"Old woman, I ain't getting paid to snuff you. But I'm gonna do you for free, you don't shut up. Blackwood ain't in jail, and he wouldn't rat me out."

"You can use the phone and call," said Crystal, finding her voice again. "I'll pay the long distance charges."

He tilted his long, narrow face, his mouth agape. "I ain't calling Blackwood."

"Call the police and ask them. Ask for Detective Tom Hawkins." The waver in Crystal's voice betrayed her. "Just ask if Blackwood's in jail."

"You're crazy. You're both crazy. I ain't calling no police. I'm doing both of you and boogying." He raised the gun, shifting the aim toward Crystal's head.

Chapter 58

PARALYZED, Crystal wanted to cry. The corners of the gunman's thin mouth turned up in a weird smirk.

At the periphery of her vision, she caught a glimpse of something that appeared most unlikely. She had a strange impression of a shovel — up in the air.

The end of the shovel scraped the ceiling. The man swung around, his gun tracing an arc. Rosa swung the shovel at the gunman's head. He jerked to the side. The shovel crashed down, hitting him in the shoulder as he pulled the trigger.

Crystal lowered her head and charged at the thug, hitting him in the side, just at the waist. His head snapped backward as Crystal drove his body forward. He slammed down on the utility room floor, smashing his head on the hard vinyl. But the revolver remained clutched in his hand.

Rosa had crumpled to the floor and lay motionless.

Crystal tried to move around to get the gun. But the killer, though stunned, half turned and swung the pistol in her direction.

"Stop right there," yelled Eula. "This is a long boning knife that's about to slice your kidney. And if it does, you'll bleed to death before an ambulance could even start out here. If we bothered to call one. Drop the gun right now, or I'll skewer you. And don't think for one moment I won't. I'd do it as quick as I'd kill a rattlesnake." She pressed a little harder and the sharp blade cut through his clothes and into his skin.

The gun hit the floor with a clatter. Crystal snatched it

and scrambled to her feet. None too gently, she pressed it against the back of his neck. "One move out of you and I'll blow your head off. Nana, check on Rosa."

Eula bent over the Mexican woman, feeling for a pulse on the side of her neck. "She's alive, that's all I can say. Looks like she got hit in the stomach. Lots of blood." She grabbed a towel from the top of the dryer, folded it and pressed it against the red tide oozing from Rosa's midsection. She crossed the young woman's hands over the towel to hold it in place. "I'll call Darcey. That worm so much as wiggles, pull the trigger."

In less than a minute, Eula had summoned the emergency medical unit from the Wooden Nickel Hospital. She went back to Rosa. "The emergency medical people are on their way. Hold on. They'll be here in no time." She checked that Rosa had the towel pressed tightly over the wound. "They're coming to help you, Rosa. You just hold on." Eula laid her hand gently on the young woman's cheek.

Eula opened a cabinet and pulled out a length of nylon cord. "Darcey said they'd be here in ten minutes," she said quietly to Crystal. "'Course they won't. Take at least fifteen. Let's hogtie this scum, then I'll call Billy Goat."

The gunman remained face down on the floor. Crystal had forced him to hold on to his belt in the center of his back, threatening to shoot him if he let go. She moved beyond his head, the pistol pressed against his left temple. Eula quickly secured his hands, then his feet. She tied a rope to the one binding his feet, and with that, pulled his feet up and tied the rope to his hands.

"That'll hold him. Here, I'll take the pistol and watch him." Eula jabbed the gun roughly into the thug's back. "Frankly, I'd like for you to move a bit so I'd have an excuse to blow your head off. Crystal, call Billy Goat and tell him we've got another sack of manure for him to take care of."

Crystal managed to get through to Sheriff Bill Glothe and explained what had happened.

She had just hung up the phone when Rosa made a low, mumbling noise. In an instant, she and Eula were hovering over the bleeding woman.

"Don't try to talk," said Crystal softly as she patted one of Rosa's hands. "The emergency medical people are on their way. They'll be here any minute to take you to the hospital."

"*Gracias.* Thank you . . . for . . . all," said Rosa, her voice soft, less than a whisper, her breathing labored and rough, like air bubbling through water. "You save me. You save . . . Lucita . . . and her *niñas*. No one . . . ever good to me as you." Her face contorted with pain, she struggled to smile for Crystal and Eula.

"Just rest. Doctors will be here soon," said Eula.

"I no make it. I know I die." Her body shuddered ever so slightly and her face twisted in pain as she coughed. Blood seeped out the corner of her mouth. "But you make me . . . happy for little time."

Once more, a tremor ran through her body and pain forced her eyes closed. "I go see my Miguel." For a moment, a smile graced her face, only to be torn away by the pain. "*Gracias.*"

Crystal and Eula sat on the floor, each holding a small, brown hand, patting it lovingly, tears running down their faces. Crystal pressed the blood-soaked towel tightly against the wound.

She looked at the gunman and thought about loosening his bonds so he might try to escape. Then she could extract an eye for an eye.

#

Bill Glothe and deputy Slim Rogers arrived shortly after the EMS. The medical technicians had worked on Rosa briefly, then stopped. She was dead. They offered condolences, packed up their gear, and left.

While Slim shot pictures from every conceivable angle,

Glothe called Willa Walters, the Justice of the Peace, to come pronounce the victim dead. Eula called Bark Holderman, who ran the Wooden Nickel Funeral Home, to come pick up the body.

"You know I gotta send the body in for an autopsy," Glothe said, almost apologetically.

"Why? There's two of us who can tell you exactly how she died."

"I know. But I gotta follow regulations. All deaths unattended by a doctor gotta have an autopsy."

"Waste of money."

"I'm not arguing the point, Eula, just telling you the regulation."

"So, when can I arrange a funeral?"

"What's today? Friday? I guess we can send it on tonight." The sheriff ticked days off on his fingers. "How about Tuesday?"

"Seems like a long time. Not like we got to gather relatives."

Glothe reached in his pocket, pulled out a toothpick, and stuck it in his mouth. "Well, body's gotta go to Dallas. They usually release the body in forty-eight hours. That'd be Sunday night. I reckon you could have it Monday morning. Late."

"I'm all done, Sheriff," said Slim.

Glothe looked at his deputy. "You read him his rights?"

The deputy nodded.

"Let's load him up, then. Gonna have to take the sack of manure by the hospital, have him checked over."

"What for?" Eula asked. "He barely got hit on the shoulder."

"Don't want no big city lawyer saying we questioned—

beg your pardon, interviewed—him when he wasn't completely healthy."

Glothe checked the handcuffs. None too gently, he and his deputy escorted Eric Lithgow out to the patrol car.

A minute later, Glothe stuck his head in the back door. "Be best if you two can come down and give your statements tonight. You'll remember more details tonight than tomorrow."

Chapter 59

SHERIFF Bill Glothe looked at his prisoner, then began to recite. "You have the right to remain silent. Anything . . ."

"You already read me my rights last night, Dumbo."

". . . you say can, and will, . . . "

"Yeah, yeah. I know all that."

Glothe continued until he had finished the complete Mirandizing. "I know, but I want to make double sure. I mean, now that the doctor says you got all your faculties. Don't want no slip-ups, just in case Blackwood brings in a high-powered lawyer." The trace of a smile came and went on the sheriff's face. "'Course, my thinking is he'll distance himself from you like a bird from a cat. Never admit he ever knew you."

The prisoner's eyes shifted slightly at the mention of Blackwood, but he said nothing.

"Why don't you tell me what happened?" Glothe stood, resting one foot on the seat of a chair, a mug of coffee too hot to drink in his right hand, his left hand resting on his knee.

Seated on the other side of a table, Eric Lithgow maintained a dark scowl on his face as if maybe he could intimidate the backwoods lawman.

"I come out here to shoot some quail. I go in the house when someone says 'Come in.' Then, the Mexcan comes at me with a shovel and when I turn to dodge, this other woman hits me in the back. The pistol went off and hit the Mexcan. Accident. Plain and simple."

Glothe nodded a few times. "That's the trouble with being a city boy. Country boy'd know you don't use hollow points on quail. You even know what a quail is?" He studied the criminal for a minute before continuing. "I really meant your connection with Blackwood and how he figured into the attempts on Crystal's life. See, I ain't concerned about what happened last night. That's an open and shut case. You're convicted already."

"Don't have trials in this hick county?"

"Oh, there'll be a trial. But you see, I got two eyewitnesses. Already got their statements and they're both clear on what happened."

"Who's gonna believe them two bitches?" sneered Eric.

"Now, you watch your mouth, or I'll have them slap you back in handcuffs and leg irons. You like that?"

The sullen man said nothing.

"And to set the record straight for the big city boy, everybody likely to be on a jury will believe Eula without question. They'll feel the same way about Crystal. So, you see, you got a problem."

"Well, maybe my lawyer'll get a change of menu, or whatever they call it."

The sheriff laughed. "That ain't gonna happen. You got Judge Graham, and she don't like that stuff. She says, you kill somebody here, you face the court here."

Now, Eric laughed. "You're blowing smoke, old man. You brought me in Friday night. This is Saturday. You don't know who the judge will be."

"Wrong. That's your city upbringing getting in the way, again. I just called my niece, who sets these things up. She says 'Life or Death' Lucy is gonna to be your judge."

A faint tinge of worry clouded Eric's face. "What's that mean, 'Life or Death' Lucy?"

"That's what they call her. Well, not to her face. She's partial to giving out life sentences when she don't give the death penalty."

"I thought the jury decided that."

"Oh, they do. They do. After the judge gives her instructions. Juries in her court just seem to come up with life or death."

Eric squirmed in his chair. "The most you can get me on is accidental shooting. I didn't mean to shoot the Mexcan, and even your old bitch friends will tell you that was an accident."

"Well, no. That's not what they said." Glothe took a drink of coffee. "Crystal believes since Rosa escaped from Blackwood, you were sent to kill her, as well as Crystal. Eula said you deliberately shot the girl. I think a jury might go along with that."

"Ain't true. I didn't even know the wetback was there."

"But you knew Crystal was there."

"I didn't say that."

"Lying is just postponing the truth. The truth *will* come out," Glothe said patiently. "You see, you got a problem. Since you tried to kill Crystal twice before coming out here for a third try, that becomes stalking, premeditated murder . . . all sorts of things. Eric, you've got a serious problem."

"Whatcha mean, tried to kill her twice before?"

"You're playing dumb, and you've got a talent for it. But the problem is, I got the evidence. We got the rifle you used. Got the bullets." Glothe didn't mention that the slugs were too damaged to be conclusive in identifying the gun that fired them. "We've got other ammo from your car that matches. We got someone who saw you on your first attempt, the one outside where she works. Remember that one? You was up on the roof of a building. Well, someone saw you there. And we got the casing you left up there. Got tire prints that put you at the scene of the second attempt on her life. And body impressions in the dirt. 'Course, that body print ain't conclusive. But it'll fit you and just add another nail to your coffin, so to speak."

Bill paused and stared at his prisoner. "You see, we got it all. Smoking gun, eyewitnesses, more evidence than we need. So, I'm not working on that aspect at all. You're convicted, sure as cows shit. Whether you get life in prison or death, well, I don't know. I was thinking maybe life, but everybody I've talked to says I'm crazy, that you're certain to get the death penalty. 'Course, they won't *all* be on the jury."

Beads of sweat formed on Eric's forehead and upper lip, but he tried bravado. "Accidental shooting, that's all. Maybe five years.

"No, son. Unless you manage to plead out something by giving up Blackwood on a conspiracy to commit murder charge, you're never getting out of prison alive."

Glothe reached down on the chair and picked up several sheets of paper. "I'm going to leave these with you and let you read them for a few minutes while I get some more coffee. Would you like a cup?"

Eric nodded.

"These are my only copies, so don't tear them up."

"What the hell are they?"

"Newspaper stories telling about some cases in 'Life or Death' Lucy's court. You'll see life ain't good for the bad." He tapped the top page. "This one shows a guy getting seventy-five years for holding a woman and kid hostage for an hour. No one got killed. Just held the two at gunpoint. The others are about the same." Glothe started to leave, then turned back. "How old are you, thirty-three? Thirty-three and seventy-five makes 108. Let's see, if they knocked off twenty-eight years for good behavior, you'd be out when you're eighty. 'Course, you won't live that long in prison."

Glothe gave Eric Lithgow ten minutes to think about it

before returning with the coffee. He put a cup down in front of the prisoner.

"Another deputy came in, so I polled him. Death penalty. Right now, the poll's running eleven to two for the death penalty. I'm about to give up and switch over to the death penalty side myself."

The sheriff glanced down at the papers. It looked like Eric had read them, or at least shuffled through them. Every story told of a defendant assessed long prison terms or the death penalty. The seventy-five-year sentence was the least penalty in any of the five newspaper articles.

"So, you get life or the death penalty, and Blackwood plays golf at the country club. Ain't fair, is it? 'Course, life ain't always fair. Maybe Blackwood deserves to sail his boat on the lake while you fight off other killers in prison, I don't know."

Eric gulped some of the coffee. "The Moore bitch said Mr. Blackwood was in jail on drug charges."

"That *was* true. But, he got out today. I imagine he's dining at some five-star restaurant about now. Then off to the theater or something. While you rot in jail, waiting for 'Life or Death' Lucy."

Eric said nothing, just stared at his hands. Drops of sweat made little circles on the wooden table.

"Actually, when they released him, the police told him you were in jail in Wooden Nickel. Know what he said? He didn't know any Eric Lithgow." Glothe sucked his teeth. "Ain't that the way it goes? You get in trouble and your friends desert you. At least we don't have to worry about him sending a big-time lawyer down here to defend you. Smart as he is, he knows it's an open-and-shut case. Why waste the money? Anyway, you don't know him and he don't know you. So, I guess it's back to the cell for you. You got nothing to bargain with."

"Don't the DA usually decide that?"

Glothe had started to leave, but he turned back. "Yeah.

But Willard sees a case like this, he won't give you a chance to plea bargain. He's coming up for re-election. He sees an easy conviction with a life term or death, he'll be happy as a pig in slop. This'll make him look good, win him some votes. Won't be much work, either. He won't want to plea bargain this, you can bank on that."

The sheriff paused at the door. "Since Crystal's a friend of mine, I just wanted to know if Blackwood was behind it. And if he was, nail him. But if he ain't, I'll just turn you over to Willard." He opened the door. "Slim, put him back in the cell."

#

Glothe came into the office on Sunday to see his prisoner. When he got there, he found out Lithgow wanted to see him. "Did he make his call?"

"Yeah," said the deputy.

"And?"

"Well, I couldn't hear too good. But purty soon he started yelling, 'Course you know me. Ask Blackwood.' Then he's saying, 'Are you there? You still there?' And he slams the phone down. That was it."

"Didn't think Blackwood would admit knowing him. Or send a lawyer."

The sheriff walked down to the cell and looked in.

"We ain't got nothing to say, Eric."

"You could talk to Willic. Tell him I've got information could get him a bigger fish," said the prisoner.

"Name's Willard, and he don't like people mispronouncing it."

"Okay. Okay. Willard. You talk to him."

Glothe looked disinterested. "Willard's probably reading the report now. Knows he's got a slam-dunk conviction."

Eric put a nervous smile on his face and tried to look

confident. "I can get him a whale of a fish."

"A whale in Dallas ain't going to help his re-election as much as a small fry like you right here at home. Tell me what you got, what you can prove, what we can check out. If it's any good, I'll see what I can do."

Eric brightened a bit. "Blackwood did put out the contract on Crystal. And he's into drugs. Not a user, a supplier. Big time. And he brings in wetbacks and holds them as slaves, threatening to kill their families back in Mexico if they don't stay where he puts them." The gunman looked pleased.

"Nothing I didn't already know, Eric."

"Yeah, but I'll testify. Give dates and numbers and stuff. I know a lot."

"Sorry. They've already got Blackwood on drugs and illegals. You got to do better than that." Glothe's face remained impassive. If Eric would testify on the murder contract, that would be worth a lot. But the sheriff just gave his prisoner a blank stare.

Now, Eric was fidgeting. Tiny beads of sweat formed on his face and his breathing became shallow and rapid. He leaned his head against the steel bars and looked at the floor. Glothe just stared at the man. *He's got to speak first*, thought Glothe. *He speaks, I win. He remains silent, it's a draw.* For a long time, neither said anything. Glothe decided to play his last card. Without a word, he turned and walked out the door.

Glothe refused to see Eric the rest of the day.

#

Monday, Bill arrived at 8:00.

"The prisoner sure is anxious to talk to you, Sheriff," said Deputy Rogers before Glothe had a chance to get a cup of coffee.

"He can wait awhile. But you might let it slip that I'm here."

At 10:15, Glothe ambled back to Eric's cell. "Eric, we got nothing to talk about. What you got's as useless as teats on a boar hog. I'll see you at the arraignment." The sheriff turned to leave.

"Wait! I got more. But I got to know I get something back."

"You got something worthwhile, it might keep you off death row."

"I need more than that. I might not get on death row anyway."

"You willing to take that chance, then have at it." Again, the sheriff started to leave.

"I got some good stuff. Can't you do better?" Eric was whining now.

"No, I can't. Willard can. Might. Hard to say. Tell me what you think you got that's worth a cow patty and if I agree, I'll talk to him."

Eric leaned his head against the cold bars. Glothe stood very still, watching the prisoner trying to decide what to do. Eric gripped the bars tightly, his knuckles white. He kicked the bars with the toe of his right shoe. Slowly, he turned his face up to look at the sheriff.

"What if I could tell you 'bout the phony company he uses to launder his drug money? And I could tell who a bunch of his big customers are?"

Glothe reached in his shirt pocket, pulled out a toothpick and stuck it in the corner of his mouth. That information would be helpful. But he said nothing and looked like he might doze off at any moment.

"Okay. Suppose I could tell you where to find the body of that policeman what disappeared in Dallas last year?"

Glothe bit down on the toothpick, preventing the shock from surfacing. Slowly, he removed the wooden pick from his mouth. "If the body's there, I'll put in a good word for you to Willard. Who killed the policeman? If you supply some information that helped nail the killer . . ." Glothe stopped and glared at Eric. "Wasn't you, was it?"

"No. No! But I knowed who Blackwood gave the contract to."

"Any proof?"

"Hell, man. I'm telling you where the body is and who to go after. Ain't that enough?"

Glothe turned his meanest look on Eric. "Not if you got more you ain't telling."

"I ain't got no proof. But the guy claimed he killed him."

Chapter 60

AT 11:00, in the little Catholic Church in Wooden Nickel, a funeral was held for Rosa Bonita Lopez. Mark and Tom had driven out to join Crystal and Eula. The four of them, along with the priest, a young altar boy, and two stooped women with Mexican origins, made up the entire group of mourners.

The priest, not knowing the deceased, had asked Eula to say a few words.

"All I gotta say is, Rosa was the kindest, most thoughtful, sweetest girl I ever met. She deserved better'n she got, that's for sure. But she died happy. As she started to check out, she said she was happy to be free and happy that now she could be with her Miguel in heaven. I have to believe she's there now. Dear Lord, take good care of Rosa. She brought joy to all of us and taught us to appreciate what we have."

At the cemetery, Crystal placed a rose on the casket before it was lowered into the ground. She had already ordered a small headstone to be engraved:

"Rosa Bonita Lopez

A flower, bringing joy, too soon gone."

#

After the funeral, Crystal, Eula, Mark, and Tom stopped by Glothe's office to see what progress the sheriff was making with Eric.

"Well, course there's no question of his guilt on shooting the Lopez woman. We got that tied up tighter'n a brand new boot." He stuck a toothpick in the corner of his mouth and turned his attention to Tom. "What we're working on now is clearing up some of *your* problems in Dallas."

"I like the way this is going," said Tom, grinning. "Which of our problems are you solving?"

"Several. Soon's I can get a lawyer in to advise him, he's ready to plea bargain to stay off death row, maybe get out when he's seventy. He'll give you more ammo on Blackwood. Says he can testify on Blackwood's drug dealings, money laundering, smuggling of illegals, and holding people against their will. I think that's called kidnapping."

"Or slavery," added Crystal.

Tom nodded. "Hunter Blackwood is very well-connected, and has damn good attorneys. We can use all the help we can get. What about conspiracy to commit murder?"

"Yep. That, too."

"Bill, that's worth lunch, if you've got time," said Tom.

"Worth lunch, huh?" Glothe stuck his thumbs in his belt and studied Tom for a few seconds, a faint grin playing around the corners of his wide mouth. "What's it worth if I tell you where to find the body of that policeman you lost last November?"

Tom's mouth dropped open. He turned to look at Mark, then back at the sheriff. "You mean Officer Tanner? C. W. Tanner?"

"Yep. And who put the contract out on him and who probably killed him?"

"My God. We've made no progress on that case in, what? Eleven, nearly twelve months? Where? Where's the body?"

Bill Glothe reached into his desk drawer and pulled out a sheet of paper. "Here's directions to a field where Eric Lithgow says you can find the body."

Tom studied the paper, shaking his head. "I can't believe this. Bill, you come to Dallas and I'll take you to the finest restaurant in town."

"You ain't asked who put out the contract on him."

"I'm so excited over the possibility of locating the body, I wasn't even hoping for more. My attention is all yours."

"You've got to prove it, of course. But I'll give you a witness who'll testify it was Hunter Blackwood. Gave the contract to a Sammy Malvern. You know Sammy?"

"Yeah. We got a file on Sammy Malvern. We can probably pick him up."

"Well, Sammy has bragged he killed the policeman. Leastwise, that's what old Eric says. Eric ain't too great a witness. But if you find the body where he says, sure be a good start."

#

Tuesday morning, Eula stood watching her granddaughter pack. "I know you got to get back to work, but I do 'preciate your staying last night," Eula said. "I'm really going to miss Rosa."

Crystal gathered the last few things into her bag. "I've been away from work so much in the last month, I'm really behind. Mark has been terrific, but it's about time I started earning my salary."

"I've seen you doing a lot of work on that computer thing while you were here. Besides, knowing how Mark feels about you, I'm sure he's not worrying about it."

Crystal glared at her Nana. "What does that mean?"

"What does what mean?"

"You know what I'm talking about. What's this 'knowing how he feels about you' bit? I work for him, do a good job for him. That's all."

"Don't con your grandmother. He likes you. Grandmothers can tell. And you like him. *Anybody* can tell that. Even Rosa commented on it. You two going out?"

Color rose rapidly on Crystal's cheeks. "Yes. But I need some things that are private, don't I?"

"Not that kind of stuff. Your old grandmother is seventy-five. I'd like to see a great-grandchild before I move on to another life."

"Well, first of all, you're going to be around a long time. Secondly, I—"

The telephone rang, saving her.

"Oh, Hi, Tom. What's up?"

"Thought you'd like to know, we found a body that is probably Officer Tanner, exactly where Lithgow said it would be. Forensics is working on a positive ID. We should know anytime now. But the main reason I called is to say that we are going to pick up Blackwood this morning. The chief wanted to make double sure, which is why we didn't get him yesterday. Blackwood has some important connections and the Chief got some high-level pressure applied to his butt when we had Hunter in jail before."

"The man's scum," interrupted Crystal.

"Yeah. So, we wanted to wait until Lithgow had signed the documents and made his bargain with the DA down there. But the Chief's completely with me now and we're going after Blackwood. And since you're the one who got us started on this, I thought you deserved to know we're bringing him in."

"Thanks for calling, Tom. You want me to pass this on to Bill?" Crystal asked.

"Already called him. Had to tell him my next promotion would be primarily due to his work."

Crystal filled Nana in on Tom's information.

"Don't do it, Crystal."

"Don't do what?"

"You know exactly what I'm talking about."

Crystal zipped up the case holding her lap top. "I can't leave the poor girl there. With Blackwood gone, you know INS will pick her up. She'll be on the next bus to Mexico. She's suffered enough."

"How do you know she's suffered?"

"I just do."

"And what are you going to do with her, assuming INS doesn't already have her and she'll come with you at all?"

Crystal smiled her sweetest smile. "I'll bring her to visit you. I'll work to get her a green card and we'll go from there. And if she's anything like Rosa, you'll be glad to have her."

"If she's not, I just might call the INS myself."

"No, you won't. You try to sound tough, but I know you. You're an old softie. And I love you."

#

By the time Crystal parked in front of Hunter Blackwood's house, four hours had passed since Tom had called. No police cars were around. She hadn't expected to see any. They had had ample time to pick up the criminal. The last time she rang his doorbell she was full of apprehension. This time, she smiled, and she could hardly stand still over the possibility of rescuing another innocent woman.

When they searched Blackwood's house, Tom indicated the maid was a young girl, probably not even twenty. Crystal knew the girl who opened the door was still in her teens.

"Do you understand English?"

The girl nodded.

"Good. I'm Crystal Moore. Did Mr. Blackwood bring you

up from Mexico and are you being held here against your wishes?"

The girl was pushed aside. Hunter Blackwood stood in the doorway, his face relaxed, composed. His eyes opened wide, then hardened. He gritted his teeth. He glanced over Crystal's shoulder, then reached out and grabbed her arm. Before she had time to step back or even resist, he yanked her inside the house and slammed the door.

Chapter 61

BLACKWOOD dragged Crystal down the hall. Inside his office, he threw her on the floor and stood over her.

She landed on her elbow, sending pain up and down her arm. She sat up and tried to get to her feet. He towered over her. She managed to get halfway up when Blackwood's shoe crashed into her knee, knocking her back down and shifting the center of pain from elbow to leg. "Stay down."

Crystal tried to sound forceful and confident, but her voice shook. "I will not. You can't hold me here against my wishes."

A hand shot out, hitting her in the head and knocking her against the oak desk. Blood oozed out of a small cut on her ear.

"Two of my Mexicans have disappeared. I've been hauled down to jail. I've lost five hundred grand of heroin." He glared at her with such intensity she shrank back against the desk. "All of my troubles stem from you. Before you showed up, I didn't have any problems. Now, I'm crawling with them." He glowered at her. "Apparently, Eric couldn't manage to kill you, but believe me, I can."

He looked around the room. Picking up the huge bronze dollar sign off the desk, he tested its weight in his hand. Crystal put her arm up over her head and cringed against the desk. A smirk eased onto his face as he tossed the weight up and caught it.

Then he put it down. "Shit. You're bleeding on my

carpet." He grabbed Crystal by the hair and yanked her to her feet. "Let's wash that off in the pool."

He started dragging her out the door. She wrapped her hand around a chair leg, pulling it after her. It caught on the doorframe and stopped her movement momentarily, but she thought the top of her head might be ripped off.

Both of his hands circled her neck. She let go of the chair, desperately clawing at his hands, trying to get free, trying to get air into her lungs. She dug her fingernails into the back of his hand, squeezing as hard as she could. He dropped her. He kicked her in the stomach, knocking the wind out of her, replacing it with a jolt of pain.

Blackwood grabbed her arm and began dragging her down the hall, now at a faster pace.

Her stomach churned, her pulse rate shot up, and her breath came in short gasps. Through the glass in the door just ahead she could see the swimming pool.

He opened the French door to the patio and pool area and started pulling her through. She grabbed at the door, but found nothing to get a firm grip on. She rammed her shoe into the glass, shattering it, and hooked her foot in the hole. A small piece of glass slashed her ankle. Hunter was moving faster now and as her foot caught, she slipped from his grasp. Without her feet under her, she fell to the floor. She scrambled to get up, but before she could get her footing and run he seized her again.

"The police know I'm here," Crystal stammered.

"Yeah, yeah."

He dragged her across the stone decking toward the pool. She wrapped her fingers around the leg of a chair, but it simply went with her. She let go of it and whipped her head around. She could see nothing that might help. "They're coming for you." It came out as a gasp.

"They had me and turned me loose."

He pulled her to the edge of the pool. She wrapped her legs around him and tried to get a firm grip with her one free hand. He wrenched her hand free, almost breaking her thumb, and slowly struggled to push her head and shoulders toward the water.

Her strength ebbed. Even with her legs around Blackwood, he could push her head under the water.

Her hair reached the water and her nose and mouth were only inches away. The strong smell of chlorine assaulted her and she could feel the warmth of the water as it edged up her face.

"They didn't know about Tanner then," she gasped as water covered her ears.

He stopped. "What about Tanner? Tanner who?"

"Let me up."

"Tell me, bitch, or I'll drown you right now." His voice was still hard, but contained a wariness she hadn't detected before.

"You're going to drown me anyway."

Without a word, he pulled Crystal up. She lay on the cold stone for a moment, then got up and sank into a chair. Blood seeped from her head and ran freely from the cut on her leg. Pain radiated up her arm from her thumb. How could she drag this out long enough for the police to get here? They must be coming. Tom said they were going to pick up Hunter four hours ago. Where were they?

"Let's have it. I'm not a patient man." He kept an iron grip on her right wrist. "Another minute and you're dead whether you tell me anything or not."

"Do you know why I'm here?"

"To steal from me again."

Not too fast, she cautioned herself. "No. I mean, why would I come and take the chance you'd capture me?"

"Cut the crap. What about Tanner?" He twisted her arm and she let out a small cry.

Okay. Go that way. Hold out on the clincher. Her mind ignored the foolishness of 'clincher.' She moaned, acting as though her arm hurt more than it did, trying to waste time before answering. She started slowly, whining and pausing to cry a little, every few words. Delay, delay, delay. "The police ... they found the body." Again, she hesitated as long as she thought she could. "They found ... the body of ... Officer C. W. Tanner."

His grip loosened and though he masked it, she could hear him suck air. "Why do I care about some loser?"

"They have a witness." Not too fast. She whimpered a little before continuing. "A witness who says . . ." She drew in air in several loud gasps and shivered a little. "He said you put out a contract on Tanner."

"Some punk who'd lie for a nickel bag?"

Slow down. "The witness knew where the body was." Drag it out. "And he knew you paid ..." Her mind went blank. Who did Eric say killed the policeman? She began to panic. "Sammy." She almost shouted the name. Still she couldn't come up with a last name. "They know you paid Sammy to kill Tanner."

Blackwood was quiet, his grip on her arm not as firm, but too tight for her to break free.

It came to her. "Sammy Malvern. Name sound familiar?"

Hunter's grip tightened and he pulled Crystal out of the chair. "Okay. Now it's time for your swim."

She leaned back, trying to resist the steady movement toward the water. "You never guessed why I came here now, at this particular time."

"Cause you're a stupid bitch."

"Because I was certain you wouldn't be here."

"And just how were you certain I wouldn't be here?" He stopped pulling her toward the pool, and turned to face her.

"I talked to the police four hours ago, and they said they were coming out to pick you up." She tried to sound confident. "I thought they'd already be here." Slow down. "I guess I drove a little faster than they did. They couldn't be more than five minutes behind me. You want them to come in while you're drowning me, or find me dead in your pool? They're—"

"Shut up, bitch." He stared at the ground, his hold on Crystal as tight as ever. Then, abruptly, he began pulling her again.

Heading toward a different door, he opened it and dragged Crystal in. She grabbed at the doorframe. He jerked her arm and pulled her hand from the frame, ripping fingernails off down into the quick. She let out a scream. He pulled her around to the back of a car. Holding her with his arm around her neck, he opened the trunk.

He smashed his fist into her jaw. In the instant she saw it coming, she turned. The fist caught her on the side of the face, snapping her head back. She could feel herself being shoved into the trunk. Just as her vision began to return, the trunk lid slammed shut.

Total darkness. The car rocked gently to one side and then a door closed on the vehicle. Within seconds, she heard the whining of the starter cranking the engine, felt the gentle vibration of the engine. *He's running the car with the garage door shut. He's trying to asphyxiate me!*

The grinding noise of an electric door opener dispelled that thought. The car started moving, backing, swaying a little as it crossed out of the garage and onto the driveway. Her body trembled. He was going to take her out, kill her and dump her body in some field, like they did Tanner. His body hadn't been found for eleven months, and then only because a murderer wanted to bargain for his life. She shook violently.

A weapon. She began searching in the dark for anything. After a minute, her hand found a metal rod. She tugged on it, but could not move it. Probing along its length, her fingers encountered an obstruction. A thumbscrew. She tried to turn it. She wiggled around until she could get both hands on it and put all her strength into the effort. It would not budge.

Letting out a scream of frustration, she dropped her head back down. *Think. Think.*

She twisted around and began searching the inside of the trunk lid. *It's got to have one.* Both hands swept the middle section. "Come on. Come on. Where are you? I thought they were supposed to glow in the dark."

Her right hand stopped. The left joined in feeling the object. She had found the emergency trunk release. "He's got to stop somewhere along the way. A stop sign, a red light, something." For the first time since arriving at Hunter Circle, Crystal smiled.

The car skidded to a stop. She yanked on the safety release. The trunk opened. Crystal sprang out before the lid was fully up and started to run.

He was yelling. She couldn't make out what he was saying, but she was not about to slow down. She didn't think he had a gun. They were still in a residential area, probably just at the end of the alley behind his house. Would he risk firing a gun here? Could she find an open gate?

Don't look back. Don't look back.

She couldn't help herself. She turned her head.

And then she stopped.

The man chasing her was a policeman. Another officer had Blackwood out of the car, while a third officer held a gun on him.

#

Five minutes later, Hunter Blackwood, in handcuffs, had

been read his rights and was headed for the Dallas city jail. Tom and Crystal stood by her car in front of Blackwood's house. Her hands were clasped tightly behind her back and she was breathing deeper than normal.

"So what in God's name were you doing here?" Tom asked.

"The more important question is: what took you so long? Four hours ago you said you were going to pick him up. What happened?"

"You know how things work at the Department—in slow motion. We'd double-checked everything, but the chief wanted to triple check everything to make sure Blackwood's lawyer didn't have him out on bail in thirty minutes. If there's a chance we can tie him to the murder of Officer Tanner, we don't want to be tripped up on a technicality."

Tom stepped back. "You look terrible. I think we ought to take you to a doctor. Let him look at the cut on your leg and those bruises on your face."

"No. I'm fine. I look worse than I am." Her voice ranged up and down, as if she had no control over it. Most of all, she wanted Tom to leave—now that Blackwood was being hauled off to jail. "How's Brandi?"

"Doing great. Hour by hour she gets better. I'm going to see her as soon as I get the paperwork on Blackwood turned in."

"That'll be good. I may go out to the Park and see Nana tonight." She opened the door and got in, but did not start the car.

Tom came to the window. "Everything Okay? Need any help?"

"No. Just pulling myself together before I start driving. Don't want to have a wreck." She tried to laugh a little, but it came out too shrill. "Go ahead. Don't wait. I just need a minute."

He rolled his eyes up and shook his head, but said nothing. He walked to his car, got in and left.

As soon as his car turned the corner, Crystal eased out and headed toward the house. What she really wanted to do was sit in the car with the doors locked, and cry. But crying would have to wait. Her legs were like granite and the walk extended forever.

She leaned on the doorbell and waited. Several minutes passed, with Crystal continually pushing the button. Even though she had seen Blackwood being hauled off in the back of a squad car, a small electric pulse surged through her as the heavy door swung back.

A second passed before Crystal found her voice. "Get your things quickly. You're coming with me."

The young Mexican girl just looked at Crystal without moving or saying a thing.

As soon as the words were out of her mouth, Crystal knew how harsh they sounded. This time, she spoke softly and, she hoped, in a soothing, trust-inspiring tone. "I'm a friend of Lucita and Rosa. I helped Lucita escape from *Señor* Blackwood, and get her children back. I will help you." Worry lines creased the young girl's brow. "If you stay here, the INS will come and send you back to Mexico, or some of Blackwood's men may come get you. I will help you."

The young woman took a small step, glanced to her right and left, then out the door, looking like a fawn caught in headlights. Finally, she turned and left. Was she getting her things or hiding?

While she waited, Crystal went into Blackwood's office and found her purse. She would have laughed if she didn't hurt so much. The keys to the car were in her purse.

The Mexican woman came into the living room, a cloth bag in one hand, a small purse in the other. "I do not know you. How do I know ..." Her steady gaze, increasing in intensity, bore into Crystal, begging for an answer.

Crystal placed a hand lightly on her shoulder. "You are free to leave at any time. I will even give you money to buy a bus ticket back to Mexico, if you decide that's what you want to do." She opened her purse and took out several bills. "Here, take this money and put it in your purse. If you decide you want to leave, you will have some money. You are free. But if you want me to help you, I will. What is your name?"

The young Mexican hesitated, then took the money. "I am called Alita. Alita Alverez."

"What a pretty name, for a pretty girl." Crystal took her hand. "Let's go get something to eat. I'm starving." Already, her hands had steadied and the encounter with Blackwood no longer crowded her mind.

                              #

Eula demanded a full story on Elita and how Crystal's leg got cut and why her hair was matted with blood and why she had two bruises on her face and what happened to her clothes.

Crystal described how she and Hunter had fought, bypassing his attempt to drown her and the trip in the trunk of the car. Twice, she was forced to stop for a second lest her voice revealed the terror she had experienced—the terror that still caused her legs to feel rubbery and her blood to tingle as adrenaline pumped. The brief description almost brought tears to her eyes, but she knew she could not cry in front of Eula. It would cause Nana more unnecessary worry if she thought yet another madman had almost killed her granddaughter. She would cry later.

Eula pressed Crystal to stay for dinner. Crystal started to beg off, citing all the work she had missed, how far behind she was on everything. But suddenly, she felt so completely drained she could not possibly drive back to Dallas tonight. "If we don't have to talk about Blackwood, I'll stay," she finally agreed.

By the time Crystal showered, and changed clothes, Eula

had started dinner. She and Alita were getting along very well.

#

Crystal intended to get up and leave early, but Eula fixed a big breakfast and the two of them talked with Alita for nearly an hour. At last, Crystal broke it off.

When she got to IRS, she went directly to her office, skipping her traditional stop to gossip with Sally. Today was the day to get back on a decent work schedule.

Sitting in her office was Dr. Krupe.

Chapter 62

HE looked at his watch. "Better than professor's hours," he said without a smile. "And what a nice office. Bigger than mine. Nicer desk and chairs." Now he smiled, his green eyes bright. "But I believe the view out my window, across the tree-covered campus, is better than your view of a city street."

Crystal stared icily. "Have you ever heard of calling for an appointment?" She sat down behind her desk and put her purse in the bottom drawer.

"I've called a dozen times. You are a very difficult person to reach on the telephone. I've sent you e-mails, which you did not acknowledge. You must be a *very* important woman." The smile had disappeared.

"Very busy."

"I see. Well, this can be very short. I'm en route to Pittsburgh. As you know, I've been invited to present our paper at Carnegie Mellon University Saturday. In fact, I changed my itinerary so I could stop by and visit with you. If you simply tell me you have no objections, I will leave and let you get back to your *important* projects."

Even as he is asking for a favor, he finds it necessary to put me down. Did he even know he did that? Maybe he's done it to so many people for so long, he doesn't hear it. Or maybe he needs to do that to maintain his feeling of superiority. Won't work this time.

"Lester, here's what I'm willing to agree to. You may present my paper to CMU—is that at Dr. Patrick's workshop, or just a student/faculty assembly, as you had said earlier?"

Krupe's mouth gaped slightly. "Ah, it's to the workshop."

"You may present my paper, but not as a joint paper. Only my name is to be on it. You can say I am unable to attend and asked you to present it for me. Your name is not to be on any of the slides. But, of course, my name should be shown, prominently, on the first slide." She leaned back in her chair.

His narrow shoulders sagged a bit, along with his face. Then, he began to inflate, bringing himself up as tall and large as he could. "Now, Crystal. Don't be unreasonable. Frankly, I am offended. The advisor's name is always included on the student's paper."

"You forfeited that right when you presented my paper at UT/Dallas as your own and not a joint paper."

"I've explained that mistake to you. And I have reprimanded the secretary," Krupe said. "What do you want? That I should have her fired?"

"I have no quarrel with a secretary. Only with you, Dr. Krupe."

"Besides, what I presented at UT/Dallas was *based* on your paper, but it wasn't completely your paper."

Both her voice and her blood pressure rose. "We've been through that. Do *not* try to con me. There wasn't a slide, there wasn't a word of substance that didn't come directly from my paper."

A benevolent smile descended over the professor's long face. "It's been nearly a year since that talk. I think your memory is deceiving you on that matter. And you may not have been paying close attention throughout the entire talk."

Crystal said nothing, afraid to open her mouth, letting a shriek out. Her face was flushed and her breathing rapid.

"Crystal, let's not get upset over this. All I want to do is bring your name up alongside mine on this paper. It will do you a lot more good than it will me." He ran a hand through his thick, silver-streaked black hair. "I must admit, I like the paper and it will be my pleasure to present it."

Crystal ripped open the drawer and grabbed her purse. She stood up and glowered at her visitor. "You may give it. But with my name as the only author."

She stormed out of her office.

#

"Why does he care?" asked Brandi.

Crystal was preparing lasagna, while Brandi put together a green salad. "Talks, presentations, papers, and books are how professors get brownie points. If he doesn't have tenure already at Stanford, the more brownie points he gets the better chance he has of getting tenure."

"What's the big deal about tenure?"

"Security," Crystal said. "Get tenure and basically, they can't fire you."

"Okay. But a school in Pittsburgh?"

"Carnegie Mellon is one of the top three schools in the country when it comes to computer science. Besides, I found out he's not just giving the paper before some students. CMU is hosting a workshop on IR. More points for that."

"From all you've told me, I'd have thought old Kreep already couldn't be fired." Brandi held up a plastic container. "You want green onions?"

"Sure."

"Okay. You know I'm not very smart on all this college stuff. But why can't he just give some other paper? I mean, I'm sure yours is great. But why go to all this trouble?"

"Good question. They might have specifically requested the paper he presented at UT/Dallas. But I can't believe he couldn't give another if he wanted to." Crystal popped the lasagna in the oven.

"Unless he doesn't have anything else worth reading."

"Oh, no. He's one of the top IR guys around. When I first entered graduate school, he was publishing a paper every time you turned around."

"Is or was?"

"What?"

"*Is* one of the top dogs, or *was* one of the top dogs?"

Crystal stopped dead still.

Brandi shrugged. "Maybe he ran out of ideas."

#

Twenty minutes later, the oven timer began to buzz. "I'm putting stuff on the table," Brandi yelled.

"Be right in. Need one more minute."

By the time Crystal got into the dining room, Brandi had everything sitting on the table. "What'd you find?"

Crystal slid into a chair. "That my unschooled roommate, once again, is smarter than I am."

Brandi beamed and puffed out her chest. "Great. Glad to hear that. How so?"

"I've been searching the Internet. I can't find a single paper by Krupe in the last three years. Oh, there are the dissertations of his students, with his name attached as co-author. But I found nothing that was just his. Not one. If I go back, say eight years, I find tons where he was the sole author. If I go back five years, I find lots. If I go back four years, one. Presented at some school in Germany. Nothing since."

Brandi doused her salad with Italian dressing and forked some lettuce into her mouth. "So, old Krupe is too pooped to publish."

"I don't know." Crystal helped herself to more lasagna,

not focusing on anything. "I'm going to do some more checking tomorrow. There are several people I can call."

#

Thursday morning, Crystal talked to Mark. Then she called three friends who were in the IR program at Stanford when she was. No one was aware of any new work by Krupe in the last few years. Each assured her that they weren't up on *all* new research in the field of information retrieval. They might have overlooked his work. But none could remember a single reference.

Two of her contacts asked why she was interested. Her first instinct was to tell them what had happened, that he had usurped her paper and passed it off as his own. But she refrained, simply saying she was doing a search of his work.

She had promised to see Krupe again. He arrived promptly, catching Crystal off guard. She had never known him to be punctual for anything.

He wasted no time with small talk. "Have you decided on a more reasonable approach?"

"Does that mean, have I capitulated? No."

"We used to be able to work together, Crystal. And if you will get over your snit, I think you'll admit I helped you a lot at Stanford."

"Not on this paper."

"Not as much on this paper. But think back. I did offer guidance and help on this very paper. Yes, the idea was yours. But I helped you develop it. And it was a good idea. One worthy of a dissertation. One worthy of a Ph.D."

Crystal wanted to scream.

He adjusted his position and leaned slightly toward Crystal, his smile warm and charming, his manner friendly. "If we can come to an amicable agreement on our various differences, I'm willing to go out on a limb for you. It will be risky for me, but I'll do it to get things smoothed out between us. I'll present this paper to your committee as your completed dissertation. All you'll have to do is come out to Stanford, hold your defense, and you'll be awarded your degree. It will be..." He paused just a beat. "Dr. Moore." He leaned back in his chair, crossed his long legs, folded his well-manicured hands in his lap and smiled.

Crystal closed her mouth. She couldn't believe what she had heard. She replayed his statement in her mind. Without working up a sweat, she could handle the defense of her dissertation. She knew that niche of IR better than anyone, including Dr. Krupe. She had lived and breathed the topic twenty-four hours a day for two years. She had dreamed about it, thought about it in the shower, while eating, walking to class, shopping for groceries. She knew the main streams and the tiny tributaries of the subject. Any question her committee could ask on this topic, she could answer with confidence and ease.

Her doctorate! It could be hers. Just the thought of it made her fingers and toes tingle. She felt light-headed, giddy. She had had her heart set on that since she was a freshman in college. Now, it lay within her grasp. A smile bubbled up.

Dr. Lester Krupe smiled also. "Now, if we do this, I want to be able to present the paper whenever I want to, of course. But we can work out the details. How does that sound?"

It sounded wonderful.

And yet, part of her still held back.

Why? This was what she had been after for nearly ten years. She swiveled around and stared out the window, not really seeing the West End street below. Dr. Crystal Moore. Her breathing accelerated. How many times had she dreamed of that, pictured it on her business card, imagined people introducing her as Dr. Moore? A movement broke her stare and she focused on a man pulling a reluctant toy poodle along on a leash.

Krupe reverted to professor mode. "Crystal. We need to resolve this. Are you ready to iron out the details now?"

"When do you leave for Pittsburgh?"

"Tomorrow afternoon. We could go out tonight, have a few drinks, celebrate a new relationship."

"I need a little time. I'll talk to you in the morning?"

Krupe's smile turned into a frown. "I leave the hotel at 11 in the morning. Why don't we settle the details now?"

"I'll come by your hotel before 11, Dr. Krupe."

"There's not much to think about. It's a no-brainer, really. You want your doctorate and I'm prepared to see you get it. I can guarantee you'll have no problems with your committee."

Crystal wasn't worried about defending her dissertation. But she *was* worried. "I'll be there by 10. That should give us plenty of time."

It was her office, but she needed to get away from Krupe, with no further wheedling from him. She glanced at her watch. "Right now, I've got an appointment I cannot be late for." She rose and walked around the desk, prepared to shake his hand. But when she got there, she could not force her hand to leave her purse. "Thank you for coming by."

And she left.

Chapter 63

CRYSTAL arrived home, the two sides of her brain arguing over what to do about Krupe and her paper. Brandi was watching television. "I need to talk to you, Brandi."

Brandi clicked the remote and the light on the DVR went out. "You've got the floor, but I've got the goods."

Crystal slumped down in a chair and told her housemate about the meeting with Krupe. "I don't know what to think. Or do."

"What's to think? You've been whining about not getting your Ph.D. Now, you can. And for what you've already done. What's the problem?"

"The way he puts it, I feel like I'm being bought. Or selling out, or something." Crystal threw her hands up. "It's just a piece of paper, after all. I've already got my job; I'm doing the work. I don't need the certificate to prove my worth."

"You always did think too much. Grab the paper and run."

Crystal pursed her lips, but said nothing. She kicked off her shoes and put her feet up on the coffee table. "It's just that the guy is a sleaze ball. I hate to give him anything."

"Yet, you want him to give you a Ph.D."

"Yes. No! I earned it. He's right. That paper *is* a worthy dissertation. I should have gotten the degree three years ago."

"Well, if you do the cooking tonight, I might give you a smoking gun."

Crystal cocked her head to one side and studied Brandi. "What are you talking about? And when I came in, you said something about having the goods. Come on, now. What gives?"

Brandi picked up the remote, clicked on the DVR, and hit the reverse button for about three seconds. "I can now say I've been to college. Went out to the University of Texas campus and believe it or not, I found the computer science division." Brandi batted her thick eyelashes and lowered her eyes. "Now, you know how bashful I am—"

"Yeah. Bashful like a rock star."

"Anyway, I asked enough people and guess what I found?"

"Haven't a clue."

"Someone who videoed Dr. Creep's talk. The one where he stole your paper. And I, young lady, now have a copy of that disk."

Crystal shook her head. "You never cease to amaze me."

"And I won't now, either," Brandi said. "Did you stay for the question period at the end of his talk?"

"No. I was too sick. I left as soon as he finished."

"Well, prepare to be sick all over again." Brandi pushed the play button and the screen filled with a picture of Dr. Krupe standing at the lectern, a slide showing on the screen behind him. He was talking and gesturing and then laughing.

Then, the microphone picked up the voice of a student asking Dr. Krupe a question. It also picked up Krupe's voice answering her.

After a minute, Brandi clicked off the video.

Crystal just sat there, staring at the blank screen. Finally, she sighed. "Why is it always that way? You just can't have your cake and eat it too."

"Not always true. Sometimes, when I had to take a cake to a church sale, Mom would bake two. So, we ate one and I took the other to the church. Mom said, occasionally it's nice to have your cake and eat it too."

Crystal frowned. "What's that mean?"

"Beats me. You're the smart one. You figure it out. While you cook."

#

At ten o'clock sharp, Crystal knocked on the door to Dr. Krupe's hotel room. A year ago, she wouldn't have dreamed of going to his room. He wasn't a threat now. José Allende was a threat. Hunter Blackwood was a threat. Until three days ago. Cèsar and Eric Lithgow were threats. Lester Krupe was a paper tiger.

"Crystal, come in." Krupe smiled as he pulled back the door and gestured for her to enter.

"Lester, I won't go to the dean about the sexual harassment, but I'm not giving you permission to use my paper with your name attached in any way, whatsoever."

His aloof manner collapsed. He sagged and for a moment, the confidence his eyes always exuded disappeared. Quickly, he recovered. "There never was a sexual story, Crystal. It was just your imagination, perhaps a desire to have a liaison with a famous professor."

Crystal's head snapped back. Her heart hammered against her ribs and her hands formed into tight balls. Her lips barely opened as she spat her reply. "I won't go back on my word. But, if I hear the smallest rumor you have propositioned another student, I'll go straight to the Dean of the Graduate School. And I will make it a point to stay tuned into the rumor mill at Stanford."

Some of the color drained out of Krupe's long face, but he kept his head up so he could look down his nose at his former student.

Crystal reached in her purse and pulled out the DVR disk. "This is a video of your talk at the University of Texas last year. It is word for word my paper, while the slide indicates this is the work of Dr. Lester Krupe."

"Okay. Okay," Krupe said with a sharp jerk of his head. "I've already admitted your name is not on the opening slide. And I've reprimanded the secretary who left your name off. What more do you want me to do?"

"I want you to present my paper to my committee and arrange for my defense of my dissertation."

"The deal was, I get to—"

"That was before I viewed the video of your talk. Let me play just a short piece for you."

She clicked on the TV, then placed the disk in the DVR. The disk had been cued to the proper spot. In seconds, a dewy-eyed coed in the audience was asking Krupe a question. "Dr. Krupe, did anyone work with you on this, like a graduate student or colleague?"

The camera cut back to the professor. His smile filled the screen. "No. No one, my dear. Entirely my idea, my work."

The camera stayed on the handsome professor as the woman asked another question. "How did you come up with such an idea? Work out such intricate details?"

The camera captured Dr. Krupe's leering smile. "Sometimes, when you get an idea, it becomes so clear, almost like a vision, and it flows out seamlessly, effortlessly, joyously."

Crystal shut the video off. "How would that play for the Dean? Is this about tenure time for you?"

Now, the color completely left Krupe's face. His fingers dug deep into the leather. He opened his mouth, but no words came out. His body drooped, as if the starch had been sucked from his being.

"Dr. Krupe, your name is not to be attached to my paper

in any shape, form, or fashion. And secondly, I want it presented to my committee as my *completed* dissertation."

Krupe slumped in his chair, staring at the floor. Finally, he spoke, but his eyes remained focused on the flowered carpet. "But they expect me to present a paper at the CMU workshop. T*omorrow*. People will be there from around the world. What am I to do?"

Crystal lowered her voice, but it remained as hard as flint. "You have two choices, Lester. One, you can make it crystal clear I am the author, the sole author. To borrow your words, it is entirely Crystal Moore's idea and work. If you take any credit at all, and I *will* know, I will ship this video and my paper, signed and dated by you three years ago, to the Dean of the Graduate School."

Crystal said nothing more. After several seconds, Krupe looked up. "And the second choice?"

"You can spend your time on the flight to Pittsburgh letting some new idea, *your* idea, become so clear, almost like a vision, that you just let it flow out seamlessly, effortlessly, joyously."

Krupe said nothing.

Crystal stood up, ejected the disk, and put it in her purse. "Call me, Lester, when you have presented my dissertation to the committee."

Chapter 64

"SO, give us the latest on Blackwood," Crystal asked Tom. They stood on opposite sides of a barbeque pit. Mark was grilling steaks for a Friday night cook-out, but he managed to keep one hand around Crystal's waist. Brandi was relaxing in a hammock a few feet away.

"Yeah," said Mark. "Is his slick lawyer going to get him off?"

"Not this time. We found Sammy Malvern. Good as he was at hiding the body, he wasn't good at hiding evidence. We got enough to get him to turn on old Hunter. So, we've got two ass—excuse me, ladies—two hired killers who are giving us a lot of information on Blackwood. Two hit contracts, and a lot more on his drug business. A forensic accountant is salivating over his books and says he can nail Blackie on several counts." He laughed. "The Chief says our only problem is, we won't get his annual, generous, contribution to the Policeman's Benevolent Association."

"Ah, the price of justice," said Brandi.

"How're you feeling, Crystal?" Tom asked.

"Much better. Particularly since I don't think anybody is going to be shooting at me," Crystal said, more relaxed than she had been in weeks.

"Amen to that," said Mark and leaned over and kissed Crystal on the cheek.

Tom grinned, arched one eyebrow, and said, "So, what did you need to go back into Hunter's house for? The Mexican illegal?"

Crystal's eyes narrowed. "Did Brandi tell you?"

"I did not tell him anything," Brandi protested, holding her right hand in front of her, palm toward Crystal. "He's guessing."

"I have no interest in illegal immigrants. But I'm sure you do," said Tom.

"Mark?" Crystal gave her boss a hard look.

"Remember Schultz, on Hogan's Heroes? That's me." Mark tried for his best German accent. "I know notheen. I zee notheen. I tell notheen."

"I'm a detective, Crystal. I didn't figure you were just pulling yourself together."

"I'd left my purse in Hunter's house."

Tom just smiled. "And?"

" Okay. I did go back and get the Mexican girl. She's barely sixteen."

"What's her name?" asked Mark.

Crystal looked at Tom.

He held up both hands, palms facing her. "I'm a cop, not part of the INS. I'm not going to turn her in."

"All right," said Crystal. "Her name is Alita. She has five young siblings. Her father is dead. And her mother can't support all of them. She came here to make the big Yankee dollars to send back to her mother. But of course, Blackwood paid her nothing and threatened to kidnap her little brother if she made any trouble or didn't do his bidding."

"And now?"

"She's working for Nana. And next week, Melva is giving her some work. I'm sure she'll be doing okay soon." She looked pointedly at Tom. "And I'm working on a deal to get her papers."

"Don't look at me. I just get shooters and stabbers who go after beautiful young Dallas gals."

"You need to do a better job," said Brandi. "Here's a novel thought. Try getting them *before* they attack."

The phone rang and Mark handed Tom the long-handled fork. "Don't let them burn." He picked up the portable phone from the table and talked for a few minutes. "Crystal. There's a man who wants to talk with you."

"Who would know I'm here?" Could Krupe have tracked her down? She took the phone. "Hello."

"Is good to hear your voice."

"Juan Grande! Hello." She paused for a second and a frown formed on her face. "Is anything wrong?"

"No. No, my tough, American friend. I called to say your friend, the one whose house you and I visited on two nights, now has problems. He no will meet us anymore."

Crystal's frown persisted, then gave way to a smile. "Is he, ah, did he die?"

"No. But he no can get away for visit."

"Ever?"

"I no think so," Juan Grande said.

"Is there any way he could, ah, break free to see us?"

"No. No is possible. But, I have someone who wish to speak with you."

For a moment, she heard only static.

"*Señorita* Crystal?"

"Lucita! How are you? How are the girls?" Crystal wanted to jump up and down.

"We are good. We are all good. I have good job. Have

nice house. We are very happy. Our thanks are for you."

"Oh, I have to tell you. Someone shot me." Crystal paused a beat. "Your medallion stopped the bullet. It saved my life."

"Our Lady of Guadalupe save me also. And my girls. I am happy she protect you. Keep it always." She hesitated a moment, then said in a rush, "*You* saved me, also. Thank you. Thank you."

"It's so good to talk with you. I thought I might never see you or talk with you again. I want to send you something. What is your address?"

No answer.

"Lucita? Are you there?"

After a moment, Juan Grande was back on the line. "*Señorita* Crystal, if you want send something to Lucita, send to Mercèdes at Plaza Mar. You remember Mercèdes?"

"Yes."

"It will find Lucita."

"But—"

"Ask *Señor* Bull. *Hasta luego.*"

#

Brandi and Tom had left an hour ago. Crystal had helped Mark clean up and now they sat in the den, Debussy's La Mer playing softly. Mark put his arm around Crystal and drew her close. She snuggled against him, savoring the special aroma that was his alone, not some "men's fragrance" shared by ten million other men. This was her Mark. *I wonder if he thinks of me as "his Crystal?" I could be happy wrapped in his arms for ... ever.*

"You've captured my heart, you know," Mark whispered.

She stretched up and kissed him lightly on the cheek. "I hope so."

He brought his lips to hers. It was a slow, soft kiss that lingered, neither wishing to end it. Finally realizing she had to breathe, she drew back, then nestled her head on his chest.

I know they say you should keep your feet on the ground, but I like this sensation of happiness, and lightness, and ....being on a cloud. A contented smile graced her face and her whole body felt completely relaxed, safe, and happy. *I'm just floating. Sort of like when I was flying the paraplane, sailing over the beach. Not when I had the girls with me.*

She sat bolt upright and pulled back from Mark. "I almost forgot. Juan Grande told me José Allende was locked up and probably would never get out."

"That's great."

"But when I wanted to send something to Lucita, he said to send it to Mercèdes. And then he said to ask *Señor* Bull. What did he mean?"

Mark laughed. "Of course, you must never know this in Mexico, but I guess Juan thought it okay to tell you now." He grinned. "Mercèdes is his eldest daughter."

Crystal gasped. "And George?"

"Jorge is his nephew. All the people who work with Juan are relatives. He knows he can trust them. With his life."

She thought of the times she was saved from being kidnapped. She thought of Juan putting her in the paraplane, while he stayed on the ground with Jose's armed men coming.

She remembered her last morning in Puerto Vallarta. "Does he have a relative named Diego?"

"I don't think so. I never heard him mention one. Why?"

She put her head back on Mark's chest and wrapped her arms around him, feeling very safe and happy.

"Oh, just a street vendor I met." And her eyes became moist. *A street vendor who saved my life.*

Epilogue

DR. Krupe faced the crowded auditorium on the campus of Carnegie Mellon University. "Today, I'm doing something I've never done before. I'm presenting a paper in which I had no part. It is by a very bright IR researcher, Crystal Moore of Intelligent Retrieval Systems in Dallas. I had the good fortune to help shape her when she was a student at Stanford."

Dr. Krupe looked directly at the video camera recording his talk. "But I did not, I repeat, did not have any input on this paper. However, I was so impressed with it, that I asked her if I could present it at this CMU workshop since she could not be here. She graciously has allowed me to do so. It is, in fact, her doctoral dissertation. I think you'll agree, it is worthy of a Ph.D."

The end

Please read the next page.

A Favor

If you enjoyed *The Silver Medallion*, it would be a great favor if you would write a review and post it on Amazon. After word-of-mouth support, reviews are the biggest help an author can get. A review of a few sentences will work well - your favorite character, or scene. Or simply, "A great read.". You can add one easily by visiting Amazon on-line and searching for *A Silver Medallion*. Or you can copy http://amzn.to/1eeykvG into your browser window and click on the cover of *The Silver Medallion*. Then scroll to the bottom to find "Write a Customer Review."

Thank you so much. And I would love to hear from you. You can drop me a note at: jamesrcallan@gmail.com.

A Ton of Gold

If you have not read the first Crystal Moore Suspense book, ***A Ton of Gold***, I've included an excerpt. If you have read it, then a few pages farther is the first chapter of ***Political Dirty Trick***, the next Crystal Moore Suspense.

Excerpt from *A Ton of Gold*

Crystal Moore's eyes shot wide open and she sat bolt upright. Disconnected pictures, all bleak, flashed in Crystal's mind, as a chill descended over her. "Tried to kill you!" Her voice almost failed her. Her chest felt like something was crushing it. She could feel her blood pulsing in her veins. "Are you Okay?"

"I'm fine."

"Where are you?"

"Home. Where else would I be?"

In the hospital. "What happened?"

"Some fool tried to run me off the road."

Crystal's back relaxed slightly. "Nana, I don't think he was trying to kill you."

"Were you here?"

Crystal reminded herself that this was her grandmother, her only living relative. "Okay. Tell me what happened."

"Well, I was going to town. And some redneck tried to run me off the road. Clear as could be. Meant to kill me!"

Crystal rolled her eyes toward the ceiling. She worried about her grandmother driving, or living alone, for that matter. At seventy-six, reactions slowed. Maybe her grandmother shouldn't be driving at all.

"Every week somebody tries to run me off the road while I'm driving to work. He just wasn't paying attention, that's all."

"That dog won't hunt. *I* was paying attention. I saw him. He looked right at me, then pulled over in my lane. I could see it in his eyes. He intended to run me right off the road—or hit me head-on. He cotton-pickin' meant to kill me."

"Did you call the police?"

"What for? They'd give me the same routine you are."

Crystal took a deep breath and let it out slowly. "What do you want me to do, Nana?"

"Nothing. Nothing you can do."

Crystal struggled to keep her voice as neutral as possible. She dearly loved her grandmother but Nana could be difficult sometimes. She saw the world very clearly, with seldom a doubt on how to interpret it. "Then why did you call me? Just to worry me?"

"No." Crystal detected a trace of hurt feelings in her grandmother's voice. "Because I wanted you to know somebody's trying to kill me. And if I die under questionable circumstances, I want you to tell the police it was *murder*. And make sure they *do* something. You know how old Billy Goat is. If you don't stick his nose in it, he can't find—"

"Nana!" Crystal cut her off. "Bill Glothe's been the sheriff for ten years—and your friend a lot longer than that."

"Ugly truck. One of those, ah, what-cha-ma-callits. Ah, four-by-fours. Big as a dump truck. Puce."

"Puce? They don't make puce-colored cars."

"Well, maybe he painted it, I don't know. Looked puce to me."

"Are you Okay? Is there anything I can do for you?"

"Yes and no. I'm fine and there's nothing you can do. Just remember what I told you. Anything happens, get Billy Goat on it."

Political Dirty Trick

"Powerful in its characterization, plot, and narrative interactions, *Political Dirty Trick* is the item of choice for thriller readers who like their stories steeped in realistic scenarios and possibilities."

Midwest Book Review Senior Reviewer Diane Donovan

"It reads like a fast-paced James Patterson cliffhanger"

Author William Doonan

"This book is the perfect read for any suspense lover and keeps the readers hooked till the last page."

Review from the Onlinebookclub.org

awesome suspense ...
—Author Steve Sebatka

Great characters ...
—Author John Lindermuth

Very exciting ... Callan has a
marvelous talent for dialogue ...
—Author Elaine Faber

Political Dirty Trick

Chapter 1

Saturday, March 24

She crept into the room, a mere shadow. No sound. No trace of her presence. The small flashlight she pulled from her pocket produced only a slight glow, hardly noticeable from across the room, invisible from outside. But it revealed the major objects in the room: a desk, two chairs. And the Mondrian. She studied the painting for a moment. *Why would anyone pay big bucks for this nonsense? With a canvas, a paint pallet and a bottle of vodka, I could produce the same thing in an hour or two. Would anyone pay me three hundred thou for it? Not a chance.*

No one was in the house, yet she moved with care to lift the painting off the wall. Lighter than she expected and only about three feet square. She turned and glided out of the room. Except for the missing painting, nothing had been disturbed, not even the dust. She made her way down the short hall and into the kitchen, headed out the way she came in.

She froze.

A noise, ever so slight, came from the back door. A key slipped into a lock.

The owner, at a campaign rally, shouldn't be home for another hour. Light flooded the entry room and she heard footsteps coming toward the kitchen, toward her. The room was still dark, but her eyes had become accustomed to the low light. Her mind raced as fast as her heartbeat. She started forward, then stopped. Back toward the study would leave her exposed in the hall.

The only other exit was a door on her left. She opened it. A pantry. She slipped in, and eased it shut just as the kitchen lit up.

The person walked as if familiar with the house, confident of the surroundings. Leather soles. Heavy. Probably a man. He hesitated. She held her breath. What if he opened this door? Her flashlight was too small for a weapon. The muscles in her body tightened like a boa constrictor.

The person moved on, headed down the hall. She waited, mentally counting off the number of seconds she had taken to reach the office. *Please let him go into the living room.*

She waited ten seconds, eased open the door. Light spilled from the study. She stepped out of the pantry, painting in hand. Before she could close the pantry door, she heard leather shoes pivot on hardwood floors. Now the steps had more purpose, as the man started back. She looked at the lights and the distance to the back door and took the only safe route: back into the pantry. She had just closed the door when the man reentered the kitchen.

The bright lights had destroyed her night vision and now she could see nothing. But she could hear. The man stopped, and began punching numbers into a telephone.

* * *

The thief could hear the man talking on the phone.

"Mr. Drake. You haven't moved the Mondrian have you?" A moment of silence. "Well, it's gone." Another pause. "I mean it's not in the study where it usually is. I went in to put those papers you wanted on your desk. First thing I saw was a blank space on the wall where it usually hangs."

Her heart was pounding so hard she was afraid the man could hear it. She took a deep, silent, breath. *Calm down.* Drake was still at the rally. This man would leave. She would have plenty of time to slip out before Drake returned. *Relax. It will be okay. Deep breaths.*

"Yes sir." The man was talking again. "I'll wait right here. How long before you get home? Fifteen minutes? Okay. I'll help myself to a Dr Pepper and wait."

Drake should be at his rally for another hour. It was supposed to be two hours, and those things never ended on time anyway. Fifteen minutes meant he was leaving right now.

She heard the refrigerator door open, close, and then the fizz as a soda can popped opened. *Go back into the office*, she willed. *I'm sure you'll find a much more comfortable chair there.*

Instead, she heard the creaking of a chair as the man sat down beside the kitchen table.

Buy Political Dirty Trick in digital or paperback or audio on Amazon at:

https://amzn.to/2UDjXxw

Read an Excerpt from a Father Frank Mystery

Over My Dead Body

James R. Callan

It begins on the next page.

Over My Dead Body

A Father Frank Mystery

Chapter 1

Syd snorted and thrust his chin toward his adversary. "Over my dead body."

The man almost smiled. "If you insist," he said easily.

Seventy-two year old Syd Cranzler squinted against the bright Texas October sun and scrutinized the well-dressed man in front of him. Syd was probably six inches shorter than the man, but Syd's voice had more iron in it. "Was that a threat?"

"No sir, Mr. Cranzler," Duke Heinz said.

Syd didn't like this city slicker, wouldn't have even if he weren't trying to steal Syd's homestead. Even Duke's clothes irritated him. The conservative black pinstriped suit, power-red tie and black wing-tips polished to perfection made the man look like he was posing for a magazine picture in New York City. And what was this "Duke" bit? Did he think he was John Wayne? "Why don't you just mosey on down the road a mile." He jerked his hand up and pointed. "Lots of land there."

They stood on pine needles under three towering trees. Forty feet behind them was Syd's small, frame house, looking like a giant, square tumbleweed.

Bud Wilcox, Pine Tree's City Manager took a step forward. "Syd, Pine Tree wants this shopping center *here*, inside the city limits. Think of all the tax revenue we'll get."

'Look, Pipsqueak, it ain't your house and land."

Bud reddened at the nickname Syd often used on him, but kept his mouth shut.

A mud-caked '92 Camaro rattled to a stop at the curb, and a man got out and started across the yard to where Syd was shaking his finger at Bud.

"So's you can waste even more than you do now? I ain't selling." Duke raised his hand and started to speak, but Syd cut him off. "And don't tell me again it's twice what it's worth. You don't know what it's worth to me. And what's this 'fee simple' bit?" He cocked his head to the side. "You think I'm simple? Take your money and go back to New Jersey."

Bud waggled his balding head. "It's a lot of dollars."

"He don't need your money," said the man from the Camaro. "He stole enough from me."

"Stay out of it, W.C.," Syd snapped. But his focus never left Duke. "You keep your money; I'll keep my land."

Duke spread his hands. "Mr. Cranzler, the Supreme Court says eminent domain can be used to obtain land needed for a project in the public interest."

"I know all 'bout the Supreme Court, and how they trampled all over people's property rights. I'd like to see some private company try to take the land *they* live on. They'd change their tune right fast. But that case was decided for a Yankee town. This is Texas. We still believe in property rights down here. And this ain't in the public interest. It's in Lockey Corporation's interest."

Duke smiled as he pulled a folded paper from the inside pocket of his coat. "Here's the court order, and it's signed by a judge right here in Texas." He held the paper out to Syd.

Syd ignored it. "Judge McFatage, right? He'd sign anything for a price."

Bud Wilcox leaned in. "Now, Syd, you shouldn't talk about the Honorable McFatage that way."

"Honorable, my foot. He's for sale. Common knowledge. You know what they say: he's the best judge money can buy.

And it looks like Lockey's the buyer."

"Look, Mr. Cranzler," Duke said. "We're going to start dirt work in three weeks. I'd like to have all the paperwork in order by then. You've lost this fight. You might as well recognize that. You can delay signing. But by fighting this, you may end up getting less money and paying a lot of it to lawyers. You can't stop it. This project *will* be built. And it starts in three weeks."

"Three weeks?" Syd pulled on his chin and a little smile crept onto his leathery face. "I'm bettin' my lawyer'll have my appeal filed before then. And I'm thinkin' I can tie this up for years. You sure Lockey wants to wait that long?" His head bobbed up and down as he continued. "Be a lot faster to go somewheres else." Now he laughed. "Bet they're gonna cut you loose when this don't happen. Can your butt."

Duke's smile faded and his eyes turned hard. "Two months from now, this will all be asphalt."

"Like I said, over my dead body."

Duke put the paper back in his pocket. "Old man, you'll hardly make a bump in the pavement."

About The Author

James R. Callan took a degree in English, intent on writing. When writing didn't support a family, he went to graduate school in mathematics, then pursued a career in mathematics and computer science. He has received grants from the National Science Foundation, NASA, and the Data Processing Management Association. He has been listed in *Who's Who in Computer Science* and *Two Thousand Notable Americans.*

But writing was his first love. He has published a number of books and picked up some awards along the way. *The Silver Medallion* is his eleventh book published and the second in the Crystal Moore Suspense novels. His thirteenth book is scheduled for publication in 2020.

Callan lives with his wife in east Texas and Puerto Vallarta, Mexico. They have four grown children and six grandchildren. You can contact him at www.jamesrcallan.com

www.ingramcontent.com/pod-product-compliance
Lightning Source LLC
Chambersburg PA
CBHW050911250626
47155CB00001B/195